HOUSE ONE

Nina Wilson

HOUSE ONE

Story Copyright@Nina Wilson 2023
Book Design: Copyright@Cactus Moon Publications, LLC 2023

Cover by Xee Shan

Cactus Moon Publications, LLC
2407 W Nopal Ave; Mesa, AZ 85202
www.cactusmoonpublishing.com

ISBN - 978-1-7347865-7-6

To Miss Tiny

Chapter One:

July 28, 2016

At seven in the morning, on Thursday, July 28th, it was already 79 degrees, and my first task of the day was to remove a twisted pile of roadkill from the entrance of camp. Thankfully, I had an affinity for roadkill removal. Whatever the dead animal used to be, it will end up in a mesh bag, buried somewhere on camp property until the flesh is eaten away by bugs and all that is left are the bones.

No air moved this morning. The leaves stood still. Armed with black trash bags and a set of gloves, I left the main building of Camp Kellova and moved toward the road. This camp's geography was etched deep into my mind, deep enough I could walk across the place in my sleep. At 24 years old, I'd worked at Kellova since I was seventeen, and was a camper since I was five. Since my mother was the director, it was only natural that camp became my life.

The girls from my cabin were hanging around Clark, waiting for breakfast. They'd be fine left to their own devices for a few moments, though I always had misgivings about that. Bad things happened here when children weren't watched.

The sun pierced my eyes mercilessly. I cursed myself for forgetting my hat. Squinting, I turned onto the road and the slightly sweet smell of death and decay reached me. Up the road toward the state park, a coyote lay in the ditch. Mom assumed a car hit it. When I approached, I thought otherwise. There were no signs of blunt force trauma. No blood. The body wasn't as squished as I expected, but the legs were abnormally long and broken in multiple directions. It all looked unnatural. It didn't *really* look like a coyote. Its skin was stretched over its skull tightly as though the skull had suddenly grown. A tiny hole was open between its eyes and the paws were mutilated. Despite it being dead, there were no flies or insects at all on the carcass. Nothing to shoo away. This was the fifteenth animal like this I'd found just this summer.

I put the bag on the ground and picked the coyote up by the snout. The lip moved to show teeth that were crooked and loose. This thing must have been messed-up from birth. I pushed it headlong into the large bag. It tumbled in, back over its neck. The bones crackled as it moved. My usually strong gut was about to give in.

I inched the bag up, bit by bit until the whole body was put away. As small as coyotes usually were, when dead, they were surprisingly cumbersome.

Between the early excursion and the heat, little black dots came to my vision and my body felt faint. I stood for a moment on the side of the road begging for my brain not to go all fuzzy on me, and imagining that if anyone drove by, I'd look like some serial killer trying to dispose of a body.

It was as if cotton stuffed itself into my skull and pushed out any remaining thoughts. Without thought or awareness, I made it back behind Clark where the woodshed was. I set the bag down and sat beside it, staring ahead at the broad leafed trees. *Gather your thoughts together, Laurel. Hurry up, God-damn-it.*

Some days I absolutely hated my brain and how it revolted against me. Five years ago, a traumatic brain injury from a car accident changed me. For all I knew, I wasn't the same person, and I sure as hell couldn't operate in the same way anymore. The heat got to me. Exhaustion got to me. Stress got to me. All the things a camp counselor had to handle turned my brain to fuzz. It was getting to the point that I simply couldn't do it anymore. My days were numbered here. I was in love with Camp Kellova, I really, truly was. It felt as though my very heart was in the land, and with the kids. Trying to imagine life without it was empty.

A few years ago, I thought I'd be at camp for the rest of my life, essentially following the same path my mother took. She'd been the director since 1989, since before I was born, while she was still dating my father. I have a degree in youth development and another in history. One for a career and one for a passion, in that order.

But plans change and I realized this may be my last summer and the days were quickly fading away.

Getting on my feet, I took the shovel and started to dig a temporary grave for this coyote.

Thursdays were lake days, hence the early start. I helped two other counselors, Orion and Scotty, unload the canoes from the shed and onto trailers. Lunch was packed by our kitchen manager, Marianne, in brown bags and placed into coolers which would also need to be loaded. I was ready for a nap by 7:30.

"Miss Laurel, come play gaga!" Jane yelled. A gregarious girl—even early in the morning—she jumped up and down beside the wall of the gaga pit.

"Sorry, hon, gotta get things ready for lake day!" I replied.

She didn't look as disappointed as I hoped she would, but I appreciated the invitation. Kennedy was on the porch, reading. She was almost finished with *Harry Potter and the Goblet of Fire*. This had to be her third or fourth time reading the series. Her nose was deep in the pages. Lisey sat beside her, working diligently on a friendship bracelet. She was good enough at them she could make ones with names on them. This one was for Taylor Halverson, the boy she had the world's cutest and most embarrassing crush on. Seeing the kids made me smile, but it didn't push away the exhaustion. I only hoped chugging some apple juice might help.

Marianne and I loaded the coolers. There were also boxes of apples and oranges, a giant tote of chip-bags, and another with baby carrots. The sandwiches were baloney on the world's driest bread. I made a mental note to pack my contraband peanut butter in my backpack with some contraband whole wheat bread. If it weren't for my secret stashes of food across camp, I doubted I'd make it through the summer.

Marianne gave up on breakfast this morning and resorted to cereal, but it was all-you-can-eat, in theory, and that meant I'd shove four bowls of corn flakes down my gullet before heading out.

After breakfast, songs were led by Miss Coral, a former camper turned counselor who had an infectious smile and bright pink hair. When I first met her, she had thick glasses, braces, and wore only khakis and tall tube socks. She was uncomfortable in her own skin then, terribly shy, and quiet. Since then, she has bloomed into a gorgeous human being, inside and out. She couldn't sing to save her soul, but she was confident now, confident enough to carry a tune; they were camp songs-musical ability was not required.

When she finished with 'I'm Alive, Awake, Alert, Enthusiastic' and 'I Don't Care if I go Crazy' I stepped into the center of the circular building with the mic. "Ok, when we dismiss, meet with your cabin groups in your assigned spots. Each cabin will come forward and grab your oars and life jackets. Those will be loaded onto your bus. Please, do not lean on the tip or blade of your oar! Counselors, make sure your kids have changed into their swimsuits with their clothes on top and that everyone has sunscreen and bug spray. Everyone is required to wear close-toed shoes until we get to the beach, then you can change them. I recommend you go to the bathroom here. Between the weather and the fact it's hornet season, you really don't want to have to use the latrines at the lake. Ok, when we arrive, do not go into the water until we have lifeguards ready. I say this every week, but every week someone just bolts in. Please be aware of that, and of your surroundings. Remember, care for the environment and your fellow campers. Make sure you choose a buddy before we head out and stick with them! Birdhouse cabins, since you are not canoeing, please go on the blue and green buses."

The Birdhouse cabins were named after various birds native to Iowa and housed the youngest campers, those that stayed for only a week or two versus the Treehouse cabins which were for kids above the age of ten. Those campers might stay with us the whole twelve weeks of summer.

This morning it was Miss Mia's turn to dismiss the campers by slamming on the table 'shave and a haircut.'

Chapter One: July 28, 2016

I met my campers outside under the smooth-limbed climbing tree. They had towels swung over their shoulders, smelled of sunscreen, and looked prepared. Except Ellie and Kennedy. "You didn't change," I said, turning my attention to Ellie.

"I'm not going in that mud bucket," Ellie said. "It's disgusting. Last time I got all those spots on me... I swear it's the water. Something's wrong with it. Maybe salmonella or e-coli." Her pale face crinkled up in a grimace.

"You're not going in either?" I asked Kennedy.

"Never have, never will," she replied, holding onto her bookbag. "You can't see your feet even if you're only up to your calves!"

"Didn't think you two would ever agree on anything," I muttered.

"Well I'm not saying the lake is filled with contagious diseases, but it is gross," Kennedy added.

The morning sun was white and harsh. The shade only helped a little. The heat index today would top 114, and sitting inside a metal canoe for a majority of the day without shade was not my idea of a good time.

"The rest of you, make sure you have your paddles and life jackets, come on," I yelled in the sea of campers.

We marched to the canoe garage where all the supplies were kept. The girls in my cabin who were participating, Gracia, Sadie, Lisey, and Jane set theirs aside the previous evening. Sadie is a good head shorter than the rest of the girls in the cabin and scrawny in comparison. Yet, she was a ball of nervous and energetic excitement for everything.

"I'm going to be with Arty and Eddie," Gracia said, "Can I go put my stuff with theirs?" Before I said anything, she hopped away, half skipping as she went. My mouth hung open with unspoken words.

"Then us two," Jane pointed at Lisey.

"Who are you going with?" I asked Sadie.

"Temple and Pandora. Juniper's skipping out this week on the canoeing so they said I could join them." Temple, Pandora, and Juniper were our set of triplets. Triplets with neon pink hair and hippie names to match.

With everyone finished deciding who they were canoeing with, we all got on the buses.

"I'm sitting next to you, Laurel!" Harry hollered, clambering onto the bus rather ungracefully, before redeeming himself, by vaulting into the space beside me. At twenty-two he was one of the few counselors near my age, and we just kind of clicked from day one.

"You smell rank," I said.

"Good morning to you as well," he said, laughing. "There's a bit of a bet going around to see who can go the longest without showering."

"You've never let yourself go this bad before," I replied, touching his oily, red locks of hair. "Gross." I immediately squirted hand sanitizer on my hands.

"Oh, I doubt Peter can hold out much longer. My only real competition is Orion and Scotty."

"I think Scotty could go the whole summer. Start drawing flies…" I shook my head, just thinking about it. "Well, since you've blocked me in here, I guess you're doing roll call." I handed him my clipboard. "We should have 36 kids on this bus." Harry had more energy than I. He seemed to have some secret store of it. He got through roll call well and sat back next to me.

He then belted out, "I love my aardvark my aardvark loves me!" The song started with more excitement than I could keep up with for long. Once that song finished, he immediately went toward, "Swimming, swimming, in a swimming pool, when days are hot, when days are cold, in a swimming pool . . .!" My mind knew the songs and the motions well enough I didn't have to think of them. They were comforting, familiar, a little loud and obnoxious, and they were part of me.

The drive was only fifteen minutes to Owaissa Lake. It was a sad excuse for a recreational body of water. Kennedy was correct on her observation that it was a mud bucket. From a distance, it was starkly brown in color.

We made our little camp near the lake's beach. Harry helped me carry my kayak to the edge and plopped it down with a twang that rattled the water and sent ripples through the swimming area. Pond weed clogged the edges of the lake, slowing the amount of water that could enter small creeks and the Owaissa River, which wound its way through Camp Kellova.

The river was the first place I ever participated in a mud run, got in a canoe, caught a catfish, had my first bonfire, and the location of my first, and so far, only, kiss.

The rescue kayak was ready to go. The lifeguards were prepared, buddy checks were made, another roll call, and swimming rules were checked off. A few counselors were prepared with soccer balls, footballs, and playing cards.

"Can we go to the quarry today?" Eddy asked, jogging toward me with his bunkmates close behind him.

"After lunch," I replied.

"What? Why can't we go now?" Arty interjected, his red hair glowed copper in the sunlight.

These kids were an odd group of vastly different individuals. One could say the ringleader was Taylor, fifteen years old, with long, enviously perfect hair, and boisterous. There was nothing that scared him; he wanted to try everything, and often did. He was scolded twice this summer for possession of weed, and a can of Budweiser which he decided tasted like "deer piss."

Arty was the genius of the group; he was in a number of Advanced Placement classes that he studied for throughout the summer—he enjoyed challenges. He was also openly gay and radiated bright, sparkly energy.

Eddy was the troublemaker, more so than even Taylor. I caught Eddy climbing more than a few roofs, trees, scaling rocks, and generally getting into everything he wasn't supposed to. He thought it was entertaining to play swords with every stick in sight, often causing welts on his fellow campers. I even found him in the basement of Clark a few times, stealing chocolate, a trait he learned from a previous counselor named Lukas. He knew where we kept ice cream and soda as well.

"When you go on the water, just make sure you stay where I can see you," I said. Eddy rolled his eyes, grumbled, and jogged away. The other boys joined him.

The morning was uneventful, it just continued to get hotter. The humidity was at 100 percent as the heat index climbed—a normal Iowan summer day.

I followed the canoers who were edging toward the marina on the other side of the small lake. They were inching away from me too far for my comfort, but when the lunch whistle blew, they hurried back.

For lunch, I had to eat my contraband peanut butter sandwich as there wasn't enough food for the counselors. I was hungry, and cranky, but had another hour on the water in the rescue kayak before I could take the older campers around the bend to the quarry.

I pushed off back into the muddy water, yawning all the way. Harry was in the other rescue kayak, amongst the kids. From a distance, he looked like one of them. It was probably his energy, his smile. Like Arty, he sparkled with energy and brilliance. I smiled a bit, watching him fling water on Eddy's canoe and hearing their shrill laughs and shrieks. Part of me ached with the knowledge that I wouldn't be a part of that joy after this summer. My mind was never truly made up, but my brain and body were telling me it was time to spend my summers in more air conditioning, with indoor plumbing, and regular meals.

I floated under an unhelpful overhang of trees. They provided little shade and if I continued in that direction, logs and congested debris would get me. Before pulling myself out of the muck, I noticed a large white object sticking out from a collection of slimy branches. The object was a sickening white . . . did not look like a fish. My stomach forgot the hunger and dropped down as fast as it could.

As I approached, the water became shallow enough that I could drive the ancient wooden paddle into the sand to anchor myself. Then I saw the object clearly.

Hair. An arm. Fingers.

"Code white! Code white!" I screamed over the walkie talkie. I leapt out of the kayak and toward the body. The bank couldn't have been more than twenty yards away. "Call an ambulance! Code white! Police!" I only hoped someone was listening. I couldn't hear over the pounding of blood in my ears.

My hand touched the skin of the figure. It was cold but didn't feel dead. It did feel wrong. It was wrong, like the coyote this morning. Something was just . . . off.

The body looked bruised and broken. When the face was revealed, it was past all recognition, beaten horrifically. The arm didn't put up any fight as I pulled it taut. There was no discernible pulse. I put my ear against their chest. A heartbeat. No breath, though. Not knowing where the strength came from, I heaved the body into the kayak. It flopped like the dead coyote, cumbersome and weighty.

I pushed the kayak into the water from the sand bar and swam with one arm toward the bank. There was a small, grassy area. A flat surface.

"Hang on, man," I said. Instinctually, I wanted to slap the guy, assuming he was a guy. With this amount of damage, it was hard to tell.

Dragged onto the bank, sopping wet, I called into the walkie talkie, "Get the kids out of the water and into the buses. The person, I believe male, appears to be in their early twenties or late teens, nonresponsive, not breathing, faint heartbeat . . ." I dug through my fanny pack for a first-aid kit and removed the breathing barrier. Breathing barrier in place, head back, mouth open, body flat, arms straight, elbows locked, fingers interlaced, I started CPR. As hard as I tried to go to the tune of *Staying Alive* it was Queen's *Another One Bites the Dust* that weaseled its way into my brain. *Count to thirty, breathe, keep yourself together, Laurel, keep yourself together.* Exhaustion crept in, but so did a trance-like state of desperation.

"Laurel, do you need help?" It was Harry. His voice sounded so far away.

"Just count," I said. "Is anyone coming?"

"Yes," he said, leaning over me. Drops of water hit my skin and slid down my face. He was just above the person's face. "Thirty," he said, and breathed for me.

"Miss Laurel, what's going on?" Gracia asked, her voice shook, rising up from the pounding in my ears. The other canoers would be with her.

"Go, go, all of you, help get the canoes up to the buses." Breath resisted me. It was difficult to fill my lungs.

When their voices diminished, it was easier to focus. We were out in the middle of nowhere . . . at least twenty minutes from the nearest hospital if the person driving the ambulance was going a hundred miles an hour. Desperate, I pounded right on the person's heart as hard as I could.

"Don't stop, Laurel," Harry said. His voice was calm. How could he be so calm in such a situation?

Back to straight arms, locked elbows, I threw my whole body into CPR, jamming the balls of my hands into the ribs. They crackled in a sick manner, already broken. Distantly, I heard sirens.

Chapter Two:

July 28, 2016

EMTs arrived. When they took over CPR, my body slumped back, drained of all energy. They used an AED on the waterlogged person, though most of my mind didn't register the experience. The chest heaved slightly. The dinging sound of a steadied heartbeat.

Cotton clouded my mind. I stared straight ahead, an absence seizure taking me. With the last bit of consciousness, I only hoped that Harry and I managed to keep the heart and lungs working long enough for the person to survive.

By the time I returned to the land of the living, the person I pulled out of the lake was loaded onto a gurney by EMTS and hurried away by the ambulance- sirens and all. The sirens were a good sign, the person was alive.

A police officer, Chief Travis Stevens, knelt in front of me. Harry was still beside me, as silent as my mind. I couldn't get the gears going again. I just looked right past—through him. "Laurel, it's Travis. You know me. I just need to ask you some questions."

"You're Riley's dad," I robotically said. Riley was one of my camp kids from the past few years.

"Yes, I am. I want to thank you both for working so hard on that young man. We called your mother to inform her what happened. The kids are on their way back to camp. I can drive you two. Can you tell me what happened?"

I recalled everything I could, unable to do anything but stare straight ahead as I spoke.

"Do you think he'll make it?" Harry asked Travis.

"He's not stabilized, but he's breathing. That's about all I know," Travis said. He flipped his beaten up little memo book closed and put it in his back pocket. Travis looked older than when I first met him. His son was one of the most troubled boys I ever worked with. An anorexic boy straight out of a psych ward who turned out to be suicidal. He was a sweet kid though, smart, just tormented by something. Something no one ever really came to understand. I wondered if Travis could sleep with all the worries about his son.

I doubted I'd sleep tonight.

"Laurel? Are you sure you don't need anything?"

I didn't respond.

"It's that brain injury," Harry said. "Sometimes it makes her like this." If I was fully conscious and able to properly respond, I'd smack him.

Harry and I clambered into the air-conditioned cruiser, which after weeks of going without AC, I felt frigid and it nearly knocked me out of my funk. "Will you let me know what happens?" I asked.

Travis looked back at me, surprised by my voice, before getting the car on the road. "You don't know the young man, do you?"

"No, how could I?"

"You're not family. I don't think it'd be proper; giving you many updates," he said.

I rubbed my head, feeling tired and achy. "You know me," I said.

"I don't make a habit of being unprofessional. Last summer . . . that was different. You seemed to know my son better than I did at the time."

Riley Stevens ended last summer in the hospital with third degree burns after being pulled from the inside of a burning building on camp property. "I'll let you know if he makes it, though. You deserve that much."

Camp was no more than a ten minute drive away. Owaissa Lake was just outside camp property and belonged to Kellova Hills State Park. I wanted to be back on my own territory, to get back into the groove of things and maybe forget. I leaned against Harry. There was a hidden language between counselors, especially ones that worked together as long as Harry and me. There was a level of comfort and trust that came from being around one another in the grossest of situations- heavy sweat, no indoor plumbing, poor hygiene, often in inclement weather. There was no keeping up appearances here.

My mother, the camp director, stood at the narrow entrance to camp, arms crossed tightly around her middle. It was a way of self-soothing when under a great deal of pressure. She was also as red as a tomato. It could have been the heat; it could have been the situation, but her face stood out against her white-blonde hair almost comically.

"I'm so glad you're safe," she said, taking a deep breath, but not a step forward. "Who would have thought those wilderness first-aid classes would actually save someone's life?"

"This isn't funny," I replied. Harry looked away, avoiding eye contact. "I should head up to Hawthorne. The girls are probably worried about me."

"Mia is staying with them right now. They're just fine. Why don't you get some rest, go up to the Hytte. You've had a traumatic experience."

"It'd be best if I didn't have time to think about it."

"I'm not only your mother, but your boss," Mom said stiffly. There was so much fire in her eyes, I didn't have energy to argue. "You need to rest too, Harry."

"In all honesty, Miss Winters, I didn't do any of the hard work," Harry said.

"Then you can keep her company and make sure she doesn't do anything stupid. It'll give you an opportunity to freshen up. I heard the male counselors are making a bet to see who can last the longest without a shower. I'd like you to lose that bet, Harry. Besides, Laurel has warm water in the Hytte, while I still don't have any in the house." She threw her arms up in the air as she started to walk away. As frustrated as I was, I wouldn't mind a night in the Hytte, my year-round residence.

"Why do you act like nothing happened?" I asked.

"Laurel, honey, please, just get some rest. It's no use wasting time on it now." She walked off, without a hug or anything else. Charlie, our Anatolian Shepherd, the guardian of the kids and staff, followed her back.

"That poor dog looks like he's going to flop over from heat exhaustion with all that fur," Harry started. "I'm glad Carra set up that kiddie pool for him under the deck." Harry paused before adding, "I could do with some rudimentary AC and some of those freezies."

"They're called popsicles, how many times do I have to tell you that?" I asked, the first smile of the afternoon crept up on my face.

"Popsicles have sticks, freezies are just frozen sugar water. There's a difference," he said. "Uh, Laurel . . .we're missing pizza night!" He stopped in his tracks. "I can smell the butter sponges . . ."

"Go grab some. Marianne always makes extra," I added.

Back in the cabin, I curled up on my old recliner, one that belonged to my grandmother long ago, now reduced to a shadow of its former self. The padding was nearly gone, and it was so worn in places it developed cloth callouses. But with fluffy blankets, it was perfect. The TV wasn't set up to any cable, so we had some DVDs. Harry and I decided on *The Princess Diaries* complete with pizza, butter sponges (garlic bread), popcorn, and freezer pops (we finally agreed on a name for them).

I paused the movie and looked at Harry when I couldn't focus any longer. I didn't want to think about what happened earlier in the day and if I let my mind wander, I'd just see that sickeningly white skin.

"I need honesty. Are you actually going out with Peter?"

"Are you assuming I'm gay?" he asked, pushing his voice up higher than it usually was.

"I really hope that's a joke," I said. "I saw you two in the staff lounge all cuddled up, playing footsie and everything."

"I've seen you do that with numerous guys, and it didn't mean anything," he said in an amused flippant tone, tossing popcorn into his mouth. I was only two steps away from discomfort.

"Numerous? What the hell do you mean by numerous?"

"Oh, for fuck's sake, I meant two. Ezra and the arsonist."

Now I was zero steps away from discomfort. "Lukas. He has a name," I stated, burying my head in my hands. Harry noticed.

"Sorry," he said. "I know you liked Lukas."

"I didn't like him the way you think I liked him," I said. Harry moved closer to me. I could smell myself, while Harry already showered, using my shampoo, conditioner, body wash, body scrub, and body butter. He smelled like me on a good hygiene day, and it was weird. "And I miss both of them."

"Lukas was kind of freaky," Harry said. The movie was still paused with the play button on the remote right below his big, hairy toe. "He always had that broody look on his face, looked too much at teenage girls for my comfort level, and he was always touchy-feely with you, especially after that car accident. He never seemed right." He paused and added, "Never trusted him after that incident four years ago when he slept with Emma and got her fired yet your mom went ahead and hired him."

"He's just like that . . ." I said.

"What, the world's biggest man-whore?" Harry asked.

"He's still one of the few people I trust."

"I better be on that list," Harry insisted.

"You are, or you wouldn't be in my cabin with me. Lukas though, he was different like me. We never clicked well with the rest of the staff."

"Eh, that's probably a good thing on your part, though. Most leadership staff get their heads up their asses about two weeks in and go around acting like they're better than everyone else. Lukas was just desperately trying to woo as many ladies as possible to forbidden parts of camp to defile them."

"We all knew that," I said. "But to be frank, my dear, you're a man-whore too." I patted him on the shoulder.

"And you're a fucking twenty-four year old virgin," he said, not rudely, though. "You've never gone on a single actual date, as far as I'm aware, and never kissed a guy."

"No, I did, once," I said.

"The man-whore or Ezra?"

"Ezra," I whispered. "And I can name every single guy you've hooked up with at camp since we were sixteen. Would you like me to start?"

"Well, hello stalker," he said, his pale face turned red.

"First there was Colby, but that didn't last long . . ."

"Laurel," he whined.

"Oh fine, but don't mess with Peter. He's so cute and innocent. He seems like the kind of guy that would make elaborate prom-posals or bake cookies for everyone. You're just not that romantic."

"I brought you chocolate on a bad day," Harry said indignantly.

"I want chocolate now . . ." A metallic jingling filled the brief silence.

"What the hell is that?"

"Mousetraps," I said, standing up, throwing the blanket to the side. "Thought I'd have time during free hour today to check them."

"Why . . .?"

"Gotta do it at least once a week or I get overrun," I replied. There were ten mice traps set with peanut butter sandwiches throughout the Hytte, all bedazzled with self-adhesive gems. There were six squirming mice in the first trap. Harry shivered, grossed out.

"Who do you think was in the water?" I asked.

"Could've been anyone, but whoever it was, they were in a bad state."

"In Greenville? In that lake?"

We dropped the mice into one of the many five gallon buckets on the porch for this very purpose. Dusk approached, and in this part of the forest, it got dark quickly. The sunset stretched above the grassy clearing around the Hytte. Every clear night, the sky was extraordinary, like a neon, watercolor painting.

The mice scurried in the bucket, scratching up the sides. A towel went over the top and I proceeded to empty out the remainder of the traps.

"This is disgusting," Harry muttered.

"Well, how would someone end up beaten to shit in the middle of nowhere," I asked.

"I don't know! There's Valley College, and the creamery . . .we don't know, but you really shouldn't obsess over it. You tend to."

Chapter Two: July 28, 2016

"I dragged a man out of the water, Harry, and you want me to forget about it?"

"I didn't say that," he sighed.

My eyebrows rose. "Grab two of the buckets. I need to get rid of the mice."

"You don't kill them, do you?"

"No."

"Good. Honestly, I didn't think you'd have the guts," he joked. "Granted, I don't either. Where are we taking them?"

"House One," I replied.

He froze. "All the way over there?" It wasn't the hike that scared him. It was the house.

"It's only slightly dark, and I don't like going there alone anyway," I said. With buckets full of squirming mice, we stepped away from the small wooden cabin and onto one of the mulch-covered trails.

It led steadily upward, past groups of Treehouse cabins. The trees provided a thick cover and the lullaby of insects singing. The sound was the only comforting thing about the hike. The closer to House One we came; the more tension rose in my stomach and chest. The place had a horrible vibe about it, as if darkness loomed above, around, and inside the building, as well as the land. Each year, it grew, taking more land into its grip.

Harry slowed. "I hate that house," he said. Where we stood, we couldn't even see it. The hill still needed to be crested, and until that point, all that lay ahead was the ever-darkening woods. "Do we have to go in there? Why do you drop off a bunch of fucking mice in the house?" His voice was high and whiny.

"I guess part of me hopes they'll eat the place," I mumbled, thinking back to the mangled body of the coyote. A shiver ran through my bones.

"Do you always take mice there?" he asked.

"Yeah."

There were three distinct knocks when I finished speaking. Harry and I both knew they came from the house. They were predictable. There was never a trip up this way without those knocks. We shivered.

"Ah shit," Harry said. He ran forward with the buckets swinging. He tossed the mice in and ran back to me.

"I'm not running," I said. "I'm too tired and my arms hurt too much."

"Fine!" He whined again, taking the buckets from me to repeat his action. "Can we go back now? Please? I just want to finish the movie and go to sleep with a fan on my face. For fuck's sake this place gives me the creeps." He walked twice the speed he usually did on the way down the hill; I had to nearly run to keep up.

"That's probably why Lukas tried to burn the place down, ever think of that?" I asked.

"No, he was crazy. He held a shovel up to the window and challenged the damn house."

"Yeah, but he had a point," I said.

Once upon a time, the two were quite good friends, despite Lukas's slight homophobia and extreme leanings to the right. Somehow, they made their odd friendship work even if they were completely different individuals.

"Did you know that he was going to do it?" I whispered. There was no reason to keep my voice down. We were far from any kids' prying ears and the bugs were loud enough we could yell.

"He threatened it," Harry shrugged. "He said it was possessed. It was what makes all the bad things happen here, makes kids turn crazy. He blamed it for your head injury; blamed it for Haley killing herself; blamed it for the garage burning down and blamed it for Riley seeing things . . .but you know something's off with Lukas's brain, right?"

"I still think he has a point," I pressed. We descended into the clearing.

"You don't think it was Lukas in the water, right," Harry asked. He stopped walking in the grass and looked at me with wide eyes.

"God no, he's not built like that. Whoever was in the water wasn't tall enough and didn't have the tattoo," I said.

"The tattoo?"

"The camp one, the wreath."

Camp Kellova's symbol was a laurel wreath, my namesake. My mother was so enamored with this place, I was named after it. Laurel trees weren't particularly large or good looking, but there were plenty of them around camp and some lady nearly a hundred years ago used to provide wreaths for those in camp who achieved difficult honors. On every signpost and door was a laurel wreath, just like with the Greek Olympic games.

"He can't have that tattoo, it's against the rules. He didn't become a Nomad."

"Since when did he care about the rules?" I asked, laughing nervously.

We dropped the buckets on the porch and went inside to finish the third movie and go to sleep. With all the fans on, it wasn't terribly hot in there. It was nice to have a real mattress for a night rather than vinyl cushions in the cabins. Real walls weren't a bad thing either, though I was so used to the breeze catching me, I needed the windows open. Even with all the comfort, all I could do was stare at the ceiling.

When I closed my eyes, I saw the body floating in the water. Limp and cold like a dead fish, that one hand strangely graceful in the way the fingers fell. The familiar hair paired with the disfigured and unfamiliar face.

Chapter Three:

July 29, 2019

Drowsy and cranky from a lack of sleep, I dressed in my khaki shorts, and a t-shirt. My little tin of tattoo cream was next on my list of things to do. On my left arm was a peony bush with a bluebird sitting in the center, in honor of my grandfather, who not only had a love of rare peony varieties, but also said that if I were to pout, the bluebird of happiness would come by and shit on my lip. Below it was the memorial tattoo for my father, who died overseas when I was seven. He called me his little wolf, a term I hadn't heard from my mother since his death. My dad wasn't mentioned at all, any pictures of him were hidden in the attic or in storage. To my mother, I wasn't sure he ever existed. I may as well have popped out of the ground fully formed.

The tattoo was of a white wolf lying on the ground, being guarded by a large eagle. Another memorial was on my ankle, a small bottle of Felix Felicis from *Harry Potter* with a quote from my camper Haley's favorite character, Luna, "You're just as sane as I am." I kept up on these tattoos as well as I could.

I brushed my hair with my eyes closed, braided it, and even washed my face without looking. I feared if I looked in the mirror, something would be different. My hair would be wet, or there would be a piece of seaweed, or my skin would be translucent . . .but I just kept reassuring myself that the young man pulled out of the water was alive.

What I needed was a hefty dose of sleeping pills and a good bit of sleep. My entire body was incredibly sore. It needed as much rest as my mind did.

Bumbling around didn't rouse Harry; very little in the world could. His phone would soon set off an alarm that, if not expected, could cause a heart attack. On more than one occasion in the past, I had to drag Harry from his bed to make it to breakfast on time. Even his naps were hard to wake him from. Occasionally cold water would be dumped on him if he was found snoozing, not only by me. I made my way to the porch when the alarm went off. Harry cried, "I don't want to!"

"Too bad!" I yelled back.

In the distance, across the clearing, children, some still in pajamas, were carrying toothbrushes to the bathrooms to get ready for the day. Their hair was in every direction, shoes on the wrong feet, shorts on backward. It was a regular day. Tomorrow they would go home for a night of sleep and then be right back at it on Sunday afternoon. A full twenty-one hours of freedom. For my twenty-one hours, I usually spent the first hour eating and then the next twenty sleeping to recuperate for the upcoming week.

My mind did not seem to click with my physical body. With my backpack slung across my shoulder, I trudged across the thick grassy clearing, past the kids. The creek bubbled beneath a large, flat bridge I often sat upon to read. It was a beautiful creek, a good place to play, search for cool stones, or bones, and as it went both west and east, it widened into a river. With such a hot summer, though, it was drying up.

It was the halfway point between the Hytte and Clark, and near Clark, was the camp office. At this hour, it was empty. Even the two computers connected to the internet for staff use were vacant. Mom wasn't in her office. She was awake though; Charlie was running outside while it was still cool. He often bounded through the grass, jumping, bouncing, and looking for bunnies.

I dug through a file cabinet under 'S'. The file folders were color coded, thanks to the office manager. She had bad eyesight, and I had a bad brain. Too many tabs of one color blurred together in my mind. Under the name Stevens, was Riley Stevens' file with his father's cell number. I typed the number into my phone quickly, noting that it wasn't even seven o'clock yet.

"Stevens," he answered.

"It's Laurel Winters. Did you find anything out?" I asked.

"I thought you'd call . . ." he grumbled. There was a click of a mug being set down. "With the extensive facial swelling, it was difficult to determine, visually, who he was . . . but we did gain access to his phone despite the extensive water damage. Turns out it was Ezra Concord, Laurel."

My heart nearly fled through my mouth. "What?" I cried. "Ezra? Are you sure?" My heart ran up from my chest and through to the back of my head where it pounded away. Ezra. How did I not recognize him? How did I not know?

"We did dental x-rays, and we are going to match them. Height matches, hair matches, eye color matches," He paused for a long while. "You worked with him for many years. Do you know of any family to contact?"

"He doesn't have a family, at least not anymore," I said.

"No uncles, aunts, grandparents?"

"He said he didn't know who his father was, and his mother was kind of a loner. So if he has family, he's never met them. His mother died of an overdose two years ago," I said.

The man breathed heavily and waited for a moment. Small songbirds flitted about the numerous feeders hanging outside the windows. Clark was in full view including the massive porch and all the rocking chairs made by and painted by campers.

"He was staying at Valley College as an R.A. for the summer semester programs. That's all I know."

"Have you been in close contact with him?"

"I haven't spoken to him since last summer," I said.

"Were you close with him?" Travis asked. I didn't know if his tone was polite or accusatory. It was just very cop-like. My heart flipped in my chest. I couldn't tell him.

"I trust him," I replied honestly, closing my eyes. Ezra's kind face entered my mind. Those soft brown eyes and innocent smirk glowed brightly. "We were close. I just don't know why he would end up in Owaissa, half dead."

"Laurel, someone tried to kill him. What happened to him was intentional. I need to find out who and why."

"I want to see him," I said.

My mother left her house, just south of the office. She checked her flower beds, carefully weeding and watering.

"He's not awake, Laurel. Just focus on your work and I'll let you know if there's an update."

"Thank you. Say hi to Riley for me, and please, please, if absolutely anything changes, let me know. I need to know."

"Ok,"

I followed the smell of bacon to Clark. Marianne was talking loudly to someone. "Can you start getting the juice out, Kennedy?"

I stepped into the kitchen. It was warm and humid there, although there were already four massive wire fans running at top speed.

"Miss Laurel!" Kennedy cheered. I was surprised she was here. She did tend to stick out from the crowd. She preferred to hang around the counselors rather than the other campers. Considering she was thirteen years old, a sophomore in high school, and already got a thirty-two on the ACT, she was smart as a tack academically, but not socially.

"What are you doing here?" I asked.

"She got in trouble of course!" Marianne responded. "Orion sent her my way to do some kitchen duty. She decided not to participate in anything yesterday, it seems."

"I was worried about you, Miss Laurel!" Kennedy said, carrying pitchers of juice to a large, steel refrigerator. Marianne sighed, standing at a large flattop where she was flipping pancakes. Her graying hair was styled in a bun atop her head, a blue net around it.

"Do you have any hot cocoa, Marianne?" I asked, leaning against a wall.

"Got a new tub over by the coffee maker." She waved her hand in that direction. Kennedy jogged toward me.

"It sure is better than that baking cocoa you tried to pawn off on us a few weeks ago," I said, pulling the metal seal off the Nestle powder.

"I thought adding some sugar would help," she said, chuckling.

"It definitely didn't, nothing helped it."

"Can I have some hot cocoa too?" Kennedy asked.

"Sure," I said.

"You're supposed to be helping me!" Marianne called, laughing still. I noticed that even lifting a coffee pot of hot water hurt. I was so out of shape . . .

"Ok, Kennedy, so what are we going to do differently today?"

"Don't use that tone with me," she grumbled, but there was still a smile on her face.

"Well, what got you here in the first place? You could've slept in."

"You know I'm always up before everyone else. I don't mind being here, besides, at least now I can get some extra food."

"Not if you don't help me," Marianne said. Kennedy and I put down our mugs and joined her. There were well over a hundred something kids to feed and that required a hell of a lot of pancakes. She poured, we flipped.

"Last night Ellie was convinced she just had to call her mom because she was traumatized by the whole thing. It's not like she saw anything. She's too scared of going on a canoe or kayak, she thinks it'll tip over or something. Especially kayaks, though, those things are super hard to tip. You have to commit to that." She spoke quickly, though every word had probably been thought through numerous times. "She thinks the guy is dead, but he isn't, right?"

"He's not dead," I answered.

The heat from the flattop was surprisingly nice. Later in the day, though, the temperature would go up another thirty degrees or so, but now, it was almost calming.

"Ellie's going to freak seeing pancakes. I can't believe she's never eaten pancakes or cereal before she came here; why are her parents so weird?" Kennedy asked.

"They're doing that keto diet I think," I said halfheartedly.

"It's not fair to restrict a kid's diet like that. I did research on the keto diet and it's not good for growing kids. Kids need carbs. It's not like she needs to lose weight. I think her parents are just making her into a hypochondriac." All of this was coming out of a thirteen-year-old's mouth.

"I think you need to learn to be a bit more accepting,"

"I haven't said any of this to her face!" Her voice rising a few octaves.

"You have to be one of the least chill people I know," I said, bumping into her playfully.

"Be careful in my kitchen," Marianne said. "I don't want any burns. We only have half an hour before the kids set the tables."

Being in the kitchen was a good distraction, but as soon as breakfast began, all distractions fell apart. Campers and counselors alike came to me and asked if all was well. The official statement from my mother, the director, was that we were supposed to go on as normal. As if nothing happened. Camp was a distraction from outside life, a way to unplug and grow as a person, but pretending what happened didn't happen was impossible.

Kids streamed in to set the tables. Most were in pretty rough condition: hair unbrushed, clothes not clean. Some of them were here for only a week, others for two or three, and some for all twelve. It was the latter group I really got attached to. I saw them a quarter of the year, every year, for, so far, six years of their life. The girls in my cabin, currently, I'd known since they were little, and now they were becoming young adults. It was scary to see how time worked. Yesterday and last night dragged on, but in the grand scheme of things, it was rushing by so quickly I could never figure out what hit me.

Kennedy was set up in the kitchen with three cups of hot cocoa. When Ellie arrived, she ended up with the nurse, where she sat every morning in case she showed signs of some strange ailment. Ellie was a conundrum to me. Her parents were desperate to get her out of her comfort zone, to help her be social, learn new things. When they dropped her off, we spoke at length about different camps they tried and one of them seemed to fit. They had to get her away from her phone and the TV. Anything with a screen. At home, Ellie refused to go on walks with her parents, refusing to participate in life. So, if her parents were willing to stick this out, so was I. The best feeling in the world was getting a kid to change the way they looked at the world, to see it without a screen in the way. Of all the kids I battled in this manner she was definitely at the top of the list.

Right now, her phone is locked away in the office because she kept sneaking it. The second day at camp, I found her on top of the tallest hill trying to get a signal.

"Jenny!" Harry yelled as he ran up to help.

Jenny attempted to carry four pitchers of juice and it splashed everywhere. "Just . . . don't!"

I couldn't help but laugh.

Arty and Taylor, two of the older boys sat down across from me and poured each other grape juice. "I saw it, I swear!" Taylor whispered. I looked at them directly. "And a bunch of other weird shit, just like Riley said there was."

"He wasn't exactly steady in the head, man," Arty replied. "He hallucinated a girl the whole time he was here too."

"Ask Harry, or anyone. Riley wasn't the only one to see her," Taylor said.

Arty took his baseball hat off his curly head of hair and placed it on the table. He reminded me of Harry, red-headed, pale, prone to sunburns. Taylor, on the other hand, was identical to his brother, Noah, who turned seventeen years old within the last month. Both Taylor and Noah were troubled kids and had reason to be. Losing both parents would leave any kids in dire straits. Yet, here was one of them. Long, beautiful hair, braided behind his head, tanned skin clinging close to his skull, and bright, inquisitive eyes. The only difference was that Taylor wasn't in nearly as much trouble as Noah was in his younger years.

I knew exactly what they were talking about, though. "I've seen her too," I said. "Most of us have." No one had joined us at the table yet. Kids were still hurrying around with pitchers of water and juice. "I'm assuming you're talking about the woman on the hill."

"And weird orbs of light that get way too close for comfort," Taylor added.

"What are you two talking about?" Arty asked, putting his hands on the table.

Taylor said, "I think that's why people sleepwalk up there."

"You're just trying to scare me, Taylor," Arty said. "And you're not helping."

"I told you, you're not kids. I'm not going to lie to you. I say that every summer," I replied.

"I think that girl is the one that made Riley go to the house and get burned," Taylor said.

August 2015

"Laurel!" A harsh whisper in my ear. It had to be at least midnight and all I wanted was to bury my head under my pillow. "Laurel!" It was March.

"What the hell are you doing here?" I grumbled, not moving.

"I can't find Riley," he said. That probably should have gotten me out of bed, but exhaustion was a strong force, and it was late in the summer.

"What do you mean?"

"Come on, let me talk to you outside," March said, yanking on my arm. I sat up, rubbing my eyes. He led me outside. The cool, fresh air woke me a bit and I could see more clearly. "Riley, gone, get that?"

"Yeah, you rude fuck," I said. I was at my worst when tired. March sighed and shook his head. He was usually just about the sweetest, fun dude out there, but I really wanted to slap him. Hard.

"March?" Noah and Carson were outside their cabin, Aspen. They waved to get our attention. In the dark, they were barely visible, but Noah's long hair was unmistakable, and Carson's short, muscular stature was as well.

"What?" March whispered.

"If you'd listen to me!" Noah hissed back. His eyes locked with mine. "Can I talk to you without . . . them, listening?"

"Sure," I said.

"Not me?" March asked, Noah rolled his eyes. "Fine."

Noah and I stood on the slope of the hill, on the mulch path. "I'm worried about Riley. He's been sneaking out a lot. I'm not a snitch, but I met the goddamn kid in Greenville's EDO clinic, they didn't have a bed for me anywhere else. After Haley . . .I kind of went downhill- bad. My brother caught me cutting and I landed in there. My mom was worried I wouldn't make it without help . . .Riley, he was like seventy-something pounds. His brothers called him Skeletor. He was in terrible shape, had this voice talking to him called Anna.

He said he thought it was his mother coming back from the grave to haunt him."

"What?" I asked.

Noah put his hand out like I needed to slow down. "His mother died a few years ago from this weird illness, chronic fatigue turned deadly, I don't know. He described her as evil, that she would pester him about his weight and call him a fat lazy slob and that he was a bastard, so on and so forth. He was relieved when she died, and then soon after the voice appeared."

"What does that have to do with the situation now?" I asked.

"The voice has been pestering him this whole time, it's gotten stronger. Not only that, but he's been seeing this girl, Alina around, and we don't have a girl named Alina at this camp. He's been hallucinating about her this whole time. Made her a bracelet and a necklace in lapidary and everything. He even told me he kissed her."

"Why didn't you tell me this sooner?" I asked.

"I didn't know what was going on! Taylor spilled all this during dinner. He said Riley's been sneaking out every night. He only knows that because he has too." The smell of smoke filled my nostrils.

"Where's Lukas?" I asked. Noah looked confused. "March, have you seen him?"

"Ezra, is he in his bunk?" March poked his head into Cherry. "Ezra!"

"No, he's not here," Ezra said, stepping out, rubbing his eyes. He sniffed the air too. "Ah shit, we need to get up to the house."

"What do you mean? What about the house?" Harry asked, leaving his cabin as well.

The smoke billowed down the hill, clinging to the earth. The kids began to stir too, a chorus of 'what's going on?' entered the forest. I ran up the mulch path toward the top of the hill. The thick tree-cover blocked the moonlight, and the path was almost impossible to see. Ezra was close behind me.

"Lukas! Riley!" I called repeatedly. The closer to the house I came, the more smoke filled the air, billowing up in dark, black clouds. The house wasn't on fire. The smoke only came out of the windows, which had blown out. Lukas

was dragging Riley by an arm away from the house and toward the edge of the clearing. Riley wasn't conscious. "What the hell!" I screamed at Lukas.

"He wasn't supposed to be in there, Laurel . . . but it won't burn. The damn house won't burn, it's supposed to burn," he cried.

"Lukas, look at me!" I said, putting a hand on each cheek. "Look at me." There was confusion, desperation, terror on his face. "Look. At. Me."

Ezra immediately called the police and EMS. There was no telling how they would get to this location. There were no roads leading to the house from the highway.

I called, "We need water! Bring up as much water as you can!"

A string of counselors and older kids formed. Metal pails went from person to person up the hill. In the walkie-talkie I said, "Leta, Joel, don't bring any of this up to the Birdhouse kids. Try to keep them asleep. If they wake, take them to Apple to do crafts, just keep them away from the hills. If anyone has any able bodied and willing kids, stick them in the line."

Mia and Ezra led the attack on the burning mattresses, tables, and interior furniture. Lukas stood in shock, unable to speak, or move. He simply watched the destruction. Riley was out cold. His arm looked like it was partially melted, and his shirt was burned into the skin. I placed cold cloth on him and as soon as they warmed, I replaced them, continuously pouring water on the wounds.

Coral knelt across from me. "Do you think he'll make it," she asked.

"I hope so," I said.

A heavy quiet hit everything, and the world seemed to swirl around me. People's movements slowed to the point of stopping. The air was stifling. I looked around madly, hoping to find an explanation. A luminous figure stood in the woods, watching with her lacy white dress, shoulder length hair, and a face as still as one sleeping. She watched everything. When I blinked, she disappeared, and the world returned to normal.

Riley and Lukas were hospitalized, and Lukas was arrested, but until the next day, he refused to speak. Perhaps he was unable. He was in shock, more on the mental side than the physical. Riley was unconscious and on an IV drip full of liquids and pain medication.

Ezra and I stayed in his hospital room with Officer Stevens. We still smelled of smoke, but the smell of burning flesh was even stronger. While Riley was unconscious, they cleaned his dressings a few times, debriding his wounds. Chunks of skin came off him. All three of us waited in silence.

The sheriff kept Officer Stevens from interrogating Lukas. I didn't blame the sheriff for that decision. If it was my kid who was burnt in the arson, I would have ripped his face off.

Chapter Four:

July 30, 2016

Saturday morning, Gracia and I sat on the floor of the porch of Clark with a tiny table between us. She was waiting for her parents to pick her up for the weekend. They traveled from Dubuque and were reliably late. With a deck of cards, we found plenty of games to play, and we weren't alone, Charlie was half-asleep at our feet. We had a game of slap going.

Her ukulele case sat propped beside her with a small weekend bag. She was distracted, and it showed.

"What's going on, hon?" I asked.

"I've had nightmares about what happened at the lake . . . but different. It was as if it was happening to me, that there was this ugly man beating me with anything he could get his hands on, sticks, rocks, the butt of a gun . . . and really, it's dumb; you and Harry were the ones who really had to deal with it. Have you been having bad dreams?" she asked.

"No," I said. "But I just haven't really slept. Closing my eyes is the hard part."

"You see him? Under the water?" Her discernment knocked me off my game a little. In one moment, I saw her hair wet, her face gone waxy and pale. I blinked quickly to get the image away.

I nodded. She moved and wrapped her arms around Charlie. He just smiled and his tail went nuts. "I've never seen anything like that before, I think I just got all wimpy," she said.

"I don't think being uncomfortable in the middle of a crisis defines your level of courage," I said, making eye contact.

"What if something happens again and I run?"

"Why would something else happen," I asked.

She sighed and put the deck of cards down. "Mr. Lukas, Riley, Haley, Georgie . . ." she paused. "Why do you think this all happens?"

"I wish I knew."

"If you knew, would you stop it," she asked.

I paused. "I would if I could," I replied.

"Yes. I texted Noah this morning. He's signed up for the wilderness retreat in a few weeks. He's been doing some digging, at the camp library, and the one in town, trying to get answers about what happened to Haley," she started. Her eyes watered and she rubbed it away. I patted her back. She continued, "It's still hard to . . .ugh, well, he doesn't think she killed herself, and neither do I. He . . . took his research home with him. He hasn't stopped looking for answers."

"We all need answers," I said.

"I think desperation has just pushed him forward . . . he's a wiz at research. He needs something to help him through all this. He isn't planning on college, but at least he has something to talk about other than whoever he's banging at the time."

"I think you just forgot your filter," I said.

"Yeah . . . that happens sometimes, but do you promise that if he finds out what happened, you'll help me do something about it?"

"Yes."

Once the kids were home for the weekend, the camp staff started on the mess the kids left behind: the shower houses, the pool, the lost and found, and the disaster zone that was the staff lounge. Mom was in her office going through reports, parent emails about lost items, upcoming schedules, last minute sign-ups, and most of all, dealing with the aftermath of the incident at the lake. While everyone was busy, I snuck out to my small car. It was as clean as I could keep it. It was the first major purchase of my life, other than a college education. Despite my driving it through the Kellova Hills repeatedly, it still ran as smooth as butter. Gliding up the hill with thick tree-covering on either side, it was difficult to see past the road. Deer frequently ran across the street in the hills, and it was fawn season.

From camp, the road wound every which way, past a new housing development and into town. From there, there was a single straight road toward the hospital.

This section of Greenville was beautiful, separated from the large cattle pastures, dairy farms, and the creamery that took up a majority of the town. This section was spruced up for the college. It lay to the north, looking out on the hills, nestled in an array of beautiful trees. The old brick buildings stood out in comparison to the wooden farmhouses and metal silos. Strangely enough, the hospital matched the aesthetic of the college. Its exterior was made of aging sandstone, though the inside was still sterile, ugly, tile.

While I hated the hospital and being near it made me feel like my stomach dropped a few miles into an abyss, camp kept bringing me back.

Parked outside, I passed by full flower beds with marigolds, zinnias, gerberas, and roses. It was like putting lipstick on a pig. No matter the color on the outside, it wouldn't make the inside any better.

Before going inside, I called Travis Stevens.

"Hello, Laurel," he said.

"I'm at the hospital to see Ezra," I said. "Can you tell the people at the front desk to let me back?"

"He's in the ICU, Laurel. They don't exactly have visiting hours," he replied.

"I need to see him. I dragged him out of the water."

"Laurel . . ."

"Please, I need to see him," I begged.

"Give me a moment," he replied and hung up. I went inside, everything looked artificial, from the art to the plants, and painfully uncomfortable furniture.

I approached the information desk. "Hi, I need to see Ezra Concord. He's in the ICU."

"One moment," she said, and picked up a phone. She talked quietly on the other end of the line. "He already has visitors in his room, ma'am. I'll ask you to wait until they leave."

"I told Officer Stevens I was coming, he's the visitor," I said.

Thankfully, Travis came straight from the room. "She's with me . . ." he said tiredly. The woman looked at him with eyebrows raised, unsure. "I'll keep her out of trouble."

The hospital wasn't a maze. In fact, it was quite straightforward. Last time I was here, Riley was the one out cold. Now, it was Ezra. He had an IV hooked up to him and his face was still discolored, but no longer unrecognizable. He looked like himself. My heart leapt in my heart. I needed to speak to him. I needed to tell him what I'd kept to myself for the past year. I needed to tell him the truth, and I needed to know. I needed to know what happened, a year ago, a few days ago. I was desperate, and that desperation hit me like a wall.

"Miss Laurel!" Riley exclaimed, smiling widely. He sprouted at least three inches since I saw him last summer. He brought me back to reality a bit, and I could feel my feet on the ground again. The skin on his arms was plasticized from having been burned so badly. There were places where it appeared stretched and webbed. He didn't seem to mind my eyes drifting in that direction.

"Hi, Riley," I said, and sat down beside his spot on one of the hard, maroon colored chairs. Officer Stevens, wearing his civvies, stood against a wall, arms crossed.

"I want to be here when he wakes up since he was there when I woke up last summer . . . well, you and him." Riley rubbed the back of his head. Now Riley looked good. Healthy. He wasn't pale or ashy. His face was bright and interested. He wasn't a walking skeleton. "They took the breathing tube out about an hour ago, said he could wake at any time," Riley said. "He can breathe on his own and he responded, so that's good." He leaned back in his chair, legs bouncing. He didn't stay in one place well. I understood completely. "He woke up a bit last night, but the medicine they gave him kind-a knocked him out."

I approached Ezra. I couldn't stay still any longer. "Ezra," I said softly. I touched his face. Sparse facial hair grew, and the stubble was rough. My hand then wrapped around his and I squeezed. "Ezra, can you hear me?" My heart ached in my chest.

Travis took a deep breath. "Laurel, they took an MRI of his brain. There's damage from a lack of oxygen and blunt force trauma. He might not be the same."

"He'll wake up, he's gotta wake up . . ." I muttered, sitting beside Ezra on the hospital bed. I nervously touched his face, feeling heat from the swelling, but a cold sweat that made my stomach churn.

"Hey Riley, how about we go get some coffee, I at least need some," Travis said. He reached out for Riley, and they left the room. Riley looked back at Ezra and I and waved.

Ezra breathed evenly. A few years ago, I learned how to comfort him from nightmares, most of them concerning the girl on the hill leading up to House One.

I caressed the top of his forearm. After about ten minutes, I saw his eyes flitter. "Ezra," I shook his arm gently. His eyes tried to open again, but then they stopped as though there simply wasn't enough energy to carry on.

"It's Laurel, you know me. Will you wake up? Please, Ezra," I expected him to complain about talking too much, waking him up from a nice nap. "Please . . . Ezra, wake up, wake up!"

His eyes flew open, startled, and he cried out. He shot up and screamed.

"Nurse!" I yelled. "Nurse! He woke up!" At first, I was excited, hopeful. There he was. Awake. Yet the look in his eyes showed he didn't recognize where he was. He looked at the IV in his arm and touched his face and torso.

A nurse wearing blue scrubs ran in carrying a basket with a blood pressure cuff and other instruments. "Mr. Concord, do you know where you are," she asked. She was no older than either Ezra or me. Her eyes were thickly lined with eyeliner which made her look comical. "Mr. Concord." He was completely confused, his brow furrowed and mouth agape. He looked at me. There was a flicker of recognition in his eyes. "Do you know what today is?" she asked him. His face contorted with frustration.

"You're ok, you're ok," I said. "Just sit back."

Now standing beside him, hands placed on his shoulders, I gently pulled him back so he would sit down. He shielded his eyes from the bright, fluorescent lights.

"Can't you turn them down? They're hurting his eyes," I exclaimed.

The nurse, who was clearly flustered, dimmed them. Ezra peered out from behind his hands and looked at me again. Officer Stevens and Riley jogged into the room. "I told you as soon as we walked away, he would wake up!" Riley said. "I told you! And I missed it!"

"I'll listen to you next time," Travis said, out of breath. "How is he, nurse? I need to ask him some questions."

"Well, he hasn't answered a single question I've asked him," the nurse said. She went to take his blood pressure. Ezra looked confused by what she was doing, like a child. When the cuff on his arm began to tighten, he cried and moved his arm away. "I have to take your blood pressure, Mr. Concord—please."

"It's not going to be an accurate reading with him this worked up . . ." I muttered.

"Let the woman do her job," Travis commented.

I put a hand on Ezra's free arm, though it was covered with a heavy cast. He relaxed slightly, though his body was still rigid and uncomfortable. The nurse got his blood pressure, pulse, and then took a light to look in his eyes. He winced at everything. Every touch. Every movement.

"I'll call for the doctor," she said. She looked like she hadn't signed up for this and wanted to leave.

Riley slowly approached and sat down next to Ezra in the small bit of space left on the hospital bed.

"Sorry, I wasn't here when you woke up. I tried to be, but Dad wanted coffee. Maybe when you're feeling better you can help me get through this boss level I'm stuck on."

The room stayed silent until Dr. Ragnall entered. He was a tall burly man with a buzzed head and piercing eyes. "I'm going to need you two to step out for a moment," Travis said to Riley and me.

"Why?" Riley asked. "I've been here the whole time."

"Go," Travis said. "You heard the man."

"She fished him out of the water," Riley added.

"We're not arguing about this," Travis said, rubbing his temples.

Riley and I slipped into the hallway and the door slammed shut. It wasn't very good at keeping the sound out. I knelt next to the door so I could hear.

"What are you doing? What if my dad catches you?" Riley asked.

"Just act like you're playing on your phone," I replied, and I acted like I was fixing the laces on my shoe.

"Do you know of any next of kin who could be contacted, Officer Stevens?" Dr. Ragnall asked.

"He has none. The closest family he has seems to be the two people standing in the hallway," he replied.

"But they aren't related in any way?"

"No. We are just trying to figure out what happened to this young man and get justice for him. What can you tell me?" Travis continued.

Dr. Ragnall sighed heavily and was silent for a moment. "My nurse said he's exhibiting mental disturbances, confusion, and is either unwilling or unable to answer questions. His MRI results show the damage he endured happened mainly in the left hemisphere of the brain, which is integral to speech production. His confusion may be due to the fact he doesn't know why he can't speak. There may be memory loss involved with such concussive trauma as well. Though there was also a single, sharp hit between his eyes I don't understand. It doesn't match with the rest of the blunt trauma. The MRI didn't show any damage to his frontal lobe." There was a pause. "What I'm trying to say is that whoever did this to him, intended on killing him. They at least succeeded at shutting him up." After more silence, Dr. Ragnall asked, "Have you been able to determine what caused the blows?"

"There was nothing in or by the lake that was entirely obvious. We're considering draining it to see if there were any weapons, but most likely, he was dumped there and left to die after the attack." My heart felt strangled and furious at the very thought that someone would do this to Ezra. He'd never hurt a fly, a mosquito maybe, but nothing else. At least not physically.

"As he has no next of kin, the hospital will decide his course of treatment. The swelling has been relieved from his skull and the inflammation has gone down considerably. He's breathing on his own and surprisingly stable, all good things. Next, we'll need to see if he can eat and drink on his own. We also removed some hematomas, as I mentioned with the swelling being relieved, we had to go in for surgery. His shoulder was set back in place, as well as both of his knees. I'm not so much worried about the shoulder as I am about the knees. Those were complex fractures around the actual ball of the joint." Dr. Ragnall sighed. "I'll get him on some more pain medication. If he doesn't calm down, we'll sedate. He needs time to recover, that's just the bottom line. Honestly, Officer, this man should have died."

There was silence again before he continued, "I'm going to schedule Mr. Concord for a CT, and a few follow up x-rays to see if everything was set properly. We're worried about the ribs, don't want to puncture a lung… a few orderlies will be in shortly with medication and to take him away."

Once Dr. Ragnall was gone, Riley and I returned. "Can a hospital just take over care?" I asked Travis. He leaned against a counter, his coffee cup in one hand, the other hand resting on his forehead.

"You can't keep out of anything, can you?" he asked. I assumed it was rhetorical. "He can't make decisions by himself, Laurel, and he has no family to do it for him. Now, I haven't had hardly any sleep. I need to join up with the rest of the force and speak with anyone who may have known him at Valley."

"It's summer, there can't be that many people there," Riley said.

"Still need to find out," Travis said. "Come on, let's get home, Riles."

"I don't want to go home and be there alone," Riley said with the slightest bit of whine in his voice. "Can I go to camp with Miss Laurel?"

"Not today," Travis said. "Let's go. I'll keep in touch, Laurel."

"Thanks," I said. They left the room and it hummed with machines and lights. During all this, Ezra was awake, watching us, listening perhaps. He looked so strange and mummy-like with his head plastered with bandages. His eyes followed me. A desperate longing to fix him—make him whole—came over me. He was long past my being able to fix him. He was far from ever being whole again.

Chapter Five:

August 2012

It was the final week of camp. The older kids stayed for the two weeklong wilderness retreat. The kids, Ezra, and I piled into the small parlor at the creamery for ice cream. They deserved the treat since it was the least dramatic and most successful retreat I'd ever been a part of. The kids behaved, there was no 'purpling', no contraband weapons, drugs, or electronics, and very little whining.

Lukas, 17-years-old, and as thin as a rail, had two large ice cream sundaes in front of him with more than an acceptable amount of sprinkles. Coral, who was dating him at the time, kept kissing his cheek and he smiled at her, putting an arm around her waist occasionally, pulling her close. It made me slightly nauseous to watch.

She was trying her hand at her first banana split which her grimace told me she didn't like. She switched her banana split with the small remainder of ice cream in one of Lukas's bowls.

Our youngest kid on the trip, thirteen-year-old Noah, drank so much soda, I was sure he wouldn't be able to stop burping. Orion was already finished with his ice cream and was enjoying a book in the corner of the booth with his feet planted on the chair and his eyes only inches away from the page. "Let's finish up here soon," I said. "They're going to close and kick us out." I eyed Mr. Morgenstern who ran the creamery, and he just watched us with slight disdain despite the business. I always thought people who ran ice cream places should be in good moods. There was nothing in the world better than ice cream, even the smell of an ice cream parlor was inviting.

"Almost done!" Lukas said, chugging the remnants of his mostly melted ice cream. He planted a kiss on Coral's forehead. "Let's go."

We returned to the minivan. It was dark outside, the closer to camp we got, the darker it became. "When will we get back?" Coral asked, yawning, curling up against Lukas.

"We're about twenty minutes away now," I said. Town was behind us and an unlit road ahead. Even the headlights felt dim. We crested the hill, and as we reached the point in the road where we would be the closest we would ever come to the House, a truck driving on the wrong side of the road appeared.

I laid on the horn and risked swerving out of the way, but that was when my brain stopped making memories. We were hit straight on. Despite the seatbelt, the airbag on my side never deployed. I was thrown from the van, through the crushed windshield, and landed in a ditch. From there I apparently crawled toward House One. I have no memory of why I did it. Perhaps my body felt called to go in that direction—pulled. Even then I knew it had a hold on people beyond reason.

Lukas found me inside the house, unconscious. I landed in the hospital and stayed out of it for quite some time. My mind registered nothing. I simply sat on a chair, staring at a wall. Time was not relevant. Nothing was. With the kids fine, and most of the brunt of the collision on me, there was some relief in that. The driver of the truck wasn't drunk or harmed. He claimed he had no memory of why he was on that road at all, much less why he was driving on the wrong side of it. He was a college student and alone in the middle of Kellova Hills at night. No drugs were found in his system. My mother wanted to press charges, but the decision came down to me, and even in my stupor, I said no.

Occasionally I was lucid, so Lukas came to the hospital and told me what he knew. "When Ezra and I found you, you walked like a mannequin or a doll. You just kept looking back at the house like that's where you wanted to be." Coral stood outside the room, biting her nails, looking nervously at me. Their relationship would last roughly another week. For Lukas, nothing survived past the state of infatuation. "None of us could get a signal. Orion ran down the hill to wake your mom up and she called there. They took you to the ER. I was worried you wouldn't come out of it."

"I'm sorry I screwed up the retreat," I said.

"It wasn't you, it was the douchebag driving the truck," he replied. "And all he got was a slap on the wrist and a fine. Shit, he nearly killed you."

When the campers returned home, the only person left at Kellova was Mia. She stayed behind to take care of the horses until they were sent back to their farms. We'd developed a friendship since my first year working at Kellova and she was on the small list of people I truly trusted. There was no explicit reason as to why we chose each other as friends. Maybe it was because we both saw each other as separate from the rest of the staff as a whole, but we were opposites. She was very hardworking, and I suffered from moderate depression that came with serious fatigue. I was admittedly lazy. Mia could just go and go and go, and she didn't mind visiting me.

I stayed in the hospital for only two days, and after that, stayed in my mom's house, set up on the couch. Each morning Mia would be there with coloring books, friendship bracelet string, and snacks. We watched endless episodes of Law and Order: SVU, *and* Criminal Minds. *We made hundreds of friendship bracelets together, piling them in boxes. She didn't pester me with questions, she just kept me company, and I appreciated that.*

Light was painful, loud noises hurt, my head itself throbbed from the inside. The world spun and took on a near constant sense of unreality. I didn't, couldn't, feel like myself, like I lost everything: my ability to connect with the world had been cut off.

The only way I made it through college was with the help of a neuroplasticity center that helped people with brain injuries. They were able to help me regain some things like speech, my ability to walk in a straight line, reaction time, but they couldn't stop my mind from spacing out or completely revolting on me.

Nina Wilson

It's a strange thing, not being able to trust your own brain. To feel like you have somehow allowed it to be something it never was supposed to be. One simple car accident changed so much. Not being able to trust my brain meant I couldn't always trust myself. My vision, hearing, could be skewed; my very experience of the world could be wrong. Ever since that August night, I was never quite sure what was real, or what was on my mind.

Chapter Six:

July 30, 2016

Unsurprisingly, I was not allowed to stay when Ezra was taken for tests, though I desperately wanted to stay by his side. I left the hospital, feeling guilty about leaving him there, alone. Some part of me truly believed that if I listened to Ezra at the end of last summer about the dangers of Kellova, he wouldn't be in such a terrible state.

Driving out of the parking lot in the glaring sun and suffocating heat, a piece of my heart burned with the knowledge that he was probably terrified. Trapped. Unable to speak. He could not tell us who, or what, did this to him. Yet, I had a job to do, and unfortunately that would not get my full attention. For now, my mind was far, far away and my body was on autopilot. Ezra had part of my heart, as reluctant as that heart was to be shared or even viewed.

Back at camp, Charlie the dog followed me up to the office. He had a big smile on his often dopey face and his tail wagged so hard his whole butt swung side to side. I rested my hand on his head, giving him little scratches, and he liked that. He was happy to go inside with me.

The office smelled strongly of bug spray and dust. The part-time secretary was at the computer, typing along. "Hi Laurel," she said, not taking her eyes off the computer. She was a sweet older woman, small as could be, fairly wrinkled, but she was extremely huggable, and always brought cookies to staff on Sundays before kids arrived.

"Hey Gail," I replied. Gail used to be a camper at Kellova, and a counselor. She was now a retired schoolteacher. She was also a Laurelite, another word for Nomad, one of the elites at camp. This could be seen by the laurel wreath tattoo on her wrist. Only people who earned that honor were considered for administrative positions that had access to camp information. I had avoided becoming a Nomad. The whole idea of the organization seemed off to me. I appreciated that they were supposed guardians of the history of the camp, but once again, it was just a summer camp. I knew they were hiding something.

"I sent you the list and ages of kids so we can get them sorted into cabins," she said. "That shouldn't take long for the Birdhouses, but we are having some trouble with the Treehouses. We won't be able to use Birch, apparently one of the kids decided to swing on a ceiling beam and busted a window."

"Jenny?" I asked, just imagining the tall, lanky, and often badly behaved teenage girl just ramming her Converse sneakered feet right into the screen.

"Yep," she said with a giggle. "Carra had a talk with her parents about it. Jenny claims she's just a klutz, but Mia says she was acting erratic and did it on purpose. Either way, at least she didn't burn down a picnic table this time around."

"Yet, we still have plenty of time for her to do that . . ." I muttered, remembering the summer when she decided to throw an old, wooden picnic table into a massive bonfire. She blamed it on eating too many marshmallows.

"I suppose this is as good a time as any to tell you that she's signed up for the retreat, so she'll be yours at the end of the summer," Gail said.

"What?" I cried in surprise, nearly dropping my phone. I caught it on the way down, fumbling, nearly losing it. "You've got to be kidding me. She'll find a way to get us all killed."

Gail showed me the new roster as proof. "Well… at least you know what to expect from her. This week, Asia was in the same cabin as Jenny, and she's begging not to be with Jenny again."

"Out of spite I kind of want to put her there, but I don't want to give Mia that stress . . ." I said. "She complains every week. The kids are too young, too old, too crazy . . .I'm running out of options. I'm sure she'll hate the middle-schoolers too."

"She also said she doesn't want to be with the horse kids either because of the hike up to the cabin."

"Too freaking bad," I said, walking into my office. Charlie jumped onto the old futon in the back of my office. Photographs and artwork from over the years covered the walls along with a hand-painted map of camp.

The kids who would have stayed in Birch were going to be moved to House Two, even if I preferred not using that cabin. It was too close to House One for anyone's comfort. Mia would lose her mind, but until that window was fixed, the options were very limited. I texted her about the situation, and almost immediately, I got a call.

"You're doing what? I'll go over there and fix the window myself. I'm not staying within a hundred yards of that house," she said. "I'll stitch it together by hand if that's what it takes."

"She'll just bust it out again. We probably need to replace it completely. At least House Two has actual windows and air conditioning. Brand new."

"And never used for a reason! Last time I stayed there, every single night, someone walked off in their sleep. And to get to the showers we still have to walk past House One. No one would go by themselves."

"The only other cabins we have haven't been opened in a decade, Mia," I said with a sigh. "They'll need deep cleaning with bleach and new mattresses brought up from the basement of Clark. The one that's probably in the best shape is Basswood."

"Ok, I'll go there now and get started on it."

"You're supposed to be taking a break. It's the weekend."

"Can't take a break if you're making me stay there," she replied.

"It's not me! Blame Jenny if you have to blame someone,"

"I will and I swear one of these nights I'll smother her in her sleep . . ." Mia grumbled. On the other end of the phone, her car started.

"Who do you want in the cabin with you? You and Asia have mutual-"

"That girl's a bitch. Absolutely lazy. She'd just wander off half the time and she screams every time she sees a raccoon. What was she expecting? We're in the middle of the woods! She's convinced she'll get rabies. I know Juliet is usually in the Birdhouses with the littles, but please give me her. She does her job and can make a good fire. Also, she doesn't scream when she sees raccoons."

"Juliet it is," I said with a sigh, making a note, eyes falling on the ticking of my dog themed clock. The plastic dog looked just like my previous dog Georgie. For a moment, my mind slipped away, off into nothingness before I snatched it back and looked away. "Who should I give Asia to?"

"I don't care. She's not my problem. I'm going to get to work. If you want to join me when you're done," Mia said.

"Ok," I said, and hung up. Mia and Juliet would be in Basswood. Birch would be closed. House Two would stay as it was, unused. I'd put Asia with Coral since she was just about the most patient of the female counselors I had, and they'd be in Aspen with the middle school aged girls. Coral really was a sweet girl, and I already felt bad sticking Asia with her.

While thinking about Jenny and her escapades, I saw that Ryanne would be a new addition to Aspen this week. I immediately felt sick to my stomach. She was the worst camper in recent history. The child was crazy.

June 30, 2015

The girls had gone to the restroom up the hill and brushed their teeth. Everyone was in their pajamas. I dug in my Rubbermaid tote for my bedtime story book and my lantern. I set up two lanterns near the doorway in case the girls needed them in the night. Most girls were in their bunks and ready for bed by 9:30. Ryanne hadn't changed her clothes. "Are you going to get your pajamas on?" I asked. She shook her head violently.

"Honey, you'll be much more comfortable if you do," I replied.

"I'm not changing!" she cried. I could feel all the eyes of the girls in the cabin fall on me.

The cabin was perfectly square, slightly bigger than any of the other Treehouses, and not in amongst any tree or on any stilts. It was the only carpeted cabin and the only one that included more than one lightbulb. It was a 'fancy' cabin. Leta was with me that week. When she looked at Ryanne, there was hate in her eyes.

"I'm giving you fifteen minutes," I said. "Make sure you take a buddy to the bathroom, though. If you don't listen, I'll have to talk to the director."

"I don't care," she said.

I set an alarm on my watch. Usually my threats at camp were empty because kids almost always went through with what I asked. Ryanne was different. She was a pain in the ass. Speaking to my mother in the morning would accomplish nothing, and it wouldn't get her sent home, but it could end with a tongue lashing by Ryanne's mother, Brandi, over the phone.

Leta waved me over and I sat down on the bunk in front of her. Every night she'd braid my hair. I don't know who it calmed more, me or her. I always enjoyed having people braid my hair. It was long for a reason. It was kept down to my hips and if there was nothing else for kids to do, I had numerous colorful ponytail holders, brushes, and combs. They could mess with my hair to their heart's content. Often that backfired on me, but if it ever got screwed up, I could just chop it off.

Ryanne was on a bottom bunk, and soon after Leta finished with my hair, Ryanne screamed bloody murder. I jumped up and asked, "What's wrong?"

"There's a mouse! There's a mouse! There's a mouse!" She repeated, over and over again, shrieking. Within a few moments she hit her head against the banister of the bed, on purpose.

"Ryanne, Ryanne," I said, Leta placed her hand between Ryanne's forehead and the wood of the bunk. She only hit harder until Leta had to take her hand away. "What's going on? Talk to us." I tried to pry her away from hitting her head, but she was unnaturally strong for a girl her age. She didn't talk—nothing but screams. "Do you want to go outside to speak instead?" The screams were more forced and higher pitched. Other girls in the cabin wrapped their heads in blankets, trying desperately to block out the noise.

"Ryanne! Stop it!" Leta snapped, facing her directly. Ryanne ignored her. "Ryanne! I know you're there!" She clapped her hands together and tried to make eye contact.

"Ryanne, come on, let's go outside," I said, and pulled on her arm. She pushed me aside with enough strength that I tumbled down. She continued to close her eyes and hit her head on the bunk. "You have to stop it and calm down. You're driving yourself into a frenzy."

"I'm getting Vivian," Leta said. "There's something wrong with this kid." The last part, she whispered.

She left the cabin, and I was alone with all the girls who took turns trying to console Ryanne. She listened to no one. Mom eventually came to the cabin with Vivian to do something about Ryanne. Her screams could surely be heard throughout camp. The sound reverberated through my brain at such a frequency that things felt cluttered and clogged. It was difficult to think, and anxiety hit me right in the chest.

"I'm going to step out for a moment," I told Vivian, putting my hand on her shoulder.

There was a small porch attached to the front of the cabin. A lightbulb hung above it, giving off a dull glow, but it was enough to attract plenty of moths. It must have been what attracted the luna moths I saw most mornings. The air felt good. It was chilly already and even though I could still hear

Ryanne screaming inside the cabin, it was muffled. The sharpness didn't feel like it would cause my skull to bleed—if skulls could bleed.

My eyes were closed for some time, allowing me to regain control of my mind. My arms wrapped around my knees tightly to comfort myself. If there weren't people around to judge, I may have started rocking back and forth, or crying. I was at my wit's end. But as I opened my eyes, I saw something odd.

There were large orbs of white and blue light, floating weightlessly in the air, dotting the path leading up the hill. They pulsed with energy, and some grew in size.

I'd seen them before, but never so many. There had to be at least a few dozen. Leta told me she woke up with an orb floating above her only a week ago. Scared, I went back inside. It was past eleven at night and was far too late for the kids to be awake. It was too late for me to be awake. Exhaustion was powerful, and I sat on my bunk. Vivian left and shortly after, Mom did too, kissing me goodnight.

That night, Ryanne would occasionally wake up and make a ruckus, but I ignored it and pretended to sleep. I did manage to get some sleep that night, but the girls acted weird in the morning, though secretive would be a better word. They talked in hushed tones to one another, avoided looking at me, and at Ryanne.

"What's their issue?" Leta asked. Her patience ran dry. Usually she was bubbly in the morning, and I was the one struggling to open my eyes and get moving.

"Ok girls, before we get to breakfast, someone's got to tell me what's going on," I said. "Why are you all whispering to each other?" Wide eyes and scared looks landed on me. "Girls let's go. If no one talks, we're not leaving this cabin." That threat was also empty. I fully intended on enjoying pancakes this morning. We actually had syrup this time around, not just old jelly that was supposed to be used for bagel morning.

"We had to swear not to tell you!" Temple said, putting her hand on her mouth, surprised that words came out of her at all.

"Swear to who?" I asked.

"The fairies!" Her sister, Juniper answered.

"Guys!" Pandora, the third, and eldest triplet hissed.

"Fairies? What are you talking about, fairies?" Leta asked, standing by the door, arms crossed. She looked more intrigued now than pissed, but nonetheless, if it was fairies keeping us from pancakes, I wanted this to be over with as soon as possible.

Thalia, a large, pale girl said, "There were fairies around the cabin. Just little ones, that glowed."

"Did they look like balls of light?" I asked.

"No, they looked like fairies!" Juniper insisted.

"Juni!" Pandora hissed.

"What are you so worried about, Pandora?" I asked.

Ryanne laughed darkly. "If we tell you what happened, the fairies will release their wrath upon us! And if you don't believe us, they'll release their wrath upon you!"

"Ok, that's enough crazy for this morning," I said. "Girls, there are no fairies. You were probably seeing those beautiful luna moths. They glow and have wings."

"They weren't moths!" Thalia yelled. "I know what I saw."

"See! You don't believe! They're going to come and get you!" Ryanne said.

"I'll sleep just fine tonight," I replied.

"Not if I keep you up all night again," she said. In that instant, I never had a stronger feeling that I wanted to slap someone across the face in my entire life.

I never learned what those fairies were. A few counselors in the Birdhouses stated they heard stories of visiting fairies, but that they blamed it on the 'sleeping potion' they gave the girls, which was usually maraschino cherry juice with edible glitter in it. That stuff was powerful, even if it was all in suggestion.

Chapter Seven:

July 30, 2016

In the late afternoon, Clark was all but abandoned. The only noises came from the humming equipment in the kitchen. I posted the assignments for that week: cabin rosters, lifeguard duties, kitchen duties, cleaning, etc. Schedules for events were likewise taped to the wall. Once that was completed, I walked to Basswood. It was past the swimming pool, over the river, and slightly up the hill. The single lightbulb was on and lit up the cabin warmly. It glowed amongst the dark cabins sitting on the hill. None of these cabins were equipped with glass windows, but instead, had very thick and sturdy mesh screens with canvas coverings to protect from the rain. The beds inside were built from the same wood as the cabins and Native American symbols were colorfully painted on the beds and walls. Basswood had pictures of fish throughout.

Mia already completed a great deal of work. There was a pile of dirt, dust, and raccoon droppings outside the door along with a very rough looking broom. I stepped in and knocked. Mia jumped a bit and said, "You scared the shit out of me! You could have said something!" She had her hand to her chest and breathed loudly. She was working hard enough sweat soaked through her shirt.

"You did a lot!" I exclaimed. The beds were cleaned, and fresh mattresses were put down.

"I'm not taking any chances. That, and I don't want to be alone out here when it gets dark . . ." She shook her head and picked up a cloth from a bucket of soapy water. "Help me out here. The cubbies need to be deep cleaned. Already scared a good dozen chipmunks out of here . . ."

I joined her in scrubbing. "Do you know where the others went?" I asked.

"Stepsters Arcade, I think, out on Second Street. The over-21s went to Ferris's."

"That place smells like piss and puke," I said. The bar, Ferris's, was a usual spot for counselors. It was the cheapest place in town to get a drink and had a pool table and air conditioning. There wasn't much more to ask for.

"You're already over thinking it," she said. "Can tell in your voice."

"They come back hungover, and parents expect them to be able to take care of their children. It's not ok."

"They're kids, give them some leeway. You're not twenty-one anymore," Mia said. "And neither am I for that matter."

"I'm only twenty-four," I said.

"And you seemed to skip over that whole teenage phase, so you just don't understand them. Give them a break, it'll give you a break in the process. They'll be fine tomorrow. You don't need to break out a breathalyzer or anything like that." She shrugged and reached far into a cubby hole. She brought out a handful of what looked like quartz crystals.

"Those are cool," I said, putting the filthy rag into the bucket.

"I've been finding them all over the cabin," she said. "Just think about how many there could be in all the cabins we don't use right now." She pointed to a Ziploc baggie she filled with small crystals. "Found a few in my cabin when I was cleaning it out. Usually I don't do that thorough of a job, but as soon as I found one, I kept looking."

"Huh, I guess we had a rockhound here at some point," I said.

"I wonder how long ago. Some of these cabins, like Basswood, I don't remember ever being used while I was here. Maybe over ten years? Could be fifty for all we know," she said, returning to the cubby.

"Do you think we'll ever fill these cabins up again?" I asked, scrubbing a spider-web infested broom closet.

"I don't know, but camp seems to be dying. People like their screens and amenities a lot."

"But someone built all of these," I said, hitting the wooden support post with my hand.

"It's not like they didn't get used, it's just the past decade or so is all," she sighed. "You know what, Laurel, one of these days you should try joining the other counselors."

"At a bar?" I asked. "What, have you lost your gourd?"

"Let loose, act human, that'd be great. It won't ruin you if that's what you're worried about."

"That's not what I said," I started, trying to determine what to say. "It—it'd be exhausting. I just want to get some rest when we don't have kids here."

"Some people recharge around other people," Mia said.

"That's your one psychology course talking. I don't. I know being an introvert isn't the best trait for a camp counselor to have, but I must say: sleep is way better than alcohol."

"I'd agree to that," she said. She put her hands on her hips. She was sturdy in every sense of the word. Even her voice was sturdy. "Granted, I'm just tired all the time."

"Same," I said.

After cleaning, we found ourselves sitting in the dry goods storage area of Clark, eating cereal to our heart's content. "This is much better," I said, smirking.

"So you went to see Ezra today?" she asked, making direct eye contact. "If I remember correctly, you had quite the crush on him."

"Crush? I'm not sure I've ever had a crush on anyone. Not to my knowledge."

"Everyone in the world has crushes. Five year olds get crushes."

"I'm not normal!" I exclaimed.

"You wanted to be with him all the time. That's a crush in my book," she said. "The way you looked at him . . ."

"I trust him," I said plainly, stuffing my face full of Cap'n' Crunch.

"Either way, how's he doing?"

"He looks terrible. I kind of wish I had a magic wand to just fix him. I hate seeing him all broken like that . . . The dude taught me to swim, and how to do archery, and how not to have weekly meltdowns here. He was just someone to look forward to seeing."

"I know," she said. "Especially that year after the garage went up in flames; I didn't know if you were going to get through that summer without ending up in a psych ward."

"Georgie . . . Georgie dying destroyed me, but you never told me that . . ."

"You weren't sleeping, and you started talking about seeing things after what happened . . ." She leaned back against a shelf stacked high with bulk cans of corn and beans.

"Georgie meant the world to me . . ."

"I know that whoever did it was trying to hide something in that garage, what was so important . . . I think they were trying to burn something, get rid of something, like Lukas when he tried to burn down House One."

"I don't think that's even remotely the case," she said. "The inside burned. He only used one bottle of lighter fluid; he couldn't have been all that serious. At least now kids won't ask why there's a set-but-abandoned table inside a perfectly good cabin," she said and took a deep breath, looking about the room. "You told me all summer he wanted to burn the house down."

"I didn't think he meant it. He's a pyromaniac, but doing actual damage is something else, and he wasn't irresponsible enough to do it with a kid in the vicinity."

"But he was, and he did," Mia replied, putting her now empty bowl to the side. "You going into the real world?" she asked.

"The real world . . ." I laughed.

"I wish I could leave without feeling like the place will fall apart without me," she said.

"This place has me in a stranglehold," I replied.

"It's about time we both get out of here. Gave too much of my life to this place for absolutely nothing in return,"

"You have that," I said, pointing to the laurel wreath tattoo on her wrist. "You're part of the cult," I whispered in amusement.

"I thought I ought to do that since half my blood's in this ground anyway. Just wanted to prove I could do it. Are you going to do it?"

I shook my head emphatically.

"Why not?"

"I don't know. Never had my mind set out to. The whole idea of it is a little freaky anyway. Besides, you don't even attend their meetings, do you?"

"No, not really. It's a lot of people who are fanatical about Kellova. I'd rather steer clear of the drama."

"Half of them didn't put as much work into camp as you have," I said.

"Doesn't seem to make a difference." There was a certain sadness in her eyes at that statement. It was true, she gave everything to Camp Kellova. All it gave back to her was a lack of sleep, plenty of sprained ankles, and a hell of a lot of exhaustion and tears.

Sleep did not come easily that night, hardly at all actually. I was exhausted. I lay down at seven, after a nice, cold shower. I was fighting the clock. My mind had a mental timer, each minute cut away at the rest I could get. Thoughts of Ryanne plagued me, as did Asia's complaints, and how I forgot to add milk to the food order. Each time I closed my eyes, I saw that girl standing on the hill to House One; the same one Taylor saw and panicked over. The same one Riley dreamt of. The one that lured Riley to House One the day Lukas decided he was going to try to burn it down. That girl, whoever it was, Alina, Linnea, whatever the name, couldn't be trusted. I didn't know if she was real or not. Collective hallucinations were always possible. She was a thing though. Always standing on that hill, wearing a lace dress, her hands turned out to show her palms, her hair dark and black, right at her shoulders. Sometimes her face was clean, sometimes it was marked with lines of tears and black eyes.

With my curtains closed, I felt safe I wouldn't see her. I didn't have a direct line of sight to the hill anyway. Alone, though, I always worried she'd come. The sound of deer walking through the trees outside sounded uncannily like human footfalls, yet I only heard her footsteps once.

Nina Wilson

June 2011

It was blazing hot, even at eleven o'clock at night. I rolled around my top bunk, unable to get comfortable, or block out the noise from the other counselors. It was only the third week of staff training and never in my life had I experienced such a hot June before. I thought I was about to sweat into nothingness. I already was stripped down to a sports bra and swimming shorts.

We were in the BS building, Bill and Coraline Buenten-Sharpe Building was its proper name, and the air conditioning didn't work, and the windows didn't open. It was stifling. Unable to handle that anymore, I grabbed a blanket and my pillow and marched out of the single room we were all staying in.

"Where are you going?" Mia called after me. She'd worked at camp for four years, and I knew her well. She was a staple in this place. She wasn't what one would call perky or upbeat, but she did her job well and I liked her for that.

"One of the Treehouses, I need air," I said.

"You're going to stay in one of them?" she asked.

"Yes," I said.

"Alone?" she added. The thought did cross my mind that it'd be spooky, but at the same time, relief was much more important at the moment.

"Yep."

"I'm coming with you," she said, grabbing her stuff as well. "I need to get my phone charger out of the staff lounge though."

The Treehouses were cleaned within the past few days, and many were ready for habitation while the Birdhouses were not ready. They hadn't been opened or aired out yet, and the dead rats and mice hadn't been discarded.

It was pitch black outside. There was no moon, and because it was cloudy, there were no stars. It simply was like stepping into a blackhole. Our flashlights helped, though mine was old and weak and gave off a beam that only helped in alerting me to the presence of some raccoons lurking around BS.

"Ok, I'm happy you're joining me," I said, thinking of walking onto that lonely hill.

Chapter Seven: July 30, 2016

"It's not like I could stand to stay in there anyway. I hate listening to some of the girls talk, it makes me want to puke."

"What were they talking about?" I asked.

"You couldn't hear them?"

"I do my best to block them out," I added. She huffed.

"They seem to be quite the fans of Harry, wait until they find out he's gay."

"Yeah? When they start flirting . . .""

"They were ogling at his six pack and shit. That guy does hard work and that's what they focus on?"

"Doesn't make much sense . . . Not to me anyway. I know they were talking about March the other night." I said.

"Him? Really? God, I met him when he was like thirteen," Mia said, shaking her head.

March's real name was Jake, but there were so many people with Jake for a first name, he just went by his last name. He was blonde and built well. He was a varied soul, doing construction for money, and theater because that was his passion. I'd seen Facebook videos of him performing in musical theater and he was extraordinary. He could sing, dance, and act, and not badly either. He and Mia went to the same high school in Des Moines, but they just missed each other by a few years. They still found it entertaining to talk about their teachers and how little changed through the years.

The staff lounge was in the basement of my mother and I's year-round residence. It wasn't anything grand, just what could have been our living room and a bathroom. This late at night, it should have been nearly empty with the curfew being midnight and all, but light poured out of the windows onto the grass surrounding the house. We quickly went in. Only four counselors were there, all guys, spread out as far as possible on the consignment shop furniture and floor.

"What are you doing?" Ezra asked, sitting up.

Jake March, the other Jake, and Maury all looked at us bleary eyed and tired.

"Going to one of the Treehouses," Mia said.

"It's impossible to sleep, too hot," I said. Of all the things that could make me angry in this world, it was the inability to get proper sleep.

"You're just going to go in one?" Jake asked, his voice was higher than usual and a little uncomfortable.

"Yep," I said. Mia took her charger from the pile of chargers beside the wall, and we left. Back on the gravel sidewalk, we left the light of the staff lounge behind. There was some light in BS up ahead, and then there was nothing except what we knew was there. The path curved past Clark, past the ball field, past the climbing tree and picnic tables, past the gaga pit, and into a large stretch of space between this part of camp and the pool.

Once near the pool, the blackness vanished. Not completely, but there were orbs of light dancing in the air. The ones above the pool reflected on the water, moving as if they were breathing. They were made of white light, almost white enough one could see all the colors within them. After staring for some time, I realized I stopped moving. Mia put her hand on my shoulder.

There was a strange tug toward these things, these orbs. They felt so alive—my hands reached for them, but they were just past the fence of the pool. More stretched into the forest surrounding it.

"You don't want to touch them," Mia said, but her voice was so distant, clouded. Despite hearing her, I didn't accept the words. My mind didn't register the instructions. I followed the fence around and went toward one that hovered near the basketball hoop. Once near, there was a warm energy surrounding it. There were no signs of life past the breathing motion, the pulsing it made, jellyfish like. "Laurel! Listen to me! Don't touch it!" I didn't even realize my fingers were only inches away from the white orb. The curiosity, the pull, was killing me. All I wanted was to know what it felt like: if it was hot, or cold, if it was smooth, if it felt like a diamond, or if it had skin. Was it just energy?

So, I touched it.

My body was sucked into what could only be described as a void. The air was ripped out of my ears and lungs. I collapsed down to my knees before a wave of air hit me and I could breathe again. I looked up and there were hundreds, thousands, of orbs surrounding me. They all pulsed and breathed. I didn't get to find out what it felt like, but I saw something far stranger. It was a galaxy of these oddities. I got the distinct impression they were souls. I wanted to be surrounded by them, encased by the light. It was so inviting and terrifying all at the same time.

Mia, though, pulled me away—physically. She yanked me out of whatever vision or hallucination I was having. Back on my feet, it was darker in the real world. There were no orbs.

"What—what did I see? What happened?" I asked.

"I don't know," she replied. She didn't sound bored or annoyed, just honest. She kept a hand firmly on my back, though, like she expected me to bolt for another one again. I may have, but there were none. There had been such a brief sense of belonging, or wholeness in that void, and now there was simply reality. Reality was never what I wanted it to be.

We walked away from the pool, along the bridge, and toward the hill that had the Treehouses. Though it seemed dark on the other side, the even thicker tree cover made it velvety in nature. Mia led the way. Feeling slightly disoriented from my weird hallucination, I didn't ask questions.

The cabin closest to the bottom of the hill that had been cleaned was Cherry. It was also the smallest, which would allow for a greater sense of security. I flung the door open, dumped my stuff on a bed and laid down. Mia was slower to get her bed set up. I was too tired to do any of that. After a day of training and cleaning and team building exercises, I wanted to be done. Besides, today was almost tomorrow.

Once we both quieted down and Mia's breathing began to settle, I heard footsteps right outside the screened-in window that made up the wall's main structure. There were very individual footfalls. I did not open my eyes. Deer sounded just like humans, but after what I saw, I could believe anything.

There were three knocks on the door of the cabin. Neither Mia nor I moved, but I knew she was awake. A giggle cut through the silent air.

Chapter Eight:

August 1, 2016

All staff met together in Clark on Sunday at noon. Mia and I sat together on one of the circular dinner tables. She had her notebook in front of her with an assortment of gel pens and was doodling flowers. Two of the counselors, Marsha and Greg, weren't there yet.

My mother, perturbed, proceeded anyway. "Ok, so those of you who've been counselors with us previously, will know Ezra Concord. He's the one who was found in the lake." My body stiffened when eyes landed on me. "He's still in the hospital in rough, but stable, condition. If you have absolutely any information about what happened, what may have landed him in that lake, please, come tell me. I want you to feel safe speaking to me about your concerns. He's one of our own, and a good young man." There was something just slightly off about her voice. It wasn't warm. It didn't feel genuine.

Her eye contact with us broke before she locked onto Marsha and Greg. She sighed. "We are going to have some new rules put in place starting this week to help protect you and our campers. The buddy system will be absolute, as well as the rule of three. There will be no deviation from it. Kids are not to be wandering around alone. They shouldn't be wandering in the first place. Don't let anyone out of your sight if you can help it. I don't need any more of you lazing around during important events, or while on the clock. I know you're tired. I know it's a hard job, and y'all are drained, but these are other people's kids we are talking about. Their safety is our number one priority. Also, no kids are allowed alone inside any building, even to grab their shoes or bug spray. Someone must go with them. Do you understand?"

There was a chorus of non-committal yeses with varying degrees of disinterest. "This week our classes will be hand arts, archery, riflery, orienteering, soccer, and nature." I noticed the lack of any water-based sports. She didn't even mention swimming lessons. "I'll list your cabin assignments if you haven't looked yet. There are a few changes."

It was then that Marsha and Greg attempted to sneak in. Mom crossed her arms very slowly, and her eyes narrowed. "Do you forget this is a job? When you're required to be here at noon, it means noon, not 12:45." They didn't respond. They mostly just looked surprised and uncomfortable. "Do any of you take this seriously? It's a summer camp, yes, but you are responsible for kids and their safety. You're their guardians. The people who teach them, make sure they eat, sleep, get dressed, brush their teeth, and you're showing up late, hungover, and you're not even paying attention! Wake up!" She screamed the last two words, enough so that all of us froze in surprise. I'd never known my mom to act like this. Her voice was threatening. She was threatening, and it wasn't simply from anger. There was something else to it.

"Wake up and do your god-damn jobs! I'm getting tired of you thinking this is a vacation for you—it's not!" She looked at Marsha and Greg once again. "Sit down," she sighed, and went on about the week's schedule.

She paced back and forth. "I'm not happy with how the incident was handled last week. As soon as Laurel called Code White with a description like the one she gave, someone should have called 911. Kids should be removed from the water immediately, taken up to the buses, and the situation dealt with swiftly." Nausea hit me like a bus. "We've trained for these very events. Three weeks of constant training, and to be quite honest, you acted like we went over it for five minutes." She knew something, it was in her voice, it was in her eyes. She wasn't telling me everything, or anything.

My eyes went to the wreath tattoo on her wrist. Maybe the nomads knew. The Laurelites and their secrets.

Mia moved beside me, shifting. She brought McDonalds to eat today rather than the baloney and government cheese on criminally dry bread. She pushed some fries in my direction. Someone nearly died last week, and no one seemed the least bit shaken.

My mother was talking about procedure, not about how to cope with the fact that one of our colleagues was found half-beaten to death in the water. My own nerves hadn't calmed or lessened since that day. Nothing felt safe. No one, save maybe Harry or Mia, could understand, and they were still as calm as ever. Other counselors were all hunched over in hoodies with sunglasses on to protect their sensitive eyes.

I didn't know how they could do it. It was already hot out in an unholy way. Mom droned on. She noticed someone got into the cereal and was hoping that a face in her crowd would flicker with guilt. Mia wasn't paying attention and I was excellent at stopping those flickers around her.

"We aren't rolling in money here. This is a not-for-profit institution. You can't waltz in and take what you want. It doesn't belong to you. We have kids to feed." Her tone continued to concern me. "Alright, get your cabins and yourselves in order. Take cold showers if you have to, I don't care. Kids will be here in two hours."

She waved us off, except for Greg and Marsha. "You two . . ."

I followed Harry out, throwing my backpack on my shoulder and jogged down the steps. "Get any sleep?" Harry asked. "You're all pale."

"I'll be fifty shades of tomato soon, and yeah, I did."

"Carra is acting nuts," he whispered, pointing back at Clark. "I mean she's never been what I'd call nice, but she went off the hinges today." He shoved his hands in the pockets of his khaki shorts. His freckles were starting to blend into his slowly tanning skin. Most of us were significantly darker than him by now.

"Maybe Ezra in the water?" I asked. He shook his head. "She freaked me out too, something else then?"

"Some people just have bad days," he replied. We passed the soccer field. Two of the male counselors were kicking a ball around. They were some of the few that looked to be in relatively good working order. Other than that, everyone else was disappearing over the creek and bridge into the cooler overhang of trees. "And there's plenty going on to make someone stressed." He scratched behind his ears, squinting in the glowing green light of early afternoon.

"I need to know what's happening here," I said.

"Kellova? At camp? Just a lot of strange shit, that's all. Don't go nuts on me, please. I need some sane people in my life."

"Thanks for the boost of support," I replied disdainfully.

"I'm just saying, you get hung up on things quickly and in a week or two, it's like there was nothing to interest you in the first place. You get that way about books, research topics, even people. Sometimes I think I know more about you than you do."

"Since I got bonked in that head, you probably do . . ." I admitted. That was true. There was a pervasive sense of disconnection between me and what was around me. Often the feeling of being grounded and steady was fleeting. Sometimes my mind floated off for moments, leaving my vision fuzzy and everything would have to be put, briefly, on autopilot.

"Did anything fun yesterday?" I asked to change the subject. The incline to the cabins began, passing the Apples Arts Center, Lapidary, the Library, and the remains of the garage.

A great big smile broke across his face. "Peter and I played laser tag. He was so good at it, talented, seriously; it was hot. When he won, I kissed him. I don't care if the people working there saw it on the cameras or whatever. It was the most amazing thing."

I smiled. "So, are you a thing, then? You two?"

"Well, he hasn't really come out of the closet."

"As if it isn't obvious," I said with a smirk. We stopped outside of Hawthorne.

"Not everything is as obvious to everyone else as it apparently is to you," Harry said. "His parents are clueless . . . but I can't stop thinking about him." He giggled. He did his little happy shiver and dance and went about fifty feet away to his cabin. He was paired with Orion. They worked well together, like a well-oiled machine. Peter, this week, had the teenage boys. Getting everyone to behave this week was going to be a challenge, but I wasn't nearly as worried about the boys as I was about Ryanne.

Hawthorne, my cabin, while the same age as the majority of the Tree-houses, was the best kept and the closest to the bathroom. It felt safe. A large eagle was painted on the single solid section of wall and my bed faced it. It felt like protection from what lived in these woods and on that hill.

The cabin was as clean as could be, which provided another feeling of safety. Years of dirt and debris were stubbornly stuck into the ground, but it was swept twice daily. The door didn't shut well and let leaves in frequently. One end was two inches off the ground and it didn't latch. It was on Greg's to-do list, but apparently so was Marsha.

All the girls' personal items were still neatly tucked away. Beds were made, fitted sheets with a sleeping bag on top, maybe another blanket folded at the end. Extra odds and ends were kept in waterproof Rubbermaid containers. The cabin almost always won cleanest cabin award, as long as the girls would participate. It was a title I was not willing to let go of.

Outside each cabin were large wooden posts drilled into the ground with white stripes painted on them. Each stripe symbolized one cleanest cabin award. This cabin had the most stripes, and thus, the most poles.

My clothes were packed in Ziploc baggies to keep out moisture. Sweat-soaked clothes could be worn again, but nothing felt or smelled worse than mildewy clothes. Moisture removers were a must to keep things fresh- all lessons learned over time. Things needed to be in the proper order. Part of my brain was convinced that something bad would happen if they weren't. That was where half my concern was, the other half was focused on my mother.

Once the cabin was in order, I hurried to the office. Her door was closed. It was never closed, but I could hear rattling inside. "Mom, it's me," I said, knocking on the door. In the past, she would find knocking offensive, claiming that I was supposed to be comfortable with sharing space and that knocking meant I was worried about intrusion. At least something of that nature. "Mom," I said again. "Mom."

Finally, I opened the door. She looked stressed and disheveled. Patches of red sprouted on her face. Her hair stuck out from her head. "What's going on?" I asked. "Mom?" She looked up at me with dagger-like eyes. "Maybe you need to sit down for a moment. I'll get you some water." I encouraged her to sit at her desk and went to the kitchenette for a bottle of water. Gail, our secretary, was already down in Clark setting up for check in. We were alone. "Why are you giving me the silent treatment? You never keep things from me," I said.

She took a long drink of water and shook her head. "Only things you don't need to know," she said. Color evened across her face after a few gulps of water.

"Excuse me? I thought we told each other everything." I sincerely hoped she was simply in a bad mood, or the stress got to her, but I didn't feel either of those vibes, just that something was off. "I can tell when you're lying."

"I haven't really said anything, Laurel, so how could I be lying?" She was harsher than I expected. Stress usually caused her short bouts of inconsolable tears, not this. "It's nothing. Nothing is going on," she said, continuing to shake her head. Her slender hand reached for the bottle again.

"Then tell me what's happening here at camp," I asked as calmly as I could. "I need to know." A jolt of, as far as I knew, unsubstantiated fear went through me. That jolt was because of her.

"What do you mean?"

"You never . . . really acknowledged to me anything about Ezra. I love Ezra, Mom, you know that; you knew that last year. And the year before that. All the nights I stayed up talking about how safe I felt with him . . . and he's found in a lake half dead, and you don't even bring it up except in a meeting to tell people to talk to you and not the cops if they suspect anything? You barely responded even last year when Riley was nearly killed after Lukas tried to burn the house down. I was heartbroken, in tears, freaked out, you name it. You quieted it down as fast as you could. The year before when Haley killed herself, at least then you cried, but you never acknowledged her since. The year when the garage burned with Georgie in it was the last time I saw real emotion out of you!"

"You put this many kids and young adults together in a limited space for twelve weeks at the same time, shit happens, Laurel."

"That's not what I'm talking about!" I cried. "I'm talking about you, Mom! I'm talking about how you don't seem to care about what happens! People get hurt here! Ezra got hurt."

"And what do you want me to say? I'm sorry? I didn't do it, Laurel. I didn't land him in that lake. I didn't take my fists to him. There's nothing I can do to fix him."

"You could at least have hugged me," I said, biting my lip. I didn't want to cry. I didn't want to show her any weakness. She didn't move. "Acknowledged it? But whatever lives here, did that to Ezra. What happens here, it sure as hell doesn't feel normal."

"You always feel crap, and it's all made up. It's stuff you imagine," Mom said, breaking eye contact, looking down at the half filled bottle of water.

"I didn't imagine finding one of my girls hanging in House One. She wrote, 'It won't let me leave' in blood on the walls, Mom. You saw it. I saw it. It was there. It existed. Haley existed."

"She was a troubled girl, Laurel, you saw all those scars on her wrists," Mom said, almost sounding whiny now. Yet, behind her, there was a picture of that girl, Haley, hugging Noah and I.

"That's your explanation? There were no signs—"

"You're not as good a judge of character as you think you are, Laurel," she said. Her eyes met mine again. "There's nothing going on here. Nothing strange. Nothing abnormal. It's probably that knock on your head. It did screw some things up."

"Excuse me?"

"You're making connections that aren't there. Maybe this is all too stressful for you."

"What are you talking about?" My voice screeched in surprise. I'd never heard her talk like that before, she was usually so encouraging and supportive.

"Laurel . . . you're unstable. If you start spouting this nonsense off to the kids-"

"I'm not spouting nonsense!" I cried. My heart hurt, my head pounded, the constriction in my chest was reminiscent of a blood pressure cuff wrapped around my ribcage. "You just want me to lie to them? If they ask a question, I'm going to answer . . ."

She looked at me for what felt like an eternity. For the first time, I didn't trust her. "I don't know who you are," I muttered.

"You're spewing nonsense," she said, turning away. She clicked on her computer monitor. Knowing the conversation was over and silence would only become more pervasive, I left. Yet I wanted nothing more than to run back to my mom and hug her tightly and get the truth out of her. If I could simply get a soft word, I would be happy.

Gail was in Clark, setting up check-in stations and new cabin assignment sheets. There was a wary look on her face when she made eye contact with me. "Is she staying this time around?" she asked, motioning her head to the office.

"Yeah," I murmured. "Was she acting odd this morning, to you?"

She straightened the papers in front of her and took a deep breath. She pursed her lips for a moment. "She's always on edge on Sundays," Gail started, smoothing down her long, silver hair. She always had a flower pin in her hair. Today it was white with a fake diamond in the center. "And of course, all the emails about the boy in the water. About Ezra. It's hit the newspapers and TV, so people have been asking all sorts of questions. It's exhausting. Every time I get a call I'm supposed to say 'no-comment.' I haven't really listened because I want them to know that none of the campers were harmed." I bit the inside of my cheek to keep quiet. To keep busy, I put up signs to direct traffic.

On cue, the first camper dropped off was Gracia Parkinson. She was always the first dropped off and the last to be picked up. Her father wore a white polo shirt with khaki shorts. He looked intensely uncomfortable in the woods. "Hope it's ok we're a tad early. Have a golf tournament to return to."

"No problem, Mr. Parkinson," I said, though every time we went through this talk, and I saw his smug face, I got the urge to smack it off. He signed the papers, handed over cash for the snack-shop and camp store. Once he left, Gracia bounced in place, holding her ukulele case in front of her.

"Can I help the counselors take the younger kids to their cabins if I get bored?"

"If it gets busy and you stay with a counselor. Otherwise I want you to stay on the porch. Can't just go wandering around right now, new rules," I said.

"Should be an old rule at this point," she replied absently. She sat on one of the colorful rocking chairs and immediately got her ukulele out and strummed away and sang. Her voice was warm, smooth, and a tad husky.

Other kids came into Clark including the Tanner triplets: Pandora, Juniper, and Temple. Their parents were fun people, easy to talk to, prepared, and attentive. Though people often stared at all five of them since the girls were colorful and the parents were covered in tattoos.

"Hi, Miss Laurel!" Temple said, running to hug me. She was a hugger. At twelve-years-old, they were growing fast and all three were as tall as me.

"Hi girls," I said, waving at the other Tanners. "Any idea what you're signing up for this week?"

"We want to get our orienteering packets done!" Pandora called. She was already looking at the schedules. Above Pandora's fading pink pigtails were dozens of photographs of campers past and present. On the far left was a photo of her and her sisters their first summer here. "Mom, look!" She waved.

"Got more sunscreen, bug spray, and new lanterns," Myla, their mom, said. She went over to look at the photograph. "Beautiful, girls," she said. "Juniper, do you have your toothpaste?" Juniper dug through her rucksack and held up the all-natural, fluoride-free toothpaste she frequently lost or left in the bathroom. "Remember to brush your teeth morning and night."

"Come on, Mom, I know," Juniper whined.

"Your cavities say otherwise," Marc, their dad said. Despite the flaming skulls and crying angel tattoos on his arms, he always gave off the vibe he was shy. "You girls behave." He kissed each girl's forehead. Their counselor Coral came into Clark, jogging.

"Hey girls! Ready to go?" Coral already had a look of dread on her face. Marsha and Ryanne all in one week.

"Keep us up to date," Myla said. "And thank you for sending out emails when they found that young man in the lake. It's good to know that the girls were kept safe and away from the scene. Also, if they need anything, or if we forgot something. God knows we always do. Pregnancy brain." She knocked the side of her head lightly.

"Oh, that's exciting! A new Tanner!" I said, smiling, genuinely happy for them.

"It was a surprise," Marc said.

"That's for sure," Myla replied. "Hoping for a boy this time around."

"I'm just hoping there's only one," Marc said, chuckling. "The house isn't big enough for any more multiples."

"I'm not nearly that stretchy anymore either, but the doc said the closer to forty you get, the higher chance you have of having multiples, and that's downright insane," she said.

They kissed their girls goodbye for a week then left the building. It wasn't long after that a large line began to form. Arty hugged me too and carried textbooks under his arms when he entered the dining room.

"What are those for?" I asked.

"Getting a head start on all my A.P. courses," he said with a wide smile. "Biology, chemistry, and psychology." He waved at his dad and ran over to the porch without another word.

"Well, bye, son!" his dad said, shaking his head. "That boy . . ."

"You have a smart young man on your hands," I said. The dad nodded, an amused, strung-out smile on his face. When I met Arty, his parents could only afford to send him to camp on a scholarship. They worked hard so he could focus on his school. The kid had a 4.0 GPA and a near perfect ACT score.

"He wants to go to Cornell or Brown," he said. "He'd be the first to go to college in the family, and he wants to go all out. How to pay for that . . . phew, I don't know." They both were well dressed, put together nicely. Arty had on a yellow, button-up short sleeved shirt and navy blue knee-length shorts. He and Gracia went to the same high school, so they were fast friends. "Keep me up to date too," he added. "I want to know if there's another incident. Something else like that, and I may need to pull him. Can't risk it getting in the way of his ability to study."

"Yes, sir," I said.

He left, and kid after kid checked in. Their counselors came to walk them to their cabins. The younger kids' parents often walked with them and the counselors to see the cabin.

Mia sat on the porch with the horse kids making friendship bracelets with my kids. I ran payments, took in health forms, and searched for lost and found items. The place was chronically understaffed, and I felt it.

Noah Halverson came by with his brother Taylor. "Hey, Miss Laurel," he said, smiling. He made sure, though, that not an ounce of emotion came through that wasn't cool. "Here's the paperwork from Mom. She couldn't get off work today."

"At least this time she really is working late," Taylor said. Noah went to grab him in a headlock, but Taylor was too fast for him.

"Where'd that come from?" I asked, pointing to a brand-new sleeve tattoo on his right arm, including a large eagle coming in for a landing.

"Nebraska," he said. "You only have to be sixteen there."

"Nice, it's epic," I replied.

"I like your eagle," he pointed. "But I went with the shading and realism here. I don't think blackwork is for me. It's only the first, but I'm hoping to find an artist closer to home I like."

"Can I go to the porch, man?" Taylor asked. "Rather than listening to you blab about that thing on your arm."

"Last I checked, you said it was awesome."

"Yeah, yeah, yeah," Taylor said.

"Go on," I replied, waving at him. He bolted off.

"Hey! Aren't you going to give me a hug or something?" Noah yelled.

"Just say hi to everyone! They miss you!" Taylor said, and the door slammed.

"Have you heard from Riley much?" I asked Noah.

"About Ezra? Yeah, Riley and I are going to visit him with Mr. Stevens. Riley said Ezra seemed to like watching him play video games. We'll keep him company for you."

"Thanks. You're a good young man."

"He was there for me, you both were," Noah said, shrugging. When he smiled, it seemed to add nearly a decade to his age. Laugh lines clung around his smile. He had so much weighing on his mind for such a young kid. "I'll see you on Saturday. Hope nothing shitty happens until then."

"You and everyone else has been telling me roughly the same thing," I said. Noah went to the porch. There were a lot of hugs.

Ellie came soon after. She glared at everyone and sat apart with a book. Her light blonde hair waved down past her shoulders and was styled. She looked pretty. And clean. But not for long. She often refused to shower because the shower house was simply 'too gross' for her.

"Had to fight to get her here," Ellie's mom, Mrs. Beal said. She handed me her daughter's phone in a baggie. "I hope she continues to warm up to this place, though. She did say some positive things, in between the complaints of spiders and bugs." Mrs. Beal did not look overly hopeful. She was a thin woman, very athletic in build. I swore all her clothing came from REI and she spent an inordinate amount of money on her outdoor attire, but that was just my disdain for people who didn't let their children eat pancakes or cereal.

On the porch, Gracia was trying to encourage Ellie to join her, but it didn't work. Kennedy was able to sit next to her though with a bag full of books, including more Tolkien. She was also perfectly happy playing Garbage or Egyptian Rat Slap with whoever would play. She got Ellie into a game which was eventually joined by Jane. Jane was eager to get into any game, especially competitive ones. She was headstrong and adventurous.

Sadie, the youngest in my cabin at thirteen, ran into the dining room. She waved at me, said nothing, and immediately ran off with Coral's kids so she could take care of the frogs and tadpoles in the nature shed by Apple Arts Center. She was on the small and undeveloped side with glasses and braces to boot. She wasn't the most popular kid here, but she didn't seem to care or notice. She found what was fun to her and got along just fine.

Lisey was the last to arrive. She kept her appearance as impeccable as one could at camp. She took part mostly in hand arts, stayed away from heat and sweat if at all possible, and had an unmistakable crush on Taylor. It was cute how she fawned over him, but I did feel a lot of second-hand embarrassment.

I was so busy, I didn't even see Ryanne get checked in. Gail told me. She also mentioned that the payment from Ryanne's mother Brandi was late and that it came in the form of a check she half expected to bounce.

The girls from Hawthorne and I made it up toward the cabin. Here the breeze was nice, and the sun was blocked out by the cover of trees. It was a reasonable temperature. The only issue was that we were one member short of our group. "Kennedy, Lisey, could you get Sadie from the nature shed?" I asked them as we neared our cabin. The lights were on in the shed and there were numerous campers in there. "I'm going to check up on Miss Marsha's cabin real fast, make sure everyone is settling in."

"We know why you're really going over there," Jane said with a heavy sigh. "It's because that gross kid is back."

"Jane, that's—that's not how you're supposed to talk," I said.

"It's not like you disagree with me." Her eyebrows raised; arms crossed. She was waiting for confirmation. My silence was enough for that. "No one disagrees with me."

"Just don't destroy anything while I'm gone," I said. "And you know what, she might be perfectly fine at home. Gotta give people the benefit of the doubt." There was a pause. "Be ready for the pool, we're going at four since it's so hot today."

"What are we doing tonight?" Ellie asked. She didn't whine. She didn't sound interested either, but it was a step in the right direction.

"I was thinking we could make glow jars," I said.

"I want to play gaga!" Jane, instead, whined.

"You can play before supper, there'll be time, like always," I said.

"I need to beat Mr. Peter's cabin," Jane said.

"The whole cabin? That's like five people who know what they're doing!" Ellie said.

"And Taylor! He hardly ever loses!" Gracia added.

"He's lost to me at least five times this summer," Jane said, crossing her arms, pouting a bit.

"I'll be back soon," I said, slipping out of Hawthorne.

Ryanne and her mother Brandi were front and center when I entered the cabin. Both looked like the kind of people I would laugh at internally if I saw them at Walmart. Brandi was overweight, or rather, morbidly obese. She wore a neon pink bra that was ill-concealed by her white tank top and shorts that were too small and scrunched up from her walk up here.

"Hi, I just wanted to see if everyone is doing well," I said. Ryanne avoided eye contact and pouted. She sat on the bed. Her suitcase had already managed to explode, and her swimsuit was beside her. "Hi, Ryanne,"

"She's reluctant is all," Bradi said. "I'll be back before you know it, babe."

"No!" Ryanne hissed, reaching out for her with claw-like hands.

"Oh, honey," Brandi sat beside her, and Ryanne clung.

"Don't leave me here! I don't like this place!" Ryanne cried. The other girls in the cabin were dueling out cards for a game of UNO.

"Do you want to join the game?" I asked. Pandora shot me a desperate 'oh don't' look.

"No, I don't want to be here!"

"We can get your bunk all set up. Is this the one you want? You'll be by your counselor," I said. The girl looked at me with pure malice. I wouldn't be surprised if I found her lurking over me in my sleep. Nonetheless, I was taught to go ahead, so I did. Marsha and I unrolled her sleeping bag.

"Aurora is my favorite princess," Marsha said, a statement that would easily get a young girl to open up.

"I don't like princesses. They're stupid," Ryanne replied.

"Well, you have all your stuff here. It's getting late. I've got to get driving home," Brandi stood up and made for the door. Ryanne just glared at her. "I'll send you mail every day. I'll miss you baby." If she could do everything wrong in the mom-book of how to avoid homesickness, she was doing so. The only thing she was missing was the spiel about how she would sleep in her kid's bed at night whilst crying.

"Let's make your bed so you won't have to do it tonight," I said, and reached for her sleeping bag.

"Don't touch my stuff!" she snapped. I backed off slightly, showing as little reaction as possible.

"It's ok, Ryanne, we just want to help you," Coral said, coming from the back of the cabin. "How about we plan what we're going to eat during our cookout. That'll be fun."

"It's just going to be gross. I don't want to do it. I don't wanna be here!"

"You don't have to be so obnoxious!" Pandora yelled, standing up from the game. "Some people are actually looking forward to stuff and want to have a good time or at least willing to try."

"It's ok, Pandora, we'll talk to her. How about you go back to your game?" I asked, giving her a look of 'stay out of it'.

"I'm just saying, all the whining is annoying," Pandora said. Temple face-palmed.

"It's going to be a long week," Temple whispered, almost inaudibly.

I whispered to Coral, "If you need any help, you know where to find me. I shouldn't leave the girls alone this long."

I returned to Hawthorne, reveling in a nice breeze that hit me smack in the face on the small path between cabins. When I entered the cabin, the girls were in a circle on the floor. They already had their towels and swimsuits out. I sat on my bed.

"We should have corn on the cob at the cookout!" Jane exclaimed.

"Last time we tried it, it was raw," Kennedy said. "Not that raw corn is bad for you, it's just weird."

"We can cook it better this time," Lisey said.

"We should have scrambled pancakes," Gracia said, laughing. "Since that didn't go very well either."

"I liked those!" Lisey said. "Didn't clean up easily, but they tasted good!"

"They were half chocolate, that's why," I added, laughing too.

"With grilled cheese, I love grilled cheese!" Jane said.

"You love everything," Lisey added, still giggling.

"Not everything, I don't like carrots!" Janey said.

They went on bickering while Gracia turned to me. "How's Ezra? Noah told me you went to see him." This was exactly what my mother was talking about, but she asked, so I was going to tell her.

"He's . . . in rough shape," I replied. The girls went quiet, and all looked at me intently. It was hard to get them all to pay attention to anything at the same time, so I was surprised. "He's broken a lot of bones, and he—he doesn't really know how to talk right now. They're going to do everything they can to help him."

"Can't talk? Why?" Gracia asked.

"He was hit in the head really badly," I replied. Her eyes were wide.

"That's insane," she said.

"He was nearly killed," Kennedy whispered, as if to herself. "Do they know who did it?"

"No," I answered. "They're looking, though, they are."

Lisey raised her hand like she was in class. "Instead of making glow jars, we were thinking we could make him get-well cards. Since we'll be in Apple anyway. Or things to brighten the room he's stuck in."

"That's a very sweet thing to do girls, I'm sure he'd love that."

"So we can do it?" Lisey asked.

"Of course!"

"Can we still have glow sticks?" Ellie asked.

"Yes," I said. "Maybe we could have some fun with them."

Our pool things were packed, and we walked past the creek and to the pool. Our age group was the second there, after the really little ones. Leta and her fellow counselors were chasing the kids down outside the pool to put sunscreen on them. Most of the little ones who were between the ages of six and ten were only at camp for a week. My backpack came complete with three bottles of spray sunscreen, and I went in and helped get everyone sprayed down and wiped some kids' faces. One thing I'd take away from camp, no matter what, was the religious application of sunscreen.

My girls went in to change, and I did too. I hated the pool house. It was humid, smelled unspeakable most of the time, and there was always standing water in the center. There was a bit of a dip in the concrete where water collected and got progressively darker and sketchier as the summer went on. It was as if the pressure washing and fifteen gallons of bleach in June did nothing.

My swimsuit, nice and crispy from being out in the sun for weeks coupled with too many days of chlorine and water, went on much easier after being stretched from frequent use. Being around the pool, though, brought Ezra to mind. He was the one who taught me to swim.

Chapter Nine:

June 2012

"You don't have to stay in the kiddie pool forever!" Ezra exclaimed, jogging down the steps from Clark with a plastic grocery sack full of peanut butter sandwiches. "I promise I won't let anything bad happen." He stopped in front of me, eye contact in full gear. It was way too difficult to say no to those soft brown eyes and gleeful expression pasted on his face. "Besides, you promised."

"Fine," I said. "I'll learn."

"Yes! It's gonna be a good day," he said, walking backwards now on his tiptoes just as we were taught in high school marching band.

"Hand over a sandwich." I reached out and he handed me one. Marianne bought this bread from Fareway and it wasn't horrifically dry like the cheapo stuff my mother usually had for Kellova. There was a surprising difference in quality.

"You look like you just took a bite of filet mignon or something," Ezra said, chuckling.

"I'm so hungry," I replied. "It's just Saturdays, like I'm starving or something."

Part of me felt so whole, though, at that moment. It was him; it was Ezra. There was a sense of absolute safety right there, between us. It was unspoken and could very easily stay that way. His joy was contagious, and soon I found myself smiling and at ease. I was about to face one of my biggest fears, the deep side of the pool. "Are you sure you're just not eating your nerves away?" he asked.

"What, can you read my mind or something? If you can, get out of there, that's my territory,"

He burst into laughter. "I don't want to read your mind!"

"What does that mean?" I asked. "It can't be that bad!"

"It sure isn't sunshine and rainbows up in there."

"Not inaccurate, but I doubt yours is either," I said.

"I'm sure you wouldn't survive the brain that is nineteen-year-old guy's,"

"No, I probably wouldn't, not even yours," I said. He walked faster, still backwards, and I had to jog to keep up with him. The pool was just ahead, and empty. It was as freshly cleaned as it could get. It was only the third week of the summer, and the kids hadn't started staying at Kellova yet. Staff training ended, and we had until Wednesday to relax and get ourselves in order before the first week.

"If you hear me screaming, you better come running," I said.

"Ezra to the rescue!" he exclaimed. His voice was so bright and yet so warm. It reminded me of the sun. His whole aura reminded me of the sun, except huggable. "Trust me, though, nothing's going to happen. You know how to swim, it's instinctual!"

"There's plenty of instinctual things I've just missed out on," I said. Near the edge of the pool gates, he pulled out his key. As a lifeguard, he was allowed a key, though technically the rules stated that there had to be at least three people in the pool to open it. Mom, though, was more than happy for me to get swimming lessons since she'd been trying for ages to get me to participate in them. None of the teachers were Ezra, so there was no reason to take them.

We went to change. Self-consciousness hit. It wasn't as if he hadn't seen me in a swimsuit before, but I wasn't exactly the fittest person on earth. I was slim, but far from toned. Previously, I couldn't have cared less. Sighing, I knocked myself on the side of the head and told myself to shut up and just get dressed. With the swimsuit pulled on and my hair in a bun, I slathered myself in sunscreen while stepping onto the pool deck. Ezra was already in the water, floating on his back.

"Don't you ever wear sunscreen?" I asked.

"Nope!" he replied.

"You'll toast like a lobster!"

"If I don't toast and roast, I don't tan!" he yelled back.

"Skin cancer!" I added.

He was still floating comfortably, sunglasses on his head, a few floaties on the side of the pool. "Just get in the pool Laurel!"

"Sunscreen! I'm not going to die of skin cancer like you!" I called back, walking up to the side of the deep end. Eleven feet. My heart jumped to the bottom of my stomach and back up to the top of my throat. "Too deep," I said, though I meant to say it just in my head.

"You can do it," he said, flopping onto his stomach, swimming to the edge, arms holding him in place.

"Sunscreen . . ." I muttered. He just smiled and shook his head.

"Sometimes I don't know what to do with you Laurel,"

"And why is that?"

"Your brilliant mind makes absolutely no sense," he said. Brilliant. I could take that compliment. I hoped it was a compliment at least. Slathered in sunscreen, I could no longer hold off going into the pool. I sat down on the edge of it. "Come on in, you can do it."

I slid into the water and held tightly onto the edge. My heart pounded in my chest, there was burning low on my neck from nerves. Part of me was sure I would puke. I swallowed down that idea and watched Ezra. "Let go, come on, I'll show you how to tread water. You'll just need to act like you're riding a bike with your legs and twirl your arms like this on the surface of the water. Your own body will keep you afloat."

"Ok." My voice cracked. I let go and immediately my hands returned to the side.

"Laurel," he said, kicking back a little so he was nearly in the middle of the pool. A gentle smile never left his face. "You can do it." So I let go and tried to tread water. At first, I thought I would sink, but was surprised that I didn't. It was serious cardio after a bit, but Ezra's pure joy hit me. "You're doing it! See! That's the first step! Let's try some strokes."

Back on the ledge, Ezra showed me freestyle and breaststroke. "Do whatever feels like it'll carry you the best. Meet me out here." Halfway through the pool, he got into a rhythm of treading. I dunked my head under, wishing I had goggles. "You can trust me." Those words were undoubtedly true. Trust was something that rarely came to me, though I did trust Ezra. I trusted him so much it scared me.

I followed his instructions to the letter, matching the strokes. I went forward, but when I got near Ezra, I faltered. "Just keep going," he said. Kicking his legs to float backwards. He made everything so graceful. "Once you get to the other side, you get a hug!"

"I deserve a damn hug," I said, keeping my head above the water best I could.

"We're going to need to work on form, though, that's for sure." He held onto the ledge. Eleven feet below me, I thought. Yet, I did feel pretty buoyant, not as though I was progressing forward.

I lost my rhythm and panicked. "Shit, shit, shit," I cried. Ezra threw a boogie board my way. "Thanks!" I hissed sarcastically.

"You gotta learn to do it on your own!" he said. "You're a grown ass woman!"

"I currently don't feel like one!" I said, holding onto the board with a death grip.

"Kick!" he said.

I made it to the other side and went in for a hug. "Nope, gotta swim all the way over to get a hug!" He swam back to the other side. Annoyed, I felt like growling. "Hold onto the side of the pool like this!" He had his arms behind him and his knees up to his chest. "Then push off under the water, see how far you go and do that breaststroke. You'll get here!"

It took a few tries until I could swim from one end of the pool to the other that day. Ezra hugged me so tightly I wanted to cry, but out of relief. My arms were tight against him, and my face buried in the cold skin of his shoulder. "See, you did it! You keep doubting yourself! It just takes practice." He looked me in the eye, and for a moment, I thought we'd kiss, but I turned away and

dunked under the water before dragging myself from the pool. He was only a few yards behind me.

I was exhausted and sat at one of the picnic tables and in the shade. Ezra sat across from me. We were still dripping with harsh pool water. He smiled at me. "Thank you. I—I'm happy I'm learning," I admitted.

"Yes! You did great!"

"So, you haven't told me, what's going on with your mom," I said. "I've seen you on the phone in the office every evening."

"I knew you'd ask that at some point," he said, rubbing his chin. It reminded me of an old man deep in thought, minus the beard. "A week ago I took her to treatment again because when I went home for the weekend, I found her passed out on the bathroom floor. She OD'd on heroin. She's damn lucky to be alive. I half just wanted to leave her there but . . ." He ran his hands through his hair.

I stood up and side-hugged him, resting my cheek against the puff of hair atop his hair. "You did the right thing. Maybe she'll get clean."

"You and I both know that's not going to happen," he said. "There's no point in getting my hopes up. She just doesn't see the point of living without it."

"She told you that?"

"She doesn't have to. She's that dependent. Besides, she's not understandable half the time," he muttered. He took a heavy breath. I went to sit down again. "She doesn't see an issue. It gets her through the day." He paused. "At this point, I don't even want to be involved anymore."

"Then don't," I said. "Get her out of your life. You don't need any negativity or toxicity. You have work and school to focus on. It's not like she's done anything to help you since you were ten. You raised yourself." He nodded slowly. "You're nineteen now."

Ezra nervously looked me in the eyes. "It leaves me with absolutely no family if I do that. No family."

"Blood's nothing. You can make your own family. Choose your family," I said. There was some silence and I patted him on the back as I went to change.

From the pool, Ezra and I went west toward the Lost Monuments Trail. He told me about the classes he was going to take in the upcoming semester and how all his belongings were stashed in his car so his mother couldn't sell any of it.

"Are you going to be able to afford housing this semester?" I asked.

"Yeah," he said. "Being poor with great grades does come in handy when it comes to merit scholarships."

Behind the office was a small opening into the trail. It was thick with foliage, including the thorns of young wild blackberries. The trail was nothing more than a deer trail at this point, pocked with hoof prints, and in some places, deep puddles of water to hop over. I was deep into talking about my research for my junior year research symposium. "So I really want to figure out the psychology of the German people during the Holocaust."

"I thought they claimed they didn't know what was going on," Ezra said.

"'Claimed' means nothing. They knew. They had to know. The rhetoric was coming straight from the horse's mouth. It was part of party doctrine. People worked at those camps. They had to go home to someone," I said. "It's the most interesting thing to me, how people can look blindly away from something that might hurt their sensibilities, or fully embrace outright extermination. That's what I just don't understand. Can't understand."

"It'll be a good way to bring your two majors together," he said.

"Are you going to come to the symposium?" I asked, hopeful.

"I might, it's all the way in April, that's nearly a year away," he said, smiling.

I knew he wasn't going to be there. After last summer, when we connected so well, he disappeared completely from my life during the school year. The only evidence he existed was from the occasional thumbs up on Facebook posts. Otherwise, I didn't exist. It hurt, honestly, but he owed me nothing. He didn't know then, and still probably was unaware of how desperate I was for someone to trust. It was like a great void in me that I'd fight to fill.

"I'm going to study William Shirer's The Rise and Fall of the Third Reich *and* Berlin Diary. *Did you know he's from Iowa? He was a CBS correspondent in Germany during the war and the Nuremberg Trials. He lived in Cedar Rapids, I think."*

Ezra let me just talk about my favorite things in the world as we plodded to the main trail to Lost Lake. This was probably the most gorgeous trail in Kellova. The light felt so enchanted. The air was soft. Bluebell flowers carpeted the ground. They were in their last bloom before the end of the season.

Near the first of the monuments, standing stones that had been carved upon were the beginnings of Lost Lake. It was in the depths of the forest, guarded by the hills and the trees, and on private land so it was never touched. Part of the water was covered in a thick layer of lime green algae. In some places, fish could be seen darting in the water. We took kids here occasionally to fish, but never kept a single fish. The only one allowed to fish was Gary, but even if he weren't allowed, he'd do it anyway.

The grass was short on one bank where the ground became more pebbles than grass. I spread a picnic blanket out. When I sat down, Ezra stared at one of the stones. "I can't read them; what if they're grave markers?" he asked.

"I think the only people who lived here were on the land Gary lives on," I said.

"Hasn't his family lived here since like 1890 something or other?"

"I don't know for sure," I replied. "But they started Camp Kellova, so I guess they could have come down here."

He shrugged and sat down to eat one of the sandwiches while I went after a granola bar. We sat beside one another, resting, watching the lake. This was what I wanted out of summer. This was peace.

Chapter Ten:

August 1, 2016

Leta passed by me and said, "Thank you for the help earlier. I know both you and Carra think I'm excellent with little kids, but they sap the energy right out of me . . ."

"I know you're tough," I said. "Hopefully next week I'll see if I can convince my mother to put you in with some older kids."

"Fifth graders would be great," she said, smiling. She disappeared into the pool house, and I approached Trisha. The sun glared down on her reddening skin, but she always was a tad red. Spending her days cleaning the pool left her hair a bleached blonde, and her skin crispy looking.

"Everything ready?" I asked.

"On point. Water's looking great; I think we can let them in." She paused to take a deep breath before taking out her whistle. The shrill noise cut straight through the air. "Ok! I'm going to need everyone who hasn't taken the swimming test yet to form a line right here!" She made a straight line with her hand. She whispered to me, "I'll take Harry to help. He's pretty good at getting them through fast." Her eyes floated over to the crowd. "Do you think we can get Ryanne into the water this time around?"

"We can try, but honestly, no. At least step one is accomplished, she's in her swimsuit which is more than I expected." The girl's swimsuit was a little too big for her body, but it was on her. She was slathered in sunscreen. That was another bit of the battle.

I exited the fenced in area and joined some of my campers underneath an awning. They sat at one of the few wooden picnic tables passing time. Kennedy was showing Ellie one of her graphic novels and Ellie seemed to be enjoying it. Gracia and Taylor were talking nearby. Lisey was watching with both longing and jealousy. Lisey probably didn't know that there was absolutely nothing going on between Gracia and Taylor. Gracia, though fifteen, seemed years above Taylor in the maturity department. Taylor just liked having someone to talk to who didn't ask much from him.

Gracia whispered to him, before I sat down, "You have got to keep your pants zipped or you're going to regret it like your brother." I briefly looked at my hands and pretended I heard nothing. Lisey, on the other hand, did hear it, and was turning a startlingly deep color of red, though I was sure none of the aforementioned need for pant-zipping had anything to do with her.

"Noah turned out fine," Taylor said in a regular voice. Gracia looked annoyed.

"Noah turned out in a psych ward a few times over," Gracia said. "Trust me, he practically texted me the whole time."

"Why does he talk to you more than he talks to me?" Taylor asked. He wasn't offended, though.

"I don't know, I wish I knew, actually," she said. "Half the time he just wants to talk about girls he meets."

"Maybe that's because he was trying to make you jealous, ever think of that?" Taylor asked, eyebrows raised.

"About him?" she asked, surprised, almost startled. "If that's what he's doing, he has the wrong idea."

"Not interested in him?" he asked. "You'd be the first girl to tell me that."

"I can assure you," Gracia laughed, holding in her breath for a moment to get her bearings. She shook her head and put her hand out. "There is absolutely no way in hell that I'd have a crush on your brother or that there will ever be one. I'd prefer it that way. He's way too messy. Love him, but—ick."

"And Noah told me all about your little intervention with him," Taylor said, pointing at me. I put my hands up.

"I know of no such intervention," I replied.

Trisha blew her whistle again. Any remaining kids who didn't need their tests done, gathered at the pool gate while she explained procedures. While she was doing that, I slipped inside the gates. Just for Ezra's sake, I jumped into the pool from the diving board, doing a full flip in the process. He would have been proud.

"Oh yea!" Gracia cheered from behind the chain-link of the fence. As soon as they were let in, she grabbed a pool noodle, and Taylor made a raft out of kickboards. Ellie clung to the side of the pool, unwilling to let go just yet.

"Now's your chance to try, Lisey!" I said. Lisey stood in her bikini near the corner of the pool, arms around her middle, eyes all scrunched up, watching, waiting.

Eddy, one of the boys in Peter's cabin, went next. "Belly flop!" he announced. We scattered out of the possible wave zone. He went fully in for it and his stomach made a sickening slap when it hit the water. He'd be severely red after that.

"Lisey!" I called. She marched up to the board, looked at it intently, and went for it.

"Cannonball!" Ellie called as Lisey hit the water. When she came up, a large smile pasted on her face.

"You did it!" I said, swimming over.

"I did!"

Coral and Marsha were on either side of Ryanne on the pool deck, getting nowhere in whatever conversation they were having. I assumed it was to get her into the pool. I swam to shallower water while Lisey got ready for another jump. "Hey, Ryanne, want to join me?" I asked. Ryanne looked at me like I was crazy, and I was. I didn't want the kid to join me. I could go the rest of my life without seeing her and be perfectly happy about it, but this was a job.

"I'm not taking any stupid test!" she snapped at Trisha, completely ignoring me.

"If you won't take the test, you can only stay in the zero-entry area," Trisha said softly, doing her best to keep her composure. That part of the pool was no deeper than a foot and a half.

"I don't care," she said. "This is stupid." Ryanne sat down on the edge of the pool, careful not to put her feet in the water. I didn't know how she did it. The pavement was blistering.

"Do you just want to try it out?" Marsha asked. "You don't have to do the test with the other kids. We can wait, right Trisha?"

"Yes," Trisha said, though she sounded a little perturbed by the situation.

"I'm not doing it!" Ryanne screamed.

"Ok, ok, then I need to put a red band on your wrist," Trisha said.

"No you won't!" Ryanne then sat on her hands.

"It's a rule that all campers have to wear a wristband so we can keep you safe while you're in the pool. Ok?" Trisha spoke kindly, although I knew her patience only went so far. She knelt next to Ryanne and was holding a red plastic band.

"I said no!" Ryanne stood up and walked off quickly, out the gate, and toward the bridge.

"Ryanne!" Coral called. "Come back! You can't just run off like that! Ryanne!"

"That girl is going to be the death of me," Marsha hissed. "This is ridiculous. Why is she even here?"

"This is her fourth summer. We keep trying. Her mom was a camper here. Wanted to continue the legacy I guess," I said.

"Do you want to go get her?" Marsha asked.

"It's your turn," I said.

"And I have more kids to test. I can't go after the crazy ones all day." Trisha blew her whistle and called the kids waiting in line to start to tread water. "Thirty seconds! Mr. Harry will be watching. If you're testing for the intermediate area, follow me."

It was nearly ten minutes later before I saw Coral and Marsha with Ryanne. Ryanne had changed back into her clothes. She still refused to get in the water, though they did manage to get a red band on her. After about an hour more in the pool, the kids were sent to change. Kennedy, who hadn't gone in the water at all, was deep into a book, her nose only a few inches from the page. I sat by her, my hair dripping wet, yet feeling straw-dry. "Any good?" I asked.

"You know I've read this like three other times, right?" she asked, not moving.

"Yep," I said. "Just trying to make conversation."

Taylor came out of the boy's shower room with his shirt draped across his shoulder. His slim physique attracted Lisey's attention once again. She turned more purple this time. "Taylor, wear a shirt for God's sake," I said.

"It's a million degrees outside!" he whined.

"Taylor," I said again. He grumbled and pulled it over his neck and stretched his arms through the sleeves.

A boy about his age in a red hat and jeans wandered off toward the bridge. He crossed it and I watched, dumbfounded. "Where are you going?" Leta asked, jogging after me as I went toward the camper.

"I think I saw a kid cross the bridge. Come with me," I said, remembering the rule of three.

"Are you sure?"

"Yeah, blue shirt, jeans, red hat," I replied. "Must be one of Peter's kids, looks about that age."

"Peter's still in the shower," Leta said and whispered, "I honestly think he's making out with Harry in there or something. No surprise, I knew they'd hook up one of these days . . ."

I asked into my walkie, "Does anyone have an older boy with a blue shirt, long blue jeans, and a red hat?" There was no response, so we crossed the bridge. The kid just kept walking, hands at his side. "Hey dude! We're going back to Clark soon for dinner! You can't go off by yourself!"

"Do you think he can hear us?" Leta asked. "We don't have a deaf kid this week, do we?"

"As far as I'm aware, no, and we didn't get any new male campers that age either," I replied. The camper opened the squeaky door and slipped into Apple.

We jogged after him, dodging a few trees, going through a brushy path. He walked past the paint covered tables and to the bathrooms.

"The bathrooms smell worse here than at the pool, why would he come here?" Leta asked.

The door closed and we stood in the hallway outside of it. Bright light poured in through all the windows, illuminating the whole building. Not a single light was on, including inside the bathroom, which had no windows. It'd be pitch black in there.

Leta looked at me with fear in her eyes. "Should we knock?" she asked. I did.

"Hey, it's just Miss Laurel. I want to make sure you're ok." There was no response. "We didn't get to see who you are."

"Are you sure he's in there? It's dark," Leta whispered. "He could be hiding around here."

"Where?" I asked. "No one in their right mind would go in those cupboards, they're gross." I knocked on the door again. "Besides, we saw him go in here." When I got no response, I opened the bathroom door. The light wasn't on, and when I flicked it on, there was no one there.

"What?" Leta cried. "No, no, yeah, you're right, we saw him go in there. We heard the door. We both did, right?"

"I saw, I heard," I replied, my heart going a bit faster in my chest. "I repeat, does anyone have a camper matching the description of male, at least five foot two, blue shirt, red hat, and jeans?"

"No," A chorus of male counselors replied. Leta nearly ran out of Apple.

I wracked my brain about who that kid could have been. He looked familiar. Familiar enough his image was almost haunting.

"Wait for me!" I called. I didn't want to be alone. She stood by the bridge. Her arms were crossed tightly around her middle and she looked at me with fear.

"I'm not going back in here," she said, shaking her head. "Ever, ever, ever."

"You'll have to." I said, almost laughing in bewilderment, but I didn't know what else to say. I went to walk over the bridge, and she didn't move.

"It's not a joke. Switch me out with someone else. See if Sasha or Kelly will teach hand arts. Anyone but me. I'll teach anything else. I'm not going back there."

"Leta, seriously?"

"There's a ghost in there!" she screeched like a bird.

"We don't know that." That was a lie of course, but I needed her to do her job.

"I'm going to talk to Miss Carra."

"That's a bad idea, Leta, please don't. She'll call you crazy. Trust me, I've been trying to tell her about things like this for years and every time she dismisses me." Leta, whose skin was usually a warm chestnut color, had gone ashy.

"You want me to act like I didn't see a thing?" she asked.

"If you can," I replied.

Chapter Eleven:

August 1, 2016

The girls and I walked across the bridge toward Apple after dinner that evening. Despite it being seven o'clock, the heat only tapered off slightly. Apple had very little circulation and would be a sweat-locker. Coral and Marsha's cabin was already there, and Coral was strategically placing fans throughout. "Thank you," I said to her. I stuck my face in front of one of the fans and let it blow my hair back behind my head. Despite the incident earlier in the day, which was written off by my mother as a hallucination of mine, shared or not, I was ok with being in here while it was packed with people. I didn't think I'd be seeing that kid wandering around, floating through tables.

"What should we make for Mr. Ezra?" Kennedy asked. "A banner? What's his favorite color?"

"He likes blue and silver, he's a Ravenclaw," Lisey said.

"Then that's blue and bronze," Kennedy said.

"Not in the movies!" Lisey whined.

"How do you know his favorite colors?" I asked. She was right, but I was still surprised.

"I pay attention," she replied. "Ok, so how about a banner with, like, pennants. We should use glitter. Glitter makes everything better."

"I like glitter!" Sadie exclaimed, giggling. Jane rolled her eyes.

Harry walked past me and whispered, "Fairy herpes." I stifled a laugh.

While they gathered construction paper, felt, string, markers, glitter, and glue, I went to the backroom, which still gave me a good look at the girls, and the hallway leading to the bathroom. I took a large handful of long, skinny glow sticks, and shoved them in my backpack. When I returned to the main room, I helped the girls cut out sizable pennants that would write out: Get Well Mr. Ezra.

Birch cabin was making new nametags in the hope Ryanne would feel included. She sat on one of the stools, doing nothing.

"I need glitter!" Ellie said, reaching out for the silver.

"I thought we decided on bronze," Kennedy mumbled, rolling her eyes.

Ellie ignored her and carefully outlined the first pendant with glue and sprinkled the glitter with care, which was refreshing. I was used to kids dumping glitter in piles.

"That will look really good Ellie," I said. She smiled at me, and my heart grew a size or two. When it came to incorporating her into our everyday life, it was very important to me.

"He likes leaf prints!" Sadie exclaimed. She had a notebook of them from various trees throughout camp. "Maybe I should make some for him."

"He'd love that," I said. She excitedly ran outside. "Make sure someone goes with you!"

"I'll go," Kennedy said. Ezra was the one that got Sadie first interested in nature. He also taught arts and crafts. I remembered days when he had glitter stuck to his face and in his dark brown hair.

Ellie focused on her glue and glitter art. I sat beside her, assisting. A heavy bang caught my attention. In this building, almost every noise was amplified. The girls didn't pay much attention. They were used to chaos. I looked to the hallway where both Marsha and Coral were standing in the doorway of the bathroom. Coral looked at me with pleading eyes. "I'll be right back," I said to Ellie.

"Ok," she said. "Can I take a picture of this when we're done?"

"Definitely."

Marsha stepped away from the door of the bathroom to make room for me and whispered, "She's going to make me insane."

"What's going on, Ryanne?" I asked.

"I went to speak with her," Coral started when Ryanne didn't respond. There was a large blue stain on Coral's shirt. "About pouring paint on me when I stopped her from messing with a lighter she found."

"Do you have the lighter?" I asked. She nodded and pulled it out of her pocket.

"She was trying to light some yarn on fire in the corner . . ."

"Ryanne, is that true? Did you pour paint on your counselor?" She was hiding in one of the stalls. The door to it wasn't closed and she was sitting on the seat. Her eyes lifted and pierced me.

"I was just asking if you wanted to make a name tag for you bunk, Ryanne," Coral said as calmly as she could manage.

"Do you want to go change, Coral?" I asked.

"Thank you," she said with a huff. She quickly left the building for Birch. I leaned against the doorway.

"Ryanne, you're old enough to know that it's not acceptable to do what you did. Coral was simply asking if you wanted to do something. There's no reason to throw paint, and you really shouldn't be playing around with lighters."

"I didn't throw paint," she said.

"Ok, you poured paint on her shirt, do you agree that you did that?" I asked.

"Leave me alone," Ryanne said harshly.

"Ryanne, you're not going to have canteen the remainder of the week," I said. "Unfortunately I know that you did this on purpose. You haven't given your counselors a chance and you are treating them unfairly and rudely."

"Oh shut up . . .you can't take away my snack!" she cried.

"You can have an apple or an orange like some of the other kids, you know that," I said. "And I can, actually." Her face scrunched up in anger and I thought she was about to burst.

"Come on and join the rest of your cabin, and stay away from fire," I said.

"No!" She stood up and for a moment, I thought she'd do what I said. That wasn't what happened.

She came at me like a bull and pushed me with both hands, hard enough I was caught off guard and slammed into the other side of the hallway. My head hit and a flash of black covered my vision. I knocked against the wall and crumbled, stunned. My poor brain was so affected by the previous traumatic brain injury that a simple hit short circuited it.

For about twenty minutes, I wasn't really with the world. I was that moveable doll. My skull felt light and empty. There were no thoughts, and absolutely no ability to focus on anything.

When I came to, at least partially, Harry was there. Ryanne was still in the bathroom being non-cooperative. "Laurel," Harry said, and looked into my eyes. He knelt next to me and waved a hand in front of my face. I slapped his hand away and he smiled. "There you are. You've been staring off into space with your eyes lolling around. I radioed Carra to get down here."

"I'll be fine . . ." I said, though my voice was slurred and that annoyed me. Any incident where my brain betrayed me was annoying.

"Sure," he said. "Well, we need to get you out of the hallway. Greg, can you stay here, make sure she doesn't go anywhere?" Harry pointed at the bathroom. My head turned to look at Greg and things swam again.

"You ok, Miss Laurel?" Gracia asked, walking up to me. The girls stopped doing their art projects and stared.

"Yeah," I said.

"Ryanne attacked her!" Kennedy whispered to Jane. Jane nodded slowly, then her eyes went to the hallway.

Harry sat me down outside in the sun, on the grass. "What happened? Marsha said you were trying to get Ryanne to participate in something and she pushed you hard enough to do this." He made a hand gesture to my head. I nodded. "I guess she's a big girl, but she must have really . . .I don't know. God, you make me worry, Laurel."

It was difficult to keep my eyes open. They felt so heavy.

"Miss Carra!" Harry called. He ran over to meet her, and I continued to lie on the grass. The buzzing in my head was loud enough I didn't hear what they said.

"Why do you keep getting in trouble, Laurel?" Mom asked while approaching.

"Yeah, I threw myself against the wall," I muttered.

"That's not what I meant, and you know it," Mom replied. Without any consolation, sympathy, or other acknowledgement, she went inside. Harry looked at me with a confused grin on his face. I tried to stand up and nearly fell over. The dizziness was pervasive and made me feel like I was coming out of anesthesia.

"Would you just take it easy for a moment? Are you capable of that?" Harry asked. Unable to argue, I just sat back down and closed my eyes. Eventually I lay down on the soft grass and felt a steady pulse go through me. The wind touched my face. It was peaceful for just a moment before the bugs started getting involved. Unable to handle being crawled on by everyone and their brother, I got up and went back to work. Harry stayed close behind me.

Mom said, "You're coming with me, Ryanne." Her voice was hard and sturdy. "And we are going to have a talk."

"No!" Ryanne whined. "I'm not going anywhere!" Her fists were balled up and she was about two shakes from trying to take my mom out. Greg, though, was behind her and managed to pull her from the bathroom.

"You don't want to stay here in this stinky hallway all night, do you?" Mom asked. It was silent. She waved Coral away, who now had a clean shirt on. Coral mouthed 'sorry' to me. I sat down at the long table with my girls and the banner they were making as well as an assortment of paper chains. It was beautiful, actually. It didn't look like it was made by kids, but that it was being carefully put together by girls who cared. Some of the pennants even had lace stenciled onto them or very intricate patterns.

"Those are mine," Lisey said, pointing out the lace ones.

"It's awesome, hon," I said.

"When we're done, it's going to need to dry for a while," Ellie said. "Or it'll be all tacky and get everywhere."

From behind me, Mom was still arguing with Ryanne. The battle of wills between the two most stubborn people in this joint. Mom said, "I know what you want, Ryanne, and you're not going to win. You're not going home. I will be speaking with your mother, however. She agreed with me before she dropped you off that you're staying the full week, no matter what fits you throw. You can either act like a young lady your age, or like a toddler throwing a tantrum for no reason. You don't need to be rude to the people trying to help you, and you sure don't need to be hurting my daughter. Laurel was hurt by what you did. Most kids consider being at camp a privilege, and I know you're not one of those kids, even if your mom worked really hard to send you here. She wants you to learn some things." Mom went quiet for a moment. Her voice returned to that of the mom I knew and remembered, the one that disappeared earlier today. "Come on, Ryanne. Stop acting like this and let's talk." Magically, Ryanne left the halfway and went with my mom outside to speak together away from the rest of the kids.

"Why is she like that?" Kennedy asked, quite loudly.

"Kenny . . ." I began.

"What? You want us to act like we didn't see anything? Didn't see you get hurt? Or see her kicking and screaming and punching when Greg hoisted her out?" The other girls nodded.

Sadie said, "She's just mean. Some people are like that." Then, her whole attitude changed, and she stuck her face in the fan and started making funny voices.

We set the banner in a safe place to dry and returned to Hawthorne. Once inside, I emptied out my backpack to show them the dozens of glow-sticks I collected. "Awesome!" Sadie exclaimed. "I saw this thing online where people wore them and danced in the dark so what you saw was just glowsticks. It was hilarious!"

"Can we do that?" Lisey asked. "Please, please, please, please, please!"

"Sure!" I exclaimed. "Let's wait until it gets dark though." In the meantime we played a few games like 'mafia' and 'honey I love you,' all to gleeful laughs and probably way too much excitement.

Once it got good and dark outside, we cracked the glow sticks. Sadie and Jane had glow sticks taped to their arms, legs, stomachs, as well as a circle around their face. I played dance music on my phone for them. They were absolutely carefree in their movements and actions. Seeing their outlines made everything funnier. I laughed so hard that I thought I would develop abs. I videotaped, shakily. Everyone wanted to try it and we had enough glow sticks to go around and do exactly that. Soon enough we had a full glow stick dance party going on.

Simple things like this, the innocent playfulness, was what this place was meant for. It was why camp existed in the first place. The girls were independent, away from home, doing what they wanted, having fun, and they were safe.

Near the end of our dance party, the girls taped glow sticks to me and I danced right along with them. It was such a peaceful state to be in, full to the brim of joy until the good type of exhaustion crept in. "What should we do with them now?" Sadie asked when we all sat down on our bunks and pulled the sticks off ourselves.

"I don't know, what do you guys want to do?" I asked.

"Do you remember when we were up at the horse cabins and we threw the glow-stick juice everywhere to make the cabin light up? We should do that again!" Sadie exclaimed.

So we did.

Sleep was never easy for me. As much as I loved sleep, both quantity and quality, there were hardly ever nights without some kind of vivid nightmare or dream. The brain injury didn't help matters. So, this night, with my head freshly bonked, was no different. In the dream, Leta and I were in Apple, right where we stood earlier that day, knocking on the door to the boy's bathroom. Leta jumped at every sound. What startled me was that there were no strange differences in this world. Everything looked as real as it did to me while awake.

"Can you come out of the bathroom? We need to go back for dinner. It's spaghetti tonight." In the dream, I was hungry.

The door opened and Riley stepped out. He looked just like he did last time I saw him, burned arm and all. He looked like he was in pain. He rubbed his forehead and was yelling something silently. He was begging . . . at that moment, it suddenly felt like tragedy was going to happen.

Riley looked out one of the many windows in Apple to his right where I could see the garage on fire. My dog was there. Georgie. I dashed outside the building and straight for the garage. I could save her now. I could do what I failed to do before.

Georgie was howling and screaming in fear and pain.

"I'm coming, baby! I'm coming!" I cried. The flames licked every surface, consuming things quickly. I was surrounded by flames. Even in a dream I could feel it, like I was in hell. The flames touched my clothing, igniting the fabric. Georgie was in the center of the garage, confused, sitting, protecting her feet, crying. When she saw me, despite her pain, her tail thumped steadily. It was on fire. Despite her being such a big dog, I dove for her and swooped her up in my arms.

It was a dream, of course, she was light enough to carry, but then there was no strength in my legs, specifically my knees. I continued to fall over. I desperately wanted to keep her safe in my arms. She yowled in pain. "I got you! I got you," I said. Tears streamed down my face. I wanted those tears to flow so heavily that they would put out the fire on my dog's fur. Fighting, with every ounce of energy I could manage, I got us out of that garage.

Collapsing on the gravel, unable to breathe, and choking in flames, I lay there with Georgie underneath me. Suddenly aware that there were bits of fur on fire, I used my shirt to suffocate the flames. I dragged myself to a spigot attached to Apple and doused her in water. She was in too much pain to walk. Her paws were burnt. Her body was too, but she was alive. My Georgina was alive. She'd be ok.

Then, I woke up.

It was the depth of night. I was unable to see anything except the light attached to the bathroom, and it's many nighttime insect visitors. I tried to crawl back to reality. Tears streamed down my face rapidly. In this world, Georgie was not alive. She wasn't asleep at the base of my bed, crawling up toward me to comfort me. I desperately missed her. At eleven, she had a good life, but that didn't make her death any less infuriating. She didn't have to go like that, so afraid and in so much pain.

When it was investigated, it was clear an accelerant was used in the garage. It was a case of arson. Georgie was just an unfortunate victim, but someone killed her. Someone was responsible for her horrible death. A latent fury and curiosity rush through me.

I turned and sat against the wall and stared into the center of the cabin. Nothing moved, and yet, I felt uneasy. The bugs were silent now, the ones that lulled me to sleep earlier in the night. Tingling crawled around my ears and down my neck. I could very well start hallucinating things. I closed my eyes and focused on my big toe. The burning and tingling feeling was terribly familiar. It was a result of my brain injury, or so the sleep specialist said. Before the TBI, I never experienced such a strange thing as sleep paralysis before, but now it was common enough it happened a couple times a week.

The summer after the brain injury occurred, sleep paralysis would come and go, but so did sleep walking and I'd end up in various places, and more often than not, that place would be House One. It was bad enough that if I didn't have kids in my cabin, either Lukas or Ezra would sleep on an air mattress in front of the door to my cabin to make sure I wouldn't wander off. Whenever sleep walking prevailed, however, I woke up screaming in terror by my surroundings- the sudden feeling of absolute dread and confusion. Most of the time, House One was locked and I didn't know how I got in, much less how to get out.

August 2014

It was Saturday night, and the kids were home for a brief period of time. The sensation of sleep paralysis hit me, my heart picked up pace, heaviness overcame me. I knew it well enough that I anticipated seeing something- usually a black blob with ruby red eyes at the foot of my bed. While I could still move, I pulled my favorite purple blanket over my eyes, so I didn't have to see anything.

Paralysis came over me and I couldn't move. The immediate need to scream came with it. I always wanted to scream, to force air out my throat to make some noise, to cry for help. There was so much anger towards whatever caused this, which I knew was irrational. I wanted to fight it. I wanted to have the chance to confront it, but it was just a medical condition- there was nothing to fight.

Something sat on the mattress beside me, heavy enough to make an inden- tation. There was something touching my exposed hair. I tried to shriek. Nothing but a whisper of air left my lips.

Focusing on my big toe, it took everything I had to pull out of that paraly- sis. I threw my blanket off, expecting to see something, someone, beside me. There was nothing there, but there was something in the woods.

I saw her. I saw what some people called Alina, others called Linnea, but most agreed she was just the girl on the hill. She was halfway up, in the trees and the brush, illuminated by the moon and something within her. Her hair was black, down to her shoulders, and she wore a white, lace dress. She simply stood. She said nothing. Did nothing.

Turning away, I covered my face with the blanket again, as if it could pro- tect me, and went back to sleep.

I did not wake in that bed.

I woke inside the screened-in porch of House One. The same place we found other kids on more than one occasion. I was lying on the bench of a picnic table. I closed my eyes tightly and begged that I could just be back in

Hawthorne, away from this place. The air was different here; it was electric and invasive.

I felt invaded.

Startled, I finally screamed. I had to scream. I searched for an exit. The screen was sound, heavy gauge wire. Knowing that the doors and the windows were locked, I tried to claw my way out.

The darkness inside the house was unnatural. The world around, though, was illuminated by the morning sun, but inside the house, the light was sucked in, destroyed. Heat rushed through my body, and I was hit with a blinding panic. I landed curled up in the corner of the porch, as far away from the house as I could manage.

My watch stopped working. Completely dead. I didn't know what time it was.

The house started knocking at me in threes. I swore something was running up and down the stairs inside. With my hands clapped against my ears, I rocked back and forth to comfort myself.

Lukas found me like that. He slammed his fist into the glass of one of the windows, when that didn't work, he took a shovel and knocked it out to crawl in.

"Laurel? What the hell? How did you get in there?" That was the first time he broke into the house. "Shut up you damned house!" he screamed. His voice was sucked up by the house as well before a horrific explosion rang out. Another window on the opposite side of the house blew out, and Lukas didn't touch it. "What the fuck?" He stared in that direction. He stood, dumbfounded. His fear was palpable. "Come on, we need to get out of here." He took my arm and got me to my feet. We both stumbled out and into the clearing when the knocking inside the house grew to the point the very ground itself shook.

Chapter Twelve:

August 2, 2016

The next morning came with a hazy fog, and I felt like I managed only half an hour of sleep. It was an almost impossible task to peel myself out of my comfortable sleeping bag and get the girls up. No one wanted to move. The night was cold and the morning, colder. Being swaddled up in blankets and hoodies was the only thing that sounded appealing. Still, one by one, we got up to brush our teeth and comb our hair. Gracia had energy nearly all the time, even in the mornings. She was the first to get ready and by the time I stood up, she had her ukulele out and was strumming away.

Kennedy had her sleeping bag wrapped around her head and was looking drearily at the day. "Come on, Kenny," I muttered. "Let's get moving. If you get to Clark on time, I'll get you hot chocolate . . ."

"Ok," she said, though her voice wasn't enthusiastic in the least.

"I just couldn't sleep last night . . ." Lisey said, rubbing her temples. "Just kept waking up every hour or so. Maybe more . . ." She yawned and nearly fell over. "I'm already looking forward to going to bed tonight."

"You and sleep just don't get along," I said. "This happens every week."

"Eh, I guess it does," she said. "Had all these wacky nightmares when I did sleep too, which was obnoxious. Can't remember most of them, just a lot of falling . . ."

With our backpacks on, and everyone ready for the day, we made our way down to Clark silently. A flash of light came from my right and I turned quickly. There was a figure in the corner of my vision- it was that red hat. There was nothing there, and no one else noticed.

Other kids were already at Clark, and they acted like nothing strange was happening. A game of gaga was about to start. Jane threw off any sleepiness left in her and went for the game. Lisey ran after her, less enthusiastic, but Taylor was playing and where Taylor was, she wanted to be.

All the other girls got seats on the porch, rocking away in the comfy chairs while I fetched hot chocolate. It really was an unwritten rule that kids couldn't have the staff hot cocoa, but I didn't care. If we ran out and people complained, I'd go buy more out of my own pocket. Even if I was making $3.74 an hour.

Sitting on that porch in the morning was one of my favorite things in the world. It was peaceful. Though, usually if it was morning and I was on that porch, I was exhausted. Most mornings I was cold but there was a certain sense of calm and serenity in the air. The sound of children playing and laughing, but not yet arguing, the slight fog hanging over the grass and clinging to the trees, and the young white sunlight . . . just for the moment I could relax fully. I could enjoy the world around me.

Once we had breakfast, the kids took time to sign up for their classes, and we returned to the cabin for a shorter cabin clean up period. "Did anyone sign up for orienteering?" I asked. The cabin went silent. I paused the music for a second. "I thought you wanted to finish your packet, Kenny."

"I'm doing lapidary," she said.

"And I signed up for soccer," Jane said. "But I know Eddy, Arty, and Taylor are doing orienteering so they can get through the advanced ones." I sighed and went back to playing music, Disturbed, specifically. It was strange that these girls preferred to listen to heavy metal music while cleaning, but anything to get another stripe on the pole.

Sadie got a broom and swept the ceiling before she got to the floor. A single spiderweb could mean a loss, and I wasn't about to lose.

One time my mother docked us points for having a complete fox skeleton Sadie and I dug up, washed, bleached, and scrubbed on the porch, and it still made me furious to this day. It was Sadie and I who found the jawbone by the archery range while picking up lost arrows. She was so enamored by it that we started digging, and eventually, the whole thing came to life. We brought it back to the cabin in a plastic grocery bag and she spent a few days following a diagram to assemble it. Jake, one of the counselors at the time, was getting his master's in comparative anatomy, and he helped her make a display for it.

"What about our towels?" Lisey asked. "I still think it looks tacky to have them hanging on the ends of the beds like this." She pointed to the array of colorful towels taking up space.

"It's never hurt us before," I said.

"We always have towels up, though, it makes the place stink," Lisey said. She crossed her arms. Though she was much more awake now, there were circles under her eyes and she looked like she could fall asleep if just given a few moments to lie down.

"If you want to take them to the shower house and hang them on the clothesline, you can, just make sure you stick together," I said. I was reluctant to let any of them out of my sight, but they weren't exactly little kids. If I started to follow them around too much to keep tabs on their every move, they'd resent me.

"You wanna come, Grace?" Lisey asked.

"Sure." The two girls took a load of heavy towels down to the pool while the rest of us finished up.

"Can't you turn down that racket?" Harry called from his cabin, laughing. "It sounds like you're having a black mass in there or something!"

"Would you rather listen to some nice Gregorian chants?" I called.

"It burns, it burns!" Harry whined. His boys laughed.

"Why can't we listen to music?" One of his kids asked.

"You get too distracted. I don't want to get last place again!" Harry exclaimed. "Clean boys, clean!"

"They'll never win," Kennedy said. "I bet it's a pigsty in there. If it's anything like the bathroom . . . Did you know this morning Peter had to clean? Ugh, it was the biggest mess ever."

"By biggest mess you mean . . . I'm almost scared to ask." Granted, it couldn't be any worse than the atrocity that was the uncleaned sanitary boxes that held a summer's worth of tampons and pads I found in the girl's restroom a few years ago.

"Some kid must have had wicked diarrhea," Kennedy said, grimacing.

"Yeah, I think I heard it too . . ." Ellie said, making a gagging motion. "It was on the wall and everything. The boys were laughing about it."

"Poor Peter," I said. Though to see him cleaning up such a mess would have been the highlight of my week. I would have paid good money for the opportunity. He had a weak stomach. Despite being one of the most highly trained people here in terms of first aid and CPR- the sight of bodily fluids, or solids, usually ended up with him puking. His gut got him into a number of problems.

"Honestly, I'd just pour bleach on everything, wouldn't touch it until everything could be power washed by a hose," Ellie said, holding her hands up. "And our bathroom is bad enough, never has enough soap, paper towels are always out, and there are spiders and bugs everywhere . . ."

"Just be thankful there isn't actual crap smeared all over the wall," Kennedy replied.

"Or that kid Michael peeing all over everything," Lisey added. "You remember that, Kenny? Like when you saw him standing on top of one of the stalls spraying like a dog."

"Thank God he hasn't had an incident this year," I said.

"I was surprised I didn't see him playing gaga this morning," Jane said. "He was camped out by Greg. He must've got in trouble."

"Thank God for that too," Lisey said. "He doesn't understand that when he gets out, he's out. He can't just stay in there and pretend like he isn't and stop the whole game up. He'll stand there with his arms crossed and refuse to move."

"Jenny acted like that this morning," Sadie said.

"It's just infuriating. If you can't follow the rules, don't play the game. It's just that simple," Lisey said.

"And you say I'm high strung . . . at least with Michael he's just a kid," Jane said.

"He spit on you last week, I saw it!" Ellie said, laughing. Lisey was finishing her bed off in a military style. I preferred if we could flick coins off the bedding, but the mattresses themselves held such little shape, it really wasn't a realistic goal.

Chapter Twelve: August 2, 2016

"He got frustrated, it happens!" I never knew Jane to be such an under-standing or patient individual, but here she was, showing understanding for the most difficult kid at camp, second only to maybe Ryanne.

What surprised me, was not hearing anything about Ryanne this morning at breakfast. Coral and Marsha had an air about them that they'd be willing to kill her for a cup of strong coffee, but I got no actual complaints from them. Ryanne ate breakfast. She wasn't going on a hunger strike just yet, and she was at least wearing shoes. They weren't tied and they didn't look very sturdy, but there was something on her feet and that was already an improvement from last summer.

After cabin cleanup was completed, I met with my group of orienteering kids at the head of the first trail we were going to take this week. It was down past my mom's house on the corner of the camp property. It was a four mile hike, which didn't sound bad, but knowing this trail so well, it was challenging.

"Ok, so make sure you have water with you," I said. "And everyone has their maps and compasses. I've gotten lost on this trail more than once, so I want to make sure, at least this time around, we stick together. I know the path well, but some of you might not. This is the Chief's Daughter trail. It can be very narrow, and right up against drop offs into the creek. There are extremely steep hills going both up and down, a lot of twists and turns, and uneven terrain. You are all advanced but watch how you walk it."

My six campers had their cheap compasses out and laminated maps of the trail. "Can someone tell me the different types of maps presented here?" I asked. The kids and I sat on the grass outside the entrance to the first trail.

"Do we have to go over this every week?" Pandora whined. "It's so hot, I just want to get moving . . ."

"Yes, we do." She rolled her eyes in response.

"One is topographic," Arty said.

"And that means?" I asked.

"It shows elevation levels by using these lines. It can tell you where the hills and valleys are. Also the shape of them. So for us, it'll show how difficult the terrain is," Arty said.

"So these topographic maps are very simple. They don't show what is wooded or what is made of grassland," I said. "For instance, right now, we are on steady ground, flat plain." I pointed to a red dot signifying where we were. "That's the beginning of the trail, and we will end in the clearing at the top of the hill by House One," I said. I wasn't looking forward to walking past that place with the kids.

"Do we have to end there?" Temple asked, clearly nervous.

"At the House?" I asked.

"Yeah," Pandora said. "It freaks her out. Well, me too."

"It freaks everyone out," Eddy said. "I bet you ten bucks it'll knock at us when we get near it."

"No . . .I don't want it to," Temple muttered. Neither did I, but to get their advanced awards in orienteering, this trail had to be checked off the list and no matter what, we'd end at the House. My stomach clenched a bit as well. It tended to act up around kids.

"We don't have to go near it," I said. "But we need to finish the trail." I wanted to sound as confident and assuring as possible. "That way you can get your honors. Ok, ok, the next map, Eddy, in that little binder, how about you explain it?"

"It's just an aerial photograph, probably from Google Maps or a drone. It's not going to show us anything except that we'll be in the woods and will be passing by Lost Lake. That's it. It's pretty much useless."

"Thank you for your enlightenment," I said. Eddy chuckled. "I want everyone to keep an eye out for any signs of erosion, storm damage, anything of that nature, and record that in your packet when we return. Everyone got that?" I got nods. That was a good sign. "Did everyone finish the animal track section?"

"Yes! Let's go already!" Pandora whined.

"Just checking, chill out," I said.

Eddy was still staring at the map when my eyes returned to him. "Well, I guess you can see the clearing is a creepy perfect circle. Could take a compass to that thing." He held the map up to Taylor whose face squished a bit in surprise.

"Uh, yep," he said, less than enthusiastic.

"I want to see!" Juniper insisted. Pandora huffed. Temple joined her to look at the map, even if they all had their own maps. "What are all those white dots on the edge of the clearing? Miss Laurel, do you know?"

"They're calla lilies," I said. They looked at me. I felt pale. "Flowers."

"Let's go!" Taylor said. "I need to see this in person. I think it's been years since I've been up there." He headed first onto the trail with Pandora quickly racing ahead.

Despite everyone's new interest in the lilies around House One, I enjoyed the Chief's Daughter trail. If I was having a particularly bad day, it was a surefire way to get away from people. No one walked this trail for leisure, other than me, and occasionally Ezra, and the challenge helped keep my mind off what was bothering me, or at least helped me work out solutions for it.

"When are we getting to Monuments?" Taylor asked, about five minutes into the walk. Monuments was a large space up near the edge of camp property in the wildest area, the most untouched, where there were a few rudimentary buildings, which went mostly unused in the modern era. Until the eighties or so, Monuments was a whole unit of camp for the older age groups where they could learn more complex wilderness survival techniques and live separate from the younger kids. The distance from other activities made it dip in popularity and die. It was abandoned now.

"We'll get there, just focus on this one," I said.

At the moment, we were on flat ground, following a winding path, surrounded by wild black raspberry bushes that would soon be in season. There were giant pines growing on one side of us, and a stretch of deciduous trees going back as far as one could see. It was a sea of woodland, interrupted only slightly by the trail.

"The Chief's Daughter was established by Miss Charlotte, who was a counselor here for many years. She was the one who first made the path we are following, starting from the director's home to Lost Lake, and then from Lost Lake to the old homestead. She used this trail to search for wildlife, gather firewood, and enjoy nature. Other trails we see or have seen are more utilitarian in nature, such as the trail leading to the Monuments, the one to the quarry, and well, I guess I can't find much of a purpose for this trail as a whole."

"Are there monuments at Monuments?" Arty asked.

"There are, actually, standing stones of a Norwegian style, probably placed there by the family of the first director Miss Amalie. She and her family came from Norway and settled here," I said. That was about the extent of my knowledge.

"Oh darn, I was hoping they'd be like Native American or something," Eddy said.

"Are they graves?" Arty asked, suddenly excited.

"It's written in Norwegian, so I don't know," I said.

"Do you know who the camp took the land from?" Arty asked. The girls were so far ahead of us they couldn't hear, but I wanted them to stay in sight, so I hurried my pace a bit.

"I know nothing about that," I said.

"Who would?" Taylor asked. "Noah's been looking into the history of the place but hasn't been able to find out how this place transitioned from Native held land to a farm to a camp."

The group fell quiet for a moment and the pathway grew thin and proceeded up a hill. The path went through two massive oak trees, one of which Eddy jumped onto, grabbing a branch, pulling himself up so he sat on the limb. "Eddy . . ." I complained. "Why do you always have to climb things?"

"What?" he said, laughing. "I'm having fun!"

Arty stood under the tree where Eddy was. The girls had already reached the top of the hill. "Wait, girls! Can't leave my sight!"

"Then get out of the tree, Eddy!" Pandora barked. "I want to see what's over there!"

"It's just Lost Lake! It's not lost and it's not a lake!" Eddy called back before swinging from the branch and onto the ground with surprising grace. He immediately picked up a stick and swung it like a sword. "Sometimes you can catch fish there, if anyone decides to teach fishing."

Chapter Twelve: August 2, 2016

"There's where I let most of the frogs go that we grow in the nature shed," I said.

"Where do you get the tadpoles?" Juniper asked. She was trailing slightly behind her sisters.

"Puddles up by the horses. I'm always worried they will dry up, so I try to save all of them." I took a large drink from my water bottle.

"I wonder if the horses accidentally drink them . . ." Eddy said thoughtfully. Pandora and Temple were up by the pond. A person could probably throw a rock from one side to another if they had a good arm. "They probably do, like the goldfish you put in the troughs." Eddy was always curious and full of questions. He also tended to get in trouble. Last year he managed to climb onto the roof of my cabin by climbing the trees beside it. He was lucky he didn't break his arm.

Lost Lake was covered in bright green algae. Large bullfrogs popped in and out of the water, watching us intently and with concern. They blended in well with the algae. Juniper was absolutely enthralled by them.

"We have to keep going, Juniper," I said. She let out a whine. "There'll be other things to look at along the way."

The standing stones were near the lake, about the size of a full grown man, their words carved into the stone but unreadable.

"I think these really are graves," Taylor said. "They have names on them." He had a finger on one of the stones.

"What does it say?" I asked.

"I think it says Linnea, like the name . . .Noah's mentioned that name before," Taylor said. My heart twisted in pain and discomfort. I wanted to get away from this place. I knew that name. The girl on the hill.

"We need to keep going," I said.

The path twisted and turned frequently, often making terraces to reach some of the tallest hills in Kellova. Despite being at the top of the hill, the tree cover still made it difficult to see any distance away. The heat grew as we walked and it pounded in my ears. My cheeks and ears felt like they were on fire. My legs weren't tired. Out of everything in my less than well-put-together body, they worked well and had stamina. It was the cardio and the heavy backpack that got to me.

While we plodded on, deer, various birds, the occasional fox, and any number of rodents came into view. Often the deer stayed still until someone stepped on a particularly loud branch. Taylor, the only one who snuck his phone this far into camp, liked to take pictures of the wildlife. "Oh, I wish Noah could see that fox . . ." Taylor whispered. "He loves foxes."

"You better not let anyone else see that phone," I said. He rolled his eyes and eventually put it deep in his backpack.

The entire hike took over two hours and ended at the clearing where House One stood. In the northwest section was a picnic table where everyone sat down. The kids had their path cards to show they successfully completed the level three trail. While most of us rested for a moment, drinking water, reapplying bug spray, Taylor walked into the long, weighed down grass of the clearing to the house.

"You know, deet is a carcinogen," Pandora said to Eddy, who was applying a great deal of Off Deep Woods. "You could die from that."

"I know what deet is and I know that your lemongrass and citronella doesn't do crap against these mosquitos,"

"At least it won't kill me," Pandora replied.

"West Nile and Zika might though," Eddy said, stuffing the aerosol can back into his bag.

"Mom says carcinogens are worse than those," Pandora replied.

"You don't even know what that word means," Eddy said.

"I do too! Carcinogen means something that causes cancer," she said.

"We're not stupid," Juniper added in a hardly audible voice.

"Guys, stop," I said.

Taylor was inspecting the cellar doors to House One. "Taylor, what are you doing?" I asked.

"Someone busted off the lock!" he called.

"What?" The words left my mouth without a single thought. I passed by the circle of flowers and into the clearing, toward the house, feeling a horrific sense of curiosity. Taylor threw the padlock into the grass and opened the door. Immediately a grimace hit his face, scrunching up from some smell. I should have said something then, but my mouth was locked shut. The kids grouped behind me.

"Miss Laurel . . ." he said, stepping into the cellar.

"Don't go in there," I responded. He ignored me and disappeared into the darkness. Though my entire body screamed not to go into that house, I did anyway.

"You have to see this, Miss Laurel," Taylor said. His voice shook with fear. In a perfect circle on the dirt floor of the cellar were dead raccoons in various stages of decay. The one that was completely skeletonized was in perfect condition. Nothing touched it or moved a single bone.

"Eddy, Arty, girls, stay up there," I said.

"Why? I wanna see," Eddy said, making his way down the stairs. Thankfully his body blocked a good deal of the sunlight.

"No, Eds, you don't," Taylor said. "Trust me."

"What is it, a dead body or something?" Eddy asked.

"Well, not a person's dead body . . ." Taylor answered.

"Come on, come on, we're getting out of here and going back to main camp," I said. "Taylor, come on." He went up the steps, pushing Eddy as he went. As I closed the cellar doors, the house knocked three times.

"I told you it would!" Eddy said. He was the only one excited about it. The rest of us hurried away.

There had to be at least a dozen raccoons in that circle. None of them looked like they were brutally killed. There was no blood. These weren't wild animal attacks. The only thing I could tell was that their legs looked longer than normal, and their snouts were a little odd. Leaving the clearing, my vision blurred, and things took on a swirling feeling. The world didn't feel solid, it moved in the air. I walked, swaying side to side, attempting to keep up with the kids. A strange pinching feeling lodged in my skull, ringing, and painful.

The sweet, musky, thick odor of death clung inside my nose and throat and made me nauseous.

"We need to tell Miss Carra, right?" Taylor asked, turning back to speak to me. I nodded. I wasn't ready for words yet. His face was too long.

"What was it?" Temple cried.

"There was this—this circle, a perfect circle, of raccoons, but they were all dead . . ." Taylor said. "I've never seen anything like that before."

"That's it?" Eddy asked, disappointed. "You sound like you found a dead person or something." His face was hard to see, all I saw was the stick he was swinging around like a sword.

"Oh shut up, fuck-face," Taylor said.

"Yo, Taylor, watch your language!" Now I was ready for words. Everything solidified at once. I stopped walking for a second and put my arms out as if I was going to fall. The kids were used to my odd behavior, so they didn't say anything, they just continued to bicker.

"He's being stupid!" Taylor responded. Eddy didn't seem the least bit offended.

"We're going to Clark. If you guys could stay on the porch while I talk to Miss Carra . . .I'll let you have my deck of cards to play with."

Back at Clark, I handed over seven decks of cards, all the ones I carried around with me. I hoped that would keep the kids occupied and in place. Taylor and I went to the office. Mom's door was open. That was a relief in and of itself to know she might be back to her normal humor. She looked sharply over when she saw us. "What did you do now, Taylor?" she asked.

"Why do you automatically assume I did something wrong?" he asked.

"Well, you kind of did," I replied.

"Yeah . . .shouldn't've gone in there, wish I hadn't, but if I didn't, you wouldn't know."

"Hold on, what are you talking about?" Mom asked, standing up from her desk. Her office was littered with files and forms and pieces of paper. Usually she was meticulous. This didn't look like her office at all.

"I kind of went into the cellar of House One when we finished our hiking trail. Someone busted the lock, so I was curious."

Taylor, that house is condemned. You shouldn't be going in there. It's dangerous," Mom said.

"And in the basement, there was this circle of raccoon bodies. Perfect. It was like they fell asleep and didn't wake up. They were just stretched out and they didn't look trapped or anything. Some of them looked like they just died, and others were skeletons . . .boy it freaked me out," he said.

"Is this a joke?" Mom asked, looking at me now.

"No, I saw it too," I replied. "Maybe a dozen, dozen and a half."

"Oh good grief," she said, putting her hand up to her forehead. "Why is it you and your brother always get into things, Taylor?"

"We do have that tendency," he agreed.

"Don't be going into condemned buildings, Taylor. Seriously. I don't want to send you home, but I'm warning you."

"Yes, ma'am," he said, though he was grinning.

"Go back with the rest of the group and let me talk to Laurel for a second." Taylor ran off and down the hill to Clark. "What kind of nonsense are you putting into that boy's mind?"

"Excuse me?" I asked. "We were just taking a rest and he decided to go in there even though I told him to stop. It was like something was pulling him."

"Did you tell him that?" she asked.

"No, I was a little too freaked out by the raccoon art display."

"And that was all you saw?" she asked.

"Yes! We weren't going to stick around," I pressed. She sat down again and took a deep breath before crossing her arms and leaning back.

"I'll get someone to clean it up," she muttered.

"Aren't you wondering who did it?" I asked. She looked at me with disdain. "Who would want to do something like that, Mom?"

"And what are your theories, Laurel?" She didn't sound like she wanted to hear any theories if I had any. "Do you really think someone decided to go kill a bunch of raccoons and arrange them in the basement of a deserted building?"

"I don't have any theories, Mom, but I'm not making it up. He saw it too," I cried. "But aren't you worried? If someone does this to animals, they can do that to people and they're at camp!"

"No one in their right mind here would do that, and no one is going to get hurt here," she said. "Now go back with the kids and drop the subject."

"No one is going to get hurt here?" I said, laughing.

"Exactly what I said, I just want you to keep your mouth shut for once in your goddamn life." She slammed her hand down on her desk. I jumped back, startled. "Don't talk about the house, don't even mention it. Do you understand me?" she snapped.

"What's wrong with you?" I asked.

"What's wrong with me? You. You're what's wrong. You're walking around putting ideas in these kid's heads. You need to keep your trap shut or I'm going to take you off staff." I didn't understand her, what was making her so furious. "Just go, Laurel . . ." she muttered.

As I left, I tried to think of who would do something like that with raccoons. The only person who came to mind was Jake, but he wasn't at camp this summer, he was in Wyoming working on his doctorate.

Chapter Thirteen:

June 2014

Jake turned me into a bone hunter.

He collected skeletons and enjoyed putting them together. His sheer happiness at each new acquisition made it worth the stink and the grime. Camp had a plethora of skeletons to dig up, clean, and put together. Jake was intelligent, hardworking, and a little awkward. Sometimes he'd sit all alone in the staff lounge reading his textbooks.

Once, Lukas and I joined him in the corner, thinking he might like a little company. Armed with fresh freeze pops, Lukas asked, "What are you working on?"

"A paper for a class I'll be taking next semester," Jake said. He pushed his glasses up a bit and took one of the blue freezer pops while I took a red one. I only liked the red ones. "It's comparing the jaw bones of ungulates in particular to small predators such as foxes and coyotes."

"So like deer?" I asked.

"Deer, antelope, horses," Jake said, pointing to a collage in the textbook.

"Why are you working on it this summer?" Lukas asked, leaning his gangly frame against the wall.

"I like to get some of the work done ahead of time, so I don't get overloaded with the course work once the semester starts, and this is the perfect place to do it." Jake smiled sheepishly. It was a rare smile. Though he clearly enjoyed his job here, a smile like that, one of comfort, was a treat.

"Some of the counselors are going to Lottie's house this weekend, wanna come?" Lukas asked. The question was out of the blue. Lukas knew I wouldn't go, and the likelihood of Jake being interested was minimal as well.

"Like a party?" he asked nervously.

"Well, yeah, there'll be a grill out and everyone's going to stay the night there."

"There will be beer and stuff?" Jake asked.

"Yeah," Lukas said plainly enough. He was only eighteen at the time.

"Uh, I really appreciate that, but I don't think I want to go."

"That's ok, Jake. I'm not going either," I said. "I don't like being around drunk people. They make me nervous." He smiled at that and nodded.

"Just thought I'd ask," Lukas said. "So what do you need for your project? Do you need actual jaw bones?"

"I have pictures here," Jake said, pointing.

"That's not like the real thing," Lukas added. "I saw part of a deer in the creek down by the entrance to the Chief's Daughter trail. I can go get it for you, and I can keep my eye out for the others."

Jake's face lit up. "Really? You'd do that?"

"Yeah. It'll be fun," Lukas said.

He had a deep voice that didn't necessarily match his exterior. His face was utterly kind, though I knew better. He looked like a boy, and he was one, but a very mature, dark, and occasionally dangerous one, but a teenage boy all the same.

"I'll go with," I said, shrugging. "Happy to help."

"Thanks," Jake said.

Lukas and I left the subpar air conditioning and re-entered into the early June air. It was hot that day, though a bit overcast. It left a glare on everything.

"We might want a garbage bag," I said. "And gloves."

"Oh, gloves are for wusses," he said, smiling. He towered above me, a good foot-and-a-half, if not more, but he was thin as a rail despite his voracious eating habits. He cast a pretty good shadow.

"You been doing ok?" I asked. It was a question I asked him a lot. He looked at me with one eyebrow up. "Just checking in, I want you to know someone cares."

"I appreciate that," he said.

"Is that a yes or a no?" I asked.

"I'm fine, Laurel," he said, looking me in the eye. I appreciated it when people looked me in the eyes. Often, they spoke looking past me, through me

even. He took my hand. I always found it platonic, a way of assuring me that all was ok. A small smile crossed my face.

We went into Clark to the dry goods room and took a garbage bag.

"Why do these smell so bad?" I asked. The smell was sharp and chemical.

"Well, it's plastic," he said. Trying to open the bag, I stumbled. My head was a little fuzzy and the world had gone blurry. It was my brain acting up again.

"You ok?" He reached out with serious speed to make sure I didn't fall.

"Oh, yeah, I'm good," I said, giggling. "Just my brain, I guess a wire was loose or something." I got back to my feet. He watched me carefully when we left Clark and headed toward the path. He often wandered alone to keep himself sane on difficult days. There were no shortages of trails to explore, but some were more interesting than others. We went off the edge of Chief's Daughter and into the creek bed.

"One second," I said, pulling my Keens off before tying them to my backpack. I jumped into ankle deep water where it was still only sand and mud. Most of the creek was littered with rock and shale. A number of places were dangerous, if not painful to walk barefoot, but my feet were calloused so roughly that I didn't feel much anymore.

"Wait!" Lukas chuckled, ripping off his shoes, throwing them on the bank. The old converse shoes looked like they were about to fall apart. He joined me in the creek. "It shouldn't be too far from here. I'm sure you'll smell it before you see it."

"Smell it? I thought we were getting a jawbone," I said, shivering from premature disgust.

He laughed a bit, under his breath. "Well, if the whole thing's there, we might as well grab it for him."

"You seem to be one of the only people nice to Jake."

"He's not that weird. I appreciate his bookishness. He's good to talk to."

The heat continued to pound in my head. Little dots of black and light showed in front of me. I held onto Lukas's arm. He paused, putting the other arm around me. His hand was on my waist. If I was completely lucid, I would have been uncomfortable with how close he was. His breath was on my neck, but he was holding me up. Logic dictated that if he wanted to do something, to hurt me (a thought always in the back of my mind when I was alone with anyone) he could. Yet, he didn't. "I'm good, I'm good," I said, getting back, steady on my feet. I hated my brain.

A few steps further, the smell hit me like a stack of bricks. It was overwhelming. I gagged. "Squeamish?" he asked, chuckling. I saw the bones on the edge of the creek, up on the bank. It looked like the deer fell from the narrow trail. I reached up and picked up the hoof, which was attached to the majority of one leg. It slid off, gelatinized.

"Well, that's . . .that's disgusting," I said.

"There's some odd marks in these legs," Lukas said. "They're all broken. Those fractures that are like twists . . .oh I can't remember the word. Con—complex?"

"Maybe something tried to eat it," I said.

"Not the way it's laid out. No bugs anywhere. You'd think the flies would be all over it." He reached out for the garbage bag, and I gave it to him. The skull was nearly clean. A good blast from a hose would do it, and a bleach bath. Lukas tossed the skull into the garbage bag and started picking through the rest.

"What do you think happened to it?" I asked.

He shrugged. "It was maybe a year old. I'm not sure if it just fell dead and had a bad fall or what . . ."

"What are we going to do with the rest of it?"

He pulled another bag from his backpack. "Guess we'll bury it and let the bugs do the hard work."

"That is nasty," I said, laughing. We picked up the body and worked our way back toward camp. "I want to wash my hands."

"Since when did you become a wimp? Come on," he pressed. Just thinking about the jelly feeling from the leg made me feel sick. We cleaned up what we could and buried the rest in a mesh bag for the bugs to take care of. It was strange taking a bag of bones to the staff lounge.

By the time we entered later that day, Jake wasn't alone, so handing him a deer skull attracted some attention. "I wonder if this is legal," Jake said. "Picking up remains like this."

"Didn't kill anything," Lukas said.

"Thank you," Jake said. I'd never seen him glow so much from pure joy.

That was the beginning of an odd summer for me. Never before did I feel so comfortable around someone, or trust someone the way I trusted Lukas. I never knew why, though. It may have been the energy surrounding him, a twinkle in his eye that drew me in. He was a perfect gentleman to me. Almost excessively so, but to know someone actually cared was precious, priceless. It was like he was able to flick a switch in me, one that calmed me down and allowed me to breathe. No walls.

On the days that were particularly difficult, or times when we didn't have kids, we'd spend our time gathering things for Jake. While teaching kids how to build a campfire up by the Houses, Lukas spotted what he believed to be either a coyote or fox skeleton. Shortly after dinner, Lukas and I ditched the main camp and started the trek up the hill. He carried a shovel on his shoulder while I had marshmallows and water bottles in my backpack. "I don't like going up here alone," I said.

"No one does. It knocks," he said, and paused. "I want to burn that fucking thing down."

"Because it feels weird?"

"It feels evil, malicious. There's just something wrong with it." His eyes lifted to the top of the hill. We were surrounded by thick, bright green foliage, dipping into ravines here and there. It was an absolutely gorgeous location. Everything about it felt almost heavenly, like this was what the world was meant to be. Free, wild, and preferably, untouched by humans. Very few man-made places could match this feeling.

"Found it," he said, putting his backpack down. The clearing we were in was flat, complete with mulch, picnic tables, and a few posts to mark the outlines. Off in the corner was the rubble of a building no one knew anything about, or at least, nothing they could or would tell me. With our things set up, I

went over to a small twig sticking up from the ground. It was placed there by Lukas to remind him where the bones were.

"It's chilly," I said. "Do you want to get a fire going?"

Without a word, he jumped to it. If there was anything I knew for sure about Lukas, it was that he loved fire, building it, tending to it, growing it. He was essentially a pyromaniac, but at the moment, it was sweet and endearing.

"Do you want my jacket?" he asked. He pulled one out of his backpack.

"Hand it over," I said, giggling.

He tossed it my way. Cologne and all, I pulled it on, though it went down to my knees. As the fire kindled, I found bones and dug in the earth with a stick. I found a jawbone, but no matter how deep or far I dug, I couldn't find the top of the skull. The spine was still held together by degraded pieces of sinew and the ribs were easy to find. By the time everything was in the bag, the fire was a massive blaze. Lukas piled up fallen logs vertically to make what resembled a pyre. "Oh my God," I said. "Lukas . . ."

"It's beautiful!" he exclaimed. I buried my head in my hands, holding back a laugh.

"At least it's warm," I responded, sitting down at one of the picnic tables. He hurried about, gathering more fuel. I reached my hands out, letting them warm. "Do you want to roast marshmallows?"

"Sure," he said, sitting down beside me. Very close. Usually, this would send nerves running up and down my back and into my throat and make me all uncomfortable. Instead, I just felt . . .safe. Roasting marshmallows, mine was golden brown, his was obliterated with fire.

"I call that a Cruella Deville," I said. "In fifth grade, my class did a camping trip and had a marshmallow eating contest. I won with fifty marshmallows or so. I think you need to eat that many." I patted his back. "You're so skinny."

"And you're short," he replied.

"Hey, I can't help that." My voice climbed to an amused whine. I rested my head against his arm, relaxing, watching the flames. He wrapped an arm around me, and we stayed like that, talking about dreams, and nightmares, and horrible campers and other counselors, and life outside of camp. We talked in a way people talk when they have stopped hiding things from one another.

August 3, 2016

Tuesday, after my girls and I had our cookout, complete with chocolate chip pancakes, of the scrambled variety, and omelets made in little baggies and boiled on a Coleman stove, we went for showers. Loaded with shower caddies, flip flops, and towels, we traveled down the hill, across the bridge, and to the pool house. The place was painted bright red with white accents, reminiscent of a barn. There were four bathrooms, two for the girls, and two for the boys. Flood lights stationed on the walls illuminated the space around it. For those waiting, picnic benches, and a makeshift basketball court kept them busy.

When the girls and I got there, Peter's cabin was already showering. Usually no one was out that late, but it was nice to have some company. I watched the last bit of sun drain out of the sky and all that was remaining were stars and a half moon. Peter sat next to me. "I want to apologize in advance. They're a little rowdy tonight, I've heard them screaming and yelling about something in there . . . but as long as no one is getting into a real fight, I'm going to leave them be. I need to conserve my energy."

"No problem for me," I said, shrugging. My main objective was to keep a close eye on Lisey and Taylor. They were flirting pretty heavily at the pool earlier in the day and if Taylor was like his brother Noah, and I knew he was, I needed to keep them away from each other. I was sure they'd mess around at some point, just out of curiosity maybe, but I didn't want it to happen on my watch.

"Taylor told me your mom lost her shit on you yesterday. He said he could hear her yelling clearly outside," Peter said, leaning on his knees.

"Yeah, I don't know what to think about that," I muttered.

"She always seemed so sweet and now she's . . . freaking scary, man," he said, shaking his head. Peter looked warily into the shower house. Laughing and yelling echoed in there.

"Will you shut up?" Kennedy yelled loud enough I could hear her like a bell.

Peter shook his head. "I shouldn't have let them eat two packages of Oreos," he said. "They'll be up all night . . . but they were having so much fun . . ."

"They'll eventually pass out, they always do."

"Yeah, tomorrow morning right before breakfast," he said with a sigh. "I already got written up twice for being late to breakfast, but some of them have to be physically dragged from their beds."

"I know someone like that . . ." I said with a giggle. He didn't get it. "Harry. I've had to pour ice water on his face, drag him by the ankles, set off alarms that sound like nuclear bombs, anything that works."

"I knew he'd tell you," Peter said. "I knew it, I knew it, I knew it."

"Ok, well, everyone knows," I said. "When you're caught making out in the shower room people just assume that you two are finally a thing. Besides, there's not a lot he doesn't tell me. He can't keep his mouth shut; it just isn't natural for him."

"He'll go around telling everyone I'm gay."

"Well, you were caught making out with a guy in the bathroom. Personally, I don't think anyone here has a problem with it if you are."

He turned to me with genuine shock pasted across his face. "Why does everyone think that?"

"People give off vibes, you especially," I said.

"At least the boys haven't said anything to me."

"What are you talking about? Arty has been out since he was eleven, it's not like they'll look at you any differently."

"Oh, this is humiliating." Peter put his face in his hands and grumbled.

"What is?" I asked.

"It was a little more than kissing," he said softly, rubbing the back of his neck.

"Ahh, well, that information wasn't leaked, so I'll keep it safe with me."

First out of the shower house was Eddy, who got a hold of the best of the basketballs we had and started shooting hoops. Peter jumped in immediately to play.

"What, are you sitting out?" Eddy asked me.

"I suck at basketball!" I replied.

"Oh, come on!" he whined. I got up from the picnic table and he threw me the ball. I did my best to aim at the backboard, but like most of the time, it bounced off. "You're getting better!" Eddy said after my third attempt. He passed the ball to Peter, who very elegantly shot the ball into the hoop without any difficulty.

"How do you do that so easily?" I asked.

"Lots of practice. I was in basketball through high school," he said, passing the ball to Eddy now. "When you're as tall as I am, your parents kind of force you."

"I can't imagine you wearing basketball shorts," I said, laughing.

"They were ugly, so ugly," he replied, shaking his head.

Almost as if it was on cue, Taylor left the shower house wearing only a pair of basketball shorts; he didn't seem to think a shirt was necessary.

"Toss it to me!" Taylor said, holding his hands out. His long, wet hair looked stringy and odd in this light. He took the ball and ran about the court, dribbling it. Eddy went after him and knocked the ball out of his hands, and it started to roll down the hill toward the creek.

"Ah come on man!" Taylor whined, chasing after it. He stopped in his tracks and cocked his head to the side. "Where are you going?"

"Who are you talking to, Taylor?" Peter asked.

"I don't know, there's some kid going down the road." He pointed and Peter and I jogged over. Blue jeans, red hat. "And it's not Arty, he'd never wear a red hat," Taylor said.

"Marcus!" Peter called, walking down the path quickly. "Marcus?"

"What are you yelling my name for?" Marcus replied, but he was in the shower house. He poked his head out from the door, sopping wet. Peter pointed at him and then to the road confused. The kid in the hat continued to disappear. Taylor walked toward him.

"Guys, stay here," I said. "We need to see who that kid is."

"I'm the one who saw him!" Taylor exclaimed.

"It's dark over there," Peter whined.

"You are such a wimp," I said. "Get your flashlight." Peter listened and got his flashlight. We lit up the road best we could, jogging down, and managed to glimpse the kid entering Apple Arts Center. The lights were off in there and stayed off.

"What the hell is going on . . ." Peter grumbled. "No kid in their right mind would want to go in there in the dark. It's freaky!"

"That it is," I said and stopped walking.

"I thought you wanted to go in there," Peter said.

"I don't think that kid is real . . ." I whispered.

"Huh? What? You think he's a ghost or something?" I explained what I saw with Leta that other day. Peter went pale and shook his head and walked back toward the pool. More kids had exited the pool, standing around, looking at us.

"Didn't find him?" Taylor asked. We shook our heads. "I swear I saw him!"

"We saw him too, Taylor," I said.

Taylor walked up to me and whispered, "He looked back at me. Miss Laurel, it was Riley. I swear."

"I believe you."

The girls and I went to bed as soon as we finished at the shower house. I was a tad shaken about seeing that figure, but it was Kellova. Odd things were just a part of being here, part of the job. The girls were tired enough there were no games of flashlight trivia, and no need to read aloud from Kennedy's copy of *Beedle the Bard*.

While I lay still for some time, hoping sleep would come to me, the girls' breathing slowed and they each fell asleep. It didn't take them long. With the sun and the activities, they had plenty to keep them busy, and plenty to exhaust them. Even a shower could drain that last bit of energy. While it always took me a bit to fall asleep, that night, I finally did. That glorious dropping off into rest was the best part of the day.

It wasn't an alarm that woke me, or birds in the morning. It was Lisey screaming.

"She's in here! She's in here! She's in the cabin!" I sat up immediately and looked around.

Sadie turned on her lantern. Lisey was on her back, thrashing about. She waved her hands madly as if she was trying to push something away from her. I ran over to her as quickly as I could and knelt down beside her.

"Lisey, it's Miss Laurel. You're safe. It's just a dream, just a dream . . ." I touched her hand. She screeched in terror briefly before her eyes opened.

"What's going on?" Ellie asked, sounding more annoyed than concerned.

"I swear she was in here, Miss Laurel! It wasn't a dream!" Lisey said, taking rapid, sharp breaths.

Sadie climbed down from the bunk above her and sat down next to Lisey, trying to be a comforting presence. All the girls were begrudgingly awake now. "We're all here. You're ok," Sadie said. "We won't let anything happen to you."

Lisey just rocked back and forth, arms wrapped around her middle. I'd never seen her so shaken up. Bad dreams were normal for her and happened frequently, but not like this.

"I saw her in this cabin . . . it was dark but she kind of glowed . . ." Lisey said quietly. She finally held onto Sadie like a security blanket. "She had this lace dress and black hair . . . she didn't look at me at all, she was looking . . . at you." She made eye contact with me. Her eyes shook and watered. "I don't know why."

I didn't want to say to a bunch of sleep deprived girls in the middle of the night that I had numerous encounters with that image before. Lisey cracked and cried into Sadie's shoulder while Sadie, being quite the champ, comforted her and rocked slightly.

Before I could say anything, the door shook, like someone was trying to open it. It was secured earlier in the night with a Rubbermaid tote so raccoons would stop wandering in and wreaking havoc. The door opened inward.

Lisey let out a scream. I turned on my flashlight immediately and swung it toward the door. Through the screen I could see a red hat and a blue jacket, hurrying off into the woods. The sound of footsteps crushing leaves and small twigs seemed so real and yet I was convinced that the apparition resembling Riley couldn't be. The girls came together, hugging one another. I pushed the Rubbermaid tote aside and stepped out. "Who are you?" I called, though I knew it'd risk waking up other cabins if the crying hadn't done that already. The figure stopped running, but it didn't turn toward me. It stayed still for the longest time. I nervously walked a tad closer, but fear overcame me before I could touch it. I walked backwards to the cabin, never letting it out of sight.

"If anyone needs to go to the restroom, let's go together, now," I said.

"And then you can pile everything against the door?" Kennedy asked.

"Yeah," I said.

Gracia said, "Lisey saw what Taylor said he saw last week!" She stepped up to me. "And you said most of the counselors have seen her too. Who is she?"

"I don't know," I said.

"The person at the door wasn't a girl," Lisey said. "It was a boy wearing a hat."

"Was it a ghost?" Jane asked. "I don't like ghosts . . ."

"It'd be scarier if it was a real person trying to break in," Ellie whispered.

"I heard people put salt around things to make it safe," Gracia said.

"What did you get that from, *Supernatural?*" Kennedy asked.

"No, my mom's friend is into all that occult stuff," Gracia responded. "We have to do something. At least it's an idea. What if Lisey really did see her in the cabin, or that guy tries to get in again?"

"Oh, I don't want to think about that . . ." Lisey said. "I don't think I could ever sleep again."

"What does salt do?" Jane asked with a huff.

"Keeps bad spirits away," Gracia said. "I don't know if it actually works, but it's worth a try if we can sleep better."

"Time to sneak into the kitchen . . ." I said. "I can't believe I'm doing this."

"Are you going now? You can't go now! You have to stay here, please, please. What if one of them comes back?" Lisey asked, begging.

"Ok, I'll wait until there's some light," I said.

August 4, 2016

Shortly after five in the morning, before Marianne arrived, I went to the kitchen. With an old five gallon pail, I took every large canister of Morton salt that was in dry goods storage. It was oddly quiet in Clark. I hated being alone there, simply because of the emptiness. The vibe was uneasy, prickly, but as soon as I stepped outside into the cool, thickly fogged air, it went away. The air was gray and tinged with light. The ground was wet with dew. My hiking boots kept my feet dry, and I hiked toward the path leading to the cabins. Nothing moved. There were deer near the creek who only looked at me with interest but didn't flee. There were seven of them, four of which were fawns with their white checked hides. At Kellova, I'd seen deer walk up to counselors to sniff them. My mom was notorious for trying to chase them away and keep them wild.

The bucket of salt was heavy. About halfway there I wondered if this procedure required table salt or if I could have broken into the new garage to see if there was driveway salt.

Exhausted from minimal sleep, my mind jumped from place to place. At times, I'd have to stop walking and blink to get my vision straight. Rubbing the back of my head, I felt a small, but growing pain, near the base of my skull. It'd be a long day. A long week.

If I just walked up to the kid with the baseball cap last night, I may have gotten answers. I may have been able to stop seeing all these crazy things. I could avoid stealing salt to surround my cabin with whatever the protective properties of Morton salt in bulk were.

When I returned, the girls were huddled together, half asleep, but clearly not comfortable. I hated seeing them feel unsafe. Camp was a sacred place: everything in me believed that. And yet, here it was, being a tool of terror.

I put the pail down and opened one of the canisters. I made a distinct line starting at the door. It didn't go nearly as far as I wanted it to. After about seven canisters, there was a circle around the whole cabin. We'd probably lose the cleanest cabin award, but oh well, safety was safety. Close counts in horseshoes, hand grenades, and salt circles.

Stepping inside, over a thick line of salt at the door, I didn't feel any different. "Maybe we should sage the place, get some crystals," Gracia said.

"Or a crucifix or two," Jane said, shrugging.

"Are you sure that's a thick enough line?" Kennedy asked.

"It looks good to me," Jane said.

"Will this help you sleep tonight, Lisey?" I asked.

"If it works," she replied.

I stepped aside and turned my phone on. Five missed calls. My heart thumped around, and I walked further up the hill, still in sight of the girls. I called the number back. "Laurel? Have you heard from Riley?" It was Officer Travis.

"What? I thought you were calling about Ezra."

"No, no, no, he wasn't here this morning. Noah drove to watch him today and he wasn't in his room. His backpack is gone, his water bottle. So he didn't talk to you? Reach out at all?"

"Why would he?" I asked.

There was a sound on the phone like a radio. He was yelling at someone and drinking coffee. "I was asking Noah what they've been up to at the library recently, neither of them is really big academics. They've been researching the camp. I can't make sense of it."

"Will you let me know what happens?" I asked, heart leaping up into my throat. I swallowed it down, eyes locked on the bathroom ahead. A few girls from another cabin were trickling that way with pajamas on and toothbrushes in hand.

"If you see him, let me know," Travis said, and hung up.

Mom was already at Clark when the girls and I got there for breakfast. It was a rarity to see her at breakfast. She usually ate in her office. She also looked less than thrilled. The girls were too tired to play gaga and went to doze off on the porch. That gave me an idea. "Would you girls like to sleep out on the porch tonight?" I asked.

"Yes!" Jane said. "That would be so much fun!"

"It'd be safer . . ." Lisey said, yawning, trying to keep her eyes open. "Today is going to be so long… I just don't want to see anything sketchy tonight. I just want to sleep."

"Ok, just hang out here for a moment." I went inside to talk to my mom. The heavy screen door screeched loudly behind me. Mom was at the kitchen counter speaking to Marianne. "Mom!" I called. She looked at me, not excited to see me. "Last night something happened, I need to-"

"What do you mean?" she interrupted.

"Peter and I saw a kid wandering off and we couldn't track him down and then later, like the middle of the night, that same kid tried to get into our cabin. The girls were freaked out and were screaming, and the kid ran off into the woods. It had to be about three this morning."

She looked at me like I was crazy. "And no one recognized him."

"No," I lied. Taylor did.

"Are you sure it was a kid?" Mom asked, leaning against the counter, looking uninterested now.

"Yes," I said. "Leta and I saw the same kid a few days ago in Apple and we looked for him but couldn't locate him."

"You're imagining things," Mom said.

"I'm not the only one that saw him!"

"Yes, but you're the common denominator here," she said. "And are you the one that stole every ounce of salt from the kitchen?" She crossed her arms, glaring at me from over her reading glasses.

"The girls were scared," I said and explained their theory and why I went about doing what I did.

"What are you? Certifiably insane? Seriously, you think that some kind of superstition like that is going to do anything? If parents see what you did… ugh, and we have no salt, Laurel. Where is your brain?"

"My girls' comfort is the most important thing," I said. "If it helps them sleep, helps them feel more comfortable, I'll do what I have to do. It's no different than making a special dream potion out of the juice of maraschino cherries, or monster spray out of water and glitter!"

"Actually, it is different. Using five gallons of salt is drastically different."

"It does the same thing, it scares away the bad dreams, the monsters," I said.

"Laurel, you believe there are monsters, that they're real, and that they're in this camp," she whispered harshly, walking into the adjacent hallway, out of view of campers and counselors.

"I just wanted to tell you what happened," I said. She rolled her eyes. I supposed this wasn't the time to tell her about Riley going missing. "As the director, you oughta know!" She ignored me. "I just wanted to tell you what happened."

She returned to the kitchen. Some of the girls, the ones that weren't half asleep, were watching through the screen door of the main dining hall. I raised my eyebrows, and they turned around quickly. Something told me I needed to call Officer Stevens again. At some point, I had to tell him I saw someone matching Riley's description at camp.

I implored the girls to clean during cabin cleanup, though I knew it would be useless with the amount of salt circling the cabin. "We can't lose our winning streak. If we do, I'll cry, and you don't want to see me cry."

Sadie was sleepy, her eyes were only half open. "It's clean . . ." she said, yawning, climbing up to her bunk.

"Just make sure all the edges of your beds are tucked in, the pillows are fluffed, and suitcases are out of the way . . . you know the drill. I'm going to make a phone call. Just don't disappear or whatever in the next few minutes." I stepped out of Hawthorne and hid behind a tree so other counselors wouldn't see me with my phone. Carefully sitting against the trunk, I called Officer Stevens. When he answered I said, "I'm happy you picked up."

"What do you need, Laurel? I'm a bit busy right now." I told him about seeing the kid with the red hat and blue jacket numerous times. He was silent for a while. "How old would you say this kid is?"

"A teenager is all I can give you, but Riley had a red hat with a flat bill, just like the one I saw." He was silent for a moment.

"Is there a reason you didn't mention this earlier?" he asked gruffly.

"Honestly, no one believes the kid is real. It sounds crazy, but no one could locate him when he went into Apple." If I slept, maybe this could all just be another bad dream that could be wished away.

"Others have seen him?" he asked.

"Yes, Leta, Peter, Taylor, my whole cabin, but Officer Stevens . . . but I really don't know if what I saw was real."

"If what you saw was real . . .?" he asked slowly. "Like you were collectively imagining what you saw? Because as you mentioned, more people than you saw this."

"The kid didn't act naturally," I said. "Disappeared at times, and I never saw his face. Taylor said he did . . ."

"We're putting out a search then," Travis said firmly. "Starting at the edges of Camp Kellova and Kellova Hills. I'll be calling your mother here shortly."

"She thinks I'm insane, when I brought this up to her, she became very angry. She's not in a good mood."

"You might be crazy, but it's really not my job to decide. If he's there, I'm going to find him. If you see anything, call me immediately. Also we've wanted to get in contact with Lukas Anderson. If you can reach him, let me know if he's heard absolutely anything. Riley seems very interested in the house he got burned in…"

"Ok, I'll let you know," I said.

"Alright, Laurel." He hung up. I opened up Messenger on my phone to talk to Lukas. I was lucky I had bars, but that's what the best service in the county got me.

It'd been ages since we last texted. I didn't know if it was because I was ashamed of his actions, or angry with him; but in truth, I didn't feel either of those things at the moment. I missed him badly, but I doubted a text would be enough to change that heavy, inflexible melancholy of something lost completely. Our friendship felt unretrievable, partially because I stayed here, and partially because he tried to destroy the place I loved so much.

Me: Hi

It said he was connected and online, so I waited and returned to the cabin.

Not cleaning? He replied.

Me: *Haven't lost yet this summer.*

Lukas: *Knew you were still there. It's not good for you.*

Me: *Can't help it. Where are you?*

Lukas: *Decorah*

Me: *Nice, camping there?*

Lukas: *Only in the state because of probation. Good spelunking here.*

Me: *How have you been doing?*

Lukas: *I'm alive.*

The girls watched me like I was doing some illegal activity. Ellie had her arms crossed and her face all pouty. "I'm trying to figure out what happened last night," I said.

"With your phone?" Gracia asked, laughing. "You don't have a good enough internet signal out here to google anything."

"No, I'm asking someone a question," I replied, coming inside to sit on my pristine bunk. I was worried I would leave a butt dent in it.

Gracia hopped over and looked at my phone before I could hide it. "Mr. Lukas? Why . . . what?" She looked at me with curiosity. "Why him? Were you two dating?"

"No."

"You might be lying . . . I'm nearly convinced you were dating," Gracia said.

"I assure you, we didn't date," I replied. "He was a very good friend of mine. Still is, I guess."

"But not since he was fired, probably," Jane said. "I mean, seriously, trying to burn down the place."

Me: *I should amend my statement. Are you taking good care of yourself?*

Lukas: *You know I really don't care, right?*

Me: *About what? Yourself? What happens to you?*

Lukas: *Yes*

Me: *You should. You know, people still care about you.*

Lukas: *Like you? You haven't spoken to me in months. Everyone acts like I'm some kind of pariah.* He wasn't wrong. I just didn't know what to say.

Me: *I'm sorry I haven't reached out. Felt betrayed.*

Lukas: *I told you what I was going to do. I didn't hide anything from you.*

Me: *I thought you were joking. Most people don't torch their places of employment.*

Lukas: *It was making everyone sick, making the land sick too. Still is.*

Me: *I can feel that. I believe you. I have a question about Riley Stevens.*

Lukas: *Do you think all arsonists keep track of each other?*

Me: *What are you talking about?*

Lukas: *Nothing*

Me: *He's missing.*

Lukas: *And you think I know what happened?*

Me: *Did he ever talk to you?*

Lukas: *No.*

I set my phone aside for a moment. The girls were still looking at me, dreary eyed, and bored. "Will you at least play some music? I'm going to fall asleep!" Jane whined.

"Ryanne!" Marsha's voice bellowed out her cabin door. I'd never heard her that loud before. "Come back! Where do you think you're going?"

"Ryanne!" Coral called.

"What's going on?" I stepped out of the cabin and toward Coral.

"After she decided to spray high deet bug spray on everything and the girls called her out on it, she sprayed it in Temple's mouth, and I had to carry her to get her mouth cleaned out. Marsha tried to keep Ryanne from running off, but obviously, she ran off."

It was just after breakfast. No one had energy, but Ryanne appeared to. Ryanne was surprisingly spryly for a girl wearing flip flops. "Come on," I said, waving for one of them to follow me. I hated running, but I did. Ryanne already passed the bridge. "I am too out of shape for this!" I said to Coral, who was picking up speed.

"I am too . . .!" she whined. "Where is she going?"

"I don't know."

We got to the open field, and she slowed down, so we approached. Her hair was a matted mess, her clothes were still the ones she had on when she came to camp. I was sure she smelled ripe.

"Ryanne! Where are you going, hon?" I asked.

"Getting away from you!" she said, though her voice trembled, and she sounded tired and afraid.

Coral rubbed her forehead. She had a look of absolute exhaustion and annoyance on her face. She was at her wit's end. This girl did that to people.

"Let's talk about this," I said. "But stop running off. We can't talk if we're out of breath."

"I don't want to talk about anything! I want to go home!" she cried.

"Ryanne, you're from Carlisle. You can't walk home," I said. She knew that. There was no reason to argue with her or try to talk. "I believe your counselors just wanted you to take care of yourself and others: wash your hair, brush your teeth, change your clothes. You'll get sick if you don't." She glared with hard, distrustful eyes. "You know as much as anyone else that we don't send campers home."

Ryanne ran again, out of the field beside Clark, around it, and toward the road. Ryanne wasn't even breathing heavily. I didn't know how that was possible.

"What the hell?" Coral asked, looking at me. We ran too. My chest whined in complaint as if it was on fire. My body felt like it was a lumbering pile of bones and blood. The grass and the gravel road weren't good to run on, but my plodding steps did get me closer to the road. The entrance to camp wasn't far away. It was Ryanne's target. I couldn't physically drag her anywhere or force her to do anything she didn't want to. I doubted I could even legally put a hand on her. So when she got to the road and just stood there, her body hunched over, animalistic, malice burned in her eyes- Coral and I stared in disbelief. She truly didn't look like herself.

"Ryanne! That's dangerous, you need to get back over here!" Coral called. Ryanne ignored her. "Ryanne, please, this is ridiculous! You're acting crazy! You need to get off the road!"

"Ryanne, your mother is going to be very disappointed in you," I said. "You don't want to do that, do you?"

It was roughly that moment I heard the ever so faint sound of a car coming. On this winding road, usually it was too late to escape if you were, say, a deer or rabbit just hanging out on the pavement.

Before I even had a chance to swoop in and move her, a man in a ghillie suit did. He knocked us both back onto the shoulder of the road. The air rushed out of my lungs and a few stars danced in my eyes. Of all the things I didn't need, it was another blow to the head, and to deal with Gary.

Gary owned the sections of land surrounding Camp Kellova and everyone, rightfully, thought he was crazy, because he was. He was certifiably insane. Any man wandering around a children's summer camp in a ghillie suit while also wearing an army hat lined with tin foil in the hopes of getting the government out of his head had to be.

"What on earth were you doing on the road?" Gary asked the girl who looked probably as dumbfounded as I. "Did you see that truck? That thing would have turned you into a steaming pile of roadkill just because you were too stubborn to listen to your damn counselors and get out of the way! What kind of stupid are you trying to be?" She just blinked rapidly like this was all a bad dream. She slowly became herself, in terms of appearance.

"Thank you, Gary. I'd uh . . . I'd appreciate it if you'd use a bit nicer language," I said, though in the moment, I felt like he had every right.

"I'll speak how I want to speak, Miss Winters. Any girl who does something like that needs a proper talking to," he said and stood up. His ghillie suit was heavily weighed down by various materials intended to make him look like a bush. I didn't want to ask what he was doing or why.

Miss Coral stood in the driveway with her head cocked to one side. I helped Ryanne over to her. "I think we may need to have another talk with my mother. If you could take her to the office, I'll be there in a little bit," I said to Coral.

Coral grunted, annoyed, but walked her over. Ryanne was in a state of shock, so she wasn't about to fight any longer. The air was stifling and still. There wasn't a single lick of wind in the sky. With nearly forty pounds of fabric on him, I was sure Gary was melting in there. "What are you doing all the way down here?" I asked.

"Tracking some suspicious behavior," he replied, eyes darting around. I was aware he had previous military experience, probably too much of it. Mom said he used to be in special ops and recon of some kind, so he had skills. Somehow, he fell from that high and mighty to a crazy, scared hermit in the middle of nowhere Iowa.

"A person?" My heart jumped. "Have you seen someone around here with a red hat and a blue hoodie, wearing jeans?"

"The police chief's kid they're talking about on the scanner?" he asked. "Hell no, I bet that's just a figment of the house."

"What are you talking about?" I murmured, regretting I said anything in the first place.

"They'll find that kid dead, I can assure you that," Gary said, his dark eyes peering uncomfortably into mine. My stomach lurched forward and twisted around. That was the last thing on earth I wanted.

"Why . . .?"

"In this heat, it's not the time to talk, Miss Winters,"

"Do you know much about the house?" I asked.

"I know everything there is to know about the house. Come up to the farm sometime, I'll tell you what I can. Someone's got to know before it gets to me."

Before I could ask what he meant, he disappeared back into the brush. That was just about the longest conversation I ever had with that man. Usually he disappeared much faster into the woods before I had a chance to ask any questions.

I stood on the side of the road, baking for a moment, getting my mind back together as well as I could, before heading up the gravel path. Each step was unusually loud, a buzzing grew in my ears. I rubbed my temples, trying to get the noise to slow or cease, but it didn't help.

I crumbled into the shade beside the archery shed, my head continued to pound. The sheer age of the camp struck me then. I was stepping on land that had been camped on for well over a hundred years. In some ways, it made me aware that this land had a mind of its own.

His words about Riley hurt. I thought of the stout kid with a narrow smile that never showed his teeth. He didn't like his teeth- the tiny gap between his front teeth and the fact he was bulimic. His hair was always impeccable, and his clothes were always new and clean. He was intensely competitive and loved sports. He won an every-man-for-himself game of dodgeball at camp multiple times. He never gave up when it came to that . . .but he was so troubled. I could remember seeing him trying to puke up his lunch into an empty soda can, or the small note about how lakes were only good for drowning in, or his threat to drink tiki torch fluid . . . he was brilliant though, he simply just didn't know what to do with his overactive brain.

One time in Apple, we all were doing a 'pieces of self' program, where we traced ourselves and then filled the figures in. He wrote 'stupid' on his head. It broke my heart. He carried so much pain, but last time I spoke to him at camp he discussed the future for the first time I'd ever known him. He wanted to be a basketball player or a search and rescue person.

Chapter Fourteen:

August 4, 2016

The camp office was sun-bleached and badly in need of a new paint job. It was a small, ugly, ranch style house with large oak doors that squeaked horribly when opened. There were large, horizontal windows, and a peeling green exterior. I always assumed it was supposed to look like it belonged with the forest that engulfed the back of it. If it weren't for the gardens my mother considered to be her pride and joy, it would be an unredeemable eyesore. While the grounds were maintained well on the outside, the inside was a mouse's haven. On numerous occasions, I found mouse nests inside old printers, boxes of books and files, and once underneath the sink in the bathroom. No matter how much one dusted, there would still be an abundance of dust and spiders. It just came with the territory.

I slipped in through the backdoor, hoping to make a quiet entrance to my office. During the summer, I hardly touched it simply because I didn't have the time to. "Laurel?" Mom's voice echoed through the thin walls of the building.

"Coming," I said, moving past the dusty furniture.

Mom sat with Coral and Ryanne on old red chairs in her office, which was considerably bigger than my own. Ryanne stared ahead, not blankly this time; the defiance was back. I gingerly sat beside Coral who looked visibly relieved at my presence. "Ryanne, your behavior is more than unacceptable. I'm appalled actually, and after thirty years in this business, you'd think I would've seen everything, but I've never seen someone with so much disregard for their counselors, fellow campers, and their own safety. You've been acting imma-ture, unreasonable, and unfair to all those around you. I'm going to call your mother. I am considering sending you home simply for the safety of others, but I hate to think that you will get what you want for such behavior. Do you understand that we will need to have an extensive talk with your mom?" Ryanne's face simply looked like she didn't know what else she could do. It's a good thing she wasn't around when there were buildings burning here or she would have got way too many bad ideas in her head. "Ryanne?"

She eyed my mother with hate. It didn't faze Mom a bit.

"Miss Coral will return you to wherever you're supposed to be right now while I contact your mom," Mom said suddenly. Coral stood up and the two left the office.

Mom sighed heavily. "I don't like losing," she said and dialed Brandi's phone number. The phone was on speaker, so I heard the woman breathlessly answer the phone. "Hi, Brandi. This is Ms. Winters from Camp Kellova again, just wanted to call you about another incident." She waved me away.

I didn't see Ryanne the rest of the day. It was kind of nice. Things could return to a normal pace. Leta, who begrudgingly continued to teach arts and crafts, appreciated that there was no glaring girl in the corner of the room making everyone uncomfortable. Even the time at the pool was better. While I reapplied sunscreen to some littles, my walkie turned on and Mom called for me. I stepped out of the pool area and said, "I'm here."

"I'm sending Ryanne home," she said, sounding just as defeated as I thought she would. "Pack her things if you can and bring them to the office. Her mother is on her way."

The malignant entity that was Ryanne was gone. Coral and Marsha looked beyond relief, even if they only had her for a few days. It was a long few days. A horrible part of me hoped I would never see the girl again.

After supper, we had the weekly all-camp game. It was a nice, long game of counselor hunt. At the start, Harry explained the rules; each counselor had a different value attached to them based on the number of years they'd been at camp, both as counselors and campers. I missed having Noah here. And Ezra. And Riley. And Lukas. They were half of the fun from this game.

"So, in other words, Miss Laurel here is the jackpot at a grand total of 1800 points! I come in close at 1500, Mia at 1400, Orion at 1400, Coral at 1100,

Marsha had 1000, Trish at 500, Gregory at 400, Juliet at 200, Asia, also at 200, Scotty at 200, and poor old Peter at a measly 100 points. Miss Carra will be presiding over today's events! Each time you find and capture a counselor, you must bring them to her, and she'll tally the score for your team. When your points are awarded, you must give that captured counselor a full five minutes before you can pursue them again. Now, for all the teams here, you need to stay together! If a stray camper is spotted, that team will be automatically disqualified from the rest of the game. All points lost. The start of each round will be given by the revelry call over the loudspeakers. Does everyone copy?"

"Yes!" A chorus of voices returned.

"We'll get you this time, Miss Laurel!" Arty shouted, Eddy and Taylor jeered him on.

"You haven't gotten me yet!" I called back from the porch. "No sense in getting your hopes up this time around!"

The revelry cried, half making me think I slept in before I bounded off. There was one bush I liked to hide under. A predecessor of mine found it- always brought a book with her. It was nice, shaded with soft grass, a good view of the surroundings, but for some reason, no one had ever looked there, or could see through into the brush. It was behind Clark, beside the large, open ball field. It was beside the garden patches we attempted to grow every year but failed.

I settled in with a book.

My first year as a counselor, I tried everything, even resorting to hiding in rain barrels. Lukas found me and poured a handful of frogs into said rain barrel before running off chuckling. I tried hiding underneath a canoe but a raccoon found me and it wasn't a friendly one. Mr. Maury ended up hiding under the same canoe, but he wore very strong jeans duct taped to his shoes. The faster counselors usually put less thought into their hiding places so they could run. The first person to ever catch Lukas more than once in a game was Riley. He succeeded in both Counselor Hunt and Capture the Mattress.

Ignoring my book, I took out my phone and texted Lukas. *Can you come by camp during the wilderness retreat?*

Lukas: *Why?*

Me: *I miss you.*

Lukas: *And?*

Me: *I need to figure out this house situation.* Both were equally true. They both equally hurt my heart. There was a physical grief over Lukas that I didn't understand or comprehend, much less thought it was good for me, and the need to know what was going on a House One was eating away at me from the other end of things. I hated the gnawing in my chest, the feeling of constriction and unease.

With his silence I added: *I can't let it hurt someone else. It got you, Riley, Haley, and who knows how many others? Maybe Ezra. The other night, something tried to pry its way into Hawthorne, and I know it was because of that house.* Upon more silence, I texted again: *I know it's not just me going crazy. I realize I might be crazy, but I'm not hallucinating about that house. You know that, and it's not going to burn down, no matter how much fuel we throw in it.*

Lukas: *You haven't even scratched the surface.*

Me: *Do you know something?*

Lukas: *I've done some research. Have a lot of time on my hands now. Hung out with my grandma up here.*

Me: *Is her arthritis any better?*

Stupid question, I thought, what does arthritis have to do with a dangerous house? Or this town? *She's really into paranormal junk. There's a giant map on her wall, the size of the wall, of the world. On another wall is one of the US, and then one of Iowa.* Around me, the kids were running about, passing right by me. "Check the rain barrel!" Arty called.

"She's not in there you dummy!" Eddy replied.

Taylor added, "The barrels are full, she'd have to be snorkeling or something."

"Just check . . ." Arty whined. There was a sound of plastic hitting the ground and rushing water.

"Told you so," Taylor said.

"You're so immature sometimes," Arty said.

"You didn't listen! Why don't we go look for Harry? He sucks at hiding," Taylor replied.

"Because I said I'd get Miss Laurel!" he cried.

My phone lit up. Lukas: *Of ley lines, Laurel. Do you know what those are?*

Me: *Nope*

Lukas: *They're like lines connecting energy points on the earth like Stonehenge. It sounds like a bunch of stupidity but it's interesting. My grandma looks at it like a grid because most of the places can be connected easily.*

Me: *On a flat map, yeah.*

Lukas: *Tell her that. Either way, Kellova, on the map, is smack on a ley line between the magnetic north pole and the Bermuda Triangle, two major points of energy.*

Me: *You're going to have to tell me what that means.*

Lukas: *I don't know what that means. It's just something I came across.*

Me: *Interesting.*

Lukas: *Unlike you, I do have a life outside that place.*

Me: *Once upon a time, this was your life.*

Lukas: *At twenty-four years old, you would think you'd move on to something else.*

Temple's group was no more than four feet in front of me. I held my breath and watched as they scoured the area around the large bush, but not in it. "I see Mr. Peter, let's get him!" Poor Peter, low man on the totem pole.

Lukas: *And I thank it, and I thank you, but it also majorly screwed me over.*

Me: *Then let's end it.*

Lukas: *Ok, then this better the hell be the end.*

I thanked him profusely before he disconnected from Messenger. That was his way of saying he was done talking. I hated how strained things had been throughout the last year. The incident hadn't changed anything in terms of how much I cared about him. I still trusted him. Yet his anger toward Kellova expanded toward me, as I was part of the problem. Maybe staying here, not getting away from the danger, was the reason. In fact, I was sure it was, but I couldn't abandon all these people. They could get sucked in by that house and killed, or seriously injured. Yet thinking my presence would solve anything sounded so narcissistic. How could I actually fix this century-long mess?

Picking at blades of grass to give my hands something to do, a figure approached from my left side. I held my breath again, thinking one of the boys got smart and started looking from other angles, I realized it wasn't any of the boys in Aspen. Or a camper at all.

Looking straight at me from the bush was Riley Stevens.

Riley's face was the same color as his hair, as if he was at the end of a long summer of camp. His arms were notably smooth and unburned. His eyes, though, still looked haunted and frustrated. "What are you doing here?" I asked. "The police are looking for you. Your dad is looking for you" There were so many things I could have said to him, but they didn't seem right. "Riley?" He just kept looking at me. A sickening feeling crawled beneath my skin, making me clammy and nauseous. "Riley!" I whispered harshly.

"If you think you're talking to the boy, you're not. You're talking to air," Gary's voice broke the growing tension, and I turned to see him, still in his ghillie suit. I nearly fell over in fright. "Been seeing him here, there, and everywhere since you mentioned him, but look." He pointed. When Riley was just moments ago, there was nothing. I crawled under the brush, stuffing my phone in my backpack as I went. "That wasn't really him," Gary said. "I don't know what he is, but it's not him."

"What, am I talking to ghosts now?" I asked. He chuckled, pulling off the top of the suit so his face could air out some. He was smeared in oil paint, making him look like he dipped his head in pasture mud.

"I don't know, but I think he's trying to show me something," Gary said, still looking past me. "If I keep following him, I'm sure something will turn up, always does here."

"You're not supposed to be on camp property either, especially not when there's kids."

"My family established this precious little camp and ran it until 1989. I can do whatever the hell I please," he said with a huff. "I have to live next to it and live with the consequences. I already have the goddamn military and government trying to screw with my head. I don't need this place to do any more damage to anyone,"

"Why do you think they're after you?" I asked, curious enough to indulge his crazy talk.

"They want me to keep quiet about what I did during my service, but if they don't want me to talk about it, I'll broadcast it to every single fucking person on this planet if I have to. It's stuff you were never taught in school because they were too scared that people would find out. I'll tell you what, mind control, messing with people, all that stuff's real, there's a hell of a lot they don't want you to know, and I know too much." And once again, he hopped off into the brush like a deer, fast enough to disappear.

I hunkered down where I was, waiting for the sound of the horn. Every movement around me made me jumpy, even when the only one in view was a bunny.

Time and time again, kids ran past, never looking. There was a sort of grim satisfaction in knowing that no matter how many years went by, this location was still a winner.

When the horn blew, I waited until all the kids were back in the front of Clark before I exited my spot. There was a general mumble about the group of campers when I came into view. "And it looks like no one has caught Miss Laurel!" Harry called. "However, pretty much everyone else has been. Including me, three times," he said, sighing. He had a look of amusement on his face and a begrudging smile. "Round two will give you double the points! And at the current scores, I'd say if anyone catches Miss Laurel, you would be the winner!"

No one found me in my hiding spot. Not "Riley", nor Gary, again. We ate spaghetti that night with garlic bread, nicknamed 'butter sponges'. Marianne was kind enough to provide more than enough cake for us to each have two slices. She made a gesture to me, showing me where the rest of the cake was for later, and winked. I was in a daze during dinner. Arty, Eddy, and Noah were adamantly discussing the game around me. Taylor was poking at his food.

"What's up, Taylor?" Lisey asked.

"Uh, I just feel off . . ." he said.

"What do you mean?" I asked, trying to push myself back into my senses. The building had poor circulation and it was sticky inside. The lights were dim, the whole thing felt like a feverish dream.

"No clue, just feel really off."

"Do you need to see the nurse? What if you're getting sick?" Lisey asked.

"It's not like that," Taylor replied.

"What are you psychic or something?" Eddy asked.

"For once in your life, Eddy, would you just shut up?" Taylor asked, nearly exploding. Some nearby tables looked at him warily. Eddy wasn't shaken in the least. He was good at pestering. It was his specialty.

"Well, sorry man," he said with a laugh.

"I asked you to shut up . . ." Taylor grabbed at his own hair and bore down like he was about to break.

"Maybe we should take you to the nurse's station. There're some fans there. You can at least cool off and get some water. Rest a bit," I said. Taylor rubbed at his temples and didn't stop me. The nurse, Vivian, looked him over and nodded to me.

"Yeah, if we can get him to the cabin," she said. He was stumbling on his feet. It very well could have been heat-exhaustion from running too much, but he wasn't flushed, in fact he looked ashen. "Can you tell me what's going on Taylor?"

"Head is pounding so hard . . . feels like my skull is going to break wide open," he said, hardly audible.

"Migraine maybe?" Vivian asked. "We'll get you something to help with that."

It took us both to get him there. He refused to open his eyes for even a moment. The sun was just too blindingly bright. When offered water, he started to drink, but immediately stopped to run into the closet of a bathroom to puke it up. There was nothing in his stomach besides bile and water.

When she could, Vivian took his temperature, but it was normal. It was a perfect 97.8. Regardless, we got him settled on one of the hospital-like beds, and blasted three fans on him, closed the blinds, and let him be.

"It must be exhaustion. Kids do eventually get hit by the heat," she said. "Though it seems like they're usually much more immune than us." Her sharp, dark eyes looked through the door briefly. "When he can drink water, I'll get him ibuprofen for the headache. It may just be that he needs to rest here overnight."

"That kid's tough, so I would be surprised if it's overexertion," I said quietly. "I saw him climb the rock wall a few weeks ago on every single side in one night. It was over a hundred out that day. No one else could because they were just too tired."

"Even the toughest break once in a while, hon," she said.

Vivian's office was decorated with paintings she did, usually of cats, dogs, chicks, and other cute animals. She made most of the younger campers feel at home. The number one rule of camp medicine was that water solves most problems. Water, band aids, and the occasional placebo. Our best medicine for bad dreams was monster spray which was nothing more than water filled with fine glitter that could be used to keep bad things away, like magic.

"I'll keep an eye on him. You head back to the kids."

The girls and I carried our sleeping bags and pillows to the large porch surrounding Clark. With our sleeping places picked out and set up, we each took a seat on the hand painted rocking chairs. There were a few lanterns lighting up the ever darkening space, but the girls clearly felt more comfortable here than they did in their own cabin.

"We should play 'Honey I love you!'" Sadie exclaimed. She stood up. "I'll start!"

Everyone composed themselves, forcing smiles to fade into stoic faces. The point of the game was for the person who was 'it', that being Sadie to start, to manage to make the person smile during the process of saying, 'honey I love you, will you please, please smile?'. If the person manages not to smile, they must be able to say, 'sorry honey, but I just can't smile', or something similar.

Sadie approached Lisey, put her hair in a ponytail, tried walking like a guy, and did her absolute best Taylor impression. "Honey, Lisey, I really do love you, and all I could ever want is just to see you smile. Will you please, please smile?" Lisey's face cracked in half, and she burst into laughter.

"You just had to, didn't you!" Lisey cried, rubbing her face, trying to calm down. "I will never win this game!"

"That's why I went after you!" Sadie said, sitting down cross legged, hugging her backpack. Lisey paced around, trying to decide who her next target was. She went to Jane, knelt down in front of her, hands on Jane's knees, leaning in. "Well, hello there, pretty lady. I just wanted to inform you that you are my honey."

"Oh stop!" Janey cried, laughing. "Ugh . . . no fair, nope."

The game went on for a good forty-five minutes before yawning commenced and the girls just wanted to wrap themselves in their blankets and sit in the chairs.

Lisey asked, "Miss Laurel, do you have a boyfriend?"

Surprised by the question, my chest felt acidic. "Nope," I said.

"Ever had a boyfriend?" she asked.

"Nope."

"What? But you're like, old. You really need to get out more," she said. As if I hadn't heard that before from most people.

"How can I do that when I'm here all the time?" I chuckled.

"You seem to like Harry," Sadie said innocently.

Gracia burst out laughing. "Uh, I don't think he's interested like that, Sadie."

"Why not?" she asked. There were a few more chuckles.

Chapter Fourteen: August 4, 2016

"He likes guys," Gracia said.

"Oh, well, I didn't know," Sadie said, shrugging. "There's Orion, he's nice. He's really good at archery."

"I met him when he was eleven. That would be a little weird," I said.

"She likes Ezra, Sadie," Gracia said. A little twitch happened in the center of me, just thinking about him. With all the chaos, his brokenness was always on my mind. "I'm going to take the silence as an agreement." Gracia yawned loudly and nuzzled deeper into her sleeping bag. "I think I could sit right here and sleep."

Lisey asked, "Don't counselors at camp date?"

"Plenty," I said. "Usually it's a bad idea and never works out."

"Why?" she asked.

"Camp goggles," Gracia said before I could. Her voice was muffled by the blue, puffy fabric encompassing her. Lisey's brow furrowed in interest.

"It's a term we have here that when you're around the same people for twelve weeks, 24/7, they start to look more attractive than they really are," I said.

"Huh, that's weird," Lacey said.

"I'm not sure I have those problems," I added.

"What problems? Camp goggles?" Lisey asked.

"I think for me it helps me make new friends with people I'd never usually be interested in hanging out with."

"Isn't that the whole point of camp?" Kennedy asked, also yawning.

"Yes, it is," I said.

Soon, the girls fell asleep on the deck, some staying in chairs, some on the floor. I tried sleeping flat on the floor of the porch, but I woke frequently. Someone snored. Raccoons walked around us, just curious. No one woke up screaming, thankfully. About five in the morning, though, I snuck inside and made myself a giant mug of hot chocolate and tip-toed back to my chair. There were a few books I wanted to eventually get to and I was fully awake, so I started on *The Children of Hurin*. It was one of the books Kennedy finished in June. Because of her, I was making progress through every single piece of written material by Tolkien, and greatly enjoying it. This book felt more like a story than a history book, so I sailed through it for the next two hours or so.

The girls woke, one by one, before revelry sounded. They got ready in Clark's bathroom, but hardly looked functional. I hardly *felt* functional. Sleep-deprived and exhausted, the world was foggy. Being foggy and tired wasn't much of an option, though. With all that had been happening, I had to be aware. I had to keep my eyes open.

"My back hurts," Lisey said, rubbing the small of her back. "That was uncomfortable."

"Oh, stop complaining," Jane said, pretty cranky. She went down from the porch to the climbing tree. The tree was old and easily climbed. It was bare of leaves, a lightning strike effectively killed it, leaving the bark smooth. Along with the constant climbing, it was almost like plastic.

Jane, dressed in soccer shorts and a pink t-shirt, climbed to a lower limb she thought was comfortable, and closed her eyes.

While we hung out on the porch, I saw Vivian, the nurse, walking with Taylor toward the office. "I'll be right back," I said, setting aside the book. Kennedy was sitting beside me and she didn't even look up when I hopped off the porch.

I jogged over to the pair. Taylor appeared deflated and distant. "What's up?" I asked Vivian.

"When I went to check up on him about four this morning, he wasn't in the cabin," Vivian said.

Chapter Fifteen:

August 5, 2016

"I had a sketchy feeling when I saw he was gone, so I went out and looked for him. He was at the abandoned house, cabin thing, up the hill," she said, holding onto his arm tightly.

"House One?" I asked.

"Yeah, sorry, I'm tired," she said. "He must have been sleepwalking because I don't think he remembers how he got there. He hasn't exactly been talking much either since I brought him back." She shrugged. Taylor didn't look at me. He stared straight ahead. "I'm going to see if your mother will let him hang out with me another day so he doesn't get too stressed and so I can keep an eye on him. She'll hopefully send a note to his parents about his condition, too. For now, I'm just trying to get him out of his little trance thing."

The way he walked, coaxed around like a moving doll, reminded me of myself after the brain injury, how when an episode hit, most of my major decision making capabilities were gone. Friends were able to lead me anywhere. "Did he hit his head?" I asked.

"I found him sitting on the picnic table in the screened-in porch, staring off into space like he was in his own little world, quiet as a mouse too," Vivian said, shrugging. "I haven't seen any sign that he hit his head."

Mom stepped out of her office, hands on hips. Her blonde hair was flung behind her in the early morning wind. She was perturbed. "What's going on?" she asked. Vivian told her. As soon as the house was mentioned, Mom threw her hands in the air. "Carra, that's where I found him. He's only one of a number of kids I've found up there. Kids sleepwalk, it happens."

"The place is locked tight. He probably just snuck out last night and broke in and is just trying to get out of trouble. He's just like his brother," Mom said.

"No, Carra, not in the state he was in last night." Vivian was steady. My mouth was glued shut.

Nonetheless, she looked at me. "Stay out of this," Mom said. "Bring him into my office, Vivian."

Taylor didn't come down for breakfast, though I kept looking for signs of life in the office. The girls seemed a tad concerned as well. They sat around me, looking like they could use a thirty-six-hour-long nap and a hefty dose of caffeine to follow.

Lisey asked, "She's not going to ban him from camp, is she? I mean, he didn't do anything wrong."

"Who knows with her now," Kennedy said, grumbling. "You talk back one time, and she takes away your canteen privileges."

"It wasn't just one time," Ellie said. "She did the same thing to me."

"But something happened, right? He didn't look ok last night or this morning," Lisey said.

"No, he didn't look like himself," I agreed. "I don't know, though. It's Thursday. If he can manage a few more days, he can rest over the weekend. We could all do with a good night's sleep."

That morning I taught swimming lessons to the little kids, levels one through three, before dragging a canoe into the pool for tip tests. We skipped lake day this week due to Ezra being found half-dead last week, but preparation for next week was already underway. I wasn't surprised by the lack of takers. Only the triplets came down to the pool, and they looked confused and out of place. "Where is everyone?" Juniper asked. "Did they all chicken out?"

"They're probably afraid of water zombies or something, genius," Pandora replied.

"It was Mr. Ezra in there, be nice," Temple added. "Best lapidary teacher ever."

"I thought he was better at teaching beading, personally. Either way, I guess it's just us. Don't you think so?" Pandora said. I wasn't sure who exactly she was talking to. When they got to talking, they were in their own little world.

I held the canoe by the edge of the pool with my foot. They watched me, all equal height, wearing one-piece bathing suits that had shorts and specially made life vests they brought from home. Their parents were worried the ancient orange ones we owned were choking hazards. I didn't blame them. "I don't know what other people think, Pandora. I know you did this test last year, but you have to take it again after a year passes," I said.

"Last week at the lake, the hike was so boring," Juniper started. I wasn't sure who she was talking to either. "They were hurrying through so fast and didn't take time to look at anything! Sadie and I found some toads and wanted to catch them, but Orion just complained about us being behind all the time."

"Remember, when you enter a canoe in shallow water, walk on the center-line so it doesn't flip. Hold onto the edges," I said. Pandora went first, tip toeing like an expert. Temple followed, sitting in the middle, and then Juniper, who pushed them off into the water. With their paddles, they made it to deeper water. "Do you remember how to tip the canoe?" I asked.

"Yep!" Juniper said. "On three."

They counted, leaning side to side hard enough to make the canoe rock, and on three, they flipped it completely upside down. With practice, it wasn't a difficult skill, though once in a while you got a boat that would right itself. "Remember, check in on one another!" Usually, tip tests were done with multiples of two so they could reach across the canoe with a partner, grasp hands, and check to make sure they were alright, but in this case, Pandora had each sister's hand.

"Everyone good?" she asked.

"Yep, that was fun!" Juniper exclaimed. "Miss Laurel, when we're done, can we jump out of the canoe and jump back in?"

"We'll have time," I said. "Flip it back over, make sure you can get in." With the canoe filled with water, the task was to swim back into the craft and paddle to the intermediate side of the pool with their hands. There, they got out of the boat, flipped it right side up, and hoisted it above their heads. For three young girls, it looked like quite a feat, but this was the lightest canoe in our arsenal. Then they threw the boat back onto the water. It hit with a hollow, metallic, thud. "Let's push it back into deeper water and you can try to climb in," I said.

Giggling, the three girls held onto the canoe and kicked their little legs as fast as they could go to get the canoe over to the deep end. This was the part I always struggled with, getting my butt back in. Having the upper body strength of a gerbil didn't help matters, but it was always an interesting adventure.

"Do you want to go first, Juni?" Temple asked. "Do you want a hand this time?"

"I don't need a hand," she said, offended by the mere suggestion that she might.

Kicking like mad, she flung herself up, landing her stomach on the edge of the canoe, grasping for the yoke. Eventually, she heaved herself in. "There," she said, breathing heavily. Pandora, not to be outdone by the youngest of the three, tried next. She couldn't get enough height to get past the gunwale. She tried prying, dragging, pulling, and nothing worked.

"You can do it, Pandora!" I exclaimed. "Try backing up and then kick your way in!"

"I did!" she said, frustrated.

"Just one more time, you can do it!" I cheered. As I said that, my walkie went off. A rough voice said, "Laurel, I need to see you." It was my mother.

"Doing tip tests," I replied.

"I'll send Harry down to finish them," she replied.

A flush of heat went to my cheeks, and I felt absolutely wretched. My stomach churned. Where the feeling came from, I didn't know. There had to be some explanation. Did something happen to Ezra? Or Taylor? What about Riley?

No more than a minute later, Harry was at the gates of the pool. "What's up?" I asked, not taking my eyes off the girls, though the glaring white light that came off Harry's pale skin was a bit distracting.

"As if I know. Your mother just went all drill sergeant on me." He held onto a lifeguard tube and stood beside me. He whispered, "There was a cop car there, so I'm assuming something's up."

"Lovely," I said. "Thanks, Harry." He gave me a half salute, half wave.

I was on the dirt path leading to the office and walked as quickly as my feet would take me. The cruiser was unmistakable. There was the tiniest of dents above the back right tire. It was Travis Stevens. The sun beat down fully now, and I had no cover. This had been a rough summer in terms of heat. Today had to have been in the low nineties, and if there was even a hint of wind, it'd be handleable. Unfortunately, it was dead-still. I hoped to God Riley had been found and he was just letting us know, but my rational side knew that wasn't the truth, it was just wishful thinking.

Inside my mom's office, Officer Stevens stood near the door. "Laurel," he said. My stomach churned. Mom leaned back in her chair.

"They're going to search the camp. Every cabin. Every building," Mom said.

"Based on the knowledge that numerous people have seen my son here, it's a possibility he's hiding out. I don't know why. God knows this place wasn't exactly good for him. However, he knows the terrain, the buildings, and may think this is a good place for him to go." Acid flared up in my throat. I felt nervous enough that I could puke. "We are nearing the end of the summer season. If we don't locate him here, there's no telling where in Kellova Hills or Greenville he may go." The search warrant papers were on Mom's desk, indicating to me that she'd previously refused his request.

"I want you to keep this quiet with the kids, Laurel," Mom said. "Don't go around saying that Riley is missing and might be hanging around here. We can't have that added onto the fact that I'm still getting emails from parents about Ezra." To her all these events were simply inconveniences.

"Maybe you should have listened to me when I told you someone was wandering around," I replied. She rolled her eyes. "What do you want me to say to them?" I asked. "They're going to see the police around here."

"Make something up, you're good at that. Say they're just doing a routine search to make sure that everything is up to code," she replied.

"If we did that, you'd probably be shut down," Travis said.

"You know I don't have the money to fix everything," she said.

"At the very least, you could get rid of some of the condemned buildings. You have open periods here for the older kids and they could get hurt. Riley was burnt in one of those buildings, you're lucky you don't have a lawsuit going your way," he said. His tone was gruff. I'd been saying the same thing for years.

Not missing a beat she continued, "We are hoping a donor will come along and we can restore them. They're historical buildings, Travis. Some of them are over a hundred years old. I don't know why people don't appreciate that fact. We are the oldest camp still in operation this side of the Mississippi. Hell, we might be the oldest camp still running at all, and I want to keep the history." That's what her little Laurelite club was all about, they were Kellova purists. "Just tell the kids that they're doing a safety inspection. No telling the truth this time, Laurel," Mom said. She put acid behind the word truth.

"I didn't know the truth was such a problem for you, Mom," I said, adjusting my backpack. "How's Ezra?"

"He's making strides, I've been told. He can't tell me who did that to him. We are investigating that too. Noah's watching him now."

"I'm happy someone is helping him out," I said.

"The neurologists say that Ezra's memory may come back to him, but he's just now able to get some words out. They have some neuroplasticity experts coming in to help. Riley was making homemade flashcards and everything to see if Ezra could relearn more. He's hoping for sentences soon. It's good to see him so dedicated to something other than sports. Oh God, I hope we find him; that and the monster who did that to Ezra still isn't in my grasp yet either . . ."

"Riley's a good kid, Travis. He'll turn up," I said.

"Hopefully we'll get some answers," he replied.

Chapter Fifteen: August 5, 2016

Mom didn't leave the office the rest of the day.

At dinner, I announced that the Greenville Police Department was walking the grounds for a safety inspection. Then, I disregarded my mother's orders and told the staff the truth. "All staff, I need you up here with me for a short meeting. Campers, please stay at your tables!" I called. A loud, resonating noise of chairs moving filled Clark. They approached me in a semi-circle. "They're really looking for Riley Stevens."

"He's missing?" Orion asked, eyebrows raised. "Ah, I like that kid."

"Yeah, he's been spotted around here a few times," I replied. "Even at the door to my cabin. There's a search warrant, so we can assume that things inside our cabins will be moved."

Orion shivered a bit. Coral put an arm around him amicably. She was a camper when Riley first started attending camp, Orion was as well. We all knew him well. To many, he was the model camper, always participating, enthusiastic about activities, a bundle of energy . . .

"Orion, you were in a cabin with him a few years back, do you know why he'd be here?" I asked.

"No, he told me this place gave him the creeps," Orion replied, slicking back his long hair. "He said he liked us, his friends, but that . . . I don't know, he was convinced there was something wrong with the earth, said something was attached to it, that he found something . . . but he never told me. I never pried. It was Noah and Lukas who were on him about that kind of stuff."

"They never talked," I said. "Or Lukas said they never really talked."

"Well, I know that's a load of bull," Orion muttered.

"Riley knows the nooks and crannies of this camp," Mia said.

Orion added, "I don't think he ever slept at night. He'd just sneak out and break into places, like Lukas and Noah but for more of a reason. I hope the police know where to look."

"Tonight, how about some of us go searching with them, lead them in the right direction. I'll put a paper on the window back near the cabin assignments. If you'll sign up for shifts, I'd appreciate it."

"What does Miss Carra say about this?" Marsha asked.

"All she told me to do, was to lie."

The girls felt at ease with the police walking the grounds. Before bed, we went on a hike up the opposite side of camp, away from the police, and the girls were very talkative.

"Did you finish the book yet, Sadie?" Kennedy asked, referencing the Joyce Carol Oates short story collection she loaned to Sadie.

"Yeah, it's pretty spooky, it's good though," Sadie said, picking up a suitable walking stick.

"Careful with that!" Jane exclaimed. "Don't hit me with that thing!"

"I'm careful!" Sadie said, though she was a notorious klutz. I'd seen her trip down Clark's stairs, fall off a number of stools, run into a screen door, all sorts of things. This summer she was doing much better. She was more aware of her surroundings now.

In the twilight air, everything was soft. There was no nervous, prickly energy. There was only a nice calm about us. The girls had their flashlights in case it got dark, but I doubted it would. Hiking was relaxing. It helped me feel grounded.

A few years ago when a bout of severe depression hit me, I felt like I was slogging through ten tons of mud while also feeling as though I was connected to nothing at all. Things were foggy and hard to grasp. The only thing I found that made things just slightly better was to walk, preferably barefooted, along some of these trails and stare up at the green in the trees, trying to soak in their energy. It was a combination of losing so much to this place and a brain injury that nearly destroyed me. Now, though, life wasn't nearly as daunting. The depression would likely never fully go away, but it could abate a bit. I could breathe. I wasn't in deep mud. The fog lifted slightly. I could feel enjoyment and look forward to things. But with feeling came fear. Before, I was so numb that even fear couldn't override my lack of sense. Now, it could.

Even being as close to peace as I was with these girls on the trail, there was still the fact that Riley was missing. When I thought of him, I thought of a sweet kid. Could he be lost in this maze of hills? Scared? If he hated the house so much, why would he run in its direction? It was because of that house he endured so much pain throughout the past year. It disfigured him. Last time I saw him I had no indication anything was off . . . but that's how things work, isn't it?

"Miss Laurel, can we have s'mores tonight?" Lisey asked, interrupting my train of thought.

"I'm afraid we're going to have an early night tonight. You girls are absolutely beat. You need sleep," I said.

"Ah come on," Jane said. "We're fine."

"Then for those of you who are wide awake, I'm hoping all this walking will tire you out," I said, chuckling.

"I don't think we need walking to do that," Sadie said. "I'm ok with going to bed early. I can hardly keep my eyes open . . ."

"You're always complaining about not getting enough sleep," Jane said.

"That's because I don't!" Sadie, on occasion, if she was tired enough, slept in the clothes she'd wear for the next day, so she didn't have to wake up five minutes earlier to change.

"And all of you have more energy than me," I said, laughing.

"Are you going to take our get-well stuff to Mr. Ezra this weekend?" Lisey asked.

"Yes, of course. I'll see how he's doing," I said.

"He's still in the hospital, though, isn't he?" Lisey asked.

"Yeah, it'll be a while until he's doing well enough to be on his own."

My phone buzzed and I looked down at it. I had a message from Lukas. *I'm camping in the Hills.*

Me: *In your car?*

Lukas: *Yep*

Me: *You can stay in my cabin if you want.*

Lukas: *If your mother finds me, she'll take an ax to the back of my head.*

Chapter Sixteen:

August 5, 2016

Once the girls were fast asleep in Hawthorne, Mia came by the cabin, and we left with flashlights to join a search party at Clark. Officer Stevens gave people locations to search. He was getting exceedingly anxious, gnawing on his nails, a behavior I'd only seen once- when Riley had a tube down his throat at the hospital because his airway was too swollen to breathe on his own.

Mia and I were assigned to the creek which led into the river. It was thoroughly dark that night, especially when we got into the water near the Chief's Daughter. "Lukas is in Kellova Hills," I said.

"Him again?" she sighed.

"He might know something about Riley, why he's here, what drew him back," I replied.

"You sound nuts, honey," she said. "And Lukas isn't exactly on stable ground either."

I almost blurted out that I loved him. It wasn't exactly romantic love, but it was love. "Can you get us into the Nomad meeting room? I just want to see their records. They have everything about camp buildings, who built what and who donated the money, all that stuff."

"And you think that'll solve the Riley issue?" she asked.

"I doubt it, but it might give me some insight with Riley and Ezra, maybe even Haley- everything that's happened here." I waved the flashlight in front of the water, hoping to come across absolutely nothing. The last thing I wanted was to land at the police station to discuss finding another body. That'd just be too good of a coincidence, and they'd probably think I had something to do with all this.

"All the file cabinets in that room are locked. Granted, I know where your mom keeps the key. It's next to all the maintenance keys. Scotty should be able to get it for me . . ." Mia said.

"Now you're talking," I giggled.

"I think you're a bad influence on me!" she exclaimed.

"No, no, it's the other way around. When we met, I was shyest kid ever, and you treated me like a little doll-"

"Then you got some feistiness in you," she replied.

"You gave me a freaking backbone, Mia," I said. "You helped me get through . . . crap, a shit ton of things, Haley's death for one."

"I was close to her too," Mia said, her voice quiet. "I saw a cardinal the other day and thought about her. It was up by the barn."

"She was a good kid, she wasn't some bright shining light, she seemed... felt darker, but there was something so interesting about and enlightened about her. One day we just sat in the pool and just talked . . ."

July 2014

Haley floated in a collection of pool noodles strapped together by a bungee cord. We were in the corner of the deep end, and I was holding onto a pair of boogie boards for dear life. I'd just mentioned something about fishing with my grandpa when I was younger. "I couldn't kill a fish," she said. "I'd feel so guilty. I had a betta once, it was red, his name was Dread, and I loved that thing, but my cat got it out of the tank and literally just tried to eat it." I almost laughed, but she was serious.

"I couldn't believe it. I got the cat to let go by prying her jaws open, but the fish . . . it's like you could see the light going out of its eyes. If there's light in a fish's eyes, then there's gotta be something in there."

"Like a soul?" I asked.

"I don't know if fish have souls," she said. "But they have something more than just a nervous system that gives them light, like everything else, I guess. People can't tell me that other things don't have souls, though."

"Like cats," I said.

"Even my murderous one. She… she's got the most interesting personality. You can see the gears working in her mind, and you know, there's a feeling that she's self-aware and knows everything I'm saying. So it's like that one philosopher, Renee something,"

"Descartes," I added.

"She thinks, therefore she is," she said, shrugging, flopping over on the floaties another direction. It was evening and we were at a night swim. The day was too hot to do anything else and the older kids had been so good, it was like a treat. No one was caught with contraband, there was no purpling, and very minimal back talk.

Haley's arms were cut up in neat lines, and her legs looked about the same. She knew I knew what those were and where they came from. Most of the time she covered the scars with rubber band bracelets, the same way Noah did. They were very alike in that way, but she was so comfortable here, free, with all of us that there was no need to hide.

She continued, "And when my cat Allie died, I kept having dreams about her, that she was alive. I knew in the dream that couldn't be right since she died of a heart attack, but I wanted it to be real. I just kept staring at her, worried that if I looked away, she'd disappear again. I think, though, she was just trying to tell me she was ok. Like a visitation."

"They don't disappear," I said. "I had a cat when I was a kid, she was killed by some bats that were trying to get at me. Rabies. I dreamt that she was in a big castle with a beautiful garden and a marble fountain. She loved our garden at home and loved running water. She was totally my cat. She watched over me so closely, and she died for me. I wanted our pastor to come and do a service for her. Since she had rabies, we couldn't bury her. They had to take her up to Iowa State, but I put some pictures in a bag and her favorite toys then we buried them. I still feel like she's around sometimes, watching over me."

"So, you believe in God?" she asked.

"I guess that's a complicated question," I replied.

"And one you're not supposed to talk about at camp. I know it's in your handbook."

"Since when have you known me to follow the rules?" I asked, laughing. "So, do you?"

"In a way. I'm not a hard-core religious person, but I believe in some spiritual power. The church I grew up in was big on the trinity, God, the Father, Son, and Holy Ghost, or Spirit. The Holy Spirit made the most sense to me, the thing that kind of ties us all together as people and is in everyone. A life force, but more." She nodded, keeping eye contact, actually, genuinely listening. "And I've never lost faith in there being Something. In what form or manner, I don't know. I'll have to figure that out as I go along with life."

"No one in my family agrees on any one thing," she said. "But my dad's an atheist. I think being totally alone would be scarier than some wizard looking dude on a throne in the sky."

I added, "If everything comes down to pure chance- that would scare me. Regardless, though, the very fact we exist is kind of amazing. Sometimes I walk around in awe of the fact that I'm here and I'm aware of every little detail like the gravel, or the leaves, even the sound of the pool taking in extra water and making that gulping noise."

She smiled. "Gotta get out of my head more."

"That can be a hard thing to do . . ." I said. Being in a depressive state myself, there were days I simply couldn't see anything clearly. "After my head got knocked, it's like I was reduced to nothing but what was in my skull and the parts then attached. I couldn't get anything to work properly."

"Sometimes I feel like I'm not working right either, but not in a medical way . . . like . . . I don't know, that's why I do this shit, or did, to reset myself." She held out an arm. "Noah told me to stop relying on such barbarity." She looked over at him with longing. It was something more than mere infatuation that was between them, as young as they were. "He sounds like an idiot when he talks like that, but we've both stopped. He's smarter than he lets on."

"Good."

"If he cuts again, I'll smack him." She laughed and rolled on the floating again. "He's a good guy, really is. Even if he's a pain in the ass."

"I think half his energy goes to his hair," I said, swimming to the edge of the pool to sit.

"You're not wrong about that. I've never spent time like that on mine."

"One summer you got so fed up with it you just cut it off..." I laughed, remembering. It was back when her hair was a creamy brown color, before she dyed it black.

"Marshmallow does not come out of hair! I thought it would dissolve in water or something. Couldn't stand it anymore. Good thing Miss Max had scissors."

"She shouldn't have done that!" I buried my face in the slick boogie boards.

"It doesn't say anything about that in the handbook!" She splashed at me playfully.

"Because no one's chopped their camper's hair off before," I exclaimed, still laughing.

"Well, you explained periods to the boys a few years ago, pretty sure that wasn't allowed!" She laughed and pointed at the group of boys playing in the kiddie pool, chasing each other around.

"Lapse in professional judgment, but someone had to and I'm sure health class is not the best place to learn."

"That one girl, Cindy, or Cheryl, some old name, thought she was dying when her period started," Haley said. Oddly enough, I couldn't remember the girl's name either. She wasn't the first girl with that problem and wasn't going to be the last. *"She was eleven or twelve."*

"Parents should really teach their kids about crap like that," I said quietly.

"Mine sure as hell didn't," she huffed. *"But, you know, the internet and TV,"*

"Probably not the best place to learn either," I said.

"My mom just about shit herself when I told her I needed pads."

"I think mine was way too proud about going to the store to have me pick out my own," I said, giggling. This was the world before my brain decided to be self-conscious of my body and my words.

Noah swam under the water, away from the diving board, toward us, moving swiftly and easily like a fish. When he surfaced, he slicked his hair back and kissed her. *"Get a room you two, no... actually, don't,"* I said, laughing.

"I get it," Haley said, giggling, arms still around Noah's neck.

"Killjoy," Noah said.

"You don't want to get written up for purpling," I said, standing, walking over to the picnic tables where I'd spend the rest of the evening playing cards.

Shortly before Haley's death, on a Saturday night, while I was in Apple, Noah joined me. He never went home during the summer since he drove himself and paid for his stay. While he wasn't the only kid in Kellova's history to do that, it was remarkable that he also paid for his brother to be a camper as well.

He came inside the building and sat down at one of the tables. It was about eleven at night and I was blaring music from my phone. "What're you doing?" he asked. He hoisted himself onto one of the high tables so he could swing his feet back and forth.

"Got the little ones this week. So, I'm making a welcome banner." With a plethora of glitter at my disposal, the colorful banner was coming along well. "How'd you get away from Maury?"

"He fell asleep. He wouldn't notice if I was there or not, anyway. His nose is in his Pokemon games."

I found it only a tad awkward that I was standing in my pajamas- a sports bra and shorts, around a camper, but Apple never failed to give me the creeps, so it was nice to have someone around. "What are you thinking so hard about?" I asked.

"I don't feel much like a kid anymore."

"You're sixteen, aren't you?"

"Yeah," he said. "I washed dishes all year so my brother and I could be here, pay for a car, insurance, plates, school, everything." He ran his hand through his hair, and I hopped up on the table across from him and listened. "Maybe able to graduate early. I only have a few classes to do this next year."

"That would be good, do you know what you'd want to do?" I asked.

Chapter Sixteen: August 5, 2016

He shook his head, chuckling, but nervous. His face had premature laugh lines. His skin looked like it was stretched across his skull. There wasn't an ounce of fat on that kid. He grew like a weed. "Not a clue," he said.

"What makes you happy?" I asked, crossing my arms and legs.

"Camp, weed, tattoos, books, my skateboard,"

"At least you're honest," I said.

"Never claimed not to be." He held up his hands. "And Haley."

"You could work at camp during the summer, though they do drug tests," I said. My mandatory reporter brain was going haywire, but I silenced it. "Especially if you want to go to school. Camp looks wonderful on a resume."

"College isn't for me," he replied. "Can't afford it, and I don't want to be away from Taylor."

"Well, one thing's for sure. You're a damn-good brother." He smiled a nice, genuine smile. "And how is he doing in school?"

"A wiz. In everything. He picks up on shit so easily it's ridiculous." He paused. "I'd want him to go to college if he wanted to, but I'm sure he'll just do whatever I do."

"He's your shadow. Just keep assuring him that he's his own person. You two have vastly different personalities, you're much more of a caregiver. You could always go into that."

"A long haired, pierced, tattooed, male nurse." He leaned back in laughter. "I'm gonna get this arm filled in by next summer," he said, talking about his sparsely tattooed arm. Despite his age, I let him know I supported tattoos. He was mature and enjoyed being able to safely express himself. His arm already had a forest near his wrist as a way to cover up past cutting marks, and a mountain range above that. "Ok, tattoo buddy, you gotta do the same. We can be blocked out of online photos of camp together."

All of my tattoos, though, were memorials. I personally didn't want to lose anyone in order to get more tattoos. "What more do you want on these arms?" I asked, laughing. "I'm running out of room and people."

"Oh, yeah, sorry, forgot they were all for people."

"Maybe you could be a guide for people in the mountains or on rivers. You'd really shine doing that. You love helping the younger kids while canoeing."

"There's so many options and yet so few . . ." he said. "I just don't know."

"You like art, what about being a tattoo artist?" I asked.

He shrugged. "I'm not super good at it, but maybe I could learn to pierce. That could be something. I just feel weird talking about careers already."

"You had to grow up quick," I said. "Most kids your age aren't the breadwinners for their family."

August 5, 2016

Little did I know that not long after that conversation, I would get yet another memorial tattoo. This one, in honor of Haley: a little bottle of Felix Felicis, from *Harry Potter* along with a quote from her favorite character, Luna. It said, "I'm just as sane as you are." It was beside a paw print from Georgie constructed from wildflowers. Thinking about it made me shiver, how many more tattoos would this camp give me? How many more memorials?

My brain returned to the present. I kicked around rocks with my hiking boots, Mia still beside me. If I was going to do anything, it'd be for Haley and Ezra. That house killed Haley and I was sure it had something to do with Ezra.

"Laurel, was this here when you took your orienteering kids out?" She had her flashlight pegged on a thin, blue hardcover notebook in a Ziploc baggie. It was propped up beside the water.

"No."

She grabbed it and fumbled with her light. "Let me hold that." I shined both lights at the book and she opened it. The first pages were filled with doodles, edge to edge of robots, dogs, spaceships, superheroes- normal things. A few more pages, then we saw Alina. The girl we'd all seen in the woods leading up to House One. Whoever did this, drew her in perfect detail, down to the lace pattern on her dress. She was crying black tears. On the following page was the house, I thought, though it didn't look quite right.

"Aren't there three windows on this side?" I asked Mia.

"I thought there were only two. The door's all wrong, though. The screen is supposed to be on the outside," she said, looking over my shoulder.

"No, that part's right. It's supposed to be on the inside. But it doesn't have a window like it does in the picture." The front door in the drawing looked completely different than it did in my memory. "It's just flat wood, isn't it?"

"No, it has some ribbing,"

"Are we talking about the same house?" I asked.

"House One."

"Abandoned, not used, ugly, in a clearing, right?" I asked.

"Yeah."

"Cellar and screened-in porch?"

"Yeah," she said again, quietly.

"Then why do we see it differently?"

"I don't know, Laurel . . . let's just take this back. It's Riley's. It's all but got his name on it. This means he's been here," she said. Her voice was tired, but clearly scared. It may have been stronger than fear. There was the possibility she was terrified. I was more curious than anything else. The need for sleep was washed away from my brain.

"We should go through it first," I said.

"Go through it? Why would we do that?"

"I need to know what's in here." I held on tightly to the book, not willing to relinquish it just yet.

"You're crazy, hon, you're crazy." She turned around to head back. "If you're looking at it, we should get the hell away from here." She hurried back the way we came, nearly running. I had to jog to keep up.

"Mia, can you hold a flashlight so I can see?" She didn't respond, so I held one in my mouth and flipped through the pages. After the first house, there were remarkable sketches of other kids: Noah, Carson, Eddy, Arty, as well as counselors: March, Maury, even me. Every inch of the paper was covered in images. Yet interspersed in the pages were various sketches of the house. One was reminiscent of how I remembered it, the correct number of windows, but it had a small porch attached to the front door. Another sketch of the house had the number of windows Mia mentioned, but there were other ones that just didn't seem right at all. Nothing was exactly as I saw it.

"Mia, you have to see this," I said, continuing to hurry after her. "Every single sketch of House One looks different, but it's still House One. It's like he kept seeing it change."

"The kid probably had a really active imagination," she said. "Like you."

"Every other sketch is disturbingly accurate, down to the last freckle," I urged. She stopped before we got to the edge of the forest and sighed. "If it's true that we all see it differently, how did we not notice this before?"

"Let me see," she mumbled, and went through the pages slowly.

"Maybe I should ask people how they see the house. Maybe Riley saw it differently every time he saw it!" I exclaimed.

"Give me a second," Mia said, staring at the pages. Her brow furrowed. Finally she said, "No one really talks about the features of a building with each other, Laurel, but do you really hear yourself?"

"Are you not looking at the same pictures I'm looking at?"

"They're not photographs, Laurel." She waved me away. With some moonlight available, she analyzed each page. "I'm not sure what you want me to think."

"Isn't there something here?" I asked.

"It's all too much for me," she said, shaking her head, closing the book. "Honestly, I think I just need sleep. You too." As exhausted as I was, I wasn't sleepy.

Armed with Riley's notebook, I went to the basement of Clark where I knew I wouldn't be disturbed. The basement was musty and filled with old camping equipment. Green army bear bags hung from the ceiling, and tents were folded carefully in the corners. An unusable washer-dryer set was covered in lost and found towels and goggles from the pool. The place was reminiscent of an abandoned nuclear war bunker. I warmed up some of the cake Marianne left and went about looking through the pages again. Seeing myself sketched into the paper, every small detail down to the wisps in my hair, the stars on my sunglasses, and the feathers on one of my tattoos was amazing. The kid was talented, and he saw everything.

Then, looking at Haley's picture, she was smiling, looking back at Riley in the sketch. There was life in her eyes. My heart sank and tears welled in my eyes. The day came back to me as if I hit a wall.

August 2014

Everyone at camp was in the ballfield with a massive bonfire kindling in the center. There were s'mores, soccer, catch, frisbee, and music. There were fewer kids than usual as many got involved with the state fair about this time of year. I was stationed by a table we dragged out of Clark that was the home of the s'mores supplies. A soccer ball whistled over my head, and I ducked. Carson ran past me laughing diabolically.

Before I could say anything, Noah came to me, his eyes wide and frightened. "I can't find Haley," he said. "She was acting strange all day . . . I don't know where the hell she went."

"Calm down, calm down, we'll find her," I said, stepping aside, letting Lottie handle the marshmallows. It was nearly dark out now and the moon wasn't going to be much help.

"She isn't on the green, she isn't in Clark," he said. I'd never seen him so serious in my life.

"What do you mean about her acting strange?" I asked.

"How didn't you notice?" he screeched, angry. "She's hardly talked, she hasn't been sleeping, and when she does, she has nightmares."

"Have you two been sneaking out at night? Been using anything that she could have reacted badly to?"

He looked beyond annoyed with me and shook his head. "Are you kidding me?"

"Noah, I'm not stupid. I know what you two have been doing, and I'm not trying to bust you for it. I just need to know."

"Yeah, we've been sneaking out, but it's just weed."

"No K2?"

"No, not using that stuff anymore," he said. "It helps her chill out so she's not so anxious all the time and doesn't have panic attacks. If you haven't noticed, she's not exactly the most comfortable person on earth when there's a crap-ton of people around!"

Chapter Sixteen: August 5, 2016

"Noah, I need you to think," I said. "Did she come outside with us after dinner?"

"Yeah, she did." He rubbed his forehead and stared ahead, straight through me.

"What did she say during dinner?"

"She said she had a bad headache. She went to Vivian to get some Advil, and then came back. She was kind of just staring out the window most of the time. I don't know what she was staring at. She wouldn't tell me, just kept shaking her head."

"What about this morning?"

"Uh, she's had lapidary, camp craft, archery, and swimming. I actually think lapidary was the last class, advanced lapidary, yeah . . . That's where she made me this." He held up the pendant he was wearing.

"I'm going to talk to March real fast since he taught lapidary, just stay put. Don't go running off, please," I said.

Jake March, who just went by March, was sitting by the fire, talking to a group of kids from his cabin. "Hey, March, can I steal you away for a moment?" He looked concerned from just the tone of my voice, and he immediately followed me away from the fire.

"What's going on?" he asked.

"Haley, was she acting odd today in lapidary?"

"And in camp craft. I have her in both," he said. "She was just spacey, kept looking around. She's been a little off all week. She didn't finish any of her bead projects today, why?"

"Noah said he can't find her and that she's not here."

"Did she maybe just go back to Cherry? To go to sleep?" he asked. I shrugged and shook my head. "Let's go take a look. Where'd you leave Noah?"

"Over there," I said, pointing to where there was no one. "I knew he'd run—ugh, that kid."

"You thought he'd actually stay put?" he asked.

"*Kind of,*" *I muttered. We left the ball field for the main path and toward the bridge. The flashlights we had didn't appear to do much in the hazy light.* "*I hope they're both ok.*"

"*There's no reason they're not. I don't think you can overdose on weed,*" *March said, smiling.*

"*Noah just doesn't freak out and he's freaked out,*"

"*Let's check the showers,*" *March said. We searched, but the only thing I found in the pool was a frog, and the only thing I saw in the shower house was a mouse.* "*Empty over here!*" *March called.*

"*Same!*" *I replied. We met back up underneath the basketball hoop.* "*What about the laundry room? Lottie caught them in there making out one night.*"

"*It was more than making out, hon,*" *he said,* "*You're so innocent.*" *He jogged down the hill toward the little shack. Though it was silent, nonetheless he pulled on the cord attached to the single bulb. Once again, there was nothing. This time there wasn't even a mouse, though I was sure there was a toad and some daddy-long-legs.* "*Where else have they been found?*" *he asked.*

"*Apple, the library . . . is lapidary locked?*"

"*Yeah, but so is the library,*" *March said.* "*I locked it myself after camp craft.*"

"*What were you doing in there?*" *I asked.*

"*Making cookbooks,*" *he said, shrugging. He took out his walkie, fumbling a bit.* "*Guys, keep your eyes out for Haley Macinany. She hasn't been seen after dinner. Laurel and I are out looking for her. If you see her, let us know.*"

"*I'll check the garages and office buildings,*" *Harry said.*

Lottie said, "*I'll look through the archery and riflery sheds.*"

"*Have enough people left in the ballfield to keep the kids busy,*" *I added. We turned up the hill, into the woods, and toward Apple Arts Center.* "*I'll check the basement.*"

"*It's locked too, hon,*" *March said, peering in through a window.* "*God, there's a shit-ton of dead rats down there, stuck in some overturned paint.*"

"*Ew.*"

"*I thought someone would've broken in there by now to get the spray paint,*" *he said, jogging up to the front door.*

Chapter Sixteen: August 5, 2016

"No lights on," I said.

"That doesn't mean anything," he replied. The door squeaked loudly when we entered, and it smelled distinctly of crayons and tempera paint.

"I'll check in the back room," I said. The supply room was bigger than the main room and had every craft supply a person could possibly want. I opened closets, an old refrigerator, though I knew in my heart that no one was in that room. I just didn't want to leave anything unturned. Meanwhile, March was looking in the bathrooms.

"No one?" I asked him.

"No, let's go up to the cabins, I guess."

The hill was steep, and after a long day, we were both tired and wanted nothing more than to rest for a bit. Weaving through the trees, I noticed that not a single light was on in any of the cabins. "Let's check all of them, even the ones not being used," I said. Cabin after cabin, flicking on light after light, there was no sign of Haley. Her bunk was untouched and neat. Her backpack wasn't there.

There were instances when she got so overwhelmed that she would just disappear and go to the cabin to lie down, but she'd usually tell someone. A camper. A counselor. Vivian.

While I was there, my mind moved slowly to the house. She had nightmares similar to mine. We both saw the girl, but she also saw more. She was convinced that there were animals across camp that were just . . . not right. Their proportions were wrong, their eyes looked empty or filled with something unnatural. This summer she became terrified of being alone in case one of them came at her. She claimed she saw bright orbs of light that always seemed to be calling her, pulling her. And of course I believed her. I'd seen those orbs myself.

The intensity of these nightmares, Vivian and I thought could be part of her mental illness. Depression could play havoc on the mind; I knew that well enough from personal experience. My own hallucinations came from frequent sleep paralysis that woke me numerous times a week. Haley never claimed to suffer from sleep paralysis, she simply stated that she saw these things.

"*Noah?*" *March yelled. "Is that you? Noah! Haley? Haley!" March jogged up the hill and I followed, getting closer and closer to the house. Noah stood on the edge of the clearing, amongst the calla lilies. Staring. Unmoving. "Noah?"*

"*Are you ok?" I asked, putting a hand gently on his shoulder. He jumped slightly. "Noah?"*

"*I think she's in there," he whispered.*

"*Stay with him," I said to March. There was a hole cut into the screen of the porch by garden shears. It was just big enough to fit in. I dragged myself inside, cutting my leg badly in the process. The warmth of blood ran down my leg, but there was no pain, there was only pounding in my ears. "Haley?" There was the slightest creaking noise, but no sound of breath or cries. "Haley? It's me, Miss Laurel. March and I, we're here to help."*

"*Do you see her?" March called.*

I turned my flashlight to the central room that was once a dining room. The beam of light landed on feet, dangling in the air.

The table was still set, and there were footprints on the edge of it. That's where she stepped off. She hung herself. Her neck was broken.

Her eyes protruded from her face and there was a terrible white and purple color to her skin. Her wrists were slashed vertically, and blood was everywhere, including the walls where she wrote 'it won't let me leave'. The house appeared to shudder under my feet, as if the whole structure came to life and breathed.

"*Code white . . ." I muttered into the walkie, hardly able to breathe. Staring at Haley's body, thoughts spun so quickly, they were screams. No part of me could function. I tripped backwards and sat down. "March!" I finally managed. "Call the police!"*

"*No!" Noah screamed, a painful, horrific scream of grief and terror. From a window, I could see March attempting to console him while picking up his walkie. "Let me see her!" he cried, pushing March aside, hard enough March fell. Noah rushed for the house and busted through one of the windows to climb in. When he saw her, he simply sobbed. "No, no, no, no, Haley . . . why did you do this? No!"*

Chapter Sixteen: August 5, 2016

His wailing was absorbed by the house. The house ate it.

It enjoyed his pain and grief.

After Haley was removed from the house, Noah and I were taken to the hospital. I was treated for the cut on my leg which required twenty-one stitches to close up, and a blood transfusion. We both were treated for shock. I didn't think about the stitches or the needles. My brain became a massive pile of cotton. I was nearly unresponsive and stared at the wall. When I could think, I desperately tried to see if there were signs, I missed—warnings that she may hurt herself.

In the middle of the night, I wanted to scream, scream like Noah . . . to let everything out of me.

Chapter Seventeen:

August 6, 2016

It was nearly two in the morning when I slid Riley's notebook back into my bag and hiked to my cabin. Collapsing into bed, I prayed for sleep, but when it came, it was fretful. The sketches came to life, talking, laughing. Haley was alive. Noah was down about a hundred scars. The kids were ok. There was a much lighter weight on their shoulders. How so much could happen, how so much could be allowed to happen, I didn't know.

Revelry was not welcome five hours later. "Good morning, Miss Laurel!" Lisey called. She sat on the edge of her bunk, smiling. I did my best to scrape myself out of bed, but it would've been easier if there was a giant spatula.

Friday. The kids will go home for twenty hours tomorrow. Pasting on my best counselor's face, I went about the day.

Riley still wasn't found, though camp was well-searched. Mia didn't inform anyone of the notebook, and the search spread deeper into the hills surrounding Camp Kellova.

My orienteering kids were close to finishing their packets for advanced honors. Eddy wanted to go on the Lost Lake trail, while the triplets were sure they needed to do a full day hike in Kellova Hills to get their miles in. Either option sounded exhausting. "If you're really wanting to walk through the quarry, we'll have to schedule that for next week," I said. "We can hike to Lost Lake and back, but you'll need to get your trail cards out." In the packets, there were a variety of cards that related to trails within camp boundaries, and a few in Kellova Hills. To achieve the highest level of orienteering, they needed to fill out information about hiking safety, backpacking safety, and packing, compasses, how to read maps, different kinds of maps, and to get to a certain number of miles. Just like with every skill at camp, their progress was logged throughout the summer, and throughout the years, and they had everything completed except for a handful of miles. "Everyone got theirs?"

With a choir of affirmative answers, we left from Clark to the trail, which lay at the very edge of Camp Kellova's property. Surprisingly, Arty stood near me.

"I know they're looking for Riley," he whispered. I raised my eyebrows in interest, not agreeing or disagreeing. "I was in Aspen with him. He wasn't the biggest fan of mine; I think he thought I was annoying. He and Noah would sit together during free time and just talk about the camp's history. Riley was amazed. He wanted to know everything he could get his hands on, and kept pushing Noah and Carson, too, to help him find out more. Eventually Carson abandoned ship because he said it was getting too creepy for him."

"Did anyone write anything down?" I asked.

"Well, Noah did. I don't know about Riley. He was always drawing. Always, constantly. He had a baggie filled with his used up pencils." He shrugged. We climbed up a steep hill and fell silent for a moment. I kept up with him to the best of my ability. "He spent most of his free period in that clearing around the house. Don't know why. I wouldn't go with him. He did all sorts of drawings of it, a lot in his sketchbook, a lot on scrap paper too. They all looked different, the sketches of the houses I mean. I never asked him why he was doing that though. Noah looked at all of them. There wasn't a single sketch I saw that looked exactly like the house."

"What does the house look like to you?" I asked. His face twisted in confusion. He answered. To him the shingles were blue, not brown. There was a window in the front door, though I was convinced there wasn't. He claimed the house was primarily whitish gray, which I agreed with. Arty saw three windows on the main side, and two on the other two sides, while I thought there were three windows on all the sides.

Arty said, "I really don't think he meant any harm to anyone."

"What was he trying to hide, Arty?" I asked.

He took a deep breath. "I don't know, I really don't. He must have found something in the house or the clearing . . . he found it and he had to get rid of it."

"What do you mean?" I asked.

Chapter Seventeen: August 6, 2016

"He told me at breakfast one day that he had a dream . . . and in that dream he had to burn these things in fire. I . . . I think he was the one that set the garage on fire. He was totally wrecked after that."

"What?" I kept my voice down, but I couldn't imagine Riley would ever do such a thing. Being stupid and harming property, yes, but killing my dog? No, that wasn't a possibility.

"I told you; he didn't think it would hurt anyone. I don't think he thought it would burn the building down. I think he just wanted to get rid of... I don't know what it was. He didn't tell me. But he mentioned that dream like three days before it happened."

Though we were hiking, I took out Riley's notebook from my bag. Arty's face widened in amazement. "Where? How? What?"

"I found it last night, in the creek," I muttered. "Would this tell me what he may have been trying to hide or destroy?" Would it tell me why my Georgie had to die?

"He put everything in there," Arty said. As we walked, the two of us went through each page. Arty wasn't included in the numerous portraits, but he didn't seem offended by that.

"What should I be looking for?" I asked.

"Hell if I know," he responded. Occasionally I looked up at the kids who were walking ahead of me. I wasn't doing a very good job at supervision, but my mind was elsewhere. The girls were talking in a clump ahead of us, using makeshift walking sticks as wands. Eddy and Taylor were far ahead, almost out of sight.

About halfway through the book there was a picture of a small doll. It was hardly human in appearance, very crude. It wasn't the only doll drawn. Most of them were rudimentary, sewn by hand or wrapped together with twine. They were all sketched beside a wooden box with a slide-out lid. Arty and I stopped walking for a second and looked at each other. He seemed very interested. "Do you think this is it?" I asked.

"It could be, but why would he want to burn them?" he asked. "He didn't seem totally weird . . . unless someone convinced him they were dangerous."

"Do you think Noah, Lukas, or Carson could have convinced him they were?"

"I didn't see him around Lukas much, not after he got in trouble for hooking up with Emma."

"Everyone knows about that, don't they?" I said with a sigh.

"Hard to keep secrets from us," he said, and raised one eyebrow like I was crazy for not believing that every kid here knew everything. "Besides, he was kind of a jerk."

"Did Riley ever join you guys in kind of pushing Lukas out of your group?" I asked.

"He wasn't a confrontational kind of guy," Arty replied. "That's why I was so surprised when the garage went up in flames."

"If he wanted to burn these dolls, then they must be gone," I said. The garage had turned into a pile of ash and stone. And bones. Nothing like this would have survived.

"What are they? They're creepy."

"I may need to ask Noah or Lukas if they recognize them," I said.

August 7, 2016

Saturday, after the kids left for the weekend, my first order of business was to visit Gary. All I wanted was to take a nap, but there was too much to do, too much to learn. Knowing almost nothing about Gary other than that he had many weapons at his disposal, I bought a cherry pie from the store as a way of making friends. Regardless of the pie, though, I was anxious.

Lukas came down from the hills and joined me in the parking lot. He hadn't showered in days and smelled of fish and sweat. He looked a little worse for wear. Despite all that, I hugged him so tight I was lifted off the ground. For

Chapter Seventeen: August 6, 2016

a second, or a half second, I felt almost whole. Like something clicked, things were right. It was the strangest, worst feeling because there was no 'us'. There would never be an 'us'. There was too much difference, too much separation. All those excuses aside, though, I was happy.

"Let's go talk to a maniac," I said.

"Hello to you too," he said, chuckling. "Sounds like fun, but if you think he's going to eat that pie, you're crazier than he is. He thinks everyone's trying to poison him. Girl with a pie, no different." I sighed, stared at the pie, and threw it aside. It went plop on the edge of the parking lot. "We could have eaten it," he said, shocked, still laughing.

"I don't like pie and I didn't think about that!" I exclaimed. "We can get you another one in town." Going toward the road, we left the entrance to the camp behind. Gary lived north of camp on a farm. He had fields to his name, a handful of strange concrete bunkers, and a crap-ton of gardens, but other than that, he was a pure enigma. A ghillie suit wearing, talking to ghosts kind of enigma.

"Your texts make it sound like you're about half a step from losing your goddamn mind," Lukas said.

"That's probably an accurate representation of things. Thought about Haley the other day and all the other things that could be going on with kids . . . the possible dangers . . ."

"You can't read minds and you're not a psychologist," he said. "It's not your job to save people."

"And you know how much I just love apathy."

"I didn't say to be apathetic, Laurel. Don't put words in my mouth," he said, looking straight ahead. "You have to take care of yourself or you'll burn out, and you know what happens when you burn out. Your brain turns into scrambled eggs. This place isn't good for you or anyone else."

"And yet here you are, helping," I said.

"Because I'm not going to have you waltzing up to a man who wears a tin-foil hat all alone to ask him a bunch of questions. He has more weapons stashed in and around his house than Fort Knox."

"I appreciate it," I said, and hugged him again. The feeling of a hug, one that I actually wanted to give and receive, was powerful. To me, that was also stupid. My terror of being close to people made me weak. It stopped me from doing so many things. There was no fear or curiosity here, between us, just a level of comfort I could live with.

The road to Gary's homestead was extremely steep, as were all the hills in Kellova. Tiger lilies grew abundantly on either side, along with a strange bamboo type plant I often uprooted for sword fights. I ripped one out of the ground and swatted Lukas with it. He chuckled and picked one out as well. "What have you been doing with your life?" I asked.

"Good question," he replied. "Wandering, I guess. What I do best."

"You've got to have goals or something,"

"Why?" he asked. "Do you? Staying here forever, is that your goal?"

"Lukas . . . I was hoping to take over for my mother. I think she's at her wits end, holding on for dear life."

"You could do so much better for yourself." I could tell from over a foot down he was rolling his eyes. So, I went after him again with the makeshift sword.

"You're not the only one to tell me this. Making a change in kids' lives and leaving a legacy sound good enough for me. It's part of the history of this old place," I said.

"Let me guess, Ezra gave you the same spiel, about leaving," he said.

"Yes!" I exclaimed. He twirled a stick at me, so I counterattacked.

"You think he's all goody-two-shoes. You don't even know him; you just think you do."

"What are you talking about?" I asked.

"You think you can read people, but you can't. The guy can't stand the idea of being alone. You just gravitated toward that, that's why he clings to girls when he gets to college. He gets around, Laurel."

"What does that have to do with me?" I asked.

"As if I couldn't tell you've completely fallen in love with the dude," he said. "And every time he posts some picture of himself with a girl on Facebook you feel like there is a javelin shoved through your chest." He was so accurate it scared me.

"What . . .? How—"

"He's no better than me. He drinks. He smokes weed like a fiend sometimes, and—"

"Stop, he doesn't do any of that now, he's half-dead," I said sternly. "Besides, did you ever think I thought it would work between Ezra and me? I'm not . . . normal."

"That didn't stop you ogling," he said, chuckling a bit. I smacked the back of his head with the bamboo stick.

"Stop," I said. "Either way, I don't want to spend the rest of my days in academics. Too much bureaucracy."

"Just stop making excuses," he said, looking at me. He stopped walking. "You want answers in this dump, right? Why now?"

"It destroyed you," I said. And Ezra and Haley and Riley and probably many, many, many others.

"There was no reason for you to get your hopes up with me. You knew exactly who I was when you met me. I haven't changed."

"You were thirteen when I met you, of course you've changed."

"Ok, I grew a foot and a half, my voice went down about twenty octaves, I have a criminal record, and what else? I don't see the world any differently."

"You can't go six years without having your worldview change at least a little," I said. "You have to know there's good in you. You sound so defeated. That thirteen year old kid, way back when, brought me chocolate whenever I was feeling down." He smiled.

"I still don't have the sense that I can settle down or stop moving." His words were very slow and deliberate. "And it's not like I don't have time to figure my shit out. We both do. How about in the present we just focus on not getting killed."

I nodded, looking down at my scuffed old hiking books, faithfully holding together despite all odds. Part of me wanted to take Lukas's hand, and another part wanted to slap him silly. He made his bed. He chose his life, like I chose mine. Why should either of us feel the need to change that? Yet this was the whole pivotal moment in time when decisions had to be made and changes inevitably would follow. A pang hit my gut, the one that only came with existential fear- fear that hit me every once in a while.

Gary Phillips's house was off the road, blocked from view by many rows of well-placed trees that reached far past the electric lines. It was small, painted green to match the scenery, and had a large, attached garage. There was no vehicle in sight, though I never saw one unless he was coming or going. The strangled sound of country music blared from the nearest concrete cylinder of a bunker to the left of the house. Between that and the front door was an extensive herb garden. Everything was in impeccably neat rows, well-watered, and growing despite my belief that nothing on this land planted by man could thrive.

"What'ch you doing on my property?" he screamed, bolting out his house with a rifle. My hands went up immediately. "Oh, just you. Who's the skeleton you have with you?"

"This is Lukas Anderson," I said.

"Ah, the boy who tried to burn down the house." He lowered the rifle and motioned to the door. "They didn't find that Riley boy."

"No, they didn't," I said.

"Got a police scanner here." He patted his belt. He analyzed his surroundings before punching a code into a small metal box by his front door and letting us in. On the wall there were awards and accolades from the military as well as numerous dead animals.

"You were a fucking green beret?" Lukas asked, amazed.

"Among other things," he said, putting the weapon down on the kitchen table. Family photographs dating back at least a hundred and fifty years also had their place on the walls. I didn't imagine there would be so much personality inside the home of a man so private. "They liked my style, after I retired from combat, they had me participate in shit you wouldn't even imagine." Using his black boot, he poked at the file cabinet beside his desk. "Things I'd consider crimes that they went out of their way to cover up. Crap against the Geneva Convention. I'm probably a loose end."

"Like what?" Lukas asked.

"That's not the kind of stuff I want you interested in, young man," Gary said, leaning forward. "Too dark, but I don't have a lot of people here asking. I won't get into specifics, but establishing patient zeroes for strange illnesses in unstable countries, overthrowing rulers we didn't like, sterilizing people we thought were inferior, controlling the minds of those we thought stupid, or dangers . . . Do you get the point? I got out, and I came here because it was my job, and the games still haven't ended." He looked directly at me. "I wanted to tell your mother about this land since she got the job, but she wouldn't hear it, so I suppose you're the one to tell."

"How long has your family been here, Mr. Phillips?" I asked, pointing at some of the photographs.

"Since the government seized the land from the Otoe in the area and made it available for purchase. My family came over from Norway in 1891 and bought up a fuck-ton of that land. It was the Halverson family originally. Everything that is now Kellova Hills and your precious little camp, was my family's property. My family tried not only to mine, but also to farm cattle and pigs, and they kept trying that for a good twenty years."

"Trying?" Lukas asked.

"From the beginning it seemed like that land was at odds with my family. Immediately, people started dying off and they didn't know why, livestock too. The cattle and hogs were having miscarriages or mutated births. Dying for no reason. Disappearing. My ancestors already blamed the house for all this."

"The house was here?" I asked.

"Sort of. It was a log cabin back then, but still in the clearing, just as it is now. No one in town would have anything to do with this damned place or my family. Said the land was cursed. I don't blame them, and I don't blame the Indians either, it was their land to begin with, but I sure as hell doubt they built a white man's house like that."

"Did any of your family members live in that house?" I asked.

"How stupid do you think they were?" His voice cracked. "Damn, girl, I'm only telling you this because you're sticking your nose into it and it's more dangerous than you could ever think of comprehending. People have tried to solve this before and it always ends with them dead or in a looney bin, so will you just let me speak!" I hushed up. He opened a large drawer in his file cabinet, filled to the brim with centuries-old diaries.

He continued, "I've read every one of these. Balls of light scaring all the animals, unseen forces ravaging guard dogs, animals going missing, men going missing and found dead. Animals showing up that don't look right, and the ones that do look natural act like there's something seriously wrong with them. Finally, I guess they couldn't take it and sold a great deal of the land back to the state and used that money to build the camp. They said that under the condition of sale it had to be made a state park so people couldn't live here. They owned the camp until 1989, then sold that off too, to that weird group of Nomads who put your mother in charge. My property is the last of what they purchased."

"Do you have any idea what caused all the strange occurrences here?" I asked.

"Too many people have too many ideas on that. It's above my pay grade. I simply keep it in check as much as I can. It comes from inside that house, and it has a reach as far as the property."

"We need to figure out how to stop it," I said.

"I agree, it's hurting children now. It's too hungry, and it needs to be destroyed, but you've gotta be smarter than fire," Gary said.

"What does the house look like to you?" I asked, thinking of the drawings.

His grin widened. "So you've noticed. Not many people do," he chuckled.

"What?" Lukas asked.

"We all see House One differently," Gary responded. I pulled Riley's notebook out of my bag and placed it on the kitchen table. "I've seen that before," Gary said.

"Yeah, and Riley put about twenty variations of the house in here," I said. It was then that Lukas started to pace behind me while I felt like I was picking up momentum.

"And the kid recognized the flowers too," Gary said. "Smart as a whip. The calla lilies."

"What do they mean?" I asked.

"According to my grandmother's diary, they stand for purity. So it may have initially been a means of protection, but they also represent death."

"This is insane, you get that, right?" Lukas asked.

"People have been calling me nutty my entire life, son, it's nothing new," Gary responded.

"You're wearing a helmet lined with foil, sir."

"You're right, I am," he said. "Because I'm not willing to let them into my brain. They're not going to control me. They had thirty years of my life already, and that's plenty. Now, about this ring of lilies. Only one kid, I'm aware of, has seen the girl inside of the ring."

"Riley," I answered. "She led him there."

"For what reason, I don't know. I don't know what it feeds off of, but it doesn't discriminate. Once infected with it, the person usually doesn't make it, or the animal. Somehow that boy survived, and so did you," he said, looking at Lukas.

"I wasn't infected with anything, unless hate counts," Lukas replied.

"Hate is as infectious as anything," Gary said.

"How can it infect people? It's a house," he asked.

"I was never a scientist, son, I was the one who followed orders, not come up with them. That being said, I'm not stupid either. I've lived here most of my life. I know what I've seen, and there's patterns."

"Then why do you choose to live next to it?" Lukas asked.

"I already said why, boy. Someone in my family always has to. It's our responsibility! You don't know much about responsibility, I can see that, sense that, but we Halversons do. We took the land, we're responsible for it. We're probably responsible for whatever is lurking out there." He looked directly at Lukas again. "I didn't see it myself, but what happened when you tried to burn it down, son?"

"I poured gasoline all over the place, some propane, some lighter fluid, threw a match and it went whoosh . . . There was about half a second of flame before it went out. The only things that caught were the mattresses and other pieces of furniture. Not the banisters or the tables, or the floor, or the walls."

"We've tried burning it down before," Gary said. "Always fails. You can burn something inside the house, but not the house itself. I bet if you took a wrecking ball to it, it wouldn't budge, but it's in such a strategic spot, it's impossible to bring such a thing up here without flying one attached to a helicopter."

"You smashed a window in once, and Noah smashed a window too . . ." I muttered to Lukas.

"Are there any windows smashed right this second?" Gary asked.

"No," Lukas said.

"Bingo, son," Gary clapped him on the back and Lukas nearly jumped. Grabbing his rifle, Gary opened the front door and looked about. We followed him.

"Why do you have music playing all the time?" I asked, pointing at the first bunker.

"I have radio signals going so the government can't access me," he said. Lukas rolled his eyes. "I tried using a magnetic force, but the house seems to combat that. It has its own magnetic polarity. How or why, I don't know." We passed by his colorful vegetable garden. There were tall cucumber plants, tomatoes, peas growing on trellises, and bundles of green beans. Behind his house were a few large chicken coops busting with white and black dappled chickens. Razor wire topped the coops, however, and it wasn't only a layer of chicken wire separating the chickens from the outside, but thick fencing nailed into and under the ground.

"Do you lose many chickens?" I asked.

"No wild animals get to them," he said. "But I do find the strangest eggs, double yolks in numbers higher than usual, eggs inside eggs, bloody eggs, some come out without shells, just membrane . . . and it isn't poor nutrition, they get the best quality. I've been seeing more lash eggs in the past few years now- they're just hard balls of puss in place of an egg. The hens appear to be in good condition, no infections." He peered over at them. "They love their cabbage, though, more than I do, that's for sure. Sometimes I hang it up for them and they have to chase it around, give them some good exercise."

Gary seemed incredibly lonely, like I was invited up here just so he could talk, not only about the house, but about him too. He continued, "I get my bread and other meat from the grocery store in town, otherwise, I'm not trusting all the shit they put in food these days, chemicals, refined sugars, and the like. They're trying to make people apathetic, and all those things will give you cancer." There was a compost pile deep in the woods surrounded by more chicken wire and pallets. His land was perfectly primed to keep him fed, but where the money came from to keep him stockpiled, I didn't know.

At the third concrete cylinder, Gary pulled open the door. The door was heavy enough it was on rollers. It was filled with every type of firearm one could imagine: sidearms, revolvers, rifles, shotguns, assault weapons. Lukas looked like he died and went to heaven. "Like this, huh?" Gary asked, smiling. Gary looked at one of his cameras mounted above the second bunker. "All these will let me know if anything even twitches around this land.

"Uh, Gary, there was a circle of dead racoons in the cellar of House One, do you know why?" I asked.

"There was what?" Lukas interjected.

"A perfect circle of racoons in various states of decay," I said.

Gary raised his eyebrows and he said, "Never saw anything like that. Granted, I don't go into the cellar often. Like I said, it draws things in there, living things, and uses them up. I don't know how. I don't know why."

The edge of the forest opened up into the clearing. The house stood in its center. All of its windows were intact. The paint was chipped in many places and there were plenty of colors peeking through, maybe even more than I remembered seeing in the past.

Gary said, "Catch," to Lukas. He threw him a level. "Check out the angles on the house." He threw him a compass as well, like one used in geometry class.

"I have to get close to that thing?" he asked, pointing.

"I'm not doing it," Gary replied, chuckling. Lukas approached the house and touched it first with his hands as if testing to see if it would bite. Then he looked at the angles between corners, windows, and the doors. He was silent for a long time, his face contorting deeply in confusion and interest. "Tell me, son."

"What's supposed to be ninety degrees . . . aren't ninety degrees. They're like ninety-three or eighty-seven, always just a little bit off. Same with forty-five-degree angles. Nothing's even. It's like there's just something . . ."

"Generally off about it?" Gary asked.

"Yeah."

"Come on back, son," Gary said, waving him over. Gary spied something behind the house, past the clearing. It was an old shovel once used by Lukas to knock out the windows. Gary smiled and went for it.

"What are you doing?" I asked.

"You'll see," he said, chuckling. He sounded like he was having fun. Gary took the shovel and stood beside us, at the front of the house. "Can we all agree that in this iteration of the house, there is one window near the front door?"

"Yes," Lukas and I said in unison.

"And that on every side of the house, there is at least one window on the first floor, correct?" We agreed. Gary smashed each window, laughing as he went. This was a clean, sober, crazy man. Tin foil hat and all, smashing windows. Yet, for his age, he swung that heavy shovel like it weighed nothing.

The glass shattered, yet didn't leave the direct vicinity of the house, or make much of a noise. There were no showers of glass, and it didn't seem to want to break easily. Gary used all his force to take out each one of them. "That felt good," he said, standing back. The house shuddered. You could feel its anger, it was tangible, electric.

"Ah shit, what did you do?" I muttered, stepping closer to Lukas.

Chapter Seventeen: August 6, 2016

"I swear to God Almighty that there will be nothing wrong with those windows next time you come here," Gary said, though his eyes weren't on the house. He held up his hands for us to be silent. He held tightly onto the shovel, and stepped up, turning to look past the clearing. There was a coyote approaching. It didn't look quite right either. Its legs were long, unnaturally so, and they were bent and broken looking. Nonetheless, it didn't appear to have any problem walking. "What is that?" I asked.

"It's the house being pissed off, young lady," he replied.

"Shoot it!" Lukas called.

Gary laughed. "If it's under the control of the house, my shooting it will do nothing. I could unload all my ammunition, and nothing will happen."

What used to be a coyote watched us, seemingly calm, analyzing our every breath. My heart fluttered quickly in my chest. Each step it took was ginger, and silent. It made no sound with its movement, though its breath was heavy and labored. It was clearly in pain, twisted, and mutilated. It was a sickening, sad sight. If the animal was truly being controlled by the house, it had no chance of surviving like this.

"You can't help it?" I asked.

"I've only been able to get a few out of this trance, but only if they don't look like monsters first." He raised the shovel. "And then I have to manage to hit them about half an inch above each eye and in the center. If I'm lucky, when they wake up, they're nice and sane again. Most of the time, I'm not that lucky."

As if on cue, the coyote lunged for us, and Gary swiftly hit it with the shovel as if it was a baseball. The coyote slammed to the ground but got on its feet in moments. "Back up, guys," Gary said. "We need to get back home." His voice was calm, though he was urgent. The way he acted; this was a regular occurrence. He slammed the flat end of the shovel down on the head of the coyote. It yelped in anger more than pain and growled. All Gary seemed to be managing to do was piss the coyote off more. "Run to my house. I'll keep it busy."

"Like hell," Lukas said. "Hand me that shovel."

"He does like hitting things with shovels . . ." I muttered.

Gary thought about it for half a second, cocking his head to the side and then handing it to him. Lukas walked toward the coyote, pushing it further and further back. Eventually it stood on its hind legs, frustrated, and trembling. That was a sight I could have gone without seeing. Those extra-long, mutilated legs seemed perfect to hold it upright.

"Whatever you do, don't turn your back on it," Gary said. "We're just lucky there was no fucking bear in the vicinity, or that's what would be sicced on us."

Lukas swung the side of the shovel smack into the coyote's neck as it lunged. If it was any other animal, it'd be dead or decapitated. Instead, it was just flung to its side again, giving us just enough time to run backwards toward the house. We ripped through the yard, past Gary's barriers, and into the house. There were five locks on the door, which now that I was able to really appreciate it, were a few inches thick.

"It can't get in, nothing can," Gary said with a sigh. "The windows are thick polycarbonate. The walls are reinforced with steel and concrete. I made sure this place is a fortress."

Confused and amazed, I sat down on the couch and closed my eyes for a moment, only to be interrupted by the coyote slamming itself into the glass behind me. It acted rabid, minus the foaming at the mouth. "This happens a lot?" I asked. Taking a look outside, the coyote's head lolled to the side, but it still bared its teeth and panted.

"Whenever the place gets ticked off," Gary said, leaning back in his chair. "Which could be anything from walking past it, spitting at it... Sometimes just being outside, working the land pisses it off. My existence pisses it off. Usually, though, it just uses animals up. Maybe it uses them to wander around and see things. I don't know. I don't understand its motives."

"And so you just find the bodies?" I asked.

"Frequently. I tan the hides, sell the pelts, clean the bones, sell those too, bring in some money for food."

"Ever have birds?" I asked.

"The occasional crow or eagle," he said. "When they die, I put them in a box and call the Lakota to take them."

"Maybe they could help!" I cried.

"They said this land is off limits. I deliver birds to them. They will not speak of the land or what's on it."

"Do they know what's here? Or why?" I asked.

"If they do, they won't tell."

"I hope it doesn't get to . . ."

"Shit, girl, don't use names. The only advice they gave me was to not use names," he cried. "It gives whatever the hell it is power over the person." There was pounding at the door from the coyote. It was scratching, howling, and screaming. I peered out the window and saw a strange contraption to the left of the house. It was a steel barred cage, and very large.

"What's that for?"

"Sometimes I can stick whatever's going nuts in there, let it bash itself against the bars until it croaks. Sometimes if they stand still long enough, I can wham them on the forehead and get their senses back to them." He shrugged, unconcerned. His existence was undeniably a weird one. While this was second nature to Gary, it was hardly graspable. Adrenaline was coursing through me in acidic waves.

Being in a closed off space with a man I was told my entire life was a dangerous loon only made me more anxious, as did the coyote which seemed to be breaking out of its own skin in rage. If it confirmed anything, though, it was that the house had to be destroyed. It was killing innocent animals, as well as people. The coyote, though not tame, was probably just as intelligent as my Charlie, and probably had a whole personality which was just ripped away from it arbitrarily. And replaced with mindless rage.

"Can I use your bathroom?" Lukas asked, pointing to the small closet of a restroom off the edge of the living room.

"Yeah, son," Gary said, and leaned back in his chair again. Gary looked downright exhausted.

"Do you have any information on your family when they settled here?" I asked.

"Some," he replied. "They had money, but spent it mainly on land, not photographs or paper. By the turn of the century, we have more, but it's just really old portraits." He pointed at the bottom shelf of a tall bookcase made of metal that went from floor to ceiling. The first album had a cloth cover sewn onto it, but it felt very frail. The photographs inside were like cardboard.

Lukas shrieked. "Fuck! There's a fucking snake coming up the pipes! It tried to bite me!"

"What?" Gary stood up. "How'd a snake get in my house?"

"It's a fucking possessed snake is what it is!" Lukas said, slamming the door to the bathroom shut.

"I just sat down!" Gary said.

"I'll get it," I said. There'd been many instances where I had to catch snakes- at the lake, in the pool, by the river, by the fields, and it was always left to me. "Have a stick?"

"Got my walking stick by the kitchen, pretty obvious if you can take your eyes off that door for a second," Gary said to Lukas, who jumped out of his nerves momentarily.

"You can't beat it to death if it's one of those things," Lukas said, a little shrilly.

"I'm not going to beat it to death you moron," I replied. I opened the door and saw a water moccasin striking the wall absently. It was fat and I was amazed it fit through the plumbing to begin with. I'd seen smaller snakes and rats end up in toilet bowls, but nothing like this. Its dark skin seemed to dance and tremble with energy. This thing was pure muscle. Its amber eyes were piercing and unnaturally large. Most snakes I'd been in contact with never tried to strike at me or anything else. They're rather run than fight, but this was not a usual snake.

I used the heavy stick and placed it hard on the back of its head to secure it. The tail behind writhed and flicked with panicked energy. Reaching down, I grasped the back of its head and placed my thumb on the forehead. The snake had more power than any other I'd ever handled. It did everything in its power to break my grasp. "Do you have something to put it in?" I called, stepping out with the snake in my hand. I secured the back half of the snake with the other hand, and the body around my back.

"Guess I do have to stand up, god-damnit. Never seen one of those snakes like that," Gary said. He looked at it with interested eyes. "It found a way past my security." He picked up a massive barrel of a plastic trash can and deposited it in front of me, before swiftly picking up a pistol. "Not even my fucking toilet is off limits now, I suppose."

"What are you going to do with that?" I asked.

"Hoping I get a clear shot on its forehead. It doesn't look like it's too far gone. Besides, that's one ugly hide on that mother fucker, wouldn't be able to sell it for much anyway." I dropped, or rather, nearly threw, the snake in and stood back. It slammed its head against the side of the trashcan. Gary patiently watched it, waiting for the right moment. It seemed like twenty minutes passed before the deafening blow of a gunshot washed through the house. There was a slight response to it. I looked inside the trash can. Beside the snake, which was still alive, was a smashed bullet.

"You've got to be kidding me," I said, looking in. "Lukas, come here."

He stepped forward with a hand on my back, probably to comfort himself. "Now shoot that thing out there," Lukas said. "I can't stand the screaming anymore."

"If I get a clear shot, it won't save it, too far gone unfortunately," Gary said.

"Then get it in its right mind, and then take it out," Lukas said. "If you don't, I will."

"Brave all of a sudden, son? I didn't think you had a compassionate side for critters," Gary said, smirking. There were many occasions where I'd seen Lukas take a shovel or really any handy object to kill raccoons, just for the sport of it. I didn't know what was so fun about the suffering and death of another animal, but my saying so had never stopped him.

Lukas reached his hand out for the pistol. Gary rolled his eyes. "So, I'm just going to open my door and you'll get it on the first shot?"

"I spend time at the gun range," Lukas said.

"Not lately you haven't. You're on probation. Technically letting you use the weapon would throw us both in jail."

"This isn't exactly a normal situation," Lukas said. Gary shrugged and handed him the gun. Lukas flung the door open as quickly as he could. The coyote backed up in startled surprise, but soon came lunging at Lukas. He took four shots, the first three hit the animal, but did nothing. One, though, landed dead center between the eyes. The coyote fell to the ground and screamed in abject agony. It whined and tried to get away. The pain was too great. Its legs were broken, as was its jaw. It turned itself to crawl away. Lukas approached, and shot it point blank in the back of the head.

"Ah, not the skull, I could have sold that!" Gary said. "Weird and all!"

"Did you not hear it? What about compassion for the critters?" I asked.

"I sure did hear it," he said. "But when you've been dealing with shit like this for most of your life, you learn to do things more efficiently." He went over to the coyote's bleeding body and hoisted it up by the legs. He carried it to one of the bunkers. That particular bunker was filled with skins, hides, pelts, and bones. The concrete surrounding it had blood stains around the concrete. Hooks from the top. It made the 'serial killer' alarm go off in my brain.

Gary slung the coyote up and cut straight into its stomach to drain out its innards. It was still steaming.

Gary gave Lukas lessons on how to clean the carcass, stating that he probably would be able to salvage some bones and the tail, but he'd try the whole hide. Not wanting to witness the process, or even hear it, I went back inside Gary's home and tried desperately to compose myself. I felt insane, grief-stricken, and yet relieved.

They cleaned up with an outdoor faucet before instructing me to go check out House One with them again. "It's going to be quiet this time, the electricity is out of the air," Gary said. I trusted his instincts more than I trusted my own.

Chapter Seventeen: August 6, 2016

As Gary predicted, all the windows were back in place. Looking at it closer, I could see the details. It wasn't built properly, like Lukas said. There were no visible nails, nor any other binding material. It was made out of wooden planks. It was clearly old, but it didn't seem like it was something that would be constructed in the middle of nowhere, especially not without nails or screws or any evident concrete. "I'm confused," I muttered.

"Just noticed that?" Gary asked, chuckling. "Yeah, I don't know how it's standing either."

"And it was here when your family moved on the land?"

"That's what I said, and that's what they wrote. I've translated as much as I could, typed up inside. I keep logs of all activity, all the animals, anything the house happens to do." He turned to his fortress of a home. "My mother said there always had to be a Halverson on this land, to guard it. Part of that job was to log everything. It's like a family business. There's just . . . not a lot of us left. It made sure of it."

"Can I read the documents?" I asked. When we returned to the house, he packed them in a canvas bag. It was heavy, bulged, and I was hardly able to carry it.

"Now, if you don't mind, I'm going to finish up with that coyote while you get yourself updated with the madness that is in that clearing. You can read those at your own leisure. If you don't give them back, I know where to find you."

"Thank you, sir," I said.

Chapter Eighteen:

August 7, 2016

I wanted answers, but my brain simply wasn't in a state to get any at the moment. Lukas drove my car back to Kellova. He faced me in the parking lot. "Do you want me to stay?" he asked. I nodded. "How am I going to get in there without your mom seeing me?" He smirked a bit. "I don't want a lecture."

I peered over at Clark, and the office. Her SUV was nowhere to be seen. "Don't think she's there."

"Good. I'll rustle up some chocolate and meet you over at the Hytte."

My steps felt a hundred pounds heavier than normal, like I was dragging myself through electrically charged mud. The last time I felt this was during a rather severe bout of depression and I didn't want to go back to that. Yet, I felt that if I were to sit down for a few moments, just a few, I'd burst right back out into tears, but I couldn't stand all day.

The Hytte, my cabin, was a welcome sight. A lonely, welcome sight. The bright and cheerful 'welcome' sign on the door made me angry. It was stupid, my anger toward it, but it was there. Once inside, I tossed my shoes off, and went to my room and lay down. In the near silence, the only sounds were that of the steadily humming AC and the bugs outside. The Xanax was taking effect, and my heart rate at least started to slow down. Desperation, though, didn't. Just lying there, I was doing nothing. I wasn't contributing to anything, nor solving anything. Riley was still missing. Ezra was still injured . . .

Once again, my thoughts were interrupted by Lukas. "I have solid chocolate, hot chocolate, popcorn, and earbuds so I can go in the other room and not bother you." He placed them by the bed.

"Thank you," I said, slightly calmed just by the mere existence of Lukas and chocolate. I took a dose of Klonopin to shut myself up. As I drifted off, my mind showed me Ezra's Facebook pictures with his girlfriends of years past. Their happy faces stuck together, cheek to cheek, or lips to lips. He was never *mine*. I was never in the business of claiming, but there was a certain level of subconscious, angry possessiveness I just couldn't help.

I whipped out my phone before the medication stupor got me. His current relationship status listed Jessica Hellinger from Lincoln, Nebraska. She was blonde, though the blonde came out of a box, and she was effortlessly thin. She may have well been a model for Maybelline. She had the normal head-to-the-side-and-one-leg-out in pictures I usually associated with "popular" kids or sorority girls. She enjoyed Instagram filters, and "relationship goal" memes, and I never hated a person more for doing nothing wrong in my life. *She* was the reason I hadn't seen Ezra in almost a year. Despite both of us residing in Greenville, he never had time.

Time after time, promises were broken, and I kept saying it was ok, maybe next time. My anger, frustration, and grief lay just under the surface, bubbling. Boiling. It may have silently exploded because once again, I sobbed and wept, beating the pillow. I didn't want to care so damn much! Why couldn't there just be a switch that just stopped the emotions, to stop believing the bullshit about how he cared, and that I was important to him. I laid my soul bare for him, for what, for silence? And now I committed myself to his care post NDE.

Where was Jessica in all this? Back in Lincoln? Did she know him like I did?

June 2015

Ezra and I sat on the porch of my mom's house with the fire pit blazing. There was a large rocking bench decked out with comfy green cushions and cupholders. We were wrapped in blankets to keep the early summer chill at bay. We were in the middle of a heated conversation. "No, no, no, they shouldn't take money from music, art, and drama out of the budget," I said. It was being considered in the 2015-2016 school year at the high school where I graduated, and he tutored.

"Even for STEM? The world's changing," he began.

"If we devalue creative endeavors, it can be detrimental," I replied.

"What did you learn in band that's done anything for you in the long run?" he asked, taking a sip from his freshly brewed sun tea.

"Uh, teamwork? Same with theater. It's more important we have a population that knows how to work with others and be able to healthily express themselves, than one that knows how to do advanced calculus."

He nodded, sincerely listening. "But the job market is changing. The world is changing. Science and technology are everything."

"What are those things worth without reasonable people with the ability to work with others? I'm not saying STEM isn't integral. I'm just saying that the money to fund it shouldn't come out of the MAD budget. How about they use some of the money for the insanely unnecessary new athletic building? It's not like we don't already have like four of them."

Ezra chuckled. "What about all that team building jargon?"

"They have plenty of money!" I exclaimed. "You don't even get paid for tutoring over there."

"True, but the best way to learn is to teach," he said. "Even if half the kids have no clue what's going on in math class. One teacher is doing everything backward- he's having the kids learn from the book, do the homework, and then go over it. It's not working well at all."

"Sounds like my Latin class from college . . . are you wanting to be a high school teacher?" I asked.

He gave a grimace and shrugged. "God, I don't know what I want to be, but in high school? There's too much bureaucracy and drama and ugh . . . I like the kids obviously, but that's about it."

"You'd get summers off though!" I exclaimed.

"And a pathetic salary considering the hours worked! I could probably make more at Walmart."

"But what would make you happy?" I asked, looking at his face. He stared at the fire before returning eye contact.

"Well, whatever I do, I need money."

"You also need to not be miserable. What's the point of spending your days unhappy?"

"Point taken, but a nice house and a good car, and I'm going to have to do that all myself, no parental help."

"I know, and I'm lucky I have my mom, even if it is just her. I have some-one who is always there and has my back," I said, looking to the flickering window of her bedroom where she was hopefully relaxing. "The tag team. Even if we argue about brands of toothpaste and toilet paper."

He nodded. "Y'all are kind of like my adopted family. I know I can come to you if I need help."

"Of course, always," I said, squeezing his arm. "That'll never change."

"Don't know if I deserve that," he said. There was no hardness to his voice, just genuine honesty.

"What do you mean?" I matched his tone, softening my voice.

"It's hard to describe, but you just took me in, no questions asked. Family dinners, movie and game nights. I never did any of that with my own mother when she was alive," he huffed and pulled his hand free of the blanket and through his hair. "You got me just as I decided not to be a shithead."

"Well, I don't know if you're not a shithead . . ." I said, laughing, bumping into him. He laughed as well. "Why wouldn't I want you over for dinners and movies?" The answer was simple, but he wasn't going to mention the fact he usually had a girlfriend, and I wasn't about to either. I pretended that it didn't bother me. His life, his decisions. Wherever I landed was just what I had to deal with.

Chapter Eighteen: August 7, 2016

Ezra sighed. "You're too forgiving."

"I didn't think forgiveness was a bad trait," I replied. "It's very hard-wired."

"Avoid conflict at all costs . . . I know, me too," he said.

"You do flee from conflict," I said.

"I feel like I shrink if I'm arguing with someone, even a camper. I feel like I don't have a leg to stand on." I thought, at that moment, I didn't have anything to stand on either, most of the time. Like I was floating on the sea, but right at that moment, I felt ok.

"You're wishy-washy, hon, and you know it."

"I do, I do," he said, still smiling. "You don't have much of a backbone yourself."

I wanted so badly to rest my head on his shoulder, or snuggle in, but two things stopped me- my own inhibitions about proximity to others, and the fact he had a girlfriend. My actions may be taken as an intrusion.

I'd have Ezra around for the next few months, and then I'd have to relinquish him to his own little world where I just sat on the fringes, patiently waiting for something, anything- a sign, a text that indeed, I existed. I'd given so many pieces of myself over to help him rebuild, I was worried I'd have little left. And a very small, much-silenced part of me hated what I did to myself.

Another part hated him for letting me.

No matter the hurt or frustration, or javelin-in-the-heart pain, just speaking to him, being beside him was a balm, and all was right. He radiated a light so genuinely, I'd yet to find it in someone else. It did not hide darkness but blinded it.

"I'm disappointed in myself, a lot," I said in the brief silence. "That I'm not where I want to be in life. That I can't be how I want to be."

"How do you want to be?" he asked. "I don't understand. What the hell would you want to change? You're brilliant." And yet, with all that, it is still not good enough for him.

"It's hard to explain. You're hard on yourself a lot too."

"For being a moron." That I could agree to. "But you just graduated from college with honors and distinction. You oughta be proud of yourself."

"I guess I am. It doesn't feel like a big deal though," I replied. "It hardly feels real at all, like all that time didn't even happen, even if it was only a month ago."

"Brain?" he asked, pointing to his own.

"I never know anymore. Some research came out saying that people with TBIs can have flare ups years after they happen. It sounds terrifying."

"Like you could lose all your progress at any moment," he said.

"Exactly,"

"But you can always come back from that. Build yourself up stronger each time," I wanted to believe him. I truly did, but the truth was, I didn't.

Chapter Eighteen: August 7, 2016

The Hytte was empty at ten in the morning. I slept for nearly fourteen hours. That gave me only six hours to work with. The medicine bottles sat nicely on my nightstand, staring at me. The javelin swiftly came back into my chest. I wanted one of those bitter Xanax for relief. Or to eat my weight in Oreos. Instead, I stared at the wooden wall until my head cleared. There was a note on my door from Lukas in his scrawling handwriting, 'getting supplies'.

I went to my bathroom, disdaining the rainbow rugs and crystal sun catchers for being cheery when I felt empty. I stood in front of the mirror. My hair was in disarray, though, as it normally was in the morning. Once combed, it lay, for the most part, limp on my shoulders. I was drained of all color and ashy. There was strangely no sense of self there, like each part of me was scattered far and unreachable. There was no sense of purpose or urgency. Nothing except that pain in my chest. I wanted to go lie back down.

I had a small bit of sense and used it to wash my face, take my antidepressants, and brush my teeth. Then I sat on the closed toilet seat and looked out over the forest. It didn't seem very green. Even color was drained from my reality.

"Laurel! I ran into someone on the way here!" Lukas called, sounding enthusiastic.

"Hey girly," Mia said. I must have been a mess if she was willing to even acknowledge his presence without first calling the cops.

"I'm fine!" I called back.

"The hell you are," Lukas said. "We've both known you long enough. We also have donuts and kringla, so, get out here."

"And the good kind of chocolate milk," Mia added. "A whole carton."

I wasn't going to be able to hide from the day. They'd make sure of that. "Mom doesn't know you're here, does she?" I asked, looking at Lukas.

"Not unless she gets access to Gary's trail cams," he said. I came out of the bathroom. Lukas recently showered, so he smelled of soap and deodorant now instead of sweat and grime.

"There's still cops all over the Hills looking for Riley," I said.

"I packed my stuff up this morning and parked at Gary's. He practically took my car apart, first looking for bugs, but my shit is hidden." I saw that all the information from Gary was strewn across my sad excuse for a kitchen table.

"You sure did make yourself at home here," I said. Mia handed me some chocolate milk in a paper cup. I'd do anything to avoid dishes.

"He filled me in on, well, your discoveries." She pointed to the table. Not only were there typed translations, but onion skin records, bound logbooks, and photographs.

"How did I sleep through this?" I asked.

"No clue," Mia said. "You're such a light sleeper, but you were out. Very, very, very out." She got me in a tight, squishy, surprisingly comforting hug. I could have cried, again, but even that seemed overwhelming. Everything did. The donuts. The campers, and most especially the House. I didn't want to see it, read about it, or acknowledge its existence. "But I guess you're less crazy than I thought," Mia said.

"I don't know about that," I replied. I genuinely felt that if the House wanted to kill me, it could, and the only consequence would be some inconvenience.

Shut up, I told myself. The intrusive voices were getting stronger.

"Well, I truly don't think these photographs were doctored," Mia said.

"I don't want to see them right now," I replied. I sat on the couch and Mia plopped down beside me, while Lukas stayed near the door like he needed a means of egress.

"At least get a donut in you," Mia said. I wasn't hungry, but I ate.

"Hate to bring this up, but the cabin assignments haven't been done," Mia added.

"Crap. Yeah, you're right. Gotta do that . . . haven't even gone to my office." I didn't care if they saw me change, I went to my room, threw on clothes, tied my hair up and packed my backpack.

"I'm going to dig through this pile of info while you're out," Lukas said.

"You think it's safe to stay?" Mia asked. He shrugged. She continued, "I got all I could find about the founding of the places and buildings from the Nomad room. Got copies so no one knows anything is missing."

"Looks like a lot of newspapers and obits," Lukas said.

"We'll see if anything is useful," Mia said.

As I entered the office Gail said, "There's a bit of a change to your cabin this week. Jenny's decided she doesn't want to do the horse program anymore, so you get her."

"Genevieve Gentry?" I asked.

"That's the one," she replied, standing up from her side of the desk. "Your mother spoke to her father yesterday about her behavior the past few weeks. I don't know how well that went. Oh, and lake day is still canceled, so I printed out a note to stick next to the cabin and class assignments."

"Thanks, Gail," I said, and went to my office. Charlie was asleep on my futon and his tail beat steadily against it. I hugged him tightly and kissed his giant black nose. "Hello, big guy." His fluffy fur was perfect to bury my face in, even if he did smell distinctly like sweat socks.

Jenny Gentry was eccentric, intense, loud, and frequently destructive. The girls in Hawthorne had been together for the past ten weeks without incident, throwing in a curveball like Jenny was not something I looked forward to.

While I wrote the assignments, my mind continued to drift away to Ezra. He was in there, somewhere. And I thought of that kiss. That singular kiss. One that never should have happened, but how safe and at peace I felt in that moment. How ready I was for proof that he did love me, and how wrong I was. That javelin got pushed a bit further into my chest. I didn't see how I was getting through the day, or the week, but I had no choice.

Charlie joined me when I posted the assignments and prepared the main room of Clark for the staff meeting. By the time I finished, I was only a little early. I sat down with a fresh notebook and started to jot down things I knew about House One. Time was running out to solve the mystery of it.

Lukas texted me: *Clark was the first building at camp, 1909. Amalie Halverson was the first director. Clark wasn't named at that point; it was eventually dedicated to two brothers: Jonathan and Matthew Clark. Apple is dedicated to another construction worker who ended up living on the property for a while. He was twenty-nine when he married one of the Halverson girls, Katrine. She was sixteen.*

Me: *Where are you getting all this?*

Lukas: *There's some announcements in the newspaper Mia got about the construction of the buildings. Clark's unique architecture attracted some attention.*

Me: *Because it's a circle?*

Lukas: *Yes. It looks like Amalie saved all sorts of letters sent to her. People seemed to think she was a little strange too. She was against the marriages of all family members who didn't plan on moving off the property. She had a family member named Kjerstin who married a man named Cain Whyte and they stayed for a bit, but she moved away when she became pregnant.*

Amalie said in one of the letters: sons are cursed.

Me: *What does that mean?*

Lukas: *I just started, but since she was the first director, I think I should begin with her.*

Me: *What about the records from when they first arrived? Maybe we should start from as far back as we can.*

Lukas: *Amalie's full name is Amalie Nilsen, and she came from Rogaland Norway along with the rest of her family when she was 21.*

Me: *Maybe she knew what was up with the House. Gary said it was there when they moved in. The meeting is going to start soon.*

I put my phone away and Mia sat next to me. "Boxes and boxes of photographs and records . . . Lukas got them from Gary, all the way from the early 1900's. It's like putting together a puzzle. That and I think half of what he's going to have to do is put things together in some sort of order because it's just a pile." Mia spoke in hushed tones, though I doubted anyone was listening.

"Laurel!" Harry exclaimed. I nearly jumped out of my seat in surprise. He hugged me from behind and hopped into a chair in some kind of leap-frog move. "So how's the Ez?"

"What?" I asked.

"Ezra. How's Ezra?" he asked.

220

Chapter Eighteen: August 7, 2016

"Oh, he's doing well. Noah's been keeping him company," I said. "What'd you do this weekend?" He blushed immediately. "Ah, ok."

"What are you insinuating?" He crossed his arms and frowned like a little kid. Peter came through the main doors and Harry turned into a beacon of light.

"That," I replied. He shook his head and sighed, his eyes all puppy-dog and cute. "If that isn't infatuation, I don't know what is." He made a goofy face and giggled before running off to sit beside Peter. They kissed each other. Everyone cheered briefly, there was clapping involved, then Mom walked in, and silence ensued.

"Oh, good, everyone is here on time for once," she said. "I wouldn't say last week went smoothly. Perhaps you're all exhausted and the work is wearing on you, but I need you to find that second wind and push through the next few weeks and then you're done. We will start closing down cabins this week that are unused. Maintenance needs to be our top priority for those on cleaning duty." She droned on, and I checked out mentally.

There were lesson plans for orienteering, arts and crafts, nature and so much else to make that I just absently started scrawling ideas in my notebook. I could feel the heaviness of my mom's eyes on me, watching. At this point, I didn't have enough energy to care what she thought or said. I was tired in every way possible.

Before she could speak to me, I left for the office as quickly as my feet would take me. "Harry! Can you help me get the check-in set up?" I didn't want to be alone. It was an unnatural fear that was deep set in my chest and mingled with exhaustion, I felt like I had no control.

"Sure," he said, almost asking a question of it. "So what's going on? You look like you've been hit by a train."

"You're full of so many compliments," I replied.

"No, seriously," he said. Harry wasn't a serious guy, but he sounded serious.

"I'm just worried about Ezra," I said. It wasn't a complete lie.

"I thought you said he was doing ok," he said. We went inside the office. Gail had our supplies stacked up on the table. We each took a milk-carton worth of stuff.

"I did, because he pretty much is, but I still want answers about what happened to him."

"He probably got jumped," Harry said, shrugging.

"I don't think that's it," I replied, making eye contact with him.

"That's the 'it has something to do with the spooky house' face."

I nodded slowly. "We have a winner. Before your kids show up, go to the Hytte."

"Why?" he asked slowly, if not apprehensively.

"Don't freak out," I said quietly. "But Lukas is there, and he'll show you what we've found."

"You're down the rabbit hole, through the looking glass, whatever, but not in reality," Harry hissed, just loud enough to be audible.

"Harry, you're doing the wilderness retreat with me. We're going to be up there, near where all this stuff has happened. You should know what's going on." I started to doubt that it was even remotely safe, but there would be kids dedicated to this cause there, as well as some not so dedicated. It would be an interesting thing to juggle.

"Why do you have to be nuts?" he asked with a heavy sigh. I didn't reply. I wasn't angry with him. It was just a matter of getting through each hour and each day. Nonetheless, I wanted him involved.

"While I get kids signed in, just look at the evidence. You can decide for yourself," I replied, feeling a lurch in my stomach.

He sighed, noncommittally. "I'll look, though wish me luck so I don't deck Lukas in the face."

"Please don't," I said.

"Fine," he said, all drawn out and disappointed.

Jenny and her dad entered Clark. She was nearly his height. Her long, blonde hair lay across her oversized t-shirt. I noticed her flip flops immediately and sighed. "Jenny, you have to have closed toed shoes," I said.

"Ah, shit," her dad said. Keith Gentry and his daughter resembled each other only in the eyes. Other than that, she was taller, slimmer, and had electric energy around her. He had a much more tired and sluggish air about him. "Come on, change your shoes, Genevieve."

"Don't call me that," she said, rolling her eyes. There was a slight look of disgust on her face, but it was usually there. She put down the water bottle she'd been chewing on to change out her shoes.

"So she's in your cabin this week," Keith said. "I hope she doesn't cause too many problems. We've talked about it dozens of times." He had his hands on his hips, a slight paunch exceeding his dad shorts. Once again, Jenny rolled her eyes. She fist-bumped him, and then went on the porch to join Gracia, the only other camper here in that age group. "I think she's still a little ticked off about the late night intervention, claiming that she hated the horse program, wanted nothing to do with it, and thankfully they got her switched over. You've known her for a while, so I hope this is a good fit."

"I'm hopeful," I lied. He handed over a stack of bills for the canteen and camp store and left. Jenny was struggling to get a phone signal, and when that failed, her face pouted a tad more and she watched Gracia strum away at her ukelele.

"Hey, I'm going to be in Hawthorne this week," Jenny said.

Gracia lightened up, surprisingly. "So, don't ask too many questions about this, but, here," Gracia opened her bag up and dug around until she got out a necklace. "It's quartz. Wear it."

Jenny looked pleasantly amused by the gift and slipped it over her head. The girls must have had quite the conversation about how to protect themselves from this place to bring in the big guns: crystals and salt circles. I didn't know what would be next, but I hoped I'd get one of those necklaces. "Thanks, it's awesome," Jenny said.

"Just don't take it off while you're here," Gracia said.

I hoped Jenny would fit in well in Hawthorne, and for the most part, she wasn't immediately a problem. She kind of threw her stuff together haphazardly, which didn't work with the girls who were just as obsessed with getting the cleanest cabin award, yet again, as me, that they practically made her bunk up for her. "I don't get the point!" Jenny whined. "It's just a stripe!"

"We don't lose!" Sadie said gruffly. "And we're not about to start now!"

"Ugh, boring!" she said, flopping onto her bunk. "When are we going to do something fun? When are we going to the pool?"

Ellie buried her head in her hands, trying to calm herself down. Where Jenny's energy came from, I didn't know, but I needed some of it for myself.

"Is it four yet?" Jenny asked.

"No," I said. "We'll go to the pool when it's time. Right now, we need to figure out what we are going to do for cabin night, and for the cookout."

"Did Mr. Ezra like his banner?" Ellie asked.

"Loved it," I said. "It brightens up the room a lot."

"What about him?" Jenny asked. All the girls' eyes turned to her. "What? Oh . . . the guy out of the lake? Yeah, he's alive?"

"Yes, he's alive," I said. "The girls were nice enough to make him a banner for his hospital room while he recovers." There was a long pause and she started to gnaw on the straw of her water bottle again. "Well, there's a few things we haven't done recently. We haven't gone on a night swim—"

"Yes! That!" Jenny called, hands in the air, making a strange dance move.

"Uh, does everyone agree that a night swim would sound like fun?" I asked if there was the general consensus that yes, it would be, and that we should see if the boys in Cherry, Peter's cabin, would like to join. I marked that down in my notebook and continued on. "Ok, for our next order of business, cookout plans. Last week worked sort of well. I was thinking we could do something a bit more adventurous this time." With each word, I was flowing back into the pattern of 'camp counselor' rather than continuing to panic. Putting this face on, and this voice, allowed me to step outside of myself for a while, while autopilot took over.

"Can we do pie-iron stuff?" Lisey asked. "Like pizzas and pies."

"All agreed?"

Chapter Eighteen: August 7, 2016

"Ugh, boring!" Jenny said. Eyes fell on her again.

"You don't like pizza?" Sadie asked, genuinely amazed.

"We have pizza on Thursdays, it's boring," Jenny said.

"What about cinnamon rolls in a pie iron," I said, thinking back to the one time I made it maybe ten years ago. I couldn't remember if it worked or not.

"With frosting?" she asked.

"You'd have to add it on after it's cooked, but yeah," I said.

"Oh yeah!" Another dance move. I didn't understand this girl. This was energy reserved for kids during their first week at camp, not suffering through the heat and constant activity for nearly three months. It should have tempered her by now.

"For those of you who are going on the wilderness retreat with Mr. Harry and I later this summer, I would recommend you start gathering a list of your favorite meals that can be cooked over a fire so we can purchase the correct ingredients. Remember, nothing can be refrigerated. That's for Jenny, Gracia, and Kennedy, I believe. There is still time to sign up if anyone else wants to join."

"No thank you," Ellie said. "I will happily be home with my indoor plumbing and cats."

"I want to, but my parents said not until I'm older," Sadie said, deflated, arms crossed.

"Can we go hiking?" Jenny asked.

"Like during the retreat or . . .?"

"No, like this week, I want to go up to that old church by the horse place," she said. I didn't know of a church.

"Uh, if you sign up for orienteering, we sure can," I said.

"Isn't that maps and compasses and stuff like that?" she asked.

"Yep,"

"Ugh, boring." She scrunched her face up, and looked down to her hands as if there was a phone there. "We could do it after dinner, like today."

"It didn't know there was an old church here," Kennedy said.

"Neither did I," Gracia added.

"Yeah, I've seen it a few times, it looks pretty cool, it's even got this wall and gate around it." She sort-of mimed what she was talking about. "One of the other girls in my cabin and I found it when we saw it light up. Someone must have been in there, so we didn't go in."

"I'll be right back," I said, and left the cabin. I typed a message to Lukas: *Do you know anything about a church or chapel on the property?*

I pretended I was going to the restroom and waited. Lukas: *Yes, there's a lot about it here. What do you want to know?*

Me: *What is it? Why?*

Lukas: *Looks like the Halversons weren't welcome in town because of where they settled. They were devout Lutherans. It was built before the turn of the century. Looks like all the children were born in it. The family cemetery is outside of it, gated in. A woman named Inne refused to leave the chapel at some point, even when the land became a camp, she didn't leave. They held chapel services up there until 1989.*

Me: *Would it be safe to go there? Girls want to hike to it.*

Lukas: *No clue, but I'm finding a lot of weird things. It looks like no male child born on the property ever lived. Only girls born inside of the chapel lived. They also had a hell of a time getting a preacher over to bless the place, and the children.*

Me: *How accurate do you think that is?*

Lukas: *Statistics, my favorite, I'll see.*

Jenny appeared to be in her element when it came to the pool. She jumped in the lane for laps and just went back and forth. I was expecting her to pull a Ryanne and sit on the edge of the pool with a look of grumpiness on her face. While I was playing Rat Slap with Eddy and Arty, Gracia came up and asked, "Can we go hiking to that chapel? I texted Noah and he said even he'd never been there."

"You have your phone?" I asked.

Chapter Eighteen: August 7, 2016

"That's what you took out of that sentence?" She crossed her arms. I had my hand over the pile of cards because the boys tried to continue the game without me.

"Can you two be patient for a second?" I asked. It was our usual Sunday afternoon time at the pool. We were here every Sunday at four o'clock playing this game. It wouldn't be the last round; they could hold their horses for just a moment.

"Ugh!" Arty said, leaning back. "I'm going to get burnt out here for nothing!"

"They should come!" Gracia said, pointing at them. "Mr. Peter's cabin."

"Where are we going?" Eddy asked.

"Some creepy chapel near the horse pastures," Gracia replied, using the exact words to entice Eddy's interest.

"Ah come on, Grace," I said.

"Oh, when are we going?" Eddy asked. "I'm in!"

"You're in for what?" Peter asked, half walking past us, half listening in.

I sighed. "Do you want to go on a hike tomorrow for unit night and then do a night swim?"

"I heard- creepy chapel," Peter said. "I don't want to go to a creepy chapel."

"Ah come on, Mr. Peter, you don't need to be such a wimp!" Eddy said.

"That's rude," I replied. "Don't make me take the cards away from you." He held them protectively.

"This place is weird enough as it is," Peter said.

"Miss Laurel can take us," Eddy said. "Whoever wants to go,"

"Ratios, Eddy, ratios. I'm only allowed to take eight of you," I said.

"I'm sure not everyone wants to go," Eddy said, his eyes were so bright, and he was terribly excited. Almost trembling with excitement... That kid needed a chill pill. Peter sat down on the one remaining seat; his towel draped around his neck. He kept looking over at Harry on the tall lifeguard stand. He could barely keep his eyes off him.

"Somebody's in love," Arty said, smirking. Peter turned a deep red color and put his sopping wet face on the table.

"Don't get my cards wet!" I cried, taking the cards away, out of the splash zone.

"If y'all would just leave me alone about all this." Peter put his hands up in the air like he was surrendering.

"If you'd stop drooling all over him, it'd be much easier," Arty added.

Peter pulled his fingers through his hair and said, "How about Miss Laurel and I take a moment to talk about unit night. Ok? Go." He waved them off and they trotted off. When they were out of earshot and in the water, we went through a plan for the following evening. I'd take the kids who wanted to go on the hike with me, up to eight of them, and the rest would have a bonfire, and wait at House Two. Afterwards, we would go swimming. "Sounds perfect. I don't have to go to a crazy building. You can do whatever the hell you want, and then: swimming." He seemed relieved. "And tonight, spaghetti."

Chapter Nineteen:

August 7, 2016

Late that evening, after I'd been asleep for about an hour, my phone buzzed from a text, waking me up. I looked at the screen and saw Lukas's name and photo. Groggily I got out of bed and sat outside. He joined me, walking up the hill with a pile of papers he couldn't possibly read in this light.

"Let's go over to the restrooms, easier to see over there," he whispered. "So I have a list of all the people who came from Rogaland, Norway." I followed him to the opposite side of the restrooms where the floodlights gave us something to see by. "We have the patriarch, Harald Halverson, and his wife Inne and their children and their children's spouses—Espen, Ingrid, Rasmus, Kjerstin, Sylvi, and Michael. As well as Harald's brother Henrik and his wife Dorothea, and their children Finn, Nora, Mari, and Tobias. Then we have Inne's sister Linnea and her husband Anders. Amalie, who is listed as the first director of Camp Kellova, is their daughter. They started having kids in 1894. In March we had a stillborn boy from Espen and Ingrid, later that year another stillborn baby came from Linnea and Anders Nilsen and was a boy. The first live birth was in June of 1896 from Finn and Nora, and her name was Karolina. Here's the whole list." The list was written by hand in a scrawling, uneven script.

Births to 1904
March 2nd, 1894, baby boy, still born son of Espen and Ingrid Halverson
December 22nd, 1894, still born son of Linnea and Anders Nilsen
June 6th, 1896, Karolina Berg, daughter born to Finn and Nora Berg
September 21st, 1896, Else Olsen, daughter born to Michael and Sylvi Ol-
sen

October 27th, 1897, Katrine Halverson, daughter born to Espen and Ingrid Halverson

November 11th, 1898, Esther and Elisabeth Berg, baby girls born to Michael and Sylvi Olsen

January 24th, 1899, still born son born to Tobias and Mari Dahl

February 1st, 1900, Charlotte Berg, daughter born to Finn and Nora Berg

November 30th, 1900, Brigita Halverson, daughter born to Rasmus and Kjerstin Halverson

May 16th, 1901, Ina Olsen, daughter born to Michael and Sylvi Olsen

September 18th, 1902, Ella Dahl, daughter, born to Tobias and Mari Dahl.

"So, no sons survived," I said. "Up to 1904."

"This lists all births and deaths up to 1957, and there are no boys who survived. Absolutely zero," Lukas said. "Isn't that odd?"

"They still bred like rabbits," I replied, shaking my head. "Especially that Michael and Sylvi duo."

"I think you're missing the point," Lukas said. "Amalie later stated that she didn't believe that this place was safe for men at all."

"But the only camper I know who has died here was Haley, a girl," I replied.

"I spoke to Noah, and he said that he's digging up the deaths of other campers from way back when, and they do seem to be mixed, but men die at a much higher rate than women. Perhaps there was some kind of curse specifically directed toward men on this land."

"Do you think it was made by the Otoe?" I asked.

He shook his head. "The House used to be a wigwam, and it was here when the Otoe were here. When the Otoe left, it became a cabin, like a log cabin." He pulled out a different piece of paper. It was copied from a notebook but showed a drawing of a log cabin. From the drawing it looked like a reasonable dwelling, with no strange angles or too many windows/doors. "This is what was there when they moved in. Harald described it initially as feeling malicious, like it was from the devil. It eventually gained the name *Huset til Fruktbarhet* or *Hus forbannet*, house of curses, or house of barrenness."

"Do you have information from the beginning?" I asked.

"Yeah, up to 1904 is what I've dug up so far. They purchased the land in 1891 and planned on farming it. Within the next two years, livestock went missing, and if they were found, the animals were mutilated with incorrect body proportions, or pieces missing. He saw strange wolf and cat-like creatures. He was warned by the locals that the land wasn't safe, and it was cursed by the tribe who lived on the land." He opened another folder and had many photographs.

"This is the Halverson clan when they moved in." Most of the initial photographs were family portraits.

The first was of Harald and Inne Halverson, it said they were aged 50 and 48 respectively. Harald had a small, well-groomed beard, and a very angular face. He did not look like an overly calm or kind man, but he looked like he could handle anything. Inne, on the other hand, had a soft face with extremely bright, intelligent eyes that looked as though she could see right into anyone. Harald stood behind her with his hands on her shoulders. She had one hand on his, showing a small bit of affection.

The next cardboard like photograph was of Espen and Ingrid Halverson, closer to their time of marriage than when they came to the United States. Espen had short-sheared hair with a nice shirt on. He was almost smiling in his photograph and his arm was around his wife, Ingrid. She had elaborately braided hair that was close to her skull. She looked so young and beautiful. It was strange to see these faces and know they were no longer around, in fact, they were probably buried on this property.

The photograph Lukas produced of Amalie Nilsen made her look like a very stern, strong individual. Her hair was dark, loose, and it lay on her shoulders. It was very thick. It matched her dark eyes. She didn't look like most of her family, including her parents, Anders and Linnea Nilsen. Linnea was a gorgeous, bubbly looking woman.

"Keep going," Lukas said. One of the only photographs of an infant was that of Charlotte Berg, in 1900, with her parents, Finn and Nora Berg, and her sisters, Karolina, Esther, and Elisabeth.

After the family portraits, there were photographs taken at the actual homestead. Hanging from a tree was a very strange animal. It appeared to be a large wolf, though there were no wolves in Iowa then or now. It had extremely long legs, scraggly fur, and an extended muzzle. It was hooked up by its rear paws with Harald Halverson standing beside it.

"What is it?" I asked.

"The back of the photograph says it is a beast he caught going after the swine, actually written as: *beist fanget mens han spiste griser*," Lukas said. "There's more." There was what used to be a mountain lion on the ground, its massive head held open by a stake. A normal mountain lion would be roughly eighty pounds, but this looked like it was three times that size with legs that were bent and broken. "This photograph says that this cat was attacking their house. Not the animals, the family home."

There were more photographs of mutilated animals, and crop damage. "Harald wrote in some letters that no one would buy any excess goods they produced. They were going to do some logging in the area, but decided not to because there would be no buyers. In the same letter he says his beloved dogs had been barking at these orbs in the forest, but every time they caught one, they'd yelp and cower." There was even a photograph of Harald with his dogs. They looked like Heelers.

"In an 1894 letter, he says none of their chickens hatched. Two women in the family give birth to stillborn sons. Harald was angry and so he and some of the other men in the family decided to burn down the cabin, but it didn't catch fire, but a great wind came, and his crops instead burned, and they had a hell of a winter," Lukas said, pointing to a photograph of a burnt field with the remnants of stalks bent and broken.

"The next year, his family members, mainly women, suffered from hysteria-like symptoms. Well, he called it hysteria at least, as well as fatigue, and stomach problems. No doctors would see them. Linnea, who is Inne's sister, ended up getting so ill she died. She's buried by Lost Lake, and they erected a standing stone in her memory," he said. There was a photograph with Harald, Inne, Anders, and Amalie near the standing stone which looked like it belonged in sixth century Sweden.

"She was buried there because Inne had a dream that Lost Lake was where Linnea needed to go. Inne then had dreams that they needed to build a chapel, and so they did, north-east of their home. Inne swore she felt safe there. Henrik Halverson was a carpenter by trade, and he built it. It was named Kirke Tilflukt or Church of Refuge. Eventually they developed a belief that only children born inside the Kirke would live. The first one was Finn and Nora Berg's daughter Karolina. Michael and Sylvi had a child later that year named Else."

"In 1897 things started badly, he claimed that with so many mouths to feed, they had to hunt, trap, and sell semi-precious stones, mainly chalcedony, quartz, and calcite. They finally got some success raising turkeys, and selling feathers, furs, pelts, and stones to native people. The native people in the area are the Dakota who call themselves the Oceti Sakowin, and the Oteo. Basically, the only way they could make money and bring home food was to travel far. The women noticed that the crazy activity quieted down when the men were gone."

"That's so strange," I said. He showed me the records Harald kept, but they were all in Norwegian. Most of them were translated. "Can you still read Norwegian?" His grandparents were from Norway, and spoke it at home, but he wasn't exactly home a lot.

"For the most part. Also, I found out that Harald kept each receipt of sale, wrote down every animal born or hatched and was meticulous. Paranoid really is a better word for it. He was trying to keep his family alive when the land was actively trying to kill them. They had nowhere else to go. They put all their money into this venture." Lukas looked at me, grasping the papers. I hadn't seen him this excited about or focused on something in ages. I loved seeing that light in his eyes. A light which told me he was still there and still fighting.

"So in 1898 all crops except for beans and squash appeared to go black overnight and were eaten from the inside out. Harald managed to contact an Otoe who agreed to come visit him. The Otoe man was a Quaker, and only would visit with him inside the chapel after he blessed it himself. This man, who wasn't named, told Harald that there was a curse sealed inside the cabin. It could not be controlled, but it had to be contained or it would spread. He made the point that the Halversons don't 'own' the land as land cannot be owned, but they were the caretakers of it. Malice and rage breathed inside the cabin, something that eats energy, all of it, especially that of which it is made- fear." Lukas's eyes twinkled with interest. He held tightly onto the leather bound journal.

"When the Otoe left, they faced extinction. They believed in the universal spirit, and believed the land around the cabin, or at their time, wigwam, meant something either sacred or cursed by this spirit. The man refers to his people as the Jiwere. He said they were forced to move off this desirable land and to Red Rock Oklahoma, but that to find the object which could hold all the malice and fear inside the house, to give it energy, would be a way to keep it contained, and that they had to devise protective measures." Lukas stopped for a moment and opened the journal again, flipping through the flimsy pages, touching the deep pressed writing.

"So Harald and Anders searched for this object. Anders blamed the house for the death of his wife, Linnea. Whatever they were looking for, they didn't find it. The day after they did their digging, they took axes to the house and noted how much it fought against the blades. The day after that, the places they had chopped were healed. So they tried filling the cabin with dirt, but the dirt was expelled. They salted the earth, but grass still grew there. Then, Anders was found dead inside the cabin. He was just lying on the ground, as if he'd fallen asleep. He was buried beside the chapel. Later that year, three more kids were born on the property, Finn and Nora Berg had twins, Elisabeth and Esther, and then Sasha Olsen was born to Michael and Sylvi."

"This is documented? That the house fought off axes, dirt, and salt?" I asked.

"There's a picture of Harald with the Otoe man, and then of a pile of dirt beside the cabin, but that's all I could find," Lukas said, eager to keep telling me the story.

"So in 1899, in January, Mari and Tobias had a stillborn boy. Later in the year, Mari got pregnant again with Lia, who would be born in December. However, Tobias was found mauled while hunting by an animal that then appeared to fall dead of its own volition. It was Henrik who found him, but he couldn't describe the animal saying it didn't look like a cat or dog or bear, but it was some kind of predator he'd never encountered before. He drew a picture." There certainly was a picture of an animal with a very prominent hunch on its back and a protruding spine. The paws were large enough they could have been reminiscent of a bear, but nothing else matched. There was little fur. In fact, the doodle made it look patchy in some places, with long pointed ears like a cat, but a very canine looking mouth.

"After seeing this thing, Henrik went to the house and blatantly cursed it, and later in the year he died from some weird variant of smallpox." Lukas shook his head. "That's insane, isn't it?"

I nodded. There was a photograph of Henrik, I assumed, on his deathbed, covered in that pox, looking distantly past the camera. He may have already been dead.

"Mari, who lost both her father and brother, planted the calla lilies around the clearing in their honor, or as a way to appease the cabin or house. I think there's a note in here where they were all surprised that the lilies grew and flourished," he said.

"I'd be surprised too," I added.

"The only one listed as being born this year is Margareta Halverson to Rasmus and Kjerstin Halverson. Even with all this nonsense they're still having kids left and right." Lukas chuckled a bit.

"Maybe they didn't have birth control?" I asked, shrugging.

"Maybe, I don't really know what they had access to. Either way, after all this madness, in 1900, Inne was so obsessed with the chapel, she refused to leave its grounds. She meticulously gardened it and the graveyard. She finally got a pastor to baptize the kids. He was Lutheran I believe, and also spoke Norwegian." Lukas flipped through the papers and showed baptismal certificates written in Norwegian.

"This year the family had two more, Charlotte was born to Finn and Nora, and then Brigita to Rasmus and Kjerstin. Baptizing everyone over again didn't seem to have any effect because the next year Michael, Sylvi's husband, was found dead, hanging halfway out a window of the cabin in March, shortly after his daughter Ina was born."

"What happened to him?" I asked. He looked through the pile of records as if he could find a photograph.

"They didn't do an autopsy or anything. There was no formal complaint filed about his death, just that he died. It's written that he was drawn to the house and died of fright, but I don't know if someone can be actually scared to death," Lukas said.

"We know that it can draw people in though . . ." I replied, thinking of Haley's feet in the air and Noah's screams. A shiver ran through me.

"Someone had the right idea though, Sylvi ended up leaving with Else and Sasha for Decorah, but left Ina for some reason, so it's like Amalie adopted her. Some of the young girls of the family were caught sleepwalking. Crops and animals were still struggling. The next odd thing that happened is that Rasmus is found dead with an ax in his skull while cutting wood all *And Then There Were None* style. So, in an attempt to protect themselves, the family members built a fence around the chapel and carved symbols of protection and prayers into it. Amalie also noted that she saw a woman around the land that looks just like her mother, Linnea."

"So, do you think the girl on the hill is her?" I asked.

He took a deep breath and sighed. "I don't know. She was much older than the girl looked when she died, but maybe it's a younger version of her? It's not like we can ask."

"Riley called her Alina, that's nearly a conglomeration of the name Linnea," I said.

"That's a stretch, even for you, Laurel," he said, chuckling.

"Well, she had to come from somewhere and she doesn't look Native American, wearing all that lace and stuff."

"So she regressed back to thirteen years old and started hitting on a camper?" he asked, now with his eyes up and a look of amusement on his face.

"This whole thing is messed up. It wouldn't be the most messed up part, now would it?"

"No . . . I suppose it wouldn't. Ok, let me keep going or I'll lose my train of thought. None of that was weird stuff though. In 1903 someone found numerous dead animals by the house in the clearing, wild and domestic, including a whole herd of deer. Most of the women told the men that the animals should be left alone, but the men didn't listen. They went ahead and tried to salvage what they could by skinning and cleaning them. By the next day, all the men were found dead. Every last one of them. Dead, in the clearing, just lying around like the animals were." My brain went blank for a moment, trying to imagine how an entire family could be removed from the face of the earth in one day. Clearly, something ticked the house off. "So, that's when Harald's records end, and I need to start piecing together other people's information," Lukas said.

"Damn. And we're on this land."

"Yep," he replied. "I'm hoping Noah will find an answer as to what those dolls were, and about the Otoe and the curses. In the meantime, I have a lot to do."

"Do you have enough food in there?" I asked.

"Food and water. Affirmative. If I'm running low, I can either sneak out or give you a text. Since Harry and Mia know I'm here, hopefully one of you three can help." He laughed a bit.

"What did Harry think when he saw all this?" I asked.

"He didn't say anything clearly, just kind of stammered a lot. He asked where I got all of this and asked if it was a joke. I told him I got the information from Gary. He was surprised we survived a trip to Gary's house. I didn't tell him everything about what happened up there since he was already pretty freaked out but said that these were from the Halverson family who were on the land prior to the camp's existence. He just kept saying how crazy this was."

"Poor kid," I said, shaking my head. "Didn't freak out seeing you?"

"He accused me of taking advantage of you and said I had no right to be here . . ." Lukas added, shrugging.

"Harry . . ."

"He has a point," Lukas defended, which was very unlike him. Usually he'd argue, saying he had every right to do everything, practically.

"Ok, well, I'm sure he'll have something to say to me tomorrow when I see him," I said. My heart beat quickly in my chest when I thought of the Halversons. "I actually feel pretty weird about all this."

"If you didn't, I'd wonder what was wrong with you," he said. "Well, I already do, but you know what I mean."

"Thanks, Lukas," I said sarcastically, but part of me was genuine. "Hopefully the chapel will be safe to hike to tomorrow."

"It doesn't make sense that you would purposefully go somewhere like that."

"But since I am, I can corroborate your story. I can get the evidence that all of this happened. It'll be on the gravestones."

"True," he said. "Get some sleep or you'll turn into the walking dead."

"I already feel that way," I replied, and hugged him tightly, but the feeling of wholeness never came. I didn't feel like anything, not even destroying this house would make me feel whole again.

Peeling myself out of bed was a near impossible task that morning after the long talk with Lukas.

Still, I managed to get the girls up and moving. I idly brushed my hair, and watched Jenny cover her face with a pillow and refuse to move. "Come on, Jenny, both of us need to get going," I said, speaking, but speaking and doing were two vastly different things. So, I got ready. "Jenny, come on," I said. By that time, I was dressed and looked mostly put together. She hadn't moved from her sleeping bag. Revelry, which was basically the 'oh shit' alarm, would sound any second.

"This isn't funny, Jenny, we're all tired, but seriously, we have to get ready." My patience was already thin, names and dates spun around in circles in my mind.

When revelry sounded, she finally got moving, and thankfully, she spent no time getting ready. She pulled on a pair of shorts, another oversized t-shirt, and slipped her shoes on. She clearly didn't plan on brushing or combing anything. I could deal with that after breakfast. "Let's go," I said.

"Do you have any coffee?" she asked while we were crossing the bridge.

"Negatory," I said.

"Ugh." I supposed that was her favorite phrase. She reminded me of a troll in that way. I wondered how Mia survived so many weeks of this. Or how her parents managed. Ellie looked like an easy camper to deal with next to her, and in fact, Ellie was, in fact, easy to manage at the moment.

Despite Jenny's disdain for getting up in the morning, she jumped right into a game of gaga with Lisey and Jane. "She didn't brush her teeth," Ellie complained.

"She can after breakfast," I said.

"During cabin cleanup? What if she doesn't clean?" she asked.

"Let's hope she does," I said. "Do you want to play garbage?" She nodded and we sat on the floor of the deck surrounding Clark, each placing ten cards in front of us.

"Are you teaching arts and crafts this week?" Ellie asked, looking up through her black-rimmed glasses.

"Yep."

"Why not Miss Leta?"

"Miss Leta decided she wanted to teach nature instead," I said. It wasn't a complete lie. Leta did want to teach nature, but she mostly wanted to get the hell away from Apple. With what I saw in those photographs and at Gary's, a ghost version of Riley hiding out in a bathroom was the least of my worries.

"Is she teaching nature art?" Ellie asked.

"That's me too," I said. No one who heard anything about the phantom boy wanted to be near Apple. I was the only one who'd take the class, and it was a class we didn't have the option to get rid of.

"Leta will be teaching lapidary this week if you want to finish your packet for your advanced honor."

"I think I will," she said. "It'll be the first one I get done. I started on beading too, so I'll work on that this week. I want to get one in music sometime, but I don't like when it's Miss Asia teaching, and she's had it the past few weeks."

"It's Miss Coral this week if that helps." Her face lit up a bit. She used a queen card to steal my ace and win that hand. I sighed. "How do you get such good luck all the time?"

"Maybe you just keep getting bad luck!" she exclaimed.

"Isn't that the truth."

Back at the cabin for cabin clean up, after the girls signed up for their classes, I won the battle of getting Jenny to brush her teeth. The next battle was to get her to clean her bunk. Her clothes and other such items had exploded everywhere. Thankfully she didn't have more than the other girls and it was a reasonable amount of stuff to manage, but in a cabin that was usually spotless, it was pretty jarring to see.

"Jenny, we've won every single week this summer, and we've gotta keep up this streak. We can't let Mr. Harry win against us because he's always only a few points behind," I said. If I could, I'd appeal to her competitive side. "Not only have we won the most stripes, but this cabin has the most poles, and the most wins consecutively of any cabin. We lost the first two weeks this summer to Bird cabins, little kids, but we aren't going to lose again."

"Yeah!" A few of the girls cheered.

Jenny looked vaguely amused and went to work. Her morning laziness abated. She and Gracia worked together to get underneath the bunks with a broom and sweep out a few pounds of dust and dirt that were hiding. She even took some water and scrubbed the walls. I was befuddled, in a good way. Impressed, even. "I assume I don't sweep away the salt, right?" she said, holding her broom at the doorway, staring at it.

"No!" Lisey cried. Surprised she made that loud noise, she covered her mouth and stood there. "Sorry, didn't mean to yell. Let's keep the salt."

"Don't you think Miss Carra will dock us for that being on the front door?" Jenny asked. "I mean I overheard her complaining about you guys taking it . . . so she might have a cow."

"Good point," Kennedy said, looking perplexed. Then they all looked at me.

Chapter Nineteen: August 7, 2016

"I honestly have no clue what to do. The salt helps everyone sleep, but no one wants to lose the contest." I paused. "Contest be darned?"

"After that speech?" Gracia asked. "I'm sure we can figure something out, right? We could cover it with a welcome mat or something."

"What about the giant one surrounding the whole place?" Jenny asked. "Looks like you're trying to keep away demons or vampires or something."

"Or something," Lisey added, muttering.

Jenny looked not the least bit concerned. She shrugged and carefully swept around the salt. "Do we have a welcome mat somewhere?" she asked. This was about as calm as I'd ever seen her.

"I . . . I'm not . . . uh," Lisey stammered. "What if it welcomes something in?"

Kennedy's eyebrows raised and most of us looked at her. Kennedy asked, "What do you mean?"

"It's a welcome mat. It says welcome," she said.

"The ones in the bathroom are for scraping mud off shoes, so that would work," I said.

"Good enough," Gracia said, and went in that direction.

I stretched out my soft, fuzzy, purple blanket until it was completely taut. My pillows were properly fluffed. The girls wouldn't even sit on their bunk when all was cleaned, they sat in the middle of the cabin. "Have you played Mafia, Jenny?" I asked.

"I want to be the narrator!" she exclaimed.

"I guess you have played before!" I said, sitting down to join the others in a circle.

"Ok, everyone, close your eyes. One tap for the mafia, two taps for the doctor, three taps for the sheriff." She repeated the mantra as she went around us in a circle. Our eyes were closed, and she made very quiet movements. I felt a singular tap on my head. I was the mafia. Earlier in June, we played mafia with everyone in camp. It was the longest, funniest game I'd ever played. My mom was the narrator and since she knew everyone, it was very creative.

"Ok, only the mafia, wake up," she said. I opened my eyes and smiled at her. "Who would you like to kill?" I deliberated for a while, but I knew getting rid of the most logical person in the group would be to my advantage. I motioned, as silently as I could, to Kennedy. She nodded. "Mafia, go to sleep. Doctor, wake up . . . who would you like to save?" Whoever the doctor was, they had the option of saving someone, though they didn't know who the target was. "Ok, now go back to sleep. Sheriff, wake up. Who would you like to accuse?" The sheriff could accuse a person of being the mafia, and the narrator could nod yes or no. "Ok, everyone wake-up." Everyone opened their eyes and raised their heads.

"So it was a bright and beautiful morning, there were no clouds in the sky, and Kennedy was going out on a walk to the library to get herself a new book."

"Ah come on," Kennedy said.

"She knew that the library was locked, so she had bolt cutters with her that she took from the garage. When she went into the library, the mafia was waiting for her, and pushed one of the big bookcases down on her and she died." Jenny was brimming with a weird sort of glee. Kennedy made a large show of playing dead. "Ok, so now you have to be silent, but you can watch the rest of it." Kennedy scooched back from her spot and crossed her arms and legs.

"Who do you guys accuse?" Jenny asked.

"Lisey was moving around a lot," Sadie said. "I think it was her."

"I don't like sitting on the floor, but that doesn't mean I did it!" Lisey exclaimed.

"Well, I'm the sheriff, so it wasn't me," Gracia said.

"You could be lying," I replied.

"Why would I be lying?" she asked, smirking.

"To save your hide," I said.

"She has a point!" Lisey said.

"You sure are defensive," Jane said.

"Because I didn't do it," she said. "Sadie was quick to point fingers, so I'll say it was her."

"I still think it was you," I said.

Jenny asked, "All who vote for Lisey?" Over half of us raised our hands. "Ok, Lisey is in jail. She can watch, but she can't say anything. She was not the mafia."

"I told you!" Lisey exclaimed, moving to sit beside Kennedy." Now that there was suspicion about both Gracia and Sadie, I had to avoid picking one of them. So when it came time to pick, I went with Ellie.

"Ok, so it was evening, after everyone went to shower. Ellie spent an extra-long time in front of the mirror, making sure her hair was just right and that her face was washed. While she was doing that, she didn't notice that the mafia let in a giant, venomous spider that bit her. There was nothing the doctor could do because she was the doctor, and she didn't have any antivenom!"

Ellie sighed heavily. "Great, and I had my own suspicions."

"Well, keep them to yourself," Jenny said. "Any accusations?"

"I still think it's Sadie," Gracia said.

"And I think it's you," Sadie replied.

"If you're the sheriff, you should know who it is," I said to Gracia.

"All I know is that it isn't Ellie, and it wasn't Kennedy, so I got nothing," Gracia said, which automatically made Jane my next target. She wasn't under any suspicion. Sadie and Gracia bickered between them while the rest of us watched them. They were both so sure they were right, which meant one of them was going to jail. Eventually it was Sadie that landed in jail.

"Congratulations, you sent an innocent townsperson to jail," Jenny said. "You guys are bad at this. Back to sleep." As I closed my eyes, I saw someone in a red hat walk behind her outside the window.

The day went well. Arts and Crafts was fun. I planned on making sun-catchers with the pounds and pounds of clear pony beads we had available. For the kids getting their beading honors, they were working on making a beaded bracelet with seed beads. Everyone else needed a project.

To make the suncatchers, I opened the windows around the ancient oven, and the kids arranged their beads into a muffin tray with one missing bead for the string to go through. Back at the Hytte, I had a good dozen or so of them hanging around my windows, mostly ones given to me by kids. They gave a nice colorful atmosphere to the place.

Once in the oven, though, the melting beads gave off a very toxic smell that wafted out of windows using our fans pointing toward the oven and the window. While they melted, we worked on a bit more reasonable crafts using perler beads, the tiny tubular ones that could be placed on trays in various shapes. It wasn't the best project for littles, but I didn't have anyone under the age of nine with me. So I sat at a table with an iron and some wax paper, flattening out the perler bead creations, churning them out at a surprising rate.

"Hey, Miss Laurel!" Temple called, staring out the back window, near the oven. "Come 'ere!"

I turned off the iron and stood up. There was a line of kids who wanted their perler bead creations done. "Can I do it?" Jenny asked.

"Just be really careful," I said. "You know how to check to see if they're done." That was against my better judgment, or rather, any of my judgment, but Temple's voice radiated fear. She was on the tiptoes of her sneakered feet.

She pointed at a figure walking through the thick brush. It was a ghillie suit. Gary. "What is it?" she asked.

"It's one of our neighbors up the hill," I said.

"Why does he look like that?" Ellie asked, behind me. I jumped a bit, startled.

"I wish I knew." I checked the oven. The suncatchers in there were finished, so I switched them out, and placed the muffin tin aside to cool.

"Ok, Ellie, don't let anyone touch the oven or the suncatchers. I'm going to see what Gary's doing and tell him to leave," I said.

I hurried out the backdoor of Apple and toward Gary. "What are you doing?" I called. "Gary! Come here!"

He looked at me, though I couldn't see his facial expression. I stepped away from the window so the girls couldn't see if they were staring out the window. "Yes, Miss Winters?" he asked. His voice sounded odd. I didn't like the sound of it.

"You're freaking out the campers. They can see you."

"I was on the trail of something," he said.

"What?"

"Riley Stevens," he replied easily.

"Real Riley?"

"No, I don't think so, but I want to see where it's going," he said, turning away, going north. The word 'it' was strange in this scenario since 'it' still resembled a child.

I watched Gary for a while until he blended in with the foliage around him. I wanted to follow him and see this 'Riley' for myself, but I had to go back inside. The girls were, as I expected, standing at the windows.

"So there's a guy who walks around here like that?" Ellie asked. I nodded.

"It's ok, he's safe," I replied, moving to sit down at my spot by the iron.

"I'm doing it!" Jenny said.

"You sure?" I asked. She nodded, focusing. If I could get her to focus on anything nondestructive, it was good. In the past she'd experimented with mixing various substances together in Apple to make gloopy liquids or sprinkling glitter over everything. This was basically harmless.

In the hallway I texted Lukas: *Gary said he's seen Riley and is following him. He was just by Apple.*

Lukas: *Really?*

Me: *It might not really be Riley. It might just be what I saw, a spirit of him.*

Lukas: *Like a ghost or something?*

Me: *I think to have ghosts the person would have to be dead. Maybe a projection made by the house?*

Lukas: *Does Gary know I'm staying at the Hytte? I didn't tell him where I was going.*

Me: *No, but if you wanted to go find him, you could see what's going on.*

Lukas: *Hiking with Gary. Sounds like the title of a horror movie.*

Me: *He's in a ghillie suit.*

Lukas: *I don't want to know why.*

At Lunch, Jenny sat next to me, and we played cards while waiting for our table to be called for food. It was Peter's turn to handle the mic. He was very awkward, but he was trying. Jenny was totally fixated on the game of Egyptian Rat Slap. She was one of the best opponents I'd ever gone against. Usually it didn't take me very long to win since I didn't *let* anyone win, but she put up a fight. We slapped each other's hands, mostly accidentally, while trying desperately to get all the cards.

"You guys are going to get hurt," Kennedy said, laughing, half-reading her *Harry Potter* book.

"I'm going to win," I said, staring intently at the stack of cards.

"You can do it, Jenny," Gracia said. "Someone needs to beat her."

Jenny smiled slyly. I slapped, got a good dozen cards and added them to my hand. She slammed her fist on the table and nearly growled. I only smiled because I'd do the same thing. "Oh, Gracie, I don't think anyone's going to beat me." I was really in the zone and smiling. Even though it'd only been a few days, it felt like forever since I felt ok. Since I felt like it was acceptable to even smile. I'd been afraid of having Jenny in my cabin for nothing.

She finally snagged a few cards and jumped up from her chair and twirled around.

"I'm gonna win, I'm gonna win!" she said repeatedly.

"The more you say that the harder I'll fight," I said, chuckling.

"Miss Laurel's table!" Peter called out.

"We're busy!" Jenny yelled back. I focused on each card placed down. It may have been a pile of twenty cards before there were two threes in a row. We both slammed our hands down, but her finger was under my palm.

"No!" I yelled, feeling something like fury for about three seconds while she greedily gathered the cards up.

"Miss Laurel's table!" Peter said again.

246

"I told you we're busy!" Jenny replied. He looked surprised and watched curiously before calling a different table.

With well over half the deck in her hands, I could not afford to lose any cards. Finally, I was able to get a few of the cards back. Jenny gripped the table so hard, I thought she'd break something, either the table, or her hand. "I wonder what would happen if we played spoons with her," Gracia said, laughing. "Or anything, Uno even."

"We can find out," I said, though I didn't want a single distraction. I kind of waved at the girls to back up so we could get back to focusing.

It may have been another ten minutes, but I got the whole deck. Next, I had to get through the entire thing before I could say I won. Within ten cards, she'd slapped back into the game. "Ahhhh!" I cried.

"Miss Laurel! Y'all are going to have to get food!" Peter said.

"Fine!" I yelled. We put our cards down and went to get our chicken nuggets. They were soggy, like expected, and the fries were too. Most of the food at camp was simply for sustenance, not enjoyment.

"I want chocolate," Jenny said.

"You can get it at canteen," I said, pushing my emptied tray aside. "Let's continue."

"I'm not done eating!" she said, hurrying through the fries. "I'm hungry, God, just give me a second."

"Second's over," Kennedy said shortly after. I smirked and Jenny put her head on the table.

"I have to watch this," Taylor said, moving to sit at the open seat at my table.

"Wh—" I started.

"Harry said I'm good to sit over here," he said.

Jenny shook her head and pushed her tray aside. Taylor kindly cleaned up the table while we started the game, basically, all over again. It could last days if we were too equally matched. I felt light and like everything was as it should have been. I was happy the heavy feeling of dread had been replaced. It only reminded me that these were the people I needed to protect, the people who could be in danger shortly during our wilderness retreat. Even Jenny, who I'd never had the chance to get to know well until now, I wanted to keep her away from any potential danger. She seemed like the kind of kid that would jump headfirst into any danger if she saw it, just out of curiosity.

Even after another ten minutes, we were no closer to finishing the game, but we were running out of time for lunch. "What about the free period?" Jenny asked. She had a small number of cards left.

"No, we can finish it right now," I said. "Go."

The last cards landed with two fives. I slapped and grabbed the cards. All I had to do was get through the rest of the deck. Considering I was in this situation once before, I wasn't sure this would accomplish anything. Nonetheless, I went for it, going as fast as humanly possible, focusing so hard that Jenny simply couldn't catch up. Once I got all the cards safely and, in my possession, the table erupted. "Ah, Miss Laurel!" Gracia said. "Still undefeated!"

"Ugh!" Jenny threw her hands up and turned around, furious. "That's not fair!"

"How not?" I asked, laughing.

"You didn't slap every time there was a double or a sandwich! You were going too fast!"

"I'm allowed to do that, Jenny," I said, speaking calmly now, though still relishing my victory. She stormed off outside and I sighed.

"Well, that was entertaining," Gracia said. "I'm going to take a nap during my free period."

"Make sure someone else is in the cabin," I said.

I went to see Lukas during the free period. He was passed out on the couch, snoring. Remarkably, he didn't wake up when I entered the room. My kitchen had been turned into what looked like a set off of the *X-Files*. Photographs were posted on the wall along with a list of family members. He was making a family tree.

I touched Lukas gently on the shoulder. He was startled awake. "Oh God, you scared me," he said, sitting up. "I didn't sleep well last night. Stayed up too late getting things done."

"I see that," I said, pointing. "Did you find Gary?"

"No," he said, shaking his head. "Got a good hike in though. I saw some birds. Nothing exciting. I did find out why Amalie started the camp though."

"Why?"

"She swore her mother, Linnea, came to her and told her to do it, that there had to be light and laughter on the land to overcome the darkness. Something like that. It was irresponsible, in my opinion. They didn't think about the kids who would be involved, that's for sure. They shouldn't have been having kids here in the first place, not with what seemed to keep happening," Lukas said.

"Did other campers die here?" I asked.

"I'm only in the 1920s, right now, but yeah," he said. "Why are you here?"

"Free period," I said.

"Yeah, but you usually spend that time helping kids finish their packets," he said.

"Didn't know you paid that much attention," I said, smiling.

"You're a creature of habit," he said, leaning against the couch. He watched me carefully, a sly smile on his face. "Honestly, I thought you'd avoid me until Saturday."

"Why?" I asked.

"You've been a little jumpy lately." He motioned to me. "Like you felt embarrassed about what happened at the hospital."

"For a bit, yeah, but not now," I said. "Just beat Jenny at a really intense game of rat slap. She pouted and threw a bit of a fit, but I didn't expect anything different."

"You know what I mean, but you don't have to be jumpy around me." I nearly glared at him but kept my face steady. "Ok, ok, I'll show you what I have so far. There are photographs of Clark when it was first built, it was just a cabin that looked a lot like House One at that time. It really was just a basic building, and kids were staying in canvas tents outside, some of them were set up like tipis, by then some of the Halverson family left for Decorah, like Dorothea, since she didn't think it was safe. There was a chapel service held every week led by Inne that the kids walked up to. They had things like swimming, canoeing, whittling, hand crafts, archery, orienteering and camp craft. I couldn't find a pamphlet on the camp, but Amalie had some letters to Dorothea she never sent."

"Why didn't she send them?" I asked.

He pointed to the copy of the letters which hung on the wall. "I think they had a falling out of some kind. Dorothea seemed pretty stern about leaving the land, while Amalie thought the family was responsible to care for it instead. Dorothea seemed to agree with you and said kids shouldn't be brought on the property, but either way, they had about forty campers that summer. Not a lot, but a good start. The next year, in 1910 a man was brought in to work on construction, named Cain Whyte, and he and his crew worked on constructing more of Clark, and some storage sheds. He taught carpentry as well. There were almost seventy kids that year. By the beginning of 1911, Cain married Kjerstin, and they built this cabin, called the Hytte. Kjerstin tried to plant a garden, but nothing grew. Other than that, things were pretty normal."

"So this cabin is over a hundred years old?" I asked, looking around me.

"Yep, and I guess Cain Whyte thought it'd be a family home. Don't know how you'd fit a whole family in here though. It's barely large enough for you." Lukas shrugged. "Well Kjerstin got pregnant pretty fast and in 1912, the cabin was infested with rats and mice. Soon after that the house, House One, transforms into an actual house overnight. Like it turned into what it is now."

"What the hell . . ." I muttered to myself. He showed me two photographs side by side, the seemingly innocuous cabin and then the house I currently knew. "Do we see the photograph differently, Lukas?"

"What?" he asked.

"Remember how we discussed that everyone sees the house differently?"

"Yeah," he said.

"Does this house look like how you see it? The one in the picture, I mean." I pointed to it. It had the same door as I knew, the same number of windows, the same structure. Everything was as I saw it today.

"Yes," he replied, slower.

"So we see it differently?" I asked. He nodded.

"How does that work? How can a photograph look different to two people? It's a photograph," he replied.

Chapter Nineteen: August 7, 2016

"It's the house, nothing makes sense, dude," I said, shaking my head. "What did they do after the house changed into its current form?"

"Well because Kjerstin was pregnant, she and Cain left with her daughters from her previous marriage, Margareta and Brigita. They moved to Greenville. She gave birth to a son, James. She wrote to Amalie that if she stayed on the land, her son wouldn't have survived. When they moved to Greenville, they were looked on as outsiders for a couple of reasons. Kjerstin was thirty-five, Cain was twenty-four, and they thought that was weird, and then she came from this land, so people thought she was cursed. Her previous husband died under sketchy circumstances, as did every other male relative. She joined the Lutheran church in town, and became super devout, and per her request, everyone in the family was rebaptized. She managed to get a job at the newspaper in printing." He shrugged.

"She seemed really relieved to get away from Kellova and into town even if people side-eyed her a lot. Back at camp, there was a lot of growth that year, despite the house turning into a house instead of a log cabin. They built bathrooms and a whole plethora of cabins: Aspen, Cherry, Wren, and Chickadee. There were 126 campers."

"Damn, Amalie was on the move, getting crap done," I said.

"And I have no idea where she was getting the money, but she was," Lukas said. "She had meticulous records of finances, just like Harald, and there are these massive deposits that are unmarked. Maybe it was from the sale of those semi-precious stones, but that isn't going to get them rolling in the dough, that's for sure." He sighed and sat down.

He adjusted himself to get comfortable before continuing. "During the next year, things kinda blew up. It starts all nice and sweet with Karolina marrying Cain's brother Abel, yeah, their parents were probably expecting one of the two to kill the other, I don't know, but Karolina and Abel Whyte move into a house beside Kjerstin. At the beginning of summer, Birch is constructed. Then they start digging to build the pool. Unfortunately, Ingrid is found dead in Lost Lake. She ends up being buried beside the lake alongside Linnea."

"Dead? Did she drown?" I asked.

"I don't know about that. Amalie wrote that she thought perhaps it was due to the land being angry about all the construction and it lured Ingrid away and drowned her. It's far-fetched in my opinion but this land likes to kill people in strange ways," he said.

"So, she did drown?" I asked again.

He shrugged. "She also had stones in her pockets, like she was trying to do it on purpose," Lukas said. "But with the camp now, news of Ingrid's death isn't published in any newspaper, and the only way I can find any hint of it is a letter between Amalie and Karolina. Amalie even asks Karolina to lie to Kjerstin and tell her that Ingrid died of something like a fever, or just in her sleep, rather than being found drowned in the lake like that."

"So she asked her to lie about it?" I asked.

"I can see why she would. The whole family was on high alert their entire lives for things like this. Not only was the family freaked out, but it also freaked out the Whyte brothers and they stepped back from the construction job and so Amalie hired a twenty-nine-year-old Edward Apple, who ended up marrying sixteen-year-old Katrine later that year. They move into here, the Hytte."

"Ew."

Lukas just kept speaking, "He ended up knowing House One pretty well and how to manage it better than anyone else. He had a night patrol with his heeler Gus and his mule Missy." He pointed at a picture of Edward Apple on Missy's back with his dog beside him. He was also carrying a very large shotgun. He was void of facial hair and looked surprisingly young.

"At first Amalie was really not ok with Edward being here. There was a letter to Dorothea that she never sent about the marriage, saying that a man shouldn't be marrying a child and that Katrine was only having lustful thoughts or something like that and it wasn't real love, and even if it was, he shouldn't live on the property because his death would only break Katrine's heart. She must have changed her mind because when she wrote to Karolina and Kjerstin, she said that she was sure the land would be safer with Edward around."

"That's just . . . that's just wrong," I said, thinking about a near thirty year old man with a sixteen-year-old girl.

"Blame it on the early 1900s?" Lukas shrugged. "I don't know, they seemed happy." He pointed to a marriage photograph of the pair. Katrine did look like a child with porcelain skin and a gorgeous smile. There were multiple photographs of the duo. One where they faced away from the camera, and she had a wreath of flowers around her head and a beautiful bouquet. Her dress was lacey and rather poofy. In the photographs, Edward didn't seem that much older.

Lukas continued, "So in 1914 Basswood, Yew, and Eagle were built. Campers were circulating stories about a woman up on the hill, complete with dreams, sleepwalking, and the like. Amalie was convinced, still, that the figure was her mother. She got super freaked out and sent a crew to House One to fence it, but they all jumped ship without explanation and never came back. So Mari and Edward tried to build a fence around it, but the house knocked, threw shit at them, and the wooden planks fell down. So they tried surrounding it with stones, but the next morning, the stones were found in a pile."

"Damn, I'd run and hide," I said.

"I think you've seen worse out of the house than it stacking some stones," Lukas said. "Amalie asked Karolina what they should do, and Karolina suggested an exorcism."

We both laughed. I imagined a scene from *The Exorcist* with the priest repeatedly saying, 'the power of Christ compels you.'

"What did Amalie say?" I asked.

"She said that'd never work. The house wouldn't listen to any Christian pastor or a priest, and that they needed an Indian shaman to get rid of it. Apparently, she sent letters out to every one she could find and they all said it was out of their hands."

"The shamans did?" I asked.

"Yes, she asked Lakota, Dakota, Otoe, Fox, Iowa, Creek, whoever she could find," he said. "It didn't stop the camp from having nearly 200 campers that year, or her resuming the build on the pool in 1915, led by Edward. Oh, and Edward hired the Clark brothers: Jonathan and Matthew. These brothers rebuild Clark, making it look like it does now." He showed me a bunch of very old, almost crumbly looking newspaper articles noting the beauty and uniqueness of the building and its construction with the Clark brothers and Edward in front of it. Following that was an article about the camp itself and how it was run by a 'family of women' teaching 'useful skills with an outdoor lifestyle'.

He pointed to another newspaper clipping. "The city awarded the camp with an endowment for their contribution to the community. I was pretty surprised about that. There're also some photographs taken from Edward's carpentry class since his students made the rocking chairs, benches, stools, picnic tables, all the stuff that's around camp."

"That's kinda cool," I said, though it wasn't terribly surprising. Everything within camp seemed to be contained. Nothing really came from the outside, and whatever came into the camp, tended to stay.

"While Karolina and Abel were visiting, Karolina was heavily pregnant. She went to see Inne and went into labor and they had their daughter Emme inside the chapel. Karolina wrote . . . oh where is it." He dug through a pile of papers. "I thought I had these in order." He finally plucked the right paper out. "She said that it was the oddest thing because the child came a month early. She hadn't been feeling any labor pains. There was no sign the baby would come early, but as soon as she stepped into the chapel, she went into labor. She was pretty much too scared to ever go there again while pregnant. She said if she were carrying a boy, she would have lost it."

"This place is weird," I said. "Remind me never to get pregnant."

"I don't think you'll have to worry about that," he replied, nonchalantly.

"What does that mean?" I asked. His eyebrows rose like I clearly didn't know what I was talking about. "Just because I'm twenty-four now and haven't dated doesn't mean I'm going to be alone forever."

"Do you really plan on getting into the dating scene?" he asked.

"Honestly, I haven't really thought about it," I replied.

"Then how are you going to get pregnant?" he asked. "That kind of re-quires sex."

"Ich," I said.

"My point."

"For all you know there's like a hundred little versions of you running around," I replied. "At least I don't have that problem."

"There are not. I'm very careful about that, thank you very much."

"You somehow managed to have sex with some French girl on a plane; how did you have time for contraception?" I asked.

"I forgot I told you about that," he mumbled.

"Yeah, you went on and on about how you didn't know if you should, and then you told me you did and I told you I didn't want to know anything about it, but you told me anyway."

He had a look of amused defeat on his face. "I'm always packing, so no worries there."

"How did you not get thrown off?"

"The plane? They're not going to push me out the door!" he said, laughing. "I don't think anyone ever knew."

I facepalmed and said, "You know what, you're weird."

"I've been told that before, ok, can I continue?" he asked.

"Yeah, yeah, yeah," I said.

"Ok, so in 1916, the Apple Arts Center was built, in honor of Edward Apple. The pool was finished, so our pool is exactly a hundred years old, pretty much. This was also the first year of the cleanest cabin award, and the first year the whole Nomad thing was introduced. Amalie, Esther, Elisabeth, and Lia and some campers earn it. So if you see their names in the Nomad room on the plaque, that's who they are. There are like 240 campers that year. So Esther earned that award, but the next year in 1917 she went on a hike to what will eventually be the quarry but didn't return. After a month of searching, which is all over the papers this time, she's found in House One, but the place was searched multiple times prior to her being discovered."

"This place is deadly . . ." I muttered.

"I'd agree with that," Lukas said.

"What'd she die of?"

"An autopsy said she drowned even though she was on dry land."

"What the fuck," I said. His eyes widened and he chuckled.

"Of all the things that have happened here, I don't know if that's the craziest," he replied.

"It's . . . it's weird,"

"Well, she's buried beside the chapel with everyone else. So the lapidary building which was finished in October of that year was dedicated to her. That's why there is a plaque that says Esther on it. I never knew until this morning. So it's just considered some kind of tragedy, even though the town paper said she was found, and the cause of death was drowning. Either way, this family reproduces like rabbits and Katrine and Edward have their first kid, a daughter named Daisy. Also, Charlotte Dahl, who is pretty young, fourteen or fifteen at this time, becomes a nomad and her project is to plant Laurel trees in honor of all the people who died. So basically, you're named after dead people."

"Thanks, Lukas," I said, shaking my head. "All the laurel trees around here are in honor of specific dead people?"

"Yep. Charlotte wrote some letters herself, mostly to a Nicholas Walker during the off season. He was a camper. She said that she put plaques with people's names on them. In 1917, Nicholas helped her create more plaques, to kind of catch up with all the dead. Also, these letters between her and Nicholas are kind of hot and heavy, as hot and heavy as you can get during 1917 in love letters." He made a funny face. "All that shit about I can't live without you, love of my life, can't wait to be in your arms kind of stuff." Now I made a face.

"Why do you have these letters?" I asked.

"They were in Gary's possession?" he replied. "I don't know where he got them from. All I know is that she had an out of wedlock relationship with him for a good four years." He held up one piece of paper. "Detailing their escapades in various buildings and locations, including the chapel, which may be sacrilege, don't know, never actually had sex in a chapel myself."

"They did what now?" I asked.

"Well, by the sounds of it, Nicholas is talking about how awesome her breasts are and how they glowed in the moonlight filtering through the windows of the chapel, and how lovely their secret love is." I hit my head on the table.

"Ew."

"And in the Hytte . . ." he said, holding up another piece of paper.

"Not my house . . ." I whined.

"Well, considering that bed is original to this location, at least a couple of children were conceived on it," he said.

"Oh God, Lukas, why . . .?" I did not move my face from the table's surface.

"That table might not even be safe by the sounds of it," he said. I lifted my head up and then remembered when I cleaned it with Lysol spray last and returned my face to its previous position. "Ok, ok, other than Charlotte and Nicholas getting busy everywhere, Elisabeth, Esther's twin, in her grief, I guess, married Matthew Clark. She moved away to Greenville where they set up shop next to Karolina and Kjerstin. Then during the summer of 1917 they tried to build that service bridge on the east side of the river, but while they're doing that there's a flash flood that washed away all their work and crushed and killed three construction workers in the process. Charlotte notes that she made plaques for them, a Henry, a Jacob, and a Joseph."

"Oh my Lord," I said. "Was that in the papers?"

"Yes," he said, pointing to an article, copied and pasted on the wall. "They had a whole candlelight vigil situation here in honor of them, but I don't have any pictures of that, just an article."

"This place is a death trap," I said.

"It sounds pretty normal to me, though, like an accident. I don't think it was caused by the house. It was just par for the course." He shrugged. "In 1918, Charlotte told Nicholas she's pregnant, and he proposed to her on the green outside the Hytte during one very pretty sunset. She of course said yes. But he's found dead before the wedding, hanging out of the library window."

"What?" I blurted out, surprised.

"He died of blood loss, according to an autopsy. Amalie told everyone to keep this quiet because it's suspicious to have so many people dying all over the place and she doesn't want to scare campers away. Charlotte's considered mentally unstable following his death, and she's sent to stay with Karolina and Kjerstin. She gave birth to a daughter named Edythe. She wrote in a letter to Amalie that she wished it was a boy, so it'd die."

"Ah, that poor girl," I said, shaking my head.

"Still, the whole line about wishing the kid would die though . . ." Lukas said. "It's a little harsh considering the kid is all she had left of Nicholas."

"How mentally unstable are we talking?" I asked.

"The equivalent of a major depressive episode today, but back then they thought it was hysteria. There are letters going back and forth from Amalie and Kjerstin considering taking her to an asylum, but thankfully they didn't. They say they have to nurse the child and all Charlotte did for a while was cry in bed. She wouldn't get up. She lost a lot of weight. She was a mess. Karolina was able to nurse the baby since she was about to give birth to her son, Harold. So then she had to nurse two children. She and Abel decide to take custody of Edythe, legally while she's still an infant, citing neglect on Charlotte's part. In 1919, Elisabeth and Matthew had their first kid, Liliana. Matthew was part of the build crew on the first attempt on the bridge, and then he attempted it again, and was successful this time. They also started work on building the office."

"So Charlotte didn't raise Edythe at all?" I asked.

"No, in family photographs, Edythe is with the rest of Karolina and Abel's clan," he said. Pushing some photographs forward. "Though they didn't change her last name, it's still Dahl."

"They must have been overwhelmed with all of this," I said.

"They had help. Ina moved in with Karolina and Kjerstin during the offseason, and Lia tried desperately to help Charlotte by working on the laurel trees."

"I still feel bad for Charlotte," I said, looking at Lukas. He sighed.

"Well, she's long dead now, so if you believe in an afterlife, she's probably with him," he said bluntly. "I don't know how she died yet, I'm not that far into putting shit together."

"This is one messed up family," I replied.

"Every family is messed up," he said. "I don't know if I've seen a well-functioning one in my life. Can I finish?" He laughed and I nodded, motioning for him to continue. "So in 1920, Mari chose to move in with Karolina and Abel, so the Apple family moved into the homestead. Nora moved to the Hytte up at House One, the whole clearing got filled with dead robins and that freaked just about everyone out." He showed me a picture of the House and the clearing was dotted with little black birds, fallen on the ground in a grid pattern. "Inne started to go blind after that, according to Amalie, and required Nora and Katrine to care for her. She still stuck to her chapel services though. She didn't really need to see; she had the whole Bible practically memorized. A lady from Kjerstin's church donated a piano to them. I have no idea how they got it up to the chapel, but they did."

There was a photograph of Inne, Lia, and Ina standing beside the piano inside the chapel. Inne looked quite worse for wear. The two girls looked fresh and happy and had their arms around each other. They wore plain dresses, but their hair was done up in an exuberant fashion. "There's a letter from Lia, actually, noting that while she was playing the piano one evening, there was a lightning storm outside, and House One was hit. It danced with flames, but there were no signs of damage. One of the cabins, though, Yew, burnt down due to the storm, but no campers were harmed. There were 400 kids that summer."

"400? In 1920? Damn," I said. "And I'm not surprised that the House didn't burn down."

He rolled his eyes. "Well, we know that now, don't we?"

"If only you knew this information last summer," I said, sighing. He pushed into me playfully and I pushed back.

"Ok, 1921, Charlotte ends up in a relationship with a male counselor named Emmett. There are lots of letters between them. They worked on maintaining and naming trails throughout camp, including the Chief's Daughter and the Lost Lake trail. She and Ina both seem obsessed with working with the land to find out what makes it happy."

"Why does everyone know about Charlotte's love life?" I asked.

"Because she writes about it, and somehow the family managed to get access to all her letters, but Emmett was getting her letters and writing back. He thought she was the most gorgeous woman on the planet, but she didn't say the same things about him in her letters. She kind of just focused on how much she trusted him and loved spending time with him."

"Maybe she was still missing Nicholas," I said.

"And all the while, she has a daughter he doesn't know about, and she isn't taking care of . . ."

"He doesn't know? Are they talking about marriage here?" I asked.

He slowly shook his head. "I don't think she was interested in marriage. I think she was just focused on finding distractions."

"But she had a solid relationship with this guy," I said. "She wasn't just sleeping around."

"Cannot confirm or deny," he replied.

"No other love letters though," I said.

He shrugged. His lanky frame folded over when he sat down at the kitchen table. "That's all I have so far. What I can say is that Emmett and Charlotte were never planning on having a life together. No boys have been born yet at the camp. Weird shit is still happening, and a lot of people have died."

"All in fifteen years. Oh, and they seem to breed like rabbits," I said.

"They also love photography. There are so many damn photographs, and I do go through them hoping to find something just strange or off about the camp, or the people. The fact that not all of them have fled yet is interesting. It sounds like they feel not only tied to this place, unable to leave, but that they are, as a family, solely responsible for it."

"I can understand the feeling of being tied here," I said, avoiding eye contact for a moment, knowing that he didn't approve.

"You have a choice," he said.

"We made that choice, both of us, to fight the house. By learning about it, we can maybe find a pattern, or what we can do to destroy it." Lukas pulled out his phone and started typing for a moment before looking at me again.

"That's why I'm here. You'd do it alone if I weren't."

I went over and hugged him tightly. "Thank you," I said. "It means… the world that you're here."

He smiled, almost sadly. "Well, I'll get back to work, and you do too,"

Peter and I met up at dinner. He sat next to me, and we hashed out the plans for that evening, once again. He was always a bit jumpy about plans and had to get them solidly in his mind. "Is there an extra counselor around who can hang out with me with the rest of the kids, so I'm not stuck with that many by myself?" he asked.

"It won't be any more kids than you're used to, hon," I said. "Eight, remember?"

"I know, but I haven't really worked with the girls in your cabin," he said nervously.

"They're not bad," Taylor said.

"Why do you always have to eavesdrop?" Peter asked. Taylor just grinned, his skin stretching across his face like his brother's, making him look older than he was. "He shows up everywhere, just listening."

"I know," I said, sighing.

"It's called curiosity, not a bad thing," Taylor said, plopping down in the chair beside Peter. "I'm going to the chapel, though. I think it'll be fun. I'm going to take pictures and send them to Noah."

"For once, I will actually allow that," I said. "I'm going to be taking pictures myself."

Kennedy ran over to me yelling, "I finished the books!" She slammed down *Harry Potter and the Deathly Hallows* onto the table.

"Damn you read fast," I said. "Only took you ten weeks to get through all seven."

"Hey, I also read all three *Lord of the Rings* books. Now onto *The Children of Hurin* and *Beren and Luthien.*"

"*The Children of Hurin* is a little *Game of Thrones* in content," I said.

"I think I can handle it," she said, laughing. "It can't be any worse than when I tried to read *Fifty Shades of Gray.*"

"Who in God's green earth let you read that?" I asked.

"The library!" she exclaimed.

Lisey, who was listening, came over and sat down as well. "I watch *American Horror Story.*"

"I'm concerned about all y'all," I said, shaking my head.

"You've seen it too?" Lisey asked, brightening up.

"Yes," I said.

"Coven is my favorite season," she said. "Though all of them are pretty good."

"I like that show too," Taylor said.

"Let me guess, you were introduced to it by your brother," I remarked.

Peter was turning red since I was offhand talking about sex scenes with a bunch of teenage campers.

"I picked it on Netflix," Taylor said. "He just had to watch it, but he started getting really worked up about the girl, Violet, dying in the first season, I think since it reminded him of Haley . . ."

I didn't think about that. He looked a bit dejected after saying that. "It's not like it was your fault, hon," I said.

"Oh, I know, but I try to avoid things that upset him about that," he said.

Chapter Twenty:

August 7, 2016

That evening while we were taking a northern path up to the chapel, Taylor said, "About the whole Haley thing earlier... I think they were actually, like, endgame, like they were going to be together forever. Like one day they were going to be married and maybe have kids, maybe even go to school together."

"I know," I said softly. Arty, Eddy, Jenny, Gracia, Kennedy, and Lisey were spread out in a line ahead of us, walking through overgrown brush. "Haley thought that way too."

"Then why'd she do it?" he asked.

"I really don't think she planned to, Taylor."

"She really hurt my brother. That destroyed him. I'm surprised he's as ok as he is now." He looked down to his feet as we walked. There was a heavy sadness about him.

"He loved her, that's for sure," I said. "But like I said, Taylor, I really don't think she meant to harm him in any way."

"She did, by dying. By killing herself." His tone was gruff and hard. "And Noah's as convinced as you are that it wasn't really her decision. That House One caused her to kill herself. I think it's . . . it's not good for him to think that way, to place the blame somewhere else, but he seems to have proof."

"Yeah, he's talked to me about that," I said softly. He looked at me, surprised. "He talked to me about a lot of things, even when he was a camper."

"Huh," he said. "But I don't get why he keeps saying he's still in love with Haley, but he has these girlfriends. Mom's never home, but he keeps bringing them over and introducing them to me and a few months later or even weeks, they're gone."

"Have you told him that this bothers you?" I asked.

"Are you kidding me?" he asked, almost laughing, but more frustrated than anything else.

"He says I'm not allowed to talk about his quote unquote love life to him," he huffed. "The only friend he keeps around that's a girl is Gracia. That's probably because she's not even remotely interested in dating him and can somehow deal with him. Now one of his only other friends, Riley, is just up and missing. I don't know if he'll be ok."

"Taylor, your brother is a good guy, ok? He's just gone through a hell of a lot of trauma and has struggled with things, but he's made it. He's still going."

"I know that," he said. "But I'm stuck with him, so he might as well make it bearable for me."

I nodded in understanding. "Half the time I talk to him, he's going on about how good you're doing and how proud he is of you. He says you're smart as a whip, and you are." He shrugged. "Do you have any plans, like what you want to do?"

"I'm fifteen. I don't have to have everything figured out yet," he said.

"Any inkling?" I asked, smiling.

"I know I don't want to work in retail, that's for sure. Washing dishes at the restaurant near us sucks. I've picked up a few gigs cleaning rooms at the inn in town and that's horrible. So I don't want to work menial labor," he chuckled. "That's what Noah calls it. So, maybe college? I might want to go into criminology or something like that."

"That would be cool!" I exclaimed.

"You went to college but you're still here," he said. "What's up with that?"

"You and everyone else has to ask me that," I muttered.

"Well?"

We walked over a large log that fell in the middle of the path. Here it was dark. The trees were so thick that the light was nearly blocked. A few kids upfront turned their flashlights on to make sure they didn't trip over anything. "I'm hoping to be the director one day, or I was," I said.

"Didn't know that."

"I don't know, though, not now, if I'll follow that path, but I've been here nearly as long as you've been alive. I don't know much else," I said.

"It'd be cool to be a counselor here, get to know all the secrets." We both laughed.

"It's an experience, that's for sure. Is Noah still thinking about being a counselor here?"

Taylor shook his head. "No. He doesn't want to be stuck for a whole summer near House One. I'm pretty sure he's only on the retreat to get dirt on it."

"Not surprised," I replied.

"I think I see it!" Lisey said.

"How?" I called back, seeing nothing in the distance but more trees.

"I have 20/20 eyesight!" she said.

"Congratulations?" Eddy said sarcastically. "I can't see shit!"

"Eddy! Language!" I called out.

"Well, I can't! If it wasn't for my flashlight, I would have run into a thorn bush or a raccoon by now." He sounded cranky, which was both unlike him and entertaining. "How can it be this far from camp?"

Jenny said, "Now you know how far the horse kids have to walk to get to dinner every day!"

"Remind me never to be one!" Eddy said. "Horses smell like . . . crap, anyway,"

"Thank you for watching your language," I said. Taylor and I hurried to catch up with the group.

Gracia said, "I think I see a steeple-like thing up there too, or just a tall pointy roof." I squinted, trying to see what they saw. I'd have to wait until we stepped out of the thick woods, before I saw what they saw. Just as mentioned before to Taylor, I'd been at Kellova as long as he'd been alive, and yet, I'd never stumbled upon this chapel. I felt like it was hiding from me before.

The chapel was intact. It was made of dark wood, and well-crafted. It reminded me of The Chapel in the Hills in South Dakota, with its Norwegian-esque architecture. This was smaller though, in scale, with a roof that was about half the size. There were two doors which one had to climb a few stairs to reach. The windows were cloudy, and beside it, within a gated space, was the cemetery. Everything here was overgrown, but the gravestones were tall and poked out of the grass. Roses that had gone wild grew in clumps in front of the chapel.

"Wow," I said. I took out my phone and took a picture of it. "It's gorgeous." There were gargoyle-like creatures sitting on the corners of the roof. It looked quaint but stately.

"Can we go in?" Jenny asked. Her voice was quiet and seemed far away.

"Carefully," I said.

She stepped up to the door and opened it. It squeaked a tad with age and wear, but opened, nonetheless. Stale air came wafting out in a cloud. It was very dusty inside, but despite that I could see all the work that went into its creation and that it was much loved. The seats were worn, and the altar was still set. A small oak cross sat in the center of the altar atop a half-eaten linen cloth that was no longer white. There were four pews, and no room for more. There was a baptismal font also carved from wood beside the altar with a large candle sitting half-melted in a tarnished silver holder. Behind the altar was a door that went into the living quarters. This was where Inne Halverson lived most of her life, and where dozens of babies were born.

"Miss Laurel!" Taylor's voice sounded off, almost breaking a holy silence.

I turned around and he pointed at something beneath the top of the altar. It was a massive Bible. "It's not in English," Arty said, squinting at it with his flashlight.

"It's in Norwegian," I said, and carefully picked it up. It was the Halverson family Bible. My jaw nearly dropped. I took more photos to send to Lukas.

"This place is beautiful," Kennedy said.

"Agreed," added Lisey. "Why'd they stop using it?"

"No clue," I said.

"Probably because this is considered a secular camp," Kennedy said.

"A what?" Lisey asked.

"Not religious," Kennedy added.

"So why is this here?" Eddy asked.

"The family who lived here built the chapel for their family," I said. Taylor was looking through the Bible.

Chapter Twenty: August 7, 2016

"Miss Laurel, why is my name here?" he asked.

"They were Halverson's. You may be related," I said.

He looked at me with confusion, and then around at the chapel. "Really? Huh. Cool. Can we take this with?"

"Without a doubt," I replied. I stepped outside, into the fresh air, and into the graveyard. There were so many graves, of infants, children, and adults alike, all of the same family tree. I noticed Esther's name and the story of how she drowned on dry land. Or of Harald and how he and every other man died from unknown causes in the clearing around the House.

I felt a compulsion to clean this land up, to give the graves the proper tending they needed. Yet, I was fully aware that no one was here. Wherever people go after they die, it's not the graveyard in which they are buried. The place felt empty, and painfully so. The dead were not there. I touched the stones, reading names that were familiar to me only from Lukas's research. Esther, Rasmus, Ingrid, Harald, and many stillborn infants.

"Am I really related to them?" Taylor asked, pointing at the graves.

"Maybe," I replied quietly. There was something compelling about this place, how it felt in the bones. It felt like it was meant to be here, like there was something holy about it.

I was reluctant to leave, but with a night swim planned, the kids eventually did get antsy to get out of there before it became wholly dark. Most people accepted cemeteries after dark, or old abandoned chapels for that matter, were creepy. So we walked back.

It was completely silent, something I was far from accustomed to when it came to this bunch of kids. Taylor held the fragile family Bible close to his chest, cradling it. I'd have to take it to the Hytte and keep it somewhere safe and find a way to preserve it. From the first page it was clear it was owned originally by Harald's parents, Sigurd and Frigida Halverson and he, and his brother, took it with him on their quest to the Americas. His baptismal record was in the front, as was his marriage certificate, and a list of all the births and deaths in the family was carefully written as a faithful account as to what occurred for almost a hundred years.

The sun drooped down to the edge of the horizon. Pinks and scarlets lit up the sky just enough for us to find our cabins, gather our swimming supplies, and head to the pool. Now the kids had more energy, more pep in their step.

"Wait up!" Lisey jogged after Taylor, he let her jump on his back and gave her a piggyback ride across the bridge. Kennedy walked beside me; her bag full of more books to read since she hardly ever went in the pool.

The kids ran to the poolside basketball area and dropped their stuff, exchanging stories. Lisey hopped off Taylor's back and looked at him with teenage awe. Or infatuation. Either way, it was cute and kind of gross. Some of the kids already started a game of basketball after changing into their swimsuits. I ducked in to change as well. I stuffed myself into the gray, floral swimsuit.

Despite knowing I was slim, I still felt too fat and was worried about the possible cellulite on my thighs, hence the swim shorts for an added layer of protection from my own negative mind.

I looked in the mirror and didn't feel good. My shoulders seemed too wide, and I wanted them to be slender, but they weren't. My midsection felt like a muffin-top at times and my arms were scrawny. My legs looked good though, they I wouldn't complain about. I was never a fan of my face, though. It always looked wrong, like it wasn't as good as it could be, and that makeup couldn't fix those imperfections. There were splotches from the sun on my skin, freckles that weren't of the cute variety, and my hair was very fine and breakable. Another javelin went through my chest. The pool always did that to me. It made me overthink my appearance, that Ezra had seen me like this, and maybe that was why he was attracted elsewhere. Maybe it was because I never instigated anything. Maybe it was just because I wasn't good enough.

I tried to push those intrusive thoughts away and focus on my job, but my heart instead raced away in my chest like it had nothing better to do and my stomach squirmed and hitched itself higher and higher until I felt like I was about to explode or puke or both. Mia opened the door, always one to interrupt me. "I'm lifeguarding," she said. "Do you want me to open in ten?"

"That'll work," I said.

"Stop sucking your stomach in, makes you look frail," she said, and closed the door. I wasn't sure what she meant by that, but I let a heavy breath go.

My mind then went to Riley, an anorexic, wondering if that's how he thought about himself. If he ever looked in a mirror and saw something atrocious, or if he ever looked in a mirror at all. Was food still his enemy? I'd never considered food to be an enemy. I just ate when I was hungry and stopped when I was full, but lately, my stress levels seem to make the full part harder to attain. The food wasn't comforting, but it was something to keep my mind occupied. "I'm seeing things," I muttered to myself, and left the thick-aired pool house.

I stood at the gates and waved my hands. "Ok! Everyone at the gate! I expect you know the rules at this point! I don't want to see any roughhousing, dunking, or holding people under the water! And seriously, no running! You don't need to slip and fall on this concrete, that'll make it a bad time for all of us. Any of that and you will be out of the pool and sitting on your towel doing nothing for the remainder of the evening! We will open the canteen at 8:30, and at that time you will be able to purchase snacks and drinks! The same rule applies as always, one snack item, one drink item! We'll keep the pool open until 10 if everyone is listening and following the rules. Understood?"

"Yes!" A chorus of voices came back to me.

"Very good," I said and opened the door. They hurried it, just on the verge of running. "Slow down, guys!"

Once the kids were inside, I went in toward the intermediate section. Despite my ability to swim, I felt most at ease where my feet could touch the ground. My eyes scanned the water, strangely, for any protruding, floating blobs, as if there would be another half-dead body. I'd been doing that every time I came near water, and I doubted that would ever change. My mind flashed to a memory of me doing CPR.

To stop the avalanche of intrusive thoughts, I cannonballed into the pool and splashed everyone in the vicinity. Dunked in the cold water, I felt refreshed. It woke me up and put a smile on my face. "Miss Laurel!" Gracia whined in the middle of a laugh. "What was that?"

"A proper cannonball," I demanded.

"Oh, that's nothing!" Eddy said.

"Belly flop contest?" I asked.

He looked shocked that I would even consider it. We both climbed out of the pool. "Who else? Taylor! Come on Taylor! Let's go!" Lisey's arms were around Taylor at the moment, but he smiled and decided to join us. He waved her forward and she shook her head.

"Come on, Lisey!" Taylor said. She rolled her eyes and clambered out of the pool. In her bikini I imagined a belly flop would hurt quite a bit.

"If I'm doing it, you have to, Grace!" Lisey said.

"Heck no! Last time that left a mark!" Gracia yelled back, bobbing up and down.

"Grace!" Lisey called again.

Gracia shook her head and climbed out of the pool. Standing side by side with their slender frames, they did not look thrilled. "Am I going first?" I asked.

"Yes!" Arty yelled from the center of the pool. "I'll judge!"

"Here goes nothing," I muttered, and leapt from the side of the pool into the deep end, arms extended, legs straight. My stomach hit with a sickening smack that radiated heat through my limbs. With my face underwater, I didn't know how well it did, but I dove under before resurfacing.

"Very good!" Arty said. "Two thumbs up! I'd do it but I'm treading water!" He chuckled, and used one hand to slick his hair back, otherwise the curls would unwind and land in his eyes. I swam to the side of the pool and watched as Taylor lightly kicked Eddy, so he floundered and flailed his way into the pool.

"That's not fair!" Eddy said. "I'm going again!"

"Agreed! That was pathetic!" Arty called.

"It was pretty sad looking," I said.

"You barely splashed at all!" Eddy said, swimming in my direction.

270

Chapter Twenty: August 7, 2016

"Arty gave me two thumbs up; I must have done well!" I replied. Eddy stuck his tongue out and went for it again, pointing at Taylor to keep his distance. Eddy did a perfectly executed belly flop, as he was the unrivaled king.

"Beat that!" he said as soon as he surfaced. "Yeah!" He fist-pumped like he won the Olympics, and swam over to Arty.

"Taylor!" Arty called. "Beat him!"

"I'm going to have the girls go first," Taylor said, nudging Lisey forward. She was shivering in the wind and had a screwed up grimace on her face, unsure about what to do and how to do it without embarrassing herself. To her, at this age, everything was embarrassing. "Just go for it Lisey!" Taylor encouraged.

"You'll do great!" Arty said, waving.

Balling up her fists for a moment, she went for it. She kind of curled in at the end to instinctively protect her stomach, but she did try. I clapped and cheered. Just making the attempt was way out of her comfort zone. "Good job, Lisey," I commended her.

She smiled and swam over to where Eddy and I sat. Gracia stepped up to the plate. She was a fearless girl and did not hesitate. I sincerely doubted many things were out of her comfort zone. She hit the water gracefully, with a smack that sounded and looked extremely painful.

"Ten out of ten!" Arty yelled. "You couldn't make a belly flop look so pretty, Eddy!"

"Belly flops aren't supposed to be pretty! They're supposed to make waves!" Eddy replied.

"There were waves!" I said, laughing.

"I'm the judge now!" Arty said, prissily. "So far, Gracia is the one to beat, Taylor!"

"You can't rule me out of my own game!" Eddy said, mouth hanging open in surprise.

"Don't be a sore loser, Ed," Lisey said. He slumped a bit next to me. Taylor looked at the water before launching himself into the air, then spread himself out, and whacked onto the surface. There was no beating that. Arty was splashed with so much water, he floundered back before getting his footing again.

"Nope, I was wrong. Taylor wins!" Arty announced.

"Ugh!" Eddy whined. He slid back into the pool.

Lisey went to congratulate Taylor with a kiss and proceeded to hold onto his neck, hanging off him like a tumor, and Gracia went to join Jenny on a large floatie. I watched everyone and felt a nervous sort of peace. It was something I could live with, but I felt out of place, and yet like I could be nowhere else. This calm evening would have to end, like everything else.

Chapter Twenty-One:

August 2015

It was well over a hundred degrees that day. There was going to be a movie at the pool because even the toughest kids were beginning to show negative effects from the heat. I was inside the snack shack while the kids got ready to swim, loading soda into the refrigerator. About twenty boxes were stacked to my right. Instead of moving, I stuck my head in the freezer for a moment, wishing I could curl up in there. Sweat dripped down every inch of my body, leaving my arms feeling dry and wet at the same time, but downright filthy. Discomfort was the name of the game.

Sufficiently cooled down, I went to work stocking the fridge. There was a nice, steady rhythm to the work, but it wasn't long before my head started to swim as the heat of the evening came back. A sense of movement came to the world and a burning hot tingle hit the back of my skull.

I stumbled backward, getting my footing, but soon found myself sitting on a pallet simply staring ahead. I was aware of what was going on, but I just couldn't move or speak. It was almost comforting, though. There were no thoughts. No chatter in my head. Nothing. It was as if it was filled with cotton, so it felt cramped like there was no space for a brain. "Laurel!" Mom's voice entered my ear. Part of me wanted to respond, but the other half simply didn't let me. "Laurel! What are you doing?" Her face fell a bit when I didn't respond. "Laurel, seriously? Laurel." She knelt next to me and touched my forehead. This happened before. The doctors said it was a possibility that with exertion I could go into an absence like state and that it wasn't anything to call an ambulance over, but moms will be moms.

She squeezed my hand. "Ok, I'm going to get you some rest, honey, send you to the house where there's AC."

Ezra and Lukas entered the snack shack at that time. "She ok?" Ezra asked.

"Yes, she just needs to go to the house. Ezra, I'm going to have you take her. Stay with her until she's lucid again. It's just the heat. Lukas, I need you as a lifeguard."

"How do I get her to your house?" Ezra asked, pointing at me. I saw the slight movement of his finger from the very side of my vision.

"You'll figure it out. I have five kids in the office cooling down right now. Lukas, let Trisha know that I'll send them down here shortly. Everyone needs to finish a cup of water before they buy soda, and everyone is required to be in the pool. I don't care if they're just lying in the water in the zero-entry area. Meanwhile, I'm going to take Scotty and see if I can dig up more fans." Those two left the snack shack and it was just Ezra and me.

He sat where Mom was, with his elbows on his knees. "Maybe you can walk if I can get you to stand?" he asked. "I feel like I'm talking to a wall, but I know you can hear me . . . I told you to take today off . . . but who listens to me? The heat will get to you- I said. What will your brain do if it starts to cook? Yep, no one listens to me . . ."

He put his arm across my back and under my armpit. I was aware of how much I sweat. He heaved me onto my feet. I was surprised that I could stand. Motor function seemed fine; it was just the mind that wasn't there. Consciousness pretty much was in order, but the pieces didn't go together. "Hey, that's a start. Now . . . to your house, I guess. Maybe we can play cards or something when you get your brain back." I wanted him to stop talking so badly. I was already embarrassed.

The way to my mom's house was long and wound around boulders, the ga-ga pit, and the climbing tree. I veered this way and that, sometimes my vision went blurry, and I just wanted to sit down in the grass. Some part of me must have known what was going on because I didn't just sit. I followed Ezra's instructions and his guidance. He ended up putting a hand on each arm of mine and led me in the correct direction. "Last thing we need is for you to hit a tree. If you do that, you might be stuck like this forever and then what'll we do?"

When Ezra finally opened the door to the house, the air conditioning hit me like a cold brick. It was a solid wall of cold. It was both uncomfortable and relieving at the same time. In some ways, it knocked me out of my funk. I still couldn't talk, and my head was still cottony, but I moved out of Ezra's grip and to the left toward the kitchen where I got myself a glass of water. "Progress already!" he said.

He let my mom know I was in the house and safe through the walkie. Everyone could hear and everyone would know. Embarrassment arose again.

For some comfort, I went after the Little Debbie's in the cupboards knowing full well my mom would tell me sugar in the heat was a bad idea and would only make things worse.

"You must be feeling better," Ezra said. I didn't respond. That part just didn't work yet. I sat on the leather couch and stared at a wall. I pointed at my cheek, hoping he'd get the gist that I couldn't get myself to talk yet. "Ok . . ." he muttered. He turned the TV on. The drone was somewhat comforting as well. I told myself I should take a nap, but that didn't happen. For what seemed like the longest time, nothing did.

Eventually I spurt out, "I can talk again." I let out a breath with it.

"Yay!" he exclaimed, smiling at me. "You know you scare me a bit when you do that."

"I scare myself," I said, shaking my head. That was a bad idea because it hurt, like my brain was sloshing around inside.

"I know, I'm just worried you'll slide into one of those and just not come back out, and then I won't have my Laurel." His Laurel. I liked the sound of that, but it made my heart-javelin pierce a little more into my chest. By the end of the month, I doubted he'd even be thinking of me.

"It's scary not being able to get myself to move or think or do anything," I replied. "Like I'm partially paralyzed."

He put his hand on my back to comfort me. I couldn't help it, I turned and hugged him tight, pressing my face into his sweaty shoulder. I didn't mind the sweat. I didn't mind the smell. I just wanted him right there, forever. Forever lasted about twenty seconds, at max, before I went to get the cards. I had a baggie full of them in a kitchen cupboard, of all different varieties.

Ezra sat on my mom's plush leather couch, practically sinking into the cushion. Charlie the dog came up to him, butt wagging. It was too hot for him to be outside. He rested his head on Ezra's lap before seeing me and bounding over. He jumped up for a hug and nearly knocked me over. "Hey big lug," I said, kissing his face. "You're my good boy, yes." He looked dumbly happy, and then walked back over to Ezra, expecting similar praise.

"Want to sit up here?" Ezra asked, patting his lap. Charlie, still thinking he was a lapdog despite being gigantic, hopped right up, and pretty much obscured Ezra from sight.

"Nice," I said, and sat down as well. Charlie's tail wagged fiercely, smacking Ezra on the arm. I laughed. "Good boy, Charlie! Good boy!"

"You're cruel!" Ezra said, chuckling.

"He probably wants to be fed," I said. "Are you hungry?" Charlie's ears pricked up and he nearly smashed into the coffee table on his way off Ezra's lap and to the kitchen. He stood by his food bowl; his tail swinging so hard that his whole back half went with it. "Table manners," I said, opening his Tupperware box full of food. He sat down politely. He got a full, giant scoop of food in the evening. It was amazing how much an Anatolian Shepherd could eat. Once the bowl was at his feet, he slammed his face into it. "I still don't understand why the person who had him before us couldn't handle him. He's a sweetheart."

"He's giant," Ezra said. "Maybe they saw a cute little puppy and didn't realize how big he'd get. It's like people wanting babies but not children because children do get bigger and older and then they hand them to us to raise for a fourth of the year."

"Is someone cranky?" I asked, sitting down beside him. There was a comfortable distance of about two feet. I did that for both our sakes, though I'd be perfectly happy crossing that boundary. However, according to Facebook, he was in a relationship with someone named Monica. Monica with luscious lips, beautiful brown locks of hair, and cute, proportional eyes. Everyone wanted a Monica.

"I'm just tired," he said. "The heat's getting to me too. Just not as badly."

While my brain still felt cottony, I asked, "Do you want to play cards?"

"Want to watch a movie first?" he asked, and I nodded. We ended up on The Avengers. It was one of those comfort movies I'd seen enough times I could say all the memorable lines at the right times and still laugh at them.

Chapter Twenty-One: August 2015

Ezra tended to hug a pillow while watching movies. He always rested his chin on it. Charlie was at our feet, fast asleep. I was starting to feel like Charlie. Between the episode and the heat, I was close to just being done for the day. Ezra put the pillow on his lap and patted it. He didn't look at me, just made the motion that it was ok. So I laid my head on the pillow and closed my eyes. His left hand rested on my shoulder. At first, I just wanted to revel in being close to him, but soon, I fell asleep.

He woke me when it was time to go back to the pool. "Hey, Laurel," he said gently. "We gotta get going." The snarky, tired side of me wanted to refute this fact, but the grateful part won over. I sat up and looked ahead but noted that his eyes were watching me.

"Yeah, we should," I replied. An illogical part of me wanted nothing more than to just be held in his arms, to stay there for hours. To listen to his heart, to feel his warmth. It was illogical because it wouldn't, couldn't happen. Part of me accepted that. The other part was telling me just to throw my arms around him and stare into his soft, brown eyes, and read his every thought. To find the truth. The truth—it was just safer not to take the risk.

"You ok, Laurel?" he asked.

"Yeah, just a bit foggy," I replied. It wasn't a lie. I couldn't think straight either because of the absence episode, or because of him. I told myself I never should have pursued this 'friendship' because all it did was give me pain. It gave me that javelin in my chest. Yet, I felt perfectly at peace a few moments ago. All was right with the world then.

A call came over the walkie from March, "Noah's jumped ship. If you're feeling up to it Laurel, I recommend you take care of it."

"Where is he?" I asked.

"House One, I'm assuming," March said.

"Ok, I'm out."

"Out."

I sighed and stretched. "Do you want me to go with you in case you get all fuzzy again?" Ezra asked.

"He's not going to calm down if there's someone else there," I said, and hugged him.

"Be careful," Ezra said. "It's dark out and that place is bad news."

I didn't say anything, just grabbed my lantern from the porch steps and went to the House the back way.

The fact it was dark didn't bother me, but the way the air at camp sucked up light did. The lantern, though expensive and highly effective in most places, gave me only a few feet of light. The dense brush scraped up to me and got into my space. About halfway there, though, I saw an orb. It was pinkish with an orange center. It floated and bobbed like it was on water. I stopped walking. My heart raced with excitement instead of fear. I wanted that orb, desperately, and I didn't know why. It was a craving, deep set within me. So, I pursued it, and it kept moving along gently, but fast enough it was always just out of reach. My pace quickened, as did my breath. It wanted to show me something, I could feel that.

The desire burned so hot in me that I threw myself to the orb and touched it. My body went limp, immediately, onto the ground, but I couldn't see. My vision was gone, my ability to move as well. I felt like every muscle in my body turned into a noodle. I felt no pain, either physically or emotionally. I just was. I existed.

Then, vision returned, but it wasn't from my surroundings. There was light, without a source, blue and hazy in some places, brighter in others. A shape that was vaguely like Lukas stepped out on my right, smiling with gentleness mixed with mischief. To my left appeared Ezra, just as I'd seen him earlier, sheepish, shy, and yet so very alive. I didn't understand what I was supposed to do.

My spirit became mobile, and I felt it leave my body. A strange sensation of lightness and freedom entered me. I was capable of anything. I felt no fear, no inhibitions. A smile crossed my face and I twirled quickly and with such ease, arms out. There was no feeling of cotton in my head or being weighed down by mud. I thought I could soar.

Once I grappled back to reality and shoved the images out of my mind, I hurried along the path. The light illuminated more than before, but the thick brush and brambles were dense enough that even in the daylight it would be difficult to see far ahead. I felt small, covered by the immense weight and age of the forest. The woods made it evident that I did not belong here. None of us did. It didn't want our disturbance or our presence.

"Noah!" I called. My voice was taken in by my surroundings, suffocated. "Noah!"

How far I went, I didn't know. The path became unfamiliar, even if it only went one direction. I was steadily going uphill. My calves ached and my breath started to get heavier. Even in the dark, the heat hadn't abated much. There was no hint of a breeze. Branches didn't rustle, they only called out with the sounds of insects.

Noah was on his knees, with quite a bit of distance between him and the house. He wasn't looking at it. He had his back to it and instead, was facing me. "Noah," I said gently, and knelt down beside him. I placed my hand on his back, and he jumped slightly, surprised. "Talk to me, Noah."

He shook his head. "I don't know what happened. There . . . there was this light. I touched it."

"It showed you what you wanted, didn't it?" I asked, speaking out of instinct.

"It showed me Haley," he said, voice cracking. "I'm a wreck. I—I—I thought I would be able to handle being here, but she died here! I can't do it."

"No one is expecting you to be a hundred percent, Noah. What you went through, no one should ever have to."

He buried his face in his hands, sniffling away the tears. "I just couldn't be around people, couldn't do it . . . started looking around, felt panicked . . ."

"Why did you come up here instead of going to your cabin?" I asked softly.

"I don't know, I don't know, I don't know . . . I think I just hoped I would see her here . . ."

The house wanted him, and he'd be easy pickings. He was broken. His wounds hadn't healed, and I doubted they ever would fully. He would simply be left with scars instead of open wounds. He cried, "I don't like feeling like part of me got ripped out and is gone . . . so much of me . . . so damn much . . . she was supposed to be by my side forever, we'd keep each other standing... People keep telling me to suck it up . . . what the fuck do they expect?"

I couldn't say that I completely understood. I'd never lost someone I loved in that way, and never in such a violent manner, but I had lost people I loved. I'd lost my dad, and in doing so, part of my mom never really returned.

"You're not alone, Noah. I know what the pain is like, and it feels like you're the only one who could ever be in that much pain, like it's all consuming. It will never fully go away, but it'll get lighter and easier to carry," I said.

He shuddered a bit. "It's barely possible to get out of bed in the morning."

"And if you need a day to do that, it's not a bad thing. Everyone recovers differently," I said. "You will recover. You'll make Haley proud. You'll make yourself proud."

"It just feels impossible right now," he said.

"I know, Noah. It feels like you're being crushed by bricks, or that you're Atlas carrying the whole world on your shoulders," I said. He nodded. "Just keep surviving. Every day may be a battle, but you have to win."

Chapter Twenty-One: August 2015

August 9, 2016

Wednesday morning I changed out my bedding, taking my favorite purple blanket and matching pillow onto the couch in the Hytte, replacing it with a red heart blanket also given to me by my father. I desperately needed to do laundry.

Tuesday went by quickly and without difficulty. With it being the last week of regular camp, I was starting to feel a strange bit of restlessness. This happened every time the summer ended, that I was losing part of myself somehow with the time passing. Soon the hills would be quiet and empty of laughter. I desperately wanted to, and needed to enjoy what time summer gave me. I never did well in winter.

Winter was gray, and lonely, and usually came with quite the case of seasonal affective disorder. Medication did help, but it only made it less awful. Even now, I was afraid of it. It was illogical, of course, but with my brain, many illogical things found their way into my consciousness.

So, of course, in arts and crafts, I planned for a favorite, making God's eyes out of yarn and popsicle sticks. They used to creep me out as a kid, but now I have a good ten of them hanging up in the Hytte, maybe for ambience, or because they reminded me of the kids who made them and brought a little color and joy. I had one from Riley and one from Haley.

While the rest of us were working on God's eyes, Jenny was working on her beading so she could finish her packet and get her honors which would be distributed on Friday night. She was doing wire work with her beading, which was extremely technical, and she only had a single book to show her what to do. Nonetheless, the challenge was good for her. She sat in the corner with a bright light, the window, a pair of pliers, and her supplies. Upon completing this task, she would be finished with her art honor progression. I stepped beside her.

"How is it going?" I asked.

"I think it's going really well," she said, holding up a partially completed bracelet. The wirework was similar to Celtic knotting.

"Beautiful, hon," I said. "You're really knocking it out of the ballpark."

"Really?" She lit up and smiled.

"Yeah! It's fantastic!" I said, not lying or exaggerating in the least. Her work was extraordinary.

"Thanks!" she said, going back to carefully twisting and knotting the wire around the glass and crystal beads.

The rest of the period was spent finding scissors, undoing knotted string, and handing out popsicle sticks. This time, my God's eye gift came from Ellie, who made one out of my favorite color: purple. "It just seems like you," she said after handing it to me.

"Thank you, Ellie, I really love it," I said. I'd hang it with the others of course. "Could you write your name on the back and the year?"

"Yeah," she said, like she was autographing something. As she signed it, her quartz necklace hung above the craft.

When it was time to clean up, it was hard to tear Jenny away from her project.

"It'll be here tomorrow, I promise," I said. She looked a bit uncomfortable, restless, about leaving it behind. "Do you want me to lock it up so we can make sure no one gets it?" She bit her lip and looked around, then finally shook her head. "Do you want to take it with you?"

"No, I'll leave it here. Just make sure no one ruins it," she said.

"Ok." I patted her on the back, warily. I didn't know her well enough to know if she accepted that kind of sign of support or not. Her face twisted up like she was going to cry. "Are you alright, Jenny?" I asked. She bit her lip again in an attempt to hold everything back, bottle it up. That could have explained all sorts of things, her behavior especially. If she didn't feel heard, the only way to get the attention she needed was to act out.

"There's people here . . ." she said. "I don't want them to look at me weird."

"We can talk about it during pool time, how about that?" I asked. "Just us."

Her eyes brightened a bit. "Ok, but you promise not to tell anyone?"

"Of course," I said. Her wanting to speak to me, trusting me, made me feel special. I wanted to be that ear for her that she needed, to help her. Jenny was an odd kid, there was no way around that. No other kid picks up picnic tables to throw them into a bonfire, or screams about an illegal gaga ball move, or swings about the banisters in a cabin until the windows get busted out. Yet, with me, she hadn't exhibited any of that behavior. She acted like a normal, high strung teenager, and that's it. One with many interests, hobbies, and opinions.

During the free period after lunch, I went to the Hytte to clean up a bit, since I left my laundry strewn on the couch. I was hoping to find Lukas and see if he managed to glean any more information about the early life of the camp and the Halversons. I hadn't got a single text in well over two days.

I quickly went up the stairs of the old, decrepit porch to the door and swiftly opened it. Lukas was there alright, with Coral. Lukas had not one bit of clothing on his body, not even socks, instead everything was on the floor in front of me. His bare ass caught the incoming sunlight. For a moment, my mind registered that it was deflated looking. My mind also registered that Coral was in a lacey bra tugged up near her neck. Coming back into reality, Lukas grunted and then they looked straight at me.

"Laurel?" Coral asked.

"Ah fuck," Lukas muttered.

"Get out," I said, at first calm, but as soon as they used my favorite pillow and blanket given to me by my father to cover themselves up, the calm was completely gone, eradicated actually. "Now!" I screamed. "Out of my house!"

"Laurel, calm down," Lukas said, reaching out for me, one hand holding my pillow to his crotch.

"You are such an asshole!" I cried. Irrationally uncertain of what to do, I darted for my room. Thankfully the previous tenant was paranoid, I locked the door, at the knob, with a dead bolt, and with a chain and threw myself on my bed. I wanted my damn dog, my solitude, a good fan, and some hot chocolate, and to curl up in bed. He'd desecrated two of my most prized possessions without even thinking. No matter how clean they could become, it'd never be the same. He knew what those things meant to me, and this was my house. He didn't ask to 'bring any friends over'. He just did. My sacred space. Ruined.

Not only that, I had a horrid picture etched or burned into my mind of those two, more of each of them than I ever needed to see. Even how his toes curled made me want to vomit.

I heard faint whispering from outside my bedroom and the door closed. Then Lukas knocked on my door. "Laurel, look," he started.

"Stop," I said. "Just stop. I don't want to talk to you." I had to control the seething anger before I could do anything, otherwise I was sure I'd either crumble into pieces or rip his head clean off his body. Or castrate him. I'd be ok with that too. I wouldn't mind that blood on my carpet. Oh, Laurel, I thought, getting out of control. Calm the fuck down.

"Laurel," he said again. "I'll leave. Where do you want me to go?" I didn't reply, just dug my face deeper into my pillow.

Half an hour later, I called into the walkie asking if Harry would take my kayaking class for the afternoon. I wasn't about to show up red and puffy faced to class. That would elicit far too many questions than I could answer.

Chapter Twenty-Two:

August 9, 2016

All I could think about was how he'd been screwing my counselors. Lukas was a guest. A once beloved and trusted guest, but . . . now? I didn't know if I trusted him at all. What happened hurt. It felt like that javelin went clear through, and now the blunt part was jabbed in there and I had to walk around with three feet of handle hanging out either side.

It wasn't that I was oblivious about his promiscuity. He mentioned it time and time again; maybe he was even addicted. Sex with strangers, sex with acquaintances, whoever he could get. And apparently sex with ex-girlfriends wasn't off limits either. Tinder was his best friend. He went through girlfriends faster than anyone I'd ever met, and after all the years working at a camp, it was difficult to avoid witnessing things that were supposed to be private. I'd once known a couple who conceived a child at camp. They ended up naming their child Aspen after the cabin they were convinced the child was made in. That same pair decided to have sex in a hammock, and that hammock ended up falling and the trees attached collapsed on them. Of course they were fine, but it seemed like a Lukas thing to do.

Yet how could I stop trusting someone I loved? Did I love him? Could I? Of course I could. Of course I did. That was the problem. I'd been telling myself for a year that he wasn't a person I could hold onto. There are just some toxic things in the world: instability, negativity, broodiness, that all kind of came off him in waves and I absorbed. I just wanted the best for him. I wanted to help.

It was never like he'd listen to my help though. I'd encouraged therapists, schools, jobs, anything and everything to get him living in a safe and secure situation, but all was met with a solid 'I'm not ready yet.' One would think a harsh winter camping would make someone ready to settle down at least a bit, but I was wrong.

I was wrong about a lot of things, because I simply didn't understand. Being the twenty-four-year-old virgin that I was, I didn't understand hook ups. I didn't understand how you could just hand over your body like a piece of meat to someone without first establishing at least a baseline of trust. In fact, I didn't understand it at all, and that was part of my problem. Maybe that was the entire problem.

Perhaps Lukas saw me as a fragile doll that needed attention and to be cared for, not as an equal. Not as a friend or partner in the traditional sense of the word. I was always meant to be saved by the ever daring, ever stupid, Lukas.

I was consumed by questions and overwhelmed. The only thing that kept me relatively sane was staring at the suncatchers in the window reflecting the light, and the beautiful expanse of green beyond that. At least in this instance, light wasn't hateful, nor color. I was just tired and confused.

I pancaked myself out of bed and washed my face with ice water to lessen the puffiness. I looked halfway acceptable but was running out of time. I promised Jenny I would be there to listen to her at swim time, and that was coming up quickly.

I noted that nothing really moved from my kitchen/dining/living area except that the clothes were off the ground, and my bedding was gone as well. Lukas had taken his backpack and shoes with him. His research, most of his belongings, and his car keys, were all still accounted for, and I honestly didn't know how I felt about that. His help was help I didn't want but needed. I simply didn't have time to figure out this mess for myself.

Outside, it was extremely bright, and I had a pounding headache. There wasn't a single cloud in the sky. It had to be 90 degrees out, and the pool sounded fantastic, but that wasn't the first priority. Jenny was.

She was at one of the picnic tables with a large, metal water bottle and a friendship bracelet in progress attached. She hadn't changed out of her oversized shirt and cut-off jeans. It was a rarity for her not to fully embrace pool time. I sat down beside her, and she looked surprised to see me. "Where were you during kayaking class?" she asked.

"There were some things I needed to do," I lied. Her eyes made it evident that my face betrayed everything. "Do you want to talk now?"

"When everyone goes inside," she said, returning to her tight knots. She was making a chevron pattern bracelet.

"Who's that for?" I asked.

She shrugged. "I don't know yet." She seemed as deflated as I felt, and I had never seen Genevieve Gentry deflated.

Trisha called for the kids to come into the pool area. She gave me a nod, and I nodded back in acknowledgement that we couldn't stay out here the whole time. Hopefully, just long enough to talk.

"So what's going on, Jenny?" I asked.

"I don't want to go home," she said.

"Is it ok if you tell me why?" I added.

"My parents, all they do is fight. Dad moved out, and Mom's gone nuts. She loses her mind over the smallest things and I . . . I don't like being yelled at. Especially since I can't be . . . good enough to get her to stop."

"What do you mean by good enough?" I asked.

She looked at me, her brow furrowed. She pushed the water bottle away. "I try really hard to do good and keep things clean and perfect for her so she can't get mad at me, but she finds a way anyways. As soon as I get home, it's going to start all over again. She didn't want me to go to camp in the first place. She said it was too expensive, and that I was avoiding her."

"That's a lot for a person to carry," I said. "For anyone, even one as tough as you."

She shook her head. "I'm not tough. People just think I am."

"Is the way your mom acting new?" I asked.

"Not really. She sulked a lot anyway, kinda hid out in the bathroom whenever she was in a bad mood, but Dad was there to kind of fix things. Now he's not. I mean, he's just across town, he's not far away. He seems really different. I don't know, it's hard to explain. I just don't want to go back."

"You still have a few weeks here," I said. "You can enjoy your summer, try all the new things, hang out with friends, but you will need to go home. You have so many activities to get back into, your sports, and clubs, and things will get better. I know it sounds stupid coming from me, but it will. Your parents will find a way to cope with the changes, and hopefully that will help you as well."

"I thought at first it'd be a good thing because they were a mess . . . but I don't like this either."

"Being your age is hard. Everything is changing, but you're truly becoming yourself. To do that, it's sometimes a pain in the butt. You will be ok, though, and you'll become the most amazing person. I know it."

She smiled a bit and nodded. She proceeded to tell me about the time her mother destroyed all of her beauty and personal care products because Jenny accidentally used her mom's bottle of face wash instead of her own. She told me that she wanted to try track this year as well as basketball, and maybe even stick with chorus. She wanted to keep her grades great, not just good, and definitely more than decent. She showed interest in theater, but it seemed like she was desperately trying to do as much as humanly possible to keep herself busy.

"You know, you're allowed time to breathe," I said. "And relax."

"Relaxing isn't relaxing," she said, laughing a bit, leaning back, holding onto the picnic table for support. "I need to do things. I don't like being able to think too much. I get overwhelmed."

I nodded, understanding that. If it weren't for her, I'd still be curled up in bed sobbing and despising reality.

"Dad keeps thinking if we keep going out and doing things that I'll like him more or something. That's not how that works."

"Does he think you're angry with him?" I asked.

She shrugged and shook her head. "No clue. It's not like he tells me any-thing like that, and if he's not with me, he's off with his so-called girlfriend."

"Maybe just tell him what you're feeling. He wants to know. He's a good dad, he's just trying to find out how to do it all to the best of his ability," I said. "Do you want to play cards?"

288

"I just want to work on my bracelet right now," she said. I went to move, and she asked, "Can you stay with me?"

"Of course."

After dinner, there was going to be an all camp game. By request, we were playing "bonkers." It was a complicated game that took up most of the space at camp. The staff was split into three, one group of crazily dressed 'bonkers' who would run around with a sock full of flour and hit campers, a group of medics who wore red, who would then go save the kids hit with flour socks and allow them to move again, and counselors who assigned tasks that could be completed for points. The kid with the least number of bonks and the most amount of tasks completed, won.

My assignment was to let an apple be shot off the top of my head with a hose. Others, like Marsha, had kids throw discs from the top of the hill, all the way down, and back up. Some required a joke that actually made them laugh.

When I went to my station at the pool with a bucket of apples, Coral passed by me. The angry javelin in my chest flared up. She looked like she was going to say something, but I just shook my head to stop her from speaking. I didn't want to hear it.

I set myself up near the pool house with the hose ready and sat on a bucket. I was able to see down the hill. There were a few of the crazily dressed counselors hiding, one behind the gaga pit, one underneath a picnic bench, and one on the roof of Clark, ready to pounce. The 'medics' spread out, their red markers in hand to save whoever got bonked. My mother, who made one of her rare appearances, rang the bell to signify the start of the round.

Children ran and laughed and screamed in glee and surprise. The sound was musical, like bells ringing through the hills and forest. A smile broke across my face, I couldn't help it.

It was Juniper who got to me first. She was out of breath, holding up a finger to show she needed a few seconds to rest. Once she was near me, she was safe from any of the bonkers. "Oh wow, Greg can run really fast . . . it's a good thing he's clumsy."

"What'd you do?" I asked.

"Made a sharp turn and he wiped out on the gravel . . ." she said. "I hope he's ok, but I wasn't about to check."

"A girl after my own heart," I said, smiling. I didn't see anyone down on the road, so I assumed he was fine, and if not, he probably didn't notice. When counselors got really into games, often the adrenaline was so great that cuts, bruises, and even more serious injuries were off the mind until the end.

I placed an apple on my head, and she aimed, badly, showering my face in water, before managing to knock the apple over. "Sorry!" she said, laughing.

"You're not sorry!" I exclaimed, also laughing.

"You're right, you're right."

She handed me her card and I wrote my initials on it.

It did turn out to be Juniper who won the whole competition. She was never hit by a bonker and completed all the challenges. We had ice cream sundaes as a treat after, accompanied by dance music blaring out from the speakers inside Clark. Those who still had energy were out dancing in the center. Everyone else was playing board games or coloring at the tables. It was crowded, and loud, and prime territory for my brain to send the wrong signals to itself.

I had my deck of cards, like always, and was playing a nice quiet game of garbage with Kennedy and Jane. "Are you going to be here next summer?" Jane asked me.

"I . . . I don't know," I replied. "I've been here a long time. I might need to do something else."

"Other counselors say they have to become real adults," Jane said, smiling.

"Yeah, things here are kind of in a vacuum," I replied. "But I'd miss you guys. I think that's why I've stuck around this long."

Chapter Twenty-Two: August 9, 2016

"Even with kids like Ryanne?" Kennedy slyly asked.

"Even with kids like Ryanne," I repeated.

"Will you visit if you're not a counselor?" Jane asked.

"Of course!" I exclaimed, placing a king down as a wild card. I won the round. They sighed and gathered their cards up diligently.

"Who'd be our counselor?" Jane asked. "I don't know if I've had a different counselor than you."

"I think you had Rasa one summer," I replied. "And I'm sure it'll still be fun, probably even more fun because I won't be there to pester you about winning the cleanest cabin award."

"I can't lose!" she cried. "Don't you know me? I don't lose!"

"You're almost as bad as Jenny at losing . . ." Kennedy said quietly while dealing out the cards.

"If it's at gaga I will lose graciously," she said, putting her nose up slightly, making us both laugh.

"No, you'll act like a referee and criticize everything everyone else does in the pit," Kennedy mentioned.

"You don't even watch the games!" Jane said.

"I can't help but listen. You're loud." Kennedy chuckled. I drew a card from the pile first since I won the last round.

"All you girls bicker like old married couples," I said.

"That's because we know each other too well," Jane said. "Without air conditioning or indoor plumbing."

"Or enough sleep . . ." Kennedy said, putting her hand up as if to say, 'give me a hallelujah'. "And through all that creepy junk. I'm glad no one has had any bad dreams lately. I don't think I could handle it."

"I'm going to sleep for a week straight when I get home . . ." Jane remarked.

"Lucky, I still have two more weeks before I get any decent sleep," Kennedy said, finishing off her row of cards. "I win!"

"That round anyway," Jane said with a tiny bit of anger in her voice. She lost twice in a row- that wasn't to her liking.

"We'll have a bit of quiet time before the actual retreat starts, and in an air conditioned building," I said.

"Woot, BS," Kennedy said. "Why didn't they name it something reasonable, or switch the names around? Like didn't they know a bunch of young adults and kids would call it BS?"

"Very well may be why that kept it that way to begin with," I said.

"Just to be funny?" Kennedy looked concerned. "I'm looking forward to it, though. Never done a wilderness retreat. There should be plenty of time to read."

"Why don't you just enjoy what's going on rather than keeping your nose in a book?" Jane asked. "Like playing gaga or soccer with the rest of us?"

Kennedy sent daggers for eyes in her direction. "I like my books."

"Don't kill me," Jane replied. While they were bickering, I did my turn, nearly completing my set of cards.

Jane's words bothered me a bit. If I wasn't going to be at Kellova the following summer, my time in these girls' lives would end. I wouldn't be able to see their progress anymore. I wouldn't be able to answer their questions, listen to their bickering, or enjoy time with them. I'd just become a memory. That would eventually happen anyway, and I knew that. Over the years, many kids had grown out of camp, and I never saw them again.

That javelin in my chest twisted around, mutilating the already inflamed skin. It was the pain attached to losing a loved one, even though I hadn't lost them yet.

Lisey jogged over, waving her hands. "Good news, Miss Laurel! I'm joining the wilderness retreat! My parents signed off on it!"

"I didn't even know you were interested," I said, surprised.

"She isn't," Kennedy said. "She's interested in Taylor."

"I see," I said, smiling. Lisey turned a few colors.

"No, I really want to do it!" she pressed, bending her knees a little bit. She giggled and pressed her hands together. "But I do need to tell Taylor!"

"I told you," Kennedy said.

"Yes, Kenny," I replied.

We had some quiet time that evening. Kennedy and Sadie were reading. Gracia was braiding Jenny's long hair. I had my notebooks out with plans for the retreat and was jotting down notes almost absently when my phone buzzed.

Lukas: *We need to talk.*

The exact words every person with anxiety loves hearing.

Me: *I agree.*

Lukas: *Can I come by Hawthorne?*

Me: *The girls are awake.*

He went quiet. I set the phone aside and stared at the floor, trying to think of what to say. Nothing reasonable came to mind. The anger was still fresh. The horrific image kept flickering back into my brain no matter how much I tried to scrub it out.

Lukas: *Let me know when you're free.*

My heartbeat quickly in my chest, but I retained what composure I could. The girls were enjoying the evening. I wasn't about to ruin or interrupt that.

Night came and the girls went to get ready to bed without prompting. Jenny, though, was restless. She walked in circles inside the cabin and jumped a bit when she finally sat down.

"You doing ok?" I asked her. She nodded in the affirmative. Yet she bounced her leg and clenched and unclenched her fists repeatedly. "Want to go run up and down part of the hill?" I asked.

"Yeah!" she exclaimed. She, Jane, and Sadie sprinted up the hill and ran down screaming. It didn't sound like anyone was scared or in pain, the laughter mingled with it made it more joyful than anything else. Jenny reached the bottom of the hill, in the clearing near the Hytte first, and then ran back up. Once she was in the grass, she rolled down like a child. It looked fun. I joined in, feeling the soft grass cradle me, and then as I tumbled, I giggled. I was transported back at least a decade, maybe more, for a few seconds, where nothing weighed on me, and I didn't have to worry about anyone else.

When I landed at the edge of the clearing, my legs out, I was breathing hard, but smiling. "Your hair!" Sadie exclaimed, pointing. I touched my hair, some leaves and twigs had dug themselves in. I lay down in the grass, still laughing, staring up at the deepening blue of the sky.

I met Lukas behind the bathroom, again, in the bug clouded yellow light. He sat down almost demurely. He kept his gaze down, kept his distance. He acted like a scared puppy. Reasonably so, my heart filled with fury just looking at him. The thought of castration still crossed my mind, but that was vulgar and to be honest, I didn't have a sharp enough blade. He'd still deserve it though.

He looked gaunt. I didn't like how thin he was, even if he'd always been that way. In this light, he looked closer to emaciation.

"Tell me the rest of the story, about the house," I said.

"Laurel—"

"I know that tone, and I don't want to hear it. Just tell me what I need to know about the house."

"What do you need to know about the house? It's deadly. That's all I got. Unless you want the full genealogy of the Halverson clan . . . during the Depression the numbers go down, during WWII most of the men they love got sent off, some die, some come back and then are subsequently killed by the house. Amalie retired in 1956 and of all people it's Charlotte Dahl who takes up the mantle, but you already know that because you work here and have seen the little history brochures. Then in 1968 Edythe took over, and by 1989 they sold the place. Charlotte didn't keep good records. The Apples' daughter Daisy was the one who took over control of the house once Edward was killed."

"What killed him?" I asked.

"A cougar, but not a normal one. According to Daisy, who had been training with her father to take over, he was sure that his time was coming to an end. His dogs had all been killed by weird looking animals, his mules died of strange illnesses . . . and he was starting to feel *off*. He kept waking up at the house, like he was sleepwalking or something. One morning when he woke up there, he was mauled and killed by a cougar. Daisy ended up shooting it right between the eyes and then shot it again to kill it. She's the first person to write down the method of killing the animals that were controlled."

"Damn . . .what happened to Emmett?"

"Charlotte's boyfriend?" he asked. I nodded. "He fell out of a tree and broke his neck. The Climbing Tree actually, in front of Clark. His family sued the camp, but apparently Amalie had some sway in the community back then, and Emmett's family lost the case. Charlotte had another bad bout of depression. She claimed she was cursed."

He took a deep breath. "Ok, Daisy took care of the land until her fifties, when she moved to Decorah, so she was here until the 1970's. She took photographs of every strange thing. Foxes, coons, bears, trees that turned black or white overnight . . . anything that might be evidence. She said she was out of her depth. She had a diagram of the house, how she viewed it. She built some of those bunkers Gary uses and started outfitting the house with all its security measures. She was serious, but also seriously terrified. When kids were at camp, her main objective was to keep them from sleepwalking, and to walk the grounds at night. She was awake all night and barely slept during the day."

"Did it work?" I asked.

"To some degree? Most of the family moved off the property by then and lived throughout Iowa. So there weren't a lot of family members to get killed off, so the house just substituted. Now that there were no construction workers either, it moved to kids."

I grimaced, making a small face. He had an envelope and opened it. It was filled with newspaper clippings. Obits. They were glued to pieces of paper. I took one out, she'd written on the back 'the real cause of death'. One I grabbed was from 1966: *Denise Wheeler, age 12, found asphyxiated in the clearing around House One.* Shivers went up and down my spine. "Haley wasn't the first."

"No, no she wasn't," he said softly.

"She needs to be the last," I said.

Lukas continued, "There was an editorial in a newspaper that made note of all the strange occurrences at Kellova, but nothing came of that. The clipping of the newspaper article was in the Nomad room. I contacted Noah and he couldn't find the same article at the library or online. However, also in the nomad room was correspondence between Edythe and a Lakota man who claims he couldn't help her with the property. She called in shamans of all kinds, white men who were practicing Native American religions, Wiccan people, ghost hunters. She went all out."

"Oh wow," I said, thinking about how desperate she may have been to rid this place of the evil that consumed her whole family.

"They all told her stuff, pretty much the same, with some differences. The Lakota man said the land had a curse placed on it after someone botched a ritual, became too bloodthirsty, and was eventually killed, but his spirit lingered inside the house. One of the white shamans claimed that the malevolent energy was impervious to sage and other kinds of smudging and that when he went home, he was covered in scratches and bruises. The Wiccans performed spells and what-not on the house but said they didn't feel the energy balance change at all, and they didn't like the feeling inside the house, it made them feel hopeless. One ghosthunter claimed that this was all the work of elementals."

"Nothing definitive, though," I said.

He shook his head. "Though the Nomad room had a bunch of articles in there about other shitty things that happened in Greenville over the years. The newest things Mia found were about the woman who was attacked by a former classmate, and then about the woman who killed her sons in the bathtub."

"Why would they keep that?" I asked.

"Hell, I don't know," he muttered. "But people go missing in Kellova Hills more than any other state or national park, and most are never found. I don't think this is contained to the camp."

He sounded defeated. I felt defeated. "It's like a damn war," I said. "Want to go through with it? I really don't think we have a choice. Lost too many people to it, won't lose anymore."

"If you're up for a fight," he said.

Chapter Twenty-Two: August 9, 2016

"What do we do?" I asked, leaning against the wall of the bathroom, staring straight ahead. "To something that can heal itself? Kill at will. Control animals and humans, and generally seems to get the giggles when shit hits the fan?"

"I don't know," he whispered.

"I'm going to ask the kids to help us," I said.

"Are you fucking kidding me?"

"Nope," I said, voice not changing. "The more minds, the better."

"Do you forgive me?" he asked.

"Haven't decided yet," I said. "Will eventually."

Chapter Twenty-Three:

August 10, 2016

Today was the final, full day of residential camp, and I knew when I woke up that it would be the last day of regular camp for me. It was the last morning of waking up on a blue, vinyl mattress thin enough to feel the wood beneath, and smell the mustiness of the cabin, preparing for a full day ahead. Resting with my legs in my fluffy sleeping bag, listening to the birds sing in the trees with cool, damp wind clinging to my skin. Tomorrow, I'd need to spur them awake early to get their things together to move out. For a few moments, though, I could take everything in. Every little nook and cranny of Hawthorne. This cabin had been my home for so many weeks, so many months, so many summers.

When I woke the girls, we had our normal morning routine. I brushed my teeth above a sink filled with half-drowned daddy long legs and flies. There were moths still clinging to the light in the bathroom. Stall three was still plugged up by someone trying to flush a barely bled-on pad. Stall two still had a stamp on the wood of the door that said in the state of California this wood was considered a carcinogen.

Walking down to Clark felt odd. Everyone was silent. Jenny just chewed away on the rubbery bit of her water bottle, while Kennedy didn't even bring a book. The sky was gray this morning. I hoped the heat wouldn't get too bad. We all had sweatshirts on from the night's chill.

It'd also be my last morning sitting on a rocking chair on Clark's deck, just breathing, watching, waiting. Even in my half-asleep stupor, I always enjoyed that view of camp. From there I could see all the kids coming from their cabins, streaming in. I could see the gaga pit, the Climbing Tree, and the ball field. My mother's house, the office, and part of the archery field were also visible.

The javelin twisted a little more into me. . . as if that was possible. Kellova made up a large part of me. To walk away, I'd leave so much behind. First, though, I needed to destroy House One first.

The girls sat at the breakfast table, cramped together to fit. Kennedy kept elbowing Gracia. "Tell her," Kennedy said.

"Why me?" Gracia whispered. This went on while I poured everyone a cup of water.

"Do it," Sadie added.

Gracia looked at me and said, "We listened in on you last night."

Now adding to the javelin was nausea. "Why . . .?"

"Because we knew you were talking about the house and all the bad things going on with it," Gracia said. "You said you were going to ask for our help, and we're going to help."

I took a deep breath and bit my lip. I had to think for a second, but no cohesive thoughts came. "I . . ."

"If you're going to fight a war, you need soldiers," Gracia said.

"Like Dumbledore's army," Kennedy added. "Or the Rohirrim,"

I smiled a bit at her references. "Soldiers get hurt, girls." And in the case of my dad, they can get killed.

"We know," Lisey said. It was her voice that surprised me the most. The only one not making eye contact with me was Ellie.

"Theoden died," Kennedy said. "So did Lupin, and Tonks, and—"

"Not helping, Kenny," Gracia said, looking at her.

"I'm just expressing the fact that I know people can get hurt," she replied very calmly.

"We don't want you to do this alone. Haley was my friend too," Gracia said.

"And we know it's done a lot to you, over the years," Lisey said.

"I . . . uh . . ."

"Whether you let us help or not isn't part of this equation," Kennedy said. "We are, and we're getting the guys to help too."

"They're already on board. Arty and Eddy are still processing some information, but they'll come to," Lisey said.

"I'm going to do a lot of research when I get home," Kennedy replied. "We all will."

"This may be beyond the power of Google to destroy, girls," I said. "It's evil, and old, and many other people have tried."

"But *we* haven't," Gracia said.

"And they didn't have Google last time they tried," Kennedy said with a shrug. "Except for Mr. Lukas, but what he did was stupid no matter which direction you look at it from."

"Fire, chopping it down, and salting it doesn't work, that's all I know," I said.

"Then we'll try something else," Kennedy said. The responsible part of me knew everything about this conversation was bad. This went against any professionalism in my body. This was child endangerment at the very least.

"I don't think you know what you're up against," I finally said.

Their eyes pierced me. "I've seen the orbs. I've seen the girl," Jenny said. "I've heard the house rumble and creak when no one's inside."

Lisey said, "And I've seen the girl too, and the boy with the hat."

Gracia said, "Haley saw the orbs and the girl, and it got her killed. We do know what we're facing, and we're not going to be alone. Noah will be there. He's looking for answers. This time, we'll be prepared," Gracia said. All sense of her happy-go-lucky ukulele playing self was gone. She was dead serious. They all were, and I couldn't argue with that. My philosophy was to treat them like adults, and against my better judgment, I stuck to that.

As promised, the kayaking class and I went to the quarry. We started in the river just east of camp and followed its narrow pathways steadily south. I stayed at the back, surveying as the kids paddled in front of me. After doing this, some of them, for years, were comfortable in this situation. Down at the quarry we'd be met by Harry and the vans to bring us back up to camp.

My mind went through all possible scenarios with the house. It could very well send every animal in Kellova Hills after us at once and leave us slaughtered. I shivered even thinking of that possibility, and yet, I didn't believe it was possible. It had to have a source of energy, and it couldn't be an unlimited supply. If we waged a steady war on it for two weeks, it would be bound to give out at some point. Having children fight a war was wrong, but I told myself I didn't have a choice. In my heart, I felt it was the only way to win.

Once out of the thickest of the woods, the banks on either side of us steadily grew steeper and steeper, showing lines of old stone that'd been carved into over millions of years of erosion. Scraggly trees grew on the edges of these sheer cliffs. The gray skies broke over our heads, glaring hazy sunlight onto us. The water here was cleaner than in Owaissa Lake. Here, I could almost see the bottom. The water wasn't very deep in most places, except for the very center, where it looked like the earth cracked all the way through the crust, only for the void to fill with water. Instead what we were kayaking over were old dredging scars that were long abandoned.

The mounds of stone looked like small mountains with their peaks and valleys. There were occasional islands in the waterway with grass and bushes growing. Geese lived here from early spring to mid-autumn, and they were just as noisy today as ever, sprinting across the water at each other, fighting over territory, completely unconcerned about our presence.

As I surveyed the landscape, Jenny screamed. I stopped immediately and turned in her direction. Her eyes were focused on the top of the tallest peak. Someone was standing there wearing jeans and a red hat.

"Riley?" Arty called. "Riley!" The figure didn't move, not even a twitch. Arty paddled in that direction and everyone gravitated toward him.

"Arty, be careful," I said.

Arty didn't turn in my direction, only continued forward. "Riley, man, what are you doing?"

"Who's Riley?" Jenny whispered. Thank God for her being clueless.

I blinked, and Riley was gone. *"Look in the basement."* A voice as harsh as winter wind whispered in my ear. I screamed, one quick gasp of breath. Everyone stopped and looked at me. I could feel him behind me but was frozen. *"Look in the basement!"* It repeated.

"Where'd he go?" Jenny asked.

All faces were pale and ashen when we reached Harry. He smiled and leaned against the door of the van. When he saw us, his face collapsed. Jenny broke the silence, "We all saw that, right? We all saw that?"

"Yes . . ." Lisey said.

"We did? We all did?" she repeated.

"Yes!" Taylor said gruffly.

Harry almost spoke, but instead, shut his trap and helped us drag the kayaks onto the sand. I didn't look behind me. I was too afraid.

The drive back to camp was no better. Instead of the chatter that usually filled these rides, it was silent. Kids stared out windows, thinking. Harry kept looking at me, as if I were about to say something, but I wasn't. By now, he should know what to expect. I was tired, almost too tired for this. Now, though, I had a lead.

The last night of regular resident camp culminated in a massive bonfire held on the ballfield beside Clark. There, all the kids who achieved honors from their classes and packets, would receive them. The fire was stacked in a log cabin pattern to be lit by torches that were taller than me and wrapped with period pads for that extra bit of flammability. Laurel leaf crowns filled baskets, alongside charms that symbolized the honor earned. Seeing them, I was filled with pride. It helped dull down the dread beating behind my heart. The dread was its own entity, separate from the rest of me.

The kids sat in a large circle surrounding the bonfire. A few of the oldest campers, Arty, Taylor, Gracia, and Jane, were to light the fire. The prayers they spoke while doing so were those of convocation and invitation, and always made me feel unsettled, like my body wasn't properly on the ground.

"Miss Laurel," Jenny whispered to me, poking me. I jumped a bit. She'd been so quiet and still. "Take this." It was the wire and crystal bracelet she finished. It was exquisite. "It'll protect you."

"Are you sure?" I asked. "Jenny, this is beautiful work."

"I'm sure," she said.

"Thank you," I said, and gave her a tentative hug. She was not a hugging type of person. I placed the bracelet on my wrist. It felt right being there.

Once the fire was lit my mother stepped up to the podium and grabbed the newly installed microphone. "Welcome all of you to the end of your journey at Camp Kellova this summer. I'm proud of all of you for learning new skills, making new friends, enduring the heat, trying new things, new foods, and being flexible. It's always an honor to watch you grow and develop your interests and personalities over the years, and what an exceptional place to do so. This marks the one hundred and fifth summer season at Kellova and all of you have helped continue the legacy established here for excellence, dedication, hard work, and fun. If you have been here before you know that tonight is the culmination of all your hard work. You'll get to look back on all the achievements of this summer and celebrate with your friends. First, I'll have the counselors from each cabin come up to say a few words about your time with them this summer, then, each craft will award its honors to their campers. Let's begin."

She called Peter up first. His kids hollered and howled at him as he chuckled and jogged up to the podium. "Ok, ok, boys of Cherry, I must say that this has been one of the most interesting and enlightening summers of my life."

"Yeah, it has!" Arty yelled.

"I'm trying to be serious guys," Peter said, turning red, laughing. "Over the weeks we have played so much mafia, gone on so many hikes, picked wild raspberries, gotten a few cases of poison ivy, got bruises playing ninja, and made unbreakable bonds. You guys are fantastic individuals. Each of you is so unique, so special. Thank you for ruining omelets for the rest of my life. I don't think I'll ever be able to eat them again."

Mason whistled. "Thank you for making me eat the charred corn out of the bottom of a can for sustenance, and that grilled cheese sandwich that fell into the fire." His voice drifted off while he laughed.

"I've never seen a package of Oreos disappear so quickly in my life. First off, Mason, you are on top of things. I know we haven't won a single week for cleanest cabin, but man did you put up a fight. Thank you for helping me clean the mess out of the bathroom this week . . ."

Mason whistled again. "I couldn't have done that without you, I thought I was going to faint. You were willing to try everything and anything this summer and you are fearless, man. Arty, you're a nerd," All the kids laughed and Arty lay back in the grass like he'd been killed. "Who brings that many textbooks to summer camp, man? You quizzed us about history and about psychology and anything else. Put me to sleep a few times to be honest... but you'll go far. You are wicked at ninja and you beat me at every card game I threw at you. I think you're some kind of genius. Let me know when you get into Harvard."

"Brown!" Arty yelled back.

"Let me know when you get into Brown," he amended. "Eddy, Eddy, Eddy, you are a loudmouth. You say what's on your mind, you don't mince your words, you don't even filter them, and I think we all learned a bit from you this summer." The boys ruffled Eddy's hair. "You are adventurous, maybe a pain in my butt, and yet, a joy. Seriously, this summer would have been way duller without you. You're a wicked good Mafia narrator, disturbingly detailed, and I think you have a flair for comedy. Taylor, my man, you are the epitome of a camper. You've done everything here. You are a master at camp craft. You can reliably light a fire with one match, I'm impressed. You have so much drive and charisma and are just the life of the party. You have some awesome dance moves that you need to teach me some time, I need to learn! I'm so happy you were in my cabin this summer."

Each cabin went by until finally it was my turn. I was nearly teary eyed as I stepped up to the podium. "Girls of Hawthorne, we have had a very interesting summer. It hasn't been boring, I can say that. We've had a lot to bond over. Let me first say I'm proud of all of you. You've all grown so much since I first met you. You are incredible people, every last one of you. I've enjoyed our excursions to collect as many lightning bugs as possible in jars, rolling down the hill, making banners, burning pizza, sleepouts, and campfire popcorn. Late night flashlight trivia has been a blast. I've learned a lot from all of you, and I think that's what I'll share.

"Jane, I've learned that there's no excuses not to get in the game and participate in everything. I've also learned that we need to put our heart into everything we do and have passion for life. Sadie, from you I've learned to be kind to the earth, curious, inquisitive, always looking for new things and adventure. You see the best in people, and never give up on that. You're a natural caretaker. Ellie, I've learned that sometimes good things happen when trying something new, and that while it can be difficult to get out of our comfort zone, we can blossom, and you have. I've learned to look at things from all angles, understanding, and patience.

"Kennedy, I've learned the entire history of Middle Earth, and more *Harry Potter* trivia than any one person should know. I've also learned that imagination is everything, and that words are powerful and that they are tools. I've learned about loyalty and support and trust. Lisey, from you I've learned to be open, excited about everything, and energetic. To take on life with both hands and let it take me for a ride. I've learned a bit of fearlessness and bravery from you too. Gracia, I've learned over the past six or so years of knowing you that creativity is the key to everything, and that being a friend is the most important thing in the world. I've learned about communication and joy and what it means to stand by people. Jenny, I may have only had you in my cabin for one week, but I know that I've learned quite a bit in a week. I've learned that we shouldn't judge. We should listen. We should express ourselves. We should say what's on our minds, and do what makes us happy, because in the end, that's what life is about."

The girls were crying. I was crying. I went and hugged them all, curled up in a plethora of arms and giggles. That was going to be a happy moment I'd never forget. Us in a cloud of bug spray, smelling of sweat, with oily hair, stinky shoes, and old clothes, and a family.

Jenny received her laurel wreath for arts and crafts, and she was thrilled. She danced all the way back to her spot in the circle. Gracia received one in music, as well as lapidary. Sadie received one for nature, and another for nature art. Kennedy also received one for nature. The twins, Taylor, Arty, and Eddy, all received their laurel wreaths for orienteering. My whole kayaking class got their kayaking honors.

"Now, will the staff make an inner circle around the fire," my mother announced. It was dark now. As we approached the fire, we were lit by the glow and heat of it. Harry was on one side of me, Mia on the other. I bumped into them both playfully.

"The job of being a camp counselor may seem thankless in the outside world, yet today you can see the impact you have made on these campers' lives and on the lives of those you've worked with. You've all grown this summer and have worked in some of the hardest conditions. You've worked eighteen hour days without air conditioning. It's a hard job, doing what you do. You take up many roles, that of a nurse, sometimes a bat-chaser, mouse catcher, lifeguard, disciplinarian, friend, teacher, artist, singer, cook, engineer, and advisor. You've come to know each other in tough conditions and have made friendships that will last a lifetime. Despite the cuts, bruises, heat exhaustion, and occasional bad meal, or cookout gone wrong, you will treasure these memories the rest of your lives. You'll remember the magic of Kellova, and hopefully, as it lingers with you, you'll return." She sounded like a robot. She sounded far from herself, but at that moment, I just smiled. I was with people I cared about. For a moment, things were ok. Things were even good. Together, we sang the counselor song, before joining the larger circle to sing taps.

Kids were ugly sobbing at this point, though they still had one more night to go, many of them were done for the summer. Ellie hugged Sadie, promising they would find each other on Facebook and exchange numbers.

We streamed into Clark to watch the photography slideshow together, alongside some music that made the ugly crying continue. Gracia sat behind me to braid my hair while the slideshow started. The first photo was of Eddy getting out of a kayak the second week of camp when he face-planted in the mud. Other photos showed kids jumping in the pool, making funny faces, finishing lapidary projects, numerous cookouts, kids in the Climbing Tree, and playing gaga. So many faces. So many individual moments.

When the girls were settled in for their last night of camp, everyone was tired, but no one was sleepy. I got out my *Grimm's Fairy Tales* and a flashlight. For old time's sake, I read a few stories, editing as I went to make them slightly less gruesome. "Will we ever see all of us together again?" Sadie asked when I finished.

"I hope so," Lisey said quietly.

"I promise, no matter what happens, we will all see each other again," I said.

"I thought you weren't coming back to camp," Jane said.

In the dark, I thought for a moment. "No, this is my last summer as a counselor, but that doesn't mean we can't see each other again. I've known some of you for ten years. It seems wrong for it all to end now."

"You'll remember us?" Sadie asked.

"I honestly don't think I could forget," I said, smiling. "I meant every word I said up there tonight. You're all so important."

Chapter Twenty-Four:

August 11, 2016

We started early in the morning, packing up the cabin. Even my own things needed to be ready to go. I glanced at Hawthorne's newest cleanest cabin pole and all the white stripes that encircled it. There was one more charm in my collection, or rather, ten of them, one for each week. I was proud of that. I touched the pole a few times while trekking kid's luggage down the hill a bit to the tractor that would carry it over to Clark and the parking lot.

Kennedy was talking about all the research she was going to do. "I'm going to have my eyes glued to my computer the whole time I'm at home," she said. "I'll learn how to break a curse."

"You seem to know just what you're looking for," Gracia said.

"What if it's like a ghost?" Sadie asked.

"It's not a ghost," Jenny replied. We all looked at her though we were all lifting up Rubbermaid tubs full of items. "It just looks like a ghost, but it's not a ghost." She shrugged her shoulders and walked on.

"What do you mean?" I asked, hurrying to keep up with her, but Ellie's tote was very heavy.

"Just what I said," Jenny responded.

"How do you know?" I asked.

"I just do." She shrugged again. "It's not a ghost."

"I need to learn how to purge a curse out of land and a house . . ." Kennedy said.

"Don't talk too much, you sound crazy," Ellie said. "The other cabins will hear you."

"I don't care," Kennedy replied. She had a notebook open on her empty bunk. The cabin looked so odd . . . and somehow smaller. There was no sense of home to it now. The girls' bedding was gone. Their lanterns, shoes, towels, books, were all packed away. It gave me an uncomfortable itch in my stomach.

My own things would later be carried across the clearing to the Hytte to be switched out and freshened for the upcoming retreat.

"You have a funny look on your face," Lisey said to me. She touched my arm and I nearly jumped.

"I'm ok," I said. "Do you need help carrying anything else?"

"Miss Laurel, there's nothing left," she said. "Let's go to Clark, get some gaga in before our parents come."

It sounded like a sentence handed down by a court, but it wasn't. It was just the end of camp. It happens every year. No year was easy, but most of the time I was excited to get closer to having a nice bed with four walls and a proper shower and hygiene and to eat what I wanted. This time was different because I knew it wouldn't happen again. The desperate desire for the summer to speed by was not there. I wanted to hold onto it instead.

Unfortunately, when we reached Clark, Jane's parents were already there. She ran toward them, and I couldn't help but smile. Somehow, she was taller than her parents. "Come 'ere!" Jane said to me. I went and joined them on the deck of Clark.

"Thanks for taking care of her all summer, hopefully she hasn't been too much of a handful," Jane's mom said, kissing her daughter's forehead.

"Oh no, I loved having her. She's a good kid. I hope she shows you all the honors she got this summer."

"I have them in my backpack," Jane said.

"I'm sure she will and talk about them all the way home."

"Oskaloosa, right?" I asked.

"Yep, all the way to Oskaloosa," her dad said. She hugged me tightly, tight enough I was either lifted off the ground, about to be broken in two, or both.

"Can we get ice cream?" Jane asked. "Dairy Queen?"

"Yes, Jane," her dad said. "Thanks again."

"Bye, Miss Laurel!" she said and disappeared through Clark.

310

Chapter Twenty-Four: August 11, 2016

Gaga really wasn't the same without Jane playing. Jenny was in the pit, covered in dust, playing with all her might against most of the boys from Peter's cabin. The other girls were by me. Gracia had her ukelele packed beside her. She and Kennedy were conspiring about potential antidotes to our situation. Ellie was finishing up a friendship bracelet for Sadie, who watched her.

"Hey, Miss Laurel! I'll see you Sunday!" Lisey said, hugging me, as soon as her mom appeared. Her older sister, who'd been my camper a few years ago, waved at me.

"Hi, Alyssa," I said.

"Hi!" She called and ran out to hug me.

"How's UNI?" I asked. "Education, right?"

"Yep!" she said. "I'm loving it. Going to be a sophomore this year. They've got me working in the library, and it's perfect."

"That's wonderful!" I hugged her again. "Make sure Lisey doesn't get into any trouble until I see her tomorrow."

"I still can't believe she wanted to sign up for the wilderness retreat, she's a wimp," Alyssa whispered.

"There's a boy she likes," I said.

"Ah, that explains everything. Taylor, I'm assuming?"

"You assumed correct."

"See ya, Miss Laurel!" Alyssa said and sauntered off with her family.

Gracia, Kennedy, and Mason were all picked up within the next fifteen minutes. Noah came to retrieve his brother.

"Taylor, get your butt out of that gaga pit!" Noah yelled.

"I'm winning!" Taylor called back. It was between him and Jenny now. The kids around the edge of the gaga pit were counting down. At the very last moment, Taylor was bonked in the knee with the ball by Jenny. "Ah come on!" Taylor whined. Jenny celebrated by dancing and jumping, full leap, out of the gaga pit.

"Come on, loser!" Noah said playfully.

Taylor lumbered over. "I'll see ya tomorrow, Miss Laurel."

Noah said, "Taylor and I are staying with Travis tonight. He'll be bringing us by tomorrow. He doesn't want me to have my car . . ." Noah sighed. "That's fine, saves me gas money."

"Tell him I said hi," I said.

"Shall do."

Lisey ran over to say goodbye to Taylor and I gravitated back to my spot. Noah looked shocked when Taylor kissed her. A look of both amusement and disgust crossed Noah's face. "Damn, boy, you better not turn out like me," I heard Noah say as they left.

Eventually, it was just Jenny, Lisey, Ellie and I on the porch. Jenny was brushing off the dust desperately, trying to get it out of her hair. Lisey offered up wet wipes for her face. "It's done!" Ellie cried, holding up the friendship bracelet. "I wanted to make sure everyone in the cabin got one." She placed it on Jenny's wrist, and Jenny lit up.

"Thank you!" she said. "It's my first friendship bracelet!"

The girls jabbered until their parents picked them up. Then I knew I had to see Ezra before proceeding. So, I gave the honor of releasing all our critters in the Nature Shed to Harry and Peter.

August 2015

Loaded with buckets, giant rubber bands, and cheesecloth, Ezra and I went to the Nature Shed. I recently returned from the hospital where I visited Riley. "How is he doing?" Ezra asked, stepping onto the bridge. He looked back at me briefly.

"He looks bad," I said. "In places where it's not so bad there are these massive blisters, and in other places, he looks like he melted and there are open wounds. I don't know how anyone could handle that amount of pain."

"I'm sure they've given him some serious pain meds," Ezra said.

"Yeah, he's on an IV. Travis said they had trouble finding a vein. He's been sleeping most of the time. I know they're going to graft on like fish skin to help him heal."

"Fish skin?" he asked, scrunching his face.

"Tilapia specifically, but that's their only tactic other than debridement. He'll be there for a while, poor thing," I said softly, shaking my head. The buckets clinked together as we walked. They were old and cumbersome, but this was just part of the routine, even if camp didn't end as expected.

"And Lukas?" Ezra asked, disdain slipping into his voice.

"Minor burns and cuts. He's in custody now," I said. "I'm just surprised Travis hasn't tried to kill him yet."

"I am too," Ezra said. "That's insane. This is all insane."

We got to the door of the Nature Shed. It was a bit bigger than a shed and quite well taken care of for an ancient building. This one did have air conditioning in it, as well as heat lamps and electricity for all the critters inside. "I'm going to miss Jethro and Jed," I said, looking at the two bull snakes we kept this summer.

"They ate so many mice," Ezra said. "An honorable service for this camp." He patted the top of each of the twenty gallon tanks the small snakes were housed in. They were each a beautiful black color, somewhat iridescent in the sunlight. After so much handling this summer, they were pretty chill with me lifting them. I gave them a look over to make sure they were healthy and deposited them in buckets.

"Let's put one under the Hytte and the other behind the office," I said.

"Right where we found them?" Ezra asked.

I nodded. I would still need to clean out the tanks they were housed in, let them dry, and get to work on everything else. It was a daunting task I had surprisingly little time to do.

"Do you think he's going to jail?" Ezra asked.

"Lukas? I . . . I hope not," I said.

"Why?"

"He doesn't deserve jail time. He deserves to get yelled at, but jail isn't going to do him any good. It's going to make him worse."

Ezra sighed and rubbed his forehead with his free hand. We crossed the clearing toward the Hytte. "He committed a crime, what usually happens when people commit crimes is they go to jail to serve time."

"I'm aware of that. Don't have to mansplain anything."

"I'm not . . . ugh," he muttered.

"I know Riley could've died," I added. "And I'm so relieved he didn't. What Lukas did was stupid, but he didn't mean for anyone to get hurt."

"Arson is arson," Ezra said, shrugging. "I know that you want to see the good in everyone, but that can be a fault as much as a strength for you. You overlook a lot."

"Maybe you overthink things too much," I said.

"I know I do." He laughed. "But I don't want you to get hurt because you're trusting people you shouldn't trust."

"I trust like five people on earth, and they've earned that trust for a reason," I sternly replied. "You know how difficult it is for me to trust anyone."

"It's possible to misplace it, Laurel," he said. I wasn't convinced. I should have been, but I wasn't. We let Jethro the snake go beneath my porch, and he slithered away, out of sight. "Now we just need to say goodbye to Jed."

Jed was a fat snake. He enjoyed eating more than any other snake I'd ever encountered. Most snakes of his size were happy with a mouse a week, but he ate every few days. As a result, he was just massive. He was housed in a fifty-gallon tank, one of the largest ones in my arsenal, and I still worried he'd feel cramped in there. When he was released, he slithered off into my mom's garden, careful not to run over any flowers or plants in the process.

"I'll miss that fellow," Ezra said, kneeling down, watching him go.

"You sure did enjoy feeding him, maybe a little too much," I said, chuckling. I put a hand on his shoulder, and he touched it as he stood. Electricity wafted through me, an electricity I was nearly afraid of. "How are you feeling, knowing that this is your last day here?"

"Not sure. A little relieved, a little sad." He took a deep breath and looked at me. We stood still for a moment before returning to the Nature Shed. "I spent so much time here. It's just become part of my schedule, and my support system. This place feels like family to me."

"Regardless, you'll always have a family," I said.

He smiled, sadly and looked to his feet as we walked. "I know that, but not having the summer to just pretend to be a kid again for a little while will be rough, but I need to get away."

"I know," I said. "I'm just not there yet."

"I wish you were," he said. "We could tackle real adulting and what not, together."

I laughed and said, "Real world, ugh, the real world is scary. Scary place."

"And this place isn't?" he asked, though comically. "House One's insides are still smoking. You were in the hospital last night for smoke inhalation,"

"I know, I know, but I'm fine. Shit like this happens, it's part of the deal," I replied.

"It shouldn't be," he said. We entered the shed. He knew it was a sore topic. "Ok, froggy frogs, let's get you to your permanent home."

There were frogs of all kinds, raised from tadpoles I took from shallow pools made by tire tracks on the service roads. So we had a mix of leopard frogs, bullfrogs, and tree frogs. There were also a handful of toads that came out of this batch as well that had been let loose a week ago. Half the responsibilities of the Nature class kids were to take care of all these frogs and provide them with food. They watched their metamorphosis with amazement every summer.

With a giant, white net, we scooped the frogs into numerous buckets. It was going to be too much to carry, so we'd just speed up to Lost Lake and the quarry with them on the four-wheeler. The buckets shook and hopped with bodies, and the cheesecloth was coming to the end of its tenure. I was sure a few of them could wriggle out if they put their mind to it. Those culprits would be the tree frogs, and honestly, they could go just about anywhere.

"I can't believe we have so many of them . . ." I said.

"If only they'd take a dent out of the mosquito population out here," he said.

"That's the hope," I replied. "I think I read somewhere that mosquitoes have no positive ecological impact whatsoever. The world would keep on turning if they were wiped out."

"Then the froggy frogs wouldn't have them to eat," Ezra said, turning on the engine. The gator roared to life beneath us, but then turned to a putter soon after.

"They'd have plenty of other bugs," I said. "If a few of them hung out around the bathrooms at night, they'd have a feast."

"They'd also be swarmed with little hands," he added, putting a finger up. "And that'd be no fun."

With a bit of a pause I asked, "What's on the docket for your last year in college?"

The gator bumped onto the southern trail leading toward Lost Lake, and we and the frogs were jostled about. "Just trying to keep my GPA up. Get that degree and run."

"I'm surprised you never joined like any real clubs there,"

"Nothing fits," he said, shrugging. "Not without trying, though. I just feel a little bit awkward there, you know?"

"Didn't click," I said. "I do know. College was horrifically lonely."

He nodded slowly in understanding. "I wish I studied abroad last year, that would have been fun."

"Can always do it during the May term," I said.

"I still don't know what to do after all this . . . nine months isn't exactly a long time to plan an entire future."

"You don't have to have it figured out immediately. Hardly anyone does, unless they have graduate school, and then it just delays the whole process."

"Sometimes I wonder if going to school will even matter when it comes to getting jobs. There's a shit ton of people with degrees working retail and low-wage jobs that just never get out."

"Do you think you'll be one of those people?" I asked, genuinely wondering. He was quiet for a moment, turning the gator onto a bumpy, rough patch. Usually, this patch was horrifically muddy, but with the drought of this summer, it was dry as a bone.

"I hate the idea of that, but ambition has never been my strong suit," he said.

"That's the truth," He raised an eyebrow and looked in my direction. "Eyes on the road!" I called.

"I'm not going to run into anybody out here!" he said, laughing.

"Racoons, deer, squirrels!" I responded.

He sighed and shook his head with a look of amusement on his face. "You weren't supposed to agree with me about the lack of ambition," he said, chuckling.

"I wasn't?" I asked. "Well, I'm not all that ambitious either. I think my key characteristic is being tired."

"Nah, there's more to you than exhaustion."

"That's a better word than tired. Well, there's more to you than a lack of ambition," he said. "When you have a job, you do it to the best of your ability, no matter what it is, so you're a hard worker. You do whatever you can for your friends when they need your help, and even when they don't."

"And you're loyal to a fault," he whispered.

"A fault?" I asked. "What's the fault?"

"Even when people don't deserve it,"

"People always deserve it," I responded. "Unless they're like Ted Bundy or a psychopath or something."

"Even if people repeatedly prove they don't deserve your loyalty."

"I know what you're talking about, and nothing's going to change," I said, looking at him harshly.

"Ok, ok," he said. We went over a hefty bump and the frogs that could vocalize to complain, did. A huff went out of me, and I held onto the seat.

"We're not on the autobahn," I said.

"There's no speed limit out here!" he exclaimed. "Don't be a party pooper!"

"I'm always a party pooper. The fun killer: Laurel!"

"Sigh," he said, but didn't slow down.

"You're crazy," I said, laughing.

"That I am. Should I put that on my resume too?"

"Put it right next to: Loves customer service."

"Oh if I had to work customer service, I really would go crazy. Like institutionalized crazy."

"Campers can be customers, you have to please them," I said. "Or at least their parents."

He shuddered. "Just think of Walmart around Christmas. That would send me flying out the door and into the arms of any other company that would take me."

"Same, same, same, or it'd send me into a downward spiral."

He parked the gator suddenly, a dozen or so yards away from the edge of Lost Lake. The place sang with life, and in this afternoon light, the place glowed green and gold. The algae were a pastel green that clung to the water's surface throughout the pond.

Ezra and I hopped out of the gator, and each took a bucket. The contents jumped and hopped energetically. I took the cheese cloth off the top and set the bucket on its side at the edge of the water. Most went right in, a few had to be coaxed by a knock on the bottom of the bucket.

"The rest goes to the quarry?" he asked. I nodded, getting back in on the passenger's side. "Have you ever kept one of them?"

"No, I'm not going to try to keep a frog in that drafty cabin. It'd freeze to death as soon as winter comes," I responded. "You could take one to school if you wanted!"

Chapter Twenty-Four: August 11, 2016

"I'm not a frog kinda guy. Maybe I could get a pet fish."

"You don't seem like a fish kind of guy either."

"Why not?" he asked, sitting up further.

"You just don't," I said. "Maybe after school you can get yourself a cat."

"Do I give off crazy cat guy vibes?" he asked, raising his eyebrows again.

"Oh definitely," I said sarcastically.

"I could see you with chickens," he added. "Lots and lots of chickens."

The gator buzzed up the hill. I still held onto the seat. "I'm not a bad driver, Laurel," he said, chuckling. "You act like you're going to fall out."

"Just a habit," I said.

"I'm not Harry, he drives like a maniac," Ezra said.

"You're not wrong," I replied. Harry's driving, both in a car and in a four-wheeler, was terrifying. He paid little attention to anything in the road, or the signs, and barely stopped at stop signs, and even played on his phone. He also didn't take well to being told to put the phone away and pay attention.

The quarry's water was clear, and as the space was much larger, we'd release more frogs here. Once upon a time, the lake was stocked with fish, but as it was so inaccessible by normal means, the fish were unbothered. There were no roads or pathways except those that led to camp, and it was difficult enough to get a van up here to load kids into. While it wasn't pristine, it was lonely.

Ezra got out of the gator and took a deep breath and stretched his arms out. I looked over at him and smiled, I couldn't help it. The vibes he gave off were calm and at ease. All was right with the world, or it could be if I pretended the past few days didn't happen, and for a little while, I could.

We each took another bucket to the edge of the water. The sun reflected off it, and a near perfect image of the sky was painted on the water which broke into ripples when the frogs made their great escape. "Look at them go!" I said, laughing.

Ezra put a hand on my back. I shivered a bit, involuntarily. "It's so nice out here," he said, looking up at the sky, shielding his face with one hand.

"It is," I replied.

"Want to just stay out here for a little bit?" he asked.

"Yeah," I said. We found a flat bit of grass near the water's edge and sat down. The sight was picturesque. The colors were bright and clear. Everything seemed clean, as if a veil were pulled up from my eyes.

"It's nice to be away for a little while," Ezra said.

"Technically we're still on camp property," I said. "But it does feel different."

"You know, I was thinking, I don't know what'd I'd do if I hadn't met you. I may have ended up a completely different person," he said, looking out on the water for a moment, before turning his eyes to me.

"I don't think you can assign your success to me."

"You at least set me up for success," he said. I sat cross legged and faced him.

"You made the choices to learn to be on your own, to stick with school, to keep good grades, to hold down a job, and not follow your mother's footsteps. With everything against you."

He smiled, sheepishly. "You wouldn't have let me fall through the cracks, though, Laurel."

"I would have kicked you in the face if you did, that's true," I said, smiling. "You have someone on your side, no matter what. Just remember how loved you are."

"I love you too," he said, putting his hand on mine. We looked at each other for a moment. His eyes were so strangely deep, a mesmerizing, soft brown color. He had a calm half-smile, half-smirk on his face that was an almost perpetual fixture on him.

He leaned closer to me, slowly, I assumed not to take me by surprise, but nonetheless, I was very much taken by surprise. He placed his lips on mine. A burning jolt of electricity raged from my chest. The first thing that came to mind was that his lips were dry, and mine probably were too. The second thing was that he tasted like our breakfast from that morning, cinnamon rolls. Then it finally hit me, Ezra was kissing me, and I was kissing him back. I wanted closer, and I moved toward him, wrapping my arms around his neck. My mind was a buzz of notes and emptiness, simultaneously. There was no sense of self-consciousness around Ezra. He was one of the few people I felt truly knew me.

He placed his fingers in my hair and I shivered. At that very moment, nothing else on the face of the earth mattered. Only Ezra. The world was quiet, but the sound of my heart beating in my ears was not. I caught a thought for a brief moment, that I felt loved, and cared for. And it was true. I smiled and could feel him smile as well. Then his hand slid from my hair and down my shirt. His calloused hands touched my waist. Every slight touch felt like gentle fire. I wished I'd showered, but I also didn't care. I let him lift the shirt off of me, and it was tossed to the side. For some reason, I found that funny. He chuckled; I could feel it reverberate deep in his chest. I thought I may as well return the favor and clumsily felt for his shirt. He lifted it off without a problem.

This strange buzz of bliss lasted only for a short while until I realized what was happening. Perhaps it was overthinking that did me in, or fear, or something else, but as soon as his hand reached down the waistband of my shorts, I panicked. "No," I said, breathless. "No." He froze in place. I moved back quickly and looked at him. "I—I—I'm sorry, I . . . uh, just, I'm not ready for that."

"I thought you wanted—"

"Not that," I replied. I felt disgustingly sick, like there was something writhing all over me. The nausea rose so quickly, I could have puked. It was terror, completely unexpected terror.

He chuckled angrily. "I thought you trusted me."

"I do," I said.

"No, no, clearly you don't." He grabbed his shirt and stood up.

"You don't understand," I said, though the words struggled to get past my lips.

"No, you're right, I don't," he replied. "You've been leading me on for years. Years."

"I what?" I asked, shocked. "No, no, no, no—"

"Those doe-eyes and how you're always trying to get closer to me," he said.

"I like you, and I love you, that's true, but I'm just not ready for anything like that," I said, but I didn't feel like he was listening. His mind was closed off. His frustration overrode anything else. "Why are you angry?"

He looked at me like I was stupid, and I felt stupid. Humiliated too. "I should go," he said.

He just left with the buckets and the gator. Once he was gone, I put my shirt back on and sat there for the longest time, trying to think. All this time, I felt he truly cared for me, and in a matter of minutes, I ended up feeling like a hunk of rotten meat. I stood up and puked near the water and felt dizzy and sick. I desperately wished I could be normal, that I could have gone along with him without fear, or even with excitement, but that wasn't the way I was wired. If I could have even pretended to enjoy it, I would have, just to make him happy, to have him decide that maybe I was worth being with.

Yet the very thought of pretending to be enough was heartbreaking. I couldn't do that to myself. What kind of person would I be? Yet I felt so freakish and alone. Nothing I could do was right. I was foolish.

I walked back to the Hytte on my own. It took three hours, but I made it. I had no water, so I went to get some from Clark. As I walked to Clark, though, I noticed Ezra's car was gone. As it so happened, I wouldn't see him again for almost a year.

Chapter Twenty-Five:

August 11, 2016

I texted Lukas to tell him where I was going. I blasted the AC and checked my phone since it buzzed in my pocket a number of times.

It's Noah, we're going to need black salt. According to google we will need sea salt, some ash from sage, and preferably just a lot of sage, and some dirt from a graveyard.

Me: *You've got to be kidding me.*

Noah: *Nope. And when you mix all of it together, visualize the House going boom, or something.*

Me: *Going boom?*

Noah: *Or disintegrating, I don't care, but visualize it being destroyed. Preferably in a very painful way.*

Me: *Ok*

Noah: *And we need mirrors, lots of mirrors.*

Me: *Why?*

Noah: *To reflect negative energy back to the house.*

I felt slightly insane, but it wouldn't have been a big change to recent events. I drove to the store. Upon parking, I texted Lukas to see if Gary had any sage we could use since he grew so many herbs. Lukas responded with: *Are we turning into ghost hunters or witches?* I didn't respond, just went inside to purchase a lot of sea salt. All of it in fact. If it weren't for self-checkout, I would have felt really silly. Not only was this weird, but I was also going broke.

Noah texted again, saying I'd need to buy ink and parchment. *There is no Diagon Alley around here, where do you think I can buy that stuff?*

Noah: *Well, the information says that blood will work for ink.*

Me: *What in the hell are you reading?*

Noah: *Books on magic. They actually spell it magick here. Gracia's been texting me things too.*

Me: *Will regular paperwork?*

Noah: *It says parchment.*

I put my phone away and focused on the soil from a graveyard. If I was going to steal the topsoil off someone's grave, I might as well make it my dad's. My mom and I weren't grave worshippers and hadn't gone to the cemetery in some time. I never saw the point. If there was somewhere to go after death, why would someone hang around a cemetery? Sure, his body was six feet beneath the dirt in a fancy coffin, probably bones by now, but that only made me feel queasy.

Greenville Cemetery was on the edge of town, like most cemeteries. People didn't like looking at them and preferred to be a comfortable distance away. Dad's grave was in a far corner, off kind of by itself beneath an overhang of trees. Mom didn't like the idea of it being crowded amongst other people. So, I drove in, past the congested alleys of graves, all crammed together up front. The further back I drove, the more space there was between plots, and the less extravagant the headstones. Even in a graveyard one could see money and class, but I doubted the dead cared anymore.

Thinking of Dad, I choked up a bit, struggling to remember his face. It was so hard to picture him well. Mom hid all his photographs, and I was so young when he died. I couldn't imagine the sound of his voice very well. All I could get was a feeling, a comforting, protective hug. I remembered him calling me his little tiger, and that I was his brave warrior. I didn't feel much like a warrior, but I blinked away the tears, and grabbed the tools I could dig up: a knife, a spoon, and a few gallon-sized baggies.

Dad's headstone was nothing special. It looked like a generic Arlington cemetery type. There was an American flag stuck in the ground beside it, and a vase meant to hold flowers that was never used.

Despite my feeling that Dad was nowhere in sight, I started talking, "Hey, Dad, I . . . I'm sorry I haven't come here often. Just didn't seem necessary, and it probably isn't. I hope you don't mind that I'm taking some dirt. There's this weird thing happening at camp and for some reason my kids think soil from a graveyard will help. I wanted to at least take the soil from someone I knew rather than a stranger. It seems wrong either way, but we're kinda desperate." I paused, plopping some dirt into the baggie. "I really wish you were still around. Mom's distant and acts like a maniac most of the time. She thinks I'm neurotic or just bat-shit-crazy, and I feel so alone. I know I'm not . . . but if you were still here . . . ugh, it's stupid to even do the what-if's. You're dead. I gotta just be ok with that . . . but I know mom's not. She hasn't been. She clings or throws me for a loop and acts like she wants nothing to do with me. There's no in-between."

I didn't realize how much I dug with the knife. There was a big scar of earth beside the grave. Quietly, I used the serving spoon to bag it up. Then I sat down, cross legged in the shade. "If you have any supernatural powers being dead and all, I could really use your help."

In the town bookstore, I managed to find some parchment and a proper ink pen. Now with my bank account depleted, I set off toward the hospital.

My heart pounded along as I drove. It wasn't the House, or the magic, or any rituals that had to be performed that bothered me; it was thinking back to the last real conversation I had with Ezra, last summer. He ignored every text I sent after the incident. I apologized repeatedly, saying that it wasn't him. It wasn't a lack of trust. It was that there was something wrong with me, and what that was, I didn't know. I told him I wished that I could have gotten past whatever fear pushed him away… but the truth was, he didn't act acceptably afterwards. He left me. He never apologized, and I was angry.

It was the first time I felt genuinely angry toward Ezra after that. Mostly, I thought he'd written me off, and it would be a long time until I'd see him again. Fate had something else in mind and it landed him in the lake for me to fish out.

My mind switched to autopilot as I drove to the hospital. When I parked, I placed my head on the steering wheel and took a few breaths, trying to ground myself. I felt flighty, like my brain could just drain out my ears. I could have stayed that way indefinitely, but I needed to complete this errand. Seeing a friend shouldn't have been an errand, but he may not have been much of a friend either.

So, I got up and went into the hospital to check in at the visitor's desk. After all this time, I imagined they were familiar with me. "He's a popular one," the lady said with a bit of a southern twang to her voice. She smiled and handed me a badly printed sticker with my driver's license picture on it and big words reading: *Visitor*.

I stepped into the wing of the hospital where Ezra had been held for three weeks. The door to his room was open, and my whole torso buzzed and burned. The police were no closer to finding answers, but I had. He'd been possessed by House One, it took control of him, and Gary saved his mind, but in the process, destroyed his body. It felt good to have answers. It was like being given a weapon in battle. Now, though, I realized that didn't fix Ezra's past behavior. It didn't erase what happened.

I stepped inside the room, but Ezra wasn't alone. A girl with blonde hair was sitting in a chair beside him, holding his hand. He was out like a light. All that buzzing and burning inside me intensified so highly I thought I was going to puke right then and there. It was Jessica.

I didn't want to be there. I didn't want to exist. I wanted to run and hide and find some cover. Maybe curl up and die there.

But she already saw me. She stood up quickly. "Hi," she said. Makeup, to a hospital, and it was on point. I hadn't showered in three days, my hair was in a tight braid, and there were four layers of deodorant on me.

"Hi," I said.

"Who are you?" she asked. Yeah, I didn't think she'd recognize me.

"Uh, my name is Laurel," I said.

"Oh! You saved Ezra's life. Thank you so much." She sounded genuine. That was nice. "You worked with him for a few years at that camp, right?" I nodded. "It took me forever to get off work to get here, I'm so happy that he's alright."

"Was he able to tell you anything about what happened?" I asked.

"He says he doesn't remember, but he's been having these nightmares according to the nurses, and even when he has naps, poor Ezzie." I'm sure he hated being called that. It was saccharinely sweet, disgustingly so. "Do you want to get some coffee or something while he rests?"

"Sure," I said. I really, really, didn't, but I might as well know more about the person that Ezra's been spending his time with despite the fact that he never bothered to mention me.

"I'm buying," she said. "You saved his life after all. I can't believe you kept CPR going that long! What kind of coffee do you like?"

"Hot chocolate?" I said nervously.

"In this weather?"

"I'm cold," I said, smiling. I was surprised. "I haven't had air conditioning in months."

"I couldn't do that, I like my air conditioning and frequent coffee breaks," she said.

"We get coffee in the morning, but it tastes like horse piss, that's why I'm fond of hot chocolate." We both laughed. "What do you go to school for, at Valley?"

"Early childhood education," she said. "I want to work with the little littles."

"I like to work with middle-schoolers to highschoolers, they're fun," I said. Why was I talking to her? Why was I discussing stuff?

"I'm not quite sure where the cafeteria is . . ." she said, smiling a bit, looking down at her shoes.

"I do, I've been here way too much," I replied. I led her through the halls and to the elevator. The cafeteria was on the third floor.

"Do you think Ezra will be ok?" she asked, looking at me with nervous hope. I didn't want to hate her, but I didn't want to like her either. And I didn't.

"Whatever happened, he's been through a lot. He has a brain injury, that'll make things difficult for him. A few years ago I was in here for a bad brain injury and I still have problems with it."

"Oh! What happened?" she asked.

I pressed the big three button on the elevator. "Car accident. Ezra was there, actually. All he got was a big bruise on his elbow, and his hip hurt for a bit. He couldn't get off the floor without whining. A few weeks after the accident, he was at my house playing cards, and we were sitting on the floor, and he just couldn't stand up or wouldn't. He said he felt like he was forty."

"So are you good friends then?" she asked. I nodded, unwilling to tell the truth. At least the full truth. The elevator landed on the third floor, and we turned right, following our noses to the smell of old hamburgers and school-carton milk. "He's not the most . . . open of people," she added.

I disagreed, but when it came to girlfriends, they were never mentioned. Everything else was fair game though. "He likes to keep some things to himself, but he can be a chatterbox, especially if he has an opinion on something."

"He seems quiet to me, like only on the outside though, like there's a million things going on in his mind that he just doesn't share."

"That's an accurate assessment," I said. Past the cafeteria was a small coffee shop newly installed two years ago by popular demand for better coffee. Officer Stevens claimed it was no better, he just had to pay for the service.

"God, I never thought anything like this could happen . . ." she said, shaking her head. "It's insane. I got a call from a police officer asking to speak to me, if I was in the area, if I knew of anyone who had beef with Ezra, or if he'd been acting strange lately."

"Had he been acting strange?" I asked.

"Usually we talk every day, either by text or calling, but he'd been weirdly quiet. I was getting on him about it, asking if everything was ok and he claimed he was fine, just busy. He wasn't acting like himself. Like, I know he's a busy guy, and has a lot going on, but he wasn't finding or making any time. It was getting on my nerves really . . ." She ordered some fancy kind of coffee, a cappuccino with vanilla soy milk. I just asked for hot chocolate. "Then it went all quiet. He wasn't reading messages, answering phone calls, now I know why. At that time I thought he was mad at me for something."

"How long have you been dating?" I asked.

"Since February," she said, and already her Facebook was all Ezra, all the time. Kind of creepy. "It was like we just clicked so well. I can tell he's the long-term kind of guy, not looking for a fling or anything, and he's just so sweet and a gentleman."

"He is," I replied. I may have been lying, but I wasn't sure. We sat down at a booth near the window. The window had some condensation from the humidity on it, and it looked streaked with fog.

"How long have you known him?' she asked.

"Probably a decade and a half," I said. "Since we were campers, and then we worked together. Sometimes it feels like forever, like . . ."

"Like you've never actually lived before you knew him." she said. I nodded. Javelin was completely through me now and I was left with a large, gaping wound. I could practically feel it bleeding. "I'm worried about losing him since he's like this."

"Me too," I said, though I didn't mean to. She looked up at me with vaguely suspicious eyes. "People change because of brain injuries. I don't know where the trauma in the brain occurred for him, but it can affect personality, memory, and we already know it's affected his speech. I had to relearn to walk in a straight line, deal with light, relearn to drive, all sorts of things."

"It's awful he doesn't have family to help," she said. "That he's so alone over here."

"He's not alone," I said. "Most days some friends of his are here all day with flashcards and trying to do their own version of speech therapy, playing video games."

"What friends?" she asked, looking confused.

"Some campers of his, mainly Noah, but he's a kid." I smiled, just thinking about them.

"He's being babysat by a teenager?" she asked. Granted, Noah was probably only two years younger than her by the looks of it.

"And everyone's rooting for him to get better at Kellova," I said. "That banner in his room was made by the girls in my cabin. Besides, he has a family. They're just not blood."

She was quiet for a moment and looked at me, analyzing me. She was smarter than I initially gave her credit for. Her blank, stupid eyes in the pictures weren't really blank and stupid, they were disturbingly intelligent. "You?"

"Yeah. I'd do anything for him, honestly. Despite everything."

She watched me closely, her gaze wasn't hard, but it wasn't soothing either. "Do you know what happened to Ezra?" she asked.

"No, not really," I said, lying. "All I know is I think it happened at Camp Kellova."

"What makes you think that?" She sipped her coffee, then proceeded to pick at the lid.

"It's just a hunch," I said, almost saying her name out loud, but the name didn't work well in my brain.

"He's everything to me, I need whoever did that to him to be brought to justice."

"By God, I hope they will be," I said, though, I thought the entity who did harm him was unseeable, and barely perceivable. Maybe it was the possessed, shapeshifting house on evil ground. I couldn't tell her that.

"And you're his family?" she asked.

"It's hard to explain," I replied, avoiding eye contact now. I was uncomfortable, and that feeling of wanting to flee was back in me. To tell her the truth was to hurt her, but it was Ezra's truth, not mine. "We should go check on him, see how he's doing."

"Why didn't he talk about you?" she asked.

"That's a good question. I guess he didn't want to," I replied quietly. My voice hitched in my throat. I pushed down the growing lump with hot chocolate.

"Why not?"

"I don't know. He never mentioned you either," I said, shrugging.

"What, do you think you're his girlfriend or something?"

"Nope, that privilege is all yours," I said. Her tone was getting harsher, and I was shrinking. "And I never was either, if you're concerned about that." She deflated a bit from whatever anger briefly boiled up inside her. "I'm just . . . I don't know what I am." *Nothing. That's what you are. Nothing.* "Thanks for the hot chocolate, I'm going to go." I stood, shaky, wanting to disappear.

"Wait!" she called. Couldn't do it. Couldn't turn around. I just kept walking. I wouldn't see Ezra after all. He had all he needed in her. I was stupid to come anyway. She jogged after me and put her hand on my arm. The feeling of beginning stages of panic started. I wanted, needed, to hide. "Hey, I didn't mean to come off that way, I just get a little jealous is all," she said.

I shook my head. "You're fine. It doesn't matter. I gotta go."

She could have him with all the disappointment, heartache, and pain that came with him.

"Laurel!" When her hand wrapped around my wrist, I was about to genuinely freak out. "Laurel, maybe we should talk. Like, about the truth. What's up with you?" I looked down to my feet and felt stupid, though the waves of panic were subsiding. "Come on, let's maybe sit in the hall."

I let her lead me to a bench. I sat as far away from her as I could. "You can have him. All yours. I don't know why I've forgotten about everything that happened . . . just when I saw him in that lake, it was like . . . everything was forgiven."

"Were you two . . . like together?" she asked.

I shook my head. "No, not really. I loved him, I still do, but not in a way he understands. I was only ever around during the summer, and then the rest of the time it was like I didn't exist. And I kept pretending it was ok, but I never took the leap of . . . following his advances I guess, because I've never been interested in that sort of thing." Why was I telling this person everything? I didn't even know her, or like her for that matter. She gave off very weird, spikey, almost sea-urchin like vibes of anxiety and jealousy. She was a wave of insecurity, but in this case, what was I?

"What do you mean by advances?"

"I think he wanted to have sex," I said, though I'd never said it out loud, or even to myself. "And when I said no, he left me a good three hour hike away from my cabin . . . and never spoke to me again." She looked horrified, which I did appreciate, but she would be in her happy little world if I hadn't said a thing. "I shouldn't have said anything," I said. "It's not fair for me to butt in like that."

"No, no," she said, looking away for a moment.

"He was probably just frustrated, that's all," I said.

"Why are you putting the blame on yourself?" she asked. I was shocked by her tone of voice. She sounded like a therapist.

"Uh . . . I don't know," I said, thinking. "It was like nothing like that happened when I saw him in the hospital . . ."

"But you blamed yourself before he was in the water," she said.

"Maybe you should go into psychology instead of early childhood education," I replied. She raised her eyebrows like she was waiting for me to speak. "I don't like to blame people for doing anything wrong. Anything anyone's ever done to me is forgivable."

"Let's go talk to him," she said, standing up briskly.

"Uh, no, no, no, no, no," I replied. She clutched her bag to her side. Her face was soft. There was no sense of jealousy left in it. Maybe pity or confusion, but there was definitely purpose.

"Let's go," she said.

I sighed. She wasn't going to budge. Unfortunately, I was the budging type. So, I followed her down the corridors to Ezra's room. He was sitting up, looking at us with wide eyes. He looked scared that we'd met each other. Perhaps this was something he'd been avoiding. I had to admit, it was awkward, and I still felt like shit about the whole situation, but his face did make me want to laugh.

"Look who I met," Jessica said.

"Hi, Laurel," he said. He could speak without halting now, or spitting out words like they were slugs in his throat.

He looked at Jessica warily. She said, "I weaseled the truth out of her, and you owe her an apology."

The tension wafting off Ezra made me want to vomit. I wanted out of that room, and back in my car with my head on the steering wheel, pretending like the world didn't exist.

"For what?" he asked. "What'd I do?"

I took a deep breath. "No use dredging up the past," I said. "I should go."

Jessica put out her hand as a signal for me not to move. "Last summer, Ez," she said.

He lowered his face and nodded. "Yeah, that was a dick move."

"That's an understatement," she replied. "She did CPR on you for . . . what did they say, like half an hour to keep you alive, and that's all you have to say?"

We both looked at Jessica, startled. "For the record, I didn't know it was him when I pulled him out of the water." I held up my hand a bit as if speaking to a teacher. Maybe she would be good around toddlers.

"You led me on, Laurel," he said, though I could hear strain in his voice in an effort to make his words fluid.

"No . . . I didn't," I said, very sure that I was telling the truth then. "I've known you for over ten years. I haven't changed, except for maybe the brain injury, but . . . I didn't, I swear, at least not intentionally." He was quiet and looked at his lap. I didn't feel like myself.

An apology wouldn't do anything. Weeks without adequate sleep, the pressures of the House, and camp in general, had left me spineless and numb.

"Ok, so we were in a miscommunication station, I get it," Jessica said, hands up as if she was above to slap both of us.

"Sorry," Ezra said. "I screwed everything up."

"Yeah, you did," I admitted.

"And I'd like to say that I paid the price for it," he said, motioning to himself.

"Yeah, I'd agree to that," I said, and sat on the bed beside him. "I'm just glad you're ok."

"That easy?" Jessica asked, looking at me.

"Can I talk to him for a moment?" I asked. She looked puzzled, but when she realized I forgot the word 'alone', she stepped out of the room.

I said, "The House did this to you. I'm going to destroy it, but not stupidly like Lukas. I'll find a way to really destroy it."

"You're crazy and going to get yourself hurt," he said.

"It tried to kill you, and it would have succeeded if . . . sheer luck hadn't intervened." I wasn't willing yet to say that it was Gary that did the saving, because that also meant he did the shit-beating. Ezra rubbed his face with his less-mutilated hand.

"So you're going to risk your life to destroy that thing?" he said, focusing on each word.

"Yes," I replied. "And I won't stop until it's gone."

"What if you don't know what you're getting into? What if it's way over your head?"

"Maybe that's what happened to you," I said. "You were on camp property. You had to have been."

"I don't remember what happened," he said. "The last thing I actually re-member was being in my room and I was looking around for my keys."

"That's it?" I asked. "Where were you going? Why did you need your keys?"

"For all I know I could've been going to the grocery store."

"Do you have your phone?" I asked.

"Yeah, the police gave it back," he said. "Waterlogged, but it mostly works."

"If you remember anything, why you were heading to Kellova, let me know, and if anything changes,"

I fiddled in my bag to find my own keys. "You're going already?" he asked.

"You've got her to take care of you," I said, and waved a bit. His mouth was half-open like he was going to say anything. I left the room and waved at Jessica and left before she could say anything either.

Chapter Twenty-Five: August 11, 2016

Back at camp, I moved some of my things to the BS building. Then it was time to prepare for check in. Getting into the rhythm of setting up the check in desk, the sign-in forms, and the canteen money box comforted me a bit. I could focus on the present. With some time to spare, I made up my bed in BS, checked the fridge to make sure it was empty, and set live mouse traps with peanut butter sandwiches. Harry walked in on me as I was doing that.

"Oh no . . ." he whined.

"Do you want to sleep here with mice running around?" I asked.

"No . . . but I don't exactly want to go all the way to the House to get rid of them," I said.

"Then we'll just put them in my mother's office," I replied. Harry laughed, but I was serious. I slipped a trap inside the stove, and another inside a cupboard with the pots and pans.

"I'm sleeping on a top bunk," Harry said. "Away from all those mice."

"I'm sure they can climb," I said.

"There's one metal bunk and it's going to be mine," he replied, slinging his overfilled bag on his shoulder.

With little time to spare after that, Harry and I went down to Clark to join Gail at the check in. Gracia was first, no ukelele in tow this time, which was a surprise.

"Don't do anything too dangerous," her dad said. "Don't try the advanced side of the climbing wall again."

"That was three years ago," she whined. "God, when are you ever going to forget that?"

"Gracia, they had to call the police department to get you down," he said. He was right and it was hilarious to remember. It was also the day she made a joke about how she thought I was thirty and would have a lot of cats because I'd be alone for the rest of my life. Good times.

Her dad hugged her and left with a wave.

"Kenny and I have some supplies," she said and brought out a three subject notebook. She slammed it on the table and opened it up.

Gail came in. "It looks like Eddy's parents backed him out. Broke his arm climbing on their roof. He slipped off and it broke in three places. Poor kid."

I sighed. "Any others jumping ship?"

"Not that I know of, but I need to get the Gentry's invoice, oh where is my brain today . . ." she muttered and briskly walked back toward the office.

"Spells," Gracia said. "We have a pretty good idea that it will work, as long as you got the right supplies."

"I did," I said.

"What is this, *The Twilight Zone*? *X-Files*, come on . . ." Harry muttered.

"How do you know anything about those? You're too young," I said.

"Parents were obsessed," he said, shrugging. "And I'm only a few years younger than you!" He looked offended, in an amused way.

Lisey arrived and ran up to Gracia and opened her purse.

"Where did you get all those?" Gracia asked.

"Mom's friend lent them to me. I sort of kind of told her that I was going to be staying in a haunted or cursed place and she brought them over. Uh . . . this one is black tourmaline, and this is malachite. She said it was used by shamans to protect against dark curses and what not so I thought that could be helpful considering the circumstances." She held up a large black, ragged stone, and another that was smooth, palm sized, and made of swirling green. "She also said amber protects and shields a person from dark energy, so if we're doing those spell things you mentioned, this could be good." She pulled out a chunk of nearly clear amber. "It's not a crystal, but it's pretty cool."

"This is awesome," Gracia said excitedly.

"Grace!" Kennedy called as she and her parents came through the door. "Porch, now!"

"Kenny! Kenny! Uh, hello?" Her mom said, arms outstretched. Kennedy hugged her and then ran out the door. "Goodbye to you too? Ugh, that girl."

I smiled and said, "She's just excited."

"She stayed up all night learning different survival techniques and recipes to cook over a fire." I doubted that was the truth, but if it made her mother more comfortable, then that was reassuring. Kennedy looked just like her mother, even had the same bob-like haircut. "At least it'll get her outside more and maybe her nose out of a book for a little while."

Chapter Twenty-Five: August 11, 2016

Arty didn't have his books with him. He still wore a pastel polo shirt and a nice pair of khakis, but without his burden of books, there was something different about him. He high fived me and hugged his dad. "Any update on the guy in the lake?" his dad asked.

"Surprisingly, yes," I said.

"They said on the news that it was Ezra Concord, Arthur's old counselor. Couldn't believe my eyes when I saw the picture, they put of him up there. Still no clue who did it to him?"

"No," I lied. "But he is doing better. He can talk now. I went and visited him earlier today."

"Good," he said. "Arthur says his favorite cabins have always been with Ezra. He's an upstanding guy. It's a shame what happened, and to think someone in this community did it to him sickens me." I nodded. "Do you know if there's a GoFundMe out there for him? I'd like to do my part to help."

"That's a wonderful idea, I'll pitch it to him."

Near three that afternoon the Halverson boys arrived. It was scary how alike they looked. Taylor was creeping up on Noah's height and the only major difference was that Noah had a slightly wider face and tattoos. Taylor ran off from his brother's side and immediately went to the edge of the deck and kissed Lisey, a little too much for anyone's comfort.

"Ah, quit it!" Harry called. Noah sniggered, making a slightly disgusted face.

"He says you're worse," I said to Noah, looking at my sheet.

"I can sign for myself," Noah said. "Been emancipated. Taylor will in a month when he gets to sixteen." He plopped a folder with papers down on the table.

"Congratulations, I think," I said. "I know it wasn't the best situation for either of you to be in. What's the next step?"

"Get us into a house or an apartment. Saving up now for a deposit." Noah shrugged and placed a very heavy backpack onto the table. "Here's my research." There had to be four inches of paper in there. "Where's Mia? Is she going to join us?"

"She'll meet up with us in BS later, but she isn't going to do the retreat. She's gotta take care of the horses." I said. "Do you have anything your mother signed for Taylor?"

He handed me a sheet of paper with a clearly forged signature. I rolled my eyes at him but put it in the file anyway. I wasn't going to argue.

"You can't prove it isn't hers," Noah said.

"Let's go," Harry said. "Everyone and your junk to BS!"

The air conditioning of BS was always a bit strange, simply because I wasn't used to it. The kids all piled their belongings in the center room of the place before picking rooms. Taylor and Lisey still hadn't separated themselves from one another. At the moment, she was sitting on his lap in one of the large chairs available for the kids to sit in. Noah was off to the side by himself, Kennedy was talking to Arty about video games.

"Ok, so we have everyone," I said, sighing. "And y'all know this isn't going to be a normal retreat. Might as well get that out there to begin with. If you're signed up for this, you're signed up for a fight. Not only the elements this time, but House One."

"Let's burn that motherfucker down," Noah said.

"Can you please watch your language, man?" I asked.

"Only said what I was thinking," he replied, shrugging.

"For the next few days, we're going to get our meal plans together, our schedules, and if we have time, plans for what we're going to do to that house," I said.

"I have ideas!" Kennedy said, waving her arms.

Harry threw his hands up in the air and went over to Taylor and Lisey. "Ok, one of you is sitting over here with us." Lisey flushed red with embarrassment, and they separated. I tried hard not to laugh.

Kennedy and Noah joined me at a foldable table with their plans. They both went over the spell-like ceremony they previously pitched to me over text.

Noah then took a different approach. "I think this thing is ancient. Older than the Otoe. Professor M at Valley said the Otoe in the area used to say something lived in the Kellova Hills called The Gatherer, and it was always mentioned in the plural. It was what made the hills, ate the earth, and controlled the animals. The Otoe worked with it, at first, when they came to this land, to establish . . . he used the word hegemony over it, but then one warrior did something. He performed a ceremony where he took the skin of an animal and wore it, and gave the animal's spirit over to the Gatherer, and promised himself as a vessel in exchange for a long life. It's said that this man grew abnormally tall, and his legs and arms were twice as long as they were supposed to be. Everyone feared him, as he supposedly would take people from other tribes and give them over to the Gatherer. He was exiled for his crimes since they couldn't kill him. No matter what they did, he wouldn't die. Their weapons were useless against him. He began to hunt them, his own family and friends instead of outsiders. To appease him, they built him a home, a wigwam. He took it, and inhabited it, but changed it to suit his needs. Over time, the stories said he began to fade, and would leave for long periods of time, until no one saw his face any longer."

He paused and flipped through the pages of his notebook before continuing. "The Gatherer liked having a body to inhabit and would frequently take the bodies of other people and animals, though briefly, often killing them in the process. The wigwam was too dangerous for people to go near, and so they brought it offerings to appease it." He leaned back, a stern look on his face, hands resting on his notes. A heavily tattooed, pierced, and gauged seventeen-year-old kid. He didn't look like a kid, he looked much older than his years. He had a death to avenge.

He said, "Those dolls that Riley found. I think they were created by the Otoe as a way to symbolize the man who went missing, and any others who followed in his footsteps to become part of the Gatherer, and they were placed in the center of the wigwam as a way to control the spirits or to appease them. When the Otoe left, their power to control the entity did as well and I guess it was up to the Halversons to figure it out. How it chose its victims, I can't tell, but it fed off them. Clearly one of them is Linnea, who Riley called Alina, and we all followed suit. And Riley must have thought that by burning the dolls, he would get rid of whatever bad energy was inside the house. He only freed a little more of it, and it grew."

Harry gently took Noah's notes and looked through them. "Why here?" Harry finally asked.

Noah shrugged. "Professor M said that there is a massive amount of limestone and quartz beneath these hills. They can be conductors of energy. There is a lot of chalcedony in the area, which is considered sacred to many Native tribes. He says it was often used to create a pathway between worlds, but always used in a benevolent way."

"Lukas mentioned ley lines," I said. "That this camp is situated on a ley line between the magnetic north pole and the Bermuda triangle."

Noah said, "To be honest, though, I don't care about the why, I care about the how the fuck we are going to take it down."

"If this is all true," Harry said, hurriedly moving his hands over the papers. "It's only been contained. It hasn't been created. If it hasn't been created, you can't just unmake it."

"Then let's weaken the shit out of it so it can't hurt anyone else," Noah said harshly. He adjusted the beanie on his head and looked away.

Overwhelmed, I said, "I'm not crazy. This is real . . ."

"I'm still convinced you're crazy, Laurel," Harry said. After a long pause he asked, "So why does it kill people?"

"It likes pain," Noah said. "It feeds off of it, gets stronger. I don't know what would happen if it was starved of people, if it would have to move or what."

"Then we should shut down the camp," Harry said.

"We don't own it, Harry," I replied. "Neither does my mom. It's held by a board, made up of Nomads who seem to think this place is going to live on forever."

"Then let's do something that will force them to shut it down," Noah said.

"I don't know what that would be to be honest, they didn't care about everything else that's happened here over the past hundred plus years," I said.

Mia came inside, her backpack was abnormally heavy. She slammed herself into a chair beside me and sighed. "Hey, Noah," she said, tiredly. "Ok, got what you wanted. Or tried, at least."

"What'd you find out?" Noah asked, eyes sparkling with interest.

"Well, this camp isn't accredited, but they have tried, multiple times over the past fifty years or so," she said, laughing. "Not surprised there. Due to the high number of incidents, they never got the ACA accreditation. The only thing in charge of Kellova is the Nomads. They keep any incidents as quiet as possible."

"The deaths?" Harry asked.

"Kellova wasn't charged with anything related to Haley's death, nor was there much of an investigation into the board. I don't think authorities have connected anything." She scratched behind her ears and finally let out a heavy breath.

"Haley's obituary didn't even mention Camp Kellova," Noah said.

"Either way, they're not about to do anything about anything, if that makes sense," Mia said.

"What do you think would have to happen for them to close this place down?" Harry asked. She looked shocked by the very question. "If it's the only way to keep people safe . . ."

"I don't think anything would get them to close it down, they have this unyielding dedication to Kellova," she said, shaking her head.

"What about a giant catastrophe?" Noah asked.

"As if there haven't been enough of those," I said.

Mia shook her head. "At the meeting I attended they were more interested in talking about future prospective Nomads than they were about the fact Ezra was found nearly dead during lake day. They don't care."

Harry rolled his eyes. "Ok, so what is their main concern?"

"Keeping their little group together, and that means keeping camp alive," Mia said. "They'll keep anything that happens quiet. So, whatever you're planning . . ."

"I don't think you want to know," Harry interjected.

"Probably not. I still have a few weeks to take care of the horses. Whatever you do, don't hurt the horses." She yawned. "I'm damn tired. I'm going to take a nap." She picked up her bag and left, waving as she went.

Chapter Twenty-Six:

August 11, 2016

The day was long. We went through our meal plans, activities, and how to set up tents. Once I finally let my head hit the pillow that night, I was out. There were still kids up and talking and playing cards in the main room, but I blocked it all out. I was drained.

My mind only became aware again when it was silent and the main door slammed shut. I sat up, heart racing in my chest. I grabbed my flashlight and went toward the door. Outside, barefooted and in her pajamas, was Lisey. She was staring at something. I was used to night terrors and nightmares from her, but sleepwalking was different.

She stood firmly on the service road between BS and Clark and was staring intently at something with her mouth hanging open slack and her head was cocked slightly to the left.

"Lisey?" I touched her shoulders. Her arm moved slowly to point to something. "What is it, hon?" She was pointing at a cat. It was white, almost glaringly so, and sat beside the back entrance to Clark. It had long white fur, and it was looking in our direction with neon yellow eyes.

When I locked eyes with it, it began to walk in our direction. The way it walked was as if its feet didn't touch the ground. It walked so smoothly. There were no strange proportions. It was a perfectly normal cat, except my instincts told me otherwise.

I knew I could not trust Kellova, and I didn't trust that cat. "Come on, let's go inside." I tried to coax Lisey in the direction of the door. She wouldn't budge. Her feet were planted. "Wake up, Lisey!" I hissed. Her eyes seemed comfortably glazed over. Then she smiled. Her smile sent shivers through me as if ice was injected directly into my bones. The smile didn't seem natural, too wide, too toothy.

I ran back into BS and woke Harry. "Lisey is outside. She's not acting right, and I can't get her back inside." He grumbled and whined and eventually to get his attention, I turned on the lights. That only led to a chorus of whines from the other boys.

"What the hell are you doing?" Taylor asked, throwing his blanket over his face.

"I need help," I cried out. "Get off your ass, Harry!"

"What . . .?" Harry whined again, no urgency in his voice.

"I need to get Lisey inside," I said.

"Huh?" Taylor woke up instantly. "What's wrong with her?"

"She's outside staring at a cat and . . . there's just something wrong."

He hopped down from his top bunk and the other boys followed. We went outside. Lisey was even closer to Clark now. Her arm was still out, pointing, and the cat was where it was when I left her.

"Lisey!" Taylor called.

The cat stared at us with far too much intelligence in its eyes. It was clean, well fed, and its limbs were all of the correct proportion, but it seemed too large for a house cat.

"I don't like that thing," Arty said. As he spoke, the cat turned its attention to Arty. "Exhibit A." He stepped back, stumbling on the stairs leading to BS. He got to his feet and went inside, the door slamming behind him. Taylor went forward and the cat hissed. He stopped in his tracks.

After Taylor's momentary sideline from the cat, he stepped forward again, and the cat went to attack him, swinging its claws in his direction. "Ah, shit!" Taylor cried, a long scratch getting him in the calf. He kicked the cat, and it was bunted back slightly, but it didn't seem fazed. The cat went after him again and Noah pushed his brother away and tried to pick the cat up by the scruff, but it was so strong that even as we all tried to fight it, it was winning.

A bark came from the distance, and I could only imagine that the house was sending hellhounds now. The cat wasn't enough, it had more in its arsenal.

"Go get Lisey, we got this," Noah said.

Chapter Twenty-Six: August 11, 2016

I didn't think he, Riley, and Harry had control of the situation at all, but Lisey was continuing to walk toward the deep ditch between the archery field and Clark. I jogged toward Taylor, but as I did, the barking intensified.

It wasn't a hellhound. It was Charlie. He slammed into the cat, and the cat reared up on its back legs. Charlie went for it with his jaws. A horrific yowling echoed from the cat. He drove it back, further, and further into the woods.

I reached Lisey and Taylor. Taylor stood in front of her, waving his hands in front of her eyes. He held onto her firmly so she couldn't walk any further, but she sure did try. "This house isn't messing around, is it?" Taylor asked, looking at me with sad eyes.

"No, it's not," I replied.

We each took one of Lisey's arms and forced her back, doing anything we could to turn her around. We ended up needing to carry her inside. Once there, in the light, we placed her on a soft chair and locked the front doors. I dragged a table to block the door, the sound of which woke everyone.

"I think it tried to take Lisey, lure her away or something," Taylor said to everyone. "It doesn't want us to fight."

August 12, 2016

The general consensus was that no one was particularly excited about camping up near the clearing. It was also clear that no one really wanted to spend another night in BS after the drama with the cat. After a silent breakfast of cereal and oatmeal, we sat in the central room of BS. Lisey was wrapped in blankets, and Taylor had an arm around her. I'd seen Noah hold Haley just like that a few years prior and the thought made grief well up in me powerfully.

"Charlie's at the front door," Harry said as he joined us. Harry moved the door so the dog could come in, tail wagging and face scratched to shit. We all had matching marks.

Charlie didn't seem fazed, he just wanted attention and was happy to sit down among the kids. "This morning I'm going to send Harry to the store to get our food supplies. Is there anything else we need?"

"Holy water," Taylor said, being snarky. No one laughed.

"Would do, if I knew where to get it," Harry said, sipping on his coffee. He still hadn't sat down yet this morning.

"Find a baptismal font in a church, or get a priest," Kennedy said absently.

"This is the world's weirdest wilderness retreat," Arty replied.

"Agreed," Harry said. He looked at his shopping list. "Do I need to get silver instruments of torture too? Maybe a stake?"

"This isn't funny," Noah said darkly, looking up at him. Harry quieted, chugged the rest of the coffee, and left.

Tents, cots, and sleeping bags were packed along with other essentials to be hiked up to our campsite. Charlie stayed happily by our side, smiling, and wagging his tail.

The August heat was brutal, and the simple transportation of our gear was absolutely exhausting. I was ready to lie under a tree and take a nap.

We were headed to the same place Lukas and I had the marshmallow roasting bonfire extravaganza, as he called it later on. I texted him, saying we were headed to the campsite, and if he wanted to join, he was more than welcome to.

His response: *Gary wants to know what your plans are to do with the house.*

I wasn't great at typing and walking at the same time, especially not while carrying my pop-up tent, but I let him know about Kennedy's plans with the black salt and the mirrors. That was all we had to start.

It wasn't even five minutes later when he said: *Gary's laughing. He said he's never tried that before but doubts it will work.*

Me: *Let me know if he has any better ideas.*

Once at the flattened site beneath the glowing green trees and amongst the ravines and tall hills of Kellova, we set our supplies down to rest.

"Ok, I'm sweating through my shirt already," Arty said, pulling the fabric away from his skin with a grimace. He then sniffed his pits but was relatively pleased with the result.

Chapter Twenty-Six: August 11, 2016

"What did you expect? It's like a hundred out and you filled your backpack with books," Gracia said. "I don't think you're going to have much time to read them either."

"I only brought a few. Bugspray, sunscreen, wipes, painkillers- those things are taking up the bulk of my bag," he said.

"We have a job to do," Noah replied. He'd already started setting his tent up with Taylor. Arty quickly joined them, taking on tarp duty. My own tent took about five minutes to put up. It simply needed to unfold it and have my bedding set inside. This time I had my red heart blanket instead of my lucky purple one.

Gracia, the queen of tent pitching, almost single handedly put up the girl's tent. Jenny didn't even try to help. She just sat at a picnic table and looked out over the ravine. She spent the entire hike singing random songs, busting out dance moves, and now she was totally silent. Even her face was placid, but knowing her, I highly doubted her mind was quiet.

Arty asked, "Can you play some music?"

"This is a wilderness retreat, listen to the wilderness!" I replied, laughing.

"Ah come on," Arty said, putting his hands on his hips.

"I don't know if I packed it, and if I did, I'd need to uncover it." I was still getting out the cover to my tent in case it rained and was triple checking to see if everything was in plastic bags, also in case of rain.

The wind whistled around us loudly, brushing through the limbs of the trees, pulling my hair behind my head. It was warm and soft, refreshing even. It was benevolent. A smile came across my face and I relaxed.

"I'm going to get some firewood," I said.

That evening, with the tents put up, a fire started, and our camping chairs out, we proceeded to argue about dinner. "We had omelets last week . . .!" Jenny whined, walking back and forth, occasionally starting to sing some rap song I never heard before.

"Grilled cheese?" I asked. "Could just bust out the Coleman stove and not have to worry about bread falling into the fire."

Arty was out of the discussion, his face planted on the table. Kennedy was nose deep into books. Noah was beside her. Taylor and Lisey were sitting too close to each other for my comfort.

"Taylor, could you go get more fuel?" I asked, just to separate them, but when he stood up, Lisey's hand was still attached to his. Harry and I just smirked at each other in a tired sort of way.

"We should have a watch set up at night, just in case," Noah said.

Arty raised his head a bit, surprised. "Why? What do you think will happen?"

"There was a violent cat last night . . ." Gracia said, yawning. "I wish Charlie stayed with us."

"I don't know, that's why I'm suggesting it," Noah answered, as if Gracia never spoke. She raised her eyebrows and looked partially offended at his lack of acknowledgement. While Arty and Noah bickered over how a night watch would work, I got the Coleman stove out and lit it. Jenny came over and helped me put together some sandwiches.

"Is this all we're going to do? This is boring," she said, making the word boring sound like an alarm-clock siren. "I thought we were going to, like, kill some ghosts or something."

"I think you've watched too much *American Horror Story*," I said.

Before it got too dark, Jenny and I managed to fill four large mixing bowls with the black salt. I put the parchment out on the picnic table with the pen and empty ink vial.

"What do we call it?" I asked.

"Call what?" Harry added.

"The house. How do we address it?" I asked again.

"Well, you could just call it by its name, House One," Taylor said.

Noah shook his head. "It's too old. It wasn't always a house."

Lisey's eyes lit up. "Have you seen that old movie, *The Exorcist*?" Harry and I laughed but nodded. "Maybe you have to find its name to get power over it."

"Guys, it's a haunted house. It can't be that complicated," Arty pressed.

"It's not a house at all. It just looks like one," Noah replied. He explained how it changed shape, how we all saw it differently.

"What about that name you mentioned, the Gatherer?" Kennedy asked.

"That name was given to it, Kenny," Noah said. "It doesn't feel right."

The sun lowered quickly. I didn't want to go near the thing in the dark. "Let's put the bowls and mirrors out to start tonight at least, put some of us at ease," I said.

"What are they supposed to do?" Arty asked. He'd gone pale from Noah's explanation of the house.

"Reflect bad energy back at the house," Kennedy said easily.

"So, hopefully, it won't bother us," Gracia added. "And we'll leave the spell to another time I guess,"

I grabbed a bowl of salt, and the others gathered various other things- mirrors, more salt, candles. A deer trail connected the two clearings together, but a significant ravine lay between them. The presence of the ravine was relatively comforting, as if it'd bar the house from getting to our campsite.

We staggered through the rough brush and fallen limbs. Some thorn bushes crept into the space, and I was thankful that for once, I wore jeans.

"Ugh! I'm getting all scratched!" Jenny whined, holding a mirror above her head. It wasn't smart of me to give her anything to carry, but it was more likely for her to dump a bowl of salt than break the small mirror, even if it was a cheap one.

"Not just you!" Lisey said, trying to hop over the stray branches.

We started up the steep hill. "We don't have to go to the quarry again, right?" Jenny asked. "If we are, I'm bailing, I'm not going there, nope, not at all."

"No," Harry and I said at the same time.

"What happened there?" Noah asked. The group was silent. The image of Riley high up on the edge of the quarry hit my mind.

Gracia explained what we saw and that the place felt as malignant as the house. As she said that, the forest's edge immediately stopped, and the calla lilies appeared before us. Past them, was the house.

"One bowl on each side of the house with a mirror facing it," I said.

Lisey was right, though, to have power over it, I had to learn what it was. All things have a name. Even things like this.

Jenny and I placed a bowl and mirror on the west side of the house, facing the front door. The bowls were set firmly inside the perimeter of the lilies but had some distance. I watched it for a moment. The house rumbled deep inside, expressing some discontent that left me thoroughly satisfied. I wanted the damn thing unhappy, and if a simple attempt such as this could do it, so be it.

So be the death of it.

Unlike any other retreat, there was no chatter late into the night. The toughest thing to do was to pry Kennedy and Noah from their books, and Taylor and Lisey from each other.

The tents felt safe, but so did the fire. I wasn't quite willing to leave it. Harry and I sat together on a fallen log. "We're going to get into a lot of trouble, aren't we?" he asked.

"Yep," I replied.

"Like breaking the law bad."

"Hopefully that's all it comes to."

"With a bunch of teenagers . . ." he muttered. "We're all gonna die."

"Stop being a diva, we're not all gonna die," I said. I nudged into him to get a smile out.

"I'm not made for this kinda stuff."

"No one is."

Chapter Twenty-Seven:

August 13, 2016

I watched with heavy eyes for the woods to react to our presence. My eyes scanned the perimeter for movement. There was none. It was just me, and the new silence of the night which was interrupted by the buzz of my phone. It was a text from Lukas saying, *I'm coming by.* A smile crept across my face. His presence would put me at ease, and hopefully unfold the unholy knot in my stomach.

Lukas walked up on the main path, barely making a sound. He had no flashlight, but he was always good at seeing in the dark. He slung his backpack off his shoulder and sat beside me. He handed me a chocolate bar. I smiled and shook my head before leaning in to his side. One chocolate bar and all was forgiven.

We split the bar and watched the fire die. "I'll take the watch. Get some sleep, Laurel," he said.

"You ok with that?" I asked.

He nodded. "Yep." I hugged him tightly.

"If you need a place to sleep, you can use my tent," I said.

He simply nodded again. I slipped into my tent and lay atop my sleeping bag with my red blanket draped over me. It took a little time before I fell asleep. But as with most nights, dreams weren't far off.

My consciousness came to me inside the old chapel. Light filtered through dusty windows, refracting into different colors. The world felt solid, substantial. Real. Sitting beside me was Haley. She looked perfectly healthy, lively, with glowing skin and her deep, dark eyes. Happiness leapt into my chest. I turned to face her on the bench and sat with my legs criss-crossed. "Hey, Miss Laurel," she said. It was her voice, a voice I thought I forgot, but as soon as I heard it, it ran straight at me. Through me. I smiled, and felt so heavy, but so safe.

"Haley . . . what, what are you doing here?"

"Thought I'd stop to say hi to you before going to see Noah," she said, a sparkle of sadness and love behind her eyes. "And it's so quiet here . . . I like the peace."

"It won't let you leave?" I asked.

She huffed, smiling sadly, and shook her head. "None of us can."

"How many of you are there?" I asked.

She shrugged just as she would in life if I asked what was for dinner. "Lots. Oodles of people," she sighed, completely at ease. "I think it keeps us around for energy. Some of the people look like they're fading. Some stay in the chapel because it feels safe." I looked around quickly, thinking I'd see more people, ghosts. I felt no fear, but apprehension crept up on me. "They don't know you, so they might hide. The house makes them afraid. Charlotte says it likes to take the people who are in love first because it tastes good."

My brow crinkled. "Charlotte Dahl?"

"Yes," she said. "That means what Noah and I had was real, right?" The sadness welled in her eyes, and her smile faded. I wanted to reach out and touch her hand, but though it all felt so real, I was afraid my hand would pass straight through.

"He still loves you, Haley, so much," I said.

"I don't want him here. The house will want him. I need to keep him safe. I *will* keep him safe."

"We're here to destroy it, to keep others safe too . . . to free you," I pressed. "And we will."

"It's not bad," Another female voice said. Stepping in from the open door was a girl I recognized from photographs as Charlotte, and her lover, Nicholas. They had their arms locked, and youth hung on them well. "We can be together, finally. You are right, though. It has done enough damage, especially to the living."

"Have you seen it truly? Do you know its name?" I asked, trying to stand, but I felt swimmy, and loose.

"Few have," Charlotte said. "But Linnea may know. Be careful. The house knows you. It may not want you, but it will do what it has to keep itself safe."

Chapter Twenty-Seven: August 13, 2016

"I'm going to see Noah, and tell him I love him," Haley said.

August 13, 2016

I woke to the sound of soft, steady breathing beside me. The pop-up tent was small, cozy for even one, but beside me was Lukas. His chest rose at an even pace. He was just in his khaki shorts, arms raised above his head, making his ribs stand out even further.

There was a note beside me: *Harry is on watch.*

Breathing a sigh of relief, I closed my eyes again. There was a buzz of energy all around me. It wasn't uncomfortable. Just being here felt important, so I fell back asleep.

I woke up curled tightly against Lukas. Startled, I ended up there, I flailed a bit. Lukas only chuckled. "Didn't want to wake you," he said. "But I don't know anyone who moves as much in their sleep as you do."

"God . . . sorry . . . didn't mean to get all up in your business," I said, sitting up now, aware of the disaster that was my hair and the crust that was probably on the corner of my mouth. "I'm a mess." I laughed and then yawned.

His eyes were still calm, a bright blue, and he just looked at me. I took my brush and made my hair acceptable. "Did anyone disappear in the night?" I asked.

"Not while I was out there," he said. "Nothing moved. I figured you may do something today, potentially stupid, and I didn't want you to do it alone."

"I'm perfectly capable of doing stupid shit on my own, thank you," I said.

"I'm aware of that," he said, both of him smiling. I reached past his bare chest to the tent zipper and clambered out. Eyes landed on me, and Jenny nearly spit out her water.

"Don't get any ideas," I said. Only half the kids were awake. Kennedy had her books, Jenny had a pile of twigs stacked up by the picnic table, and Harry was wiping sleep from his eyes.

Harry smirked. "Ugh," I grumbled at him, retrieving clothes from my plastic totes. Lisey and Gracia were still fast asleep, looking very comfortable. The morning was cool and there was a nice breeze. It reminded me more of a late September morning than August. I also didn't plan on waking the kids up at any specific time. Any normal plans had been thrown out the window.

I carried my clothes and toothbrush to the bathroom across the path at the end of the clearing. I dressed quickly, speedily brushing my teeth. The bathroom was covered thickly in insects and spiders, and the mirror was clouded and scratched.

Something touched the back of my leg, cold, and wet. I jumped. It was Charlie, tail wagging, smiling at me. "Oh, dude, make more noise when you sneak up on me."

I rubbed his shaggy back. The very idea of having to take a shower here made me anxious. Unless I could cover the place in salt and crystals and if the shower could spray holy water, being undressed in here would still make me feel vulnerable.

"Did you sleep ok?" I jumped a bit again, and turned to see Lukas, leaning against the open door. "Didn't mean to scare you, or Charlie," he chuckled. Charlie approached him for pats. "I think I should stay out here, keep everyone out of trouble."

I leaned back against the sink and rubbed my face. "I . . . the kids are going to talk."

"Let them talk," he said, throwing a ratty towel on a hook outside one of the shower cubicles. "Most of them know you're a prude."

"Excuse me?" I huffed.

"Oh, come on, you know it's true," he said and stepped into the cubicle and started to undress despite the minimal cover from a holey white curtain.

"I don't think that's quite right," I said. He turned on the water. "I'm heading out. I need to make breakfast for the kids."

"What, don't want to join me?" he asked.

"Grow up, Lukas," I said, though I laughed.

"You are absolutely no fun," he said. I left with Charlie.

Back at the campsite, it looked like the only one still asleep was Arty. Noah had a daze over him, and his hair was unnaturally unkempt. Gracia was braiding Lisey's hair and Jenny was doodling in her notebook, occasionally slamming down the pencil she was using. She was both distracted and bored. Charlie lay down beside her and placed his head on his paws. She looked at him, surprised.

"Anyone want to help me get breakfast ready?" I asked. Harry yawned loudly in response.

Jenny jumped up. "I got plenty of twigs," she said, and eagerly started to help build a fire. Charlie then followed her around with a big smile on his face. Arty, struggling with his book, put it aside and helped.

We ate cinnamon rolls made of crescent-roll dough and cinnamon sugar wrapped around roasting sticks. Harry said he'd teach advanced knot making that morning, see what they could hang from trees. By then, Lukas returned, keeping his distance from the group. Noah left the knot class and joined Lukas and me.

"I've had enough knots in my life," he said. Haley flickered to mind. Her feet off the ground, specifically. "Let's check out the cellar."

Lukas and I looked at each other and I shrugged. "And then I want to introduce you to someone," Lukas said.

"Gary?" Noah asked.

Lukas and I exchanged glances again. "Yeah, Gary." Lukas said.

Lukas had his fists shoved deep in his pockets but walked with ease. Noah shuffled his feet, twitching with nerves. He hardly looked up. Lukas put his hand on Noah's back and clapped his shoulder. Noah looked back to the campsite and blinked quickly.

"Hey, Noah, it's ok," I said.

He shook his head. "I'm not sure what you think is ok. Haley's blood is in that house." He bit down on his lip and his pace quickened. We pushed on through the thick brambles and to the clearing. "And the blood was never cleaned up, not by any human hands . . . the house just . . . fucking absorbed it." I was partially surprised the bowls and mirrors were still where we left them.

Lukas took a deep breath.

"No scorch marks," Noah said. "No blown out windows . . . this damn thing is unholy." He walked straight up to the door and slammed his fist down on it. "This fucking thing took everything from me!" Noah cried.

"Not everything," Lukas said. "Your brother is still here."

"He shouldn't be. I should send him home, get him far away from here." Noah replied.

"He wouldn't go, even if you begged him," Lukas said.

"He wants to see you get justice," I added.

Noah took a deep breath and closed his eyes for a moment. His hand still lay on the side of the house. Lukas lifted the cellar door open, and it thumped heavily on the ground. It was never locked again after Taylor opened it.

The raccoons, though, were gone. The cellar appeared open, clear, even. The dirt floor was flat and empty. All three of us walked in. The air was suffocatingly thick. It didn't feel natural. To the north was the ever present old refrigerator. It'd been there as long as I'd known about the house. It was rusty and an ugly gray, about seventy years old.

Lukas gravitated toward it and said, "Riley must have found the dolls down here. It would only make sense that a doll meant to control whatever's in the house would be down here." He paused.

"Talking doesn't sound right," Noah added.

Lukas opened the fridge, using its car-like handles. The inside only contained a few remains of mice and their nesting material. Lukas grumbled a bit and started to move the fridge to the side. Noah and I jumped in to help. The house shook. We paused for a moment.

"Keep going," I said. Noah's eyes were wide, slightly fearful. Lukas made one big heave and the fridge toppled over. Noah jumped back.

There was a wooden door with a small crack in it. "Didn't know that was there," I said, sighing. The shaking increased. Lukas rubbed his temples and winced.

"It's . . . it feels like a heartbeat . . ." Lukas said through gritted teeth.

"Did it get into your head?" Noah asked.

"No, but it's trying," Lukas said. He took a deep breath and went to open the door. He pried at the crack with his hands. He swayed a bit, as if nauseous to the point of puking.

"What's back there?" I asked, peering over his arm on my tip toes, flashlight traced on the door.

"I can't see," Lukas replied.

"Let me try," Noah said, almost pushing Lukas away, and he looked around the edges. In one hard motion, he slammed his shoulder into a weak seam. It fell into the empty space. "There," Noah clapped his hands together. "Oh God . . ."

"What?" I asked, stepping closer. Lukas had a hand on each of my shoulders. Bones. Decrepit, old, crumbling bones. "Those wouldn't happen to be—"

"Yep," Noah said.

I stepped closer. It was a fully articulated human body curled into the fetal position. I approached it, and as I did, other images flickered to mind, as if a web of tunnels emanated from one pile of bones, going deep into the earth in every direction. One blink and the image disappeared. I knelt down beside the body to see if it had anything of interest.

"You're not really going to touch that, are you?" Noah asked.

My hand shook, but I reached forward to touch the jaw. A massive piece of chalcedony was in the person's jaw. It was inside the skeleton, as if they'd been forced to eat it. Another chunk was slammed into the left side of the chest, near where the heart would be.

"Leave it there," Lukas said, a hand remaining on my shoulder. I didn't feel afraid.

The house stopped rumbling, and there was a calm pulse.

"Do you think this is him? The one who first let the . . . whatever it is, in?" I asked Noah.

"It could be, or just a dead guy," Noah said. I blinked again and the space we were in appeared so much larger. The paths were clearer. I stood, stepping deeper into the sub-cellar. There was a gray light along the paths. The question of reality never entirely hit me. Rather, it felt as though I was being pulled by a thread.

Flashes of other images came to mind, dozens, maybe more, bodies, whole, looking alive. They lay in bits of gray light, curled up. I knew intrinsically what they were. They had been used up by the house, and here they lay.

Scrambling, I looked for any sign of Haley.

Reality, as I knew it, lay far, far behind. Unseeable, silent.

Some individuals were clearly from camp in their neckerchiefs and khakis, a few looked like unfortunate hunters, but most were Native Americans. This *thing's* history was ancient. It'd been destroying as long as there were things to destroy. It was the Gatherer, it liked to hoard things, people, bodies, souls.

None of the bodies moved. They could have been asleep. The house collected them like seed pods in its roots, growing ever deeper into the black and unforgiving earth.

Shortly before turning back, I saw a glimpse of familiarity. Jeans, blue zip-up jacket, baseball cap. It was Riley Stevens. He, too, looked asleep, but he didn't look solid like the others. My heart fell. He'd been its pawn, and now, he'd been discarded. Left as a memory, maybe, but nothing more.

I backed up, not looking back as part of me feared I would see both Noah and Lukas curled on the ground as well. Yet, when I felt the hands return to my shoulders, I let out a breath. "Lukas?" I asked.

"You blacked out for a moment, Laurel," he said.

"I'm not sure that's what happened . . ." I said, moving toward the exit.

Back in the light, I explained what I'd seen. At first Noah seemed confused, then elated. We were outside the clearing, sitting on a fallen trunk of a tree, in the woods and out of view of House One. "What is it?" I asked Noah. "You have this big grin stuck on your face."

"The house didn't really get her," he said, chuckling. "She just thinks she has to stay, but she doesn't."

"What are you going on about?" Lukas asked.

"She told me the house wouldn't let her leave, that she was trapped," Noah said.

"She told me that too," I said. Noah's eyes lit up. "But Noah, I think the people I saw were actually possessed at one point."

"Who?" Lukas pressed.

"Haley!" Noah cried.

"I've experienced a lot of shit about this place, but ghosts and possession, and seed pods made of dead people is out of my league." Lukas held his hands up.

"Seems less intense than a possessed water moccasin going for your junk," I said, shrugging.

"That happened?" Noah asked.

"Yeah, in the house of a man who thinks the government is trying to eat his brains," I said with a sigh.

"He has reason," Lukas said.

"What about Riley? I saw him down there," I said.

"You said he didn't look solid, what if he's still out there and it's using him?" Noah asked. "We could still save him."

"God, I hope so," I said. "Either way, it's what we have to deal with. Until we know more, there's nothing we can tell his dad. Or anyone else. Let's keep this between us."

I was grateful for the sun and the green life, and the easiness of the air. It was the opposite of the oppressive heaviness of the cellar.

"If I showed you some obituaries and news clippings, do you think you could recognize the people you saw?" Noah asked.

"I might," I said. "But we all know my brain, it's not so reliable."

"I think it may be with this," he responded and jumped up. Unable to argue, Lukas and I went with him back to the campsite.

"Look at this!" Jenny jumped up to show me a well-executed trucker's hitch as soon as she saw us. "I'm good at knots!"

"She is," Kennedy muttered. Her paracord was a disaster and Gracia was trying to help loosen up all the unintentional knots.

"Good job, Jenny," I said and high fived her.

"If Eddy was here, he'd use this to try to climb a tree," Arty said.

"You don't need a rope to climb these trees," Jenny said, swiftly discarding the rope she was proud of a moment ago. She ran to a nearby pine.

"Jenny . . ." Harry called, sighing. He leaned over Lisey, trying to show her a quick release knot. "Jenny, come on, you promised no funny business!"

"This isn't funny business!" she exclaimed. Though she was known to be a klutz, in the tree, she was nearly graceful. Her limbs were still too long for her age, and she grew fast enough that she struggled to keep up. She swung from branch to branch. Harry couldn't help but smile. At the same time, Kennedy finally freed all her rope. She made a loud huff.

"That was infuriating," Kennedy said, rubbing her temples.

"When are we going to make bracelets out of this?" Gracia asked.

"I thought we were going to hang things from trees," Arty said. "Like to keep food away from bears."

"There are no bears in Iowa," Kennedy said.

"Well . . . they're native to Iowa. We just don't have any left. There are plenty of bears in South Dakota and that's only a few hours northwest from here," Arty replied.

"There's no bears!" Harry yelled. "We won't make bracelets until Jenny gets down from the tree!"

"I don't want to make paracord bracelets. I just want to stay up here!" Jenny said. She was resting up against the trunk of the tree, at least eighteen feet up.

"Jenny . . ." I muttered.

"I'm staying," she announced.

Noah rolled his eyes. "I have the folder in my backpack, just give me a second . . ."

I went to the base of the tree. "Do you promise to get down for lunch? I'm not going to let you act like Harry is a doormat."

"But he is!" she said.

"Jenny!" I yelled again.

"It's not like anyone stopped me," she grumbled, rolling her eyes.

"Stop acting like you own the place, Jenny!" I replied.

"Fine . . ." she said, audibly grumbling. In a few moments, she started to half sing, half rap, but she didn't leave the branch.

Noah brought his notebook and folder to the picnic table. The first piece of paper was Haley's obituary. He gently set that aside and placed it in the opposite pocket. "Before Haley, the most recent death on camp property was in 2002. A hunter was found hanging over a branch. Obviously, you can't hunt here, but maybe he got lost. His name was John Fernsby, twenty-nine years old, moved recently to Greenville to work at the creamery. Cause of death was listed as inconclusive. They made note of major internal hemorrhaging that didn't look natural." He brought out a picture of a balding man. He was knelt beside a bloody buck, holding its head by the antlers.

Like a flashbulb, I saw a man far beneath the house, curled in an eternal sleep. I nodded. "Yeah, he's there."

Noah set that file aside. "Ok, Arnold Brewer, a counselor here, twenty years old, was found in the corner of the bathroom in the Birdhouse unit. Bashed his own head in. 1996." He showed me a crime scene photograph of a wall smeared with blood and handprints. The young man was unrecognizable after all that damage. "Listed as self-inflicted," Noah said. He turned to a photograph of Brewer teaching archery. The same neckerchief I saw in the tunnel, the same dark locks. I nodded again. "Two for two, pretty good," Noah said.

"In 1991, two boys were found dead in the Lost Lake after an extensive search of Greenville. Both had many spiral fractures in their arms and legs, and they both had several broken ribs. It was labeled as most likely an animal attack or homicide. There are two reports since the parents wanted second opinions. Jerry and Aaron Rothschild, 14 and 12. Not campers, actually. There's even a *20/20* episode about this. Had theories about a human trafficking ring and everything."

"I don't think I saw any children," I said. "No . . . there were no kids that young."

Noah sucked at his lower lip. "Hmm maybe it has a hard time getting kids?" He turned the page. "Ok, well, we have Edythe Dahl. She died in 1989 and she was the director at that time and the last person related to the original settlers to work at camp. She was found in her nightgown in the woods in early November after a freak snowstorm. She had multiple spiral fractures on all limbs and had a heart attack. She was found face up in the snow. This was ruled inconclusive as well."

In the photograph, she had long graying hair, loose about her shoulders, and piercing eyes. I'd met her parents in the dream. They never mentioned their daughter. Perhaps they were too interested in reveling in their renewed youth. Yet, I remembered that nightgown with its full button down and crisp linen. I nodded. I couldn't help but think Charlotte Dahl and Nicholas Walker could have kept her safe or warned her somehow. In death, Charlotte could make up for her failings as a mother in life.

Noah continued, until I asked him to put the folder away. "Noah, we need to figure out if they have anything in common, why they were picked or chosen, and why after the thirties or so, deaths slowed down." I was exhausted. I felt like one foot was in reality, and the other was back in the tunnels.

"They slowed down because there was almost always someone like Gary around and they stopped breeding like rabbits around here," Lukas said.

I checked my watch. "Time to get back down here, Jenny!" I called. She whined. "I have your Dad's phone number, don't make me put him on speaker!"

"I'll just tell him that we put bowls of dirt you dug up at a cemetery around this devil house you're trying to blow up!" she said, crossing her arms.

I stood amongst the branches and stared up at her. The other kids quieted. They enjoyed the drama as much as the next person.

"Jenny, we need help with lunch!" I called.

"No you don't! I want to stay here!" she replied, now perfectly calm.

I sighed.

"I'll get the fire back to life," Harry said. "Ramen, right?"

"Yeah," I said.

"I've been craving Ramen," Lukas said.

The more I yelled for Jenny, the more like Forrest Gump I felt. I didn't want her to win, but I also didn't want to feel like an idiot in the process. So, while the water warmed slowly over a new fire, everyone but Jenny sat around it. "So, I was thinking we could go do low ropes this afternoon," I said.

"I thought we were here to take the house down," Taylor said. Gracia nodded in agreement.

"Yes, we are, but as Lisey said, we still don't quite know what we are dealing with. If we rush into this, someone could get hurt." There was some quiet and moving around. "But if anyone has odd dreams or sees something, I need to know. If we do the low ropes today, we can build up to being a team."

After a lunch of ramen noodles, apples, and granola, a very hungry Jenny finally graced us with her presence. Once she ate, I got everyone on the path to our low ropes course.

"I want a piggyback ride!" Lisey jumped up and down, hands on Gracia's shoulders.

"I'll fall over!" Gracia said, laughing.

"Are you calling me fat?"

"We're the same size!" Gracia exclaimed. It brought back memories of piggyback rides on Lukas's back. He was so skinny it was very uncomfortable, but it was cool to see the world from so high up.

"Come here," Taylor said, stopping so she could hop up.

Noah looked at them, smiling sadly. I wished with everything in me, that he'd be happy again- that he could be at peace.

The low ropes course began with the spider web. We all climbed in the small space, enclosed by 'spider webs' made of rope with various sized holes.

"Ok, the objective here is to get everyone out of the web. You cannot touch the rope. If you do, the hole it is a part of will be closed. You can only use each hole once." The web was at least six feet up, and about a foot off the ground. "Also, you cannot crawl underneath; any questions?"

"This looks boring," Jenny muttered.

Gracia asked, "Is Mr. Lukas the tallest?" We all agreed he was. "Maybe he should use one of these low ones to get to the other side."

"Then lift the smallest people through the higher openings?" Noah asked.

"Yeah, but we'll need to leave a space open for whoever is last, near the bottom," she added.

Lukas looked at the rope netting. It was clear it hadn't been adjusted well in a long time. Some spaces were massive, while others weren't large enough to fit a hand through. "That one?" he asked, pointing to a long, skinny opening near the tree.

"It is you-shaped," Noah said.

Lukas smirked a bit and carefully stepped through. His shoulders nearly touched one of the edges, but he managed.

"I'm bored," Jenny said. "I'm going."

"Wait!" Gracia called. Jenny ignored her and took a prime spot and stuck her top half through without considering what to do with the rest of her. If she paused to ask, we may have been able to wheelbarrow her through. Instead, she tripped and fell.

"Now that one is closed," I said.

"Ah, come on Jenny!" Kennedy whined. "We have to figure this out together."

"Ugh, this is so stupid," Jenny groaned.

"We should put Miss Laurel through one of the spots up front. She's probably the smallest, then Lisey. That way we only need one person on the other side to catch." Noah said.

"Catch?" I asked. "Another rule, no tossing."

"No one tosses a dwarf!" Kennedy said, chuckling.

"Ha ha, very funny," I sneered.

"Dwarves are taller than hobbits at least," Lukas said.

"I don't have a beard," I said emphatically. "Heh, ok, what do I need to do?"

"Don't mind us picking you up. Plank like our lives depend on it. Go all rigor mortis!" Harry said.

Chapter Twenty-Seven: August 13, 2016

"You are weird," I said. I crossed my arms around my chest and tensed all my muscles as tight as they'd go.

"Slowly just fall back, we'll get you," Harry said.

"Sure," I muttered sarcastically. I wouldn't have been surprised if I just landed on the ground. Yet madly grasping hands shakily lifted me up. I remembered why I always hated this exercise in staff training. It was like one of those weird levels of hell.

Lukas got a hold of me from the other side and gently let me down. I sighed and dusted myself off. "That was unpleasant," I said.

"Get me out of here," Jenny whined, walking around in a circle, looking up at the sky.

"Hold your horses," I said. "This is a team process."

As unhelpful as she was, the rest of the kids were smart enough to get out of the spiderweb in about half an hour. "Good job, guys!" I exclaimed. "Especially wheelbarrowing yourself out of there, Arty!" He bowed like an actor on a stage. "And the heroes of the day, Harry and Lukas, lifting every one of us out of there." They high fived. It was nice to see them get along for once.

"We going over there?" Arty asked, pointing to a variety of platforms of different sizes.

"Yep," I said. "Ok, so we will start on the largest and go to the smallest. Everyone needs to be on the platform, you must be able to stay there long enough to say, 'beam me up, Scotty.' If someone's foot hits the ground, you gotta try again."

The first platform was easy. Everyone had room to stand. The second platform was a little more difficult. "Let's have everyone just cram on and hold onto each other to not fall off." Gracia said.

"No such thing as personal space today," Noah said, looking at the platform.

"It's camp," Taylor said, hopping up with some enthusiasm. Everyone held on for dear life, arms wrapped around each other. As soon as time came, and they released it was like water being released from a dam. By the time they reached the last platform, they had about a square foot for all of them to stand.

"We should get someone in the middle, small enough not to take up much space, but for everyone to hold onto evenly distribute the weight," Harry said.

"Or we could reach across to the person opposite and just have toes on the board," Kennedy said.

"Let's go," Arty said. "Lukas in the middle."

"Me?" he asked. "I'm not small."

"You're skinny," Kennedy said.

"Exactly, go, go, go," Arty said and laughed.

Lukas lumbered up and stood still at the center. "People of equal sizes should stand opposite of each other. That should work."

They did as instructed.

Jenny stood opposite Harry. "I don't want to," she said. "There's too many bugs and everyone smells bad." She made a disgusted sniff.

"Just do this one, Jenny," I said. "Gotta get through all these together."

"But it's stupid," she said.

"Jenny," Gracia said, tiredly, sighing. She reached out for Jenny's hand. Jenny begrudgingly proceeded with the exercise, however lackluster her effort. Her foot was maybe half an inch off the ground.

"Everyone hold on!" Taylor cried; arms interlocked with Noah's. They heaved themselves together, toes on the platform, but tumbled over before they could say the magic words.

"That's it, I'm out. I want a shower," Jenny said, walking away to sit on a log.

"More space for other people's feet," Taylor muttered, Jenny looked up with piercing eyes. They tried again in a similar formation. Grappling for a few seconds, they came out victorious. They cheered and high fived one another.

Jenny, right on cue, rolled her eyes, not impressed.

"Let's go onto the tightrope," I said.

"What? I want to go back," Jenny said.

"This is what we're doing for now," I said. She dragged behind us.

The tight rope was a large cable with a rope hanging off a telephone pole at one end. "Ok, you can hold this rope. The goal is to walk to the other end without falling off. Everyone else will be on the sides, guarding you from falls. Who wants to go first?"

Taylor jumped to the challenge and wobbled almost immediately.

"Coordinate with each other, move around if you need to," I said.

"Do I get anything if I get to the other side?" Taylor asked.

"I don't have any prizes . . . bragging rights?" I asked, he just smiled. He was starting to develop the same smile lines as his brother.

In this exercise, everyone involved worked like a well-oiled machine. Granted, Taylor was nimble, which made the process easier. When Kennedy tried next, she wobbled all over the place. It was almost like a game of ping pong, tossing her from one side to the other just to get her through.

I turned around to check in on Jenny. She wasn't on the log anymore. Her water bottle, though, was left behind.

Chapter Twenty Eight:

August 14, 2016

"Did anyone see where Jenny went?" I asked, my heart picking up speed from anxiety. Everyone stopped and looked over. There were many shakes of the head.

"Ok, buddy up and let's see if we can track her down," Harry said.

"Lukas, go with Harry, check the high ropes course," I said, pointing to the north where the unlicensed course was. There were signs stating that no one should enter, but it was Genevieve Gentry, she was highly likely not to listen to warnings. Kennedy landed with me. "Ok, everyone meets back here in an hour or sooner."

"Why'd she have to run off?" Kennedy complained.

"Let's just focus on finding her right now Kenny," I said. We went toward the horse pastures. They were east of the low ropes course where the woods thinned out and more grassland popped up. There were locked outbuildings that had been abandoned for ages out here. I didn't even try to open some of the rusted locks. We just continued to call her name. Already I was wondering what I'd tell her father if I couldn't locate her, and if I did, what if something happened? Terror washed through my veins.

"Is someone going to check the shower house?" Kennedy asked. "She said she wanted to take a shower."

"Yeah, I think Gracia and Noah are heading that way," I said. The nerves grew to the point I nearly puked, and I felt color drain from my face.

"Or in the pine trees," Kennedy said, looking up into a few of them.

"You're right," I said. There were so many places she could be. It was a giant plot of land with dense forest and plenty of ravines and creeks to fall into.

As we proceeded, Kennedy hurried forward. "Wait for me, Kenny; don't get out of sight!"

"Look at this!" she said. "It's not her, but it's weird!"

I didn't want anything weird. I didn't want anything interesting. I just wanted to find Jenny and give her a piece of my mind.

Behind a line of thick white pines were tall stones, tapering at the top, in a circle. There was a flat stone in the center that was stained black in places. "Whoa," I said, unable to stop myself. I pulled my phone out and shot a few pictures.

"Did anyone know about this?" she asked.

"Not that I'm aware of . . ." I said.

"Looks ritualistic," Kennedy said.

"Yeah, like it's been used . . ." My mouth hung open for a moment, staring at it. Kennedy touched the stones and looked up, down, and around. She picked up a large stone from the side. It was a primitive knife.

"Looks like it was chiseled to be this shape. Could be obsidian. I've been doing so much research on stones lately," she said.

"Let's take it with us," I said, opening my bag.

"No . . ." Kennedy said. "I don't think that's a good idea. That's like asking this place to attack us."

My eyes lay on the blade, wanting to know what it was used for, where it came from. It must have been the Otoe when they held this land, and yet, it didn't look *old* or used. It reminded me of the obelisk that suddenly appeared in the school janitor's backyard.

For a moment, I forgot all about Jenny. Kennedy touched my arm, causing me to jump a bit in my skin. I forced myself to come back to reality, just as things started to swim. I held onto one of the stones for support but felt as though things were dematerializing in front of me. *It's just my brain*, I told myself. *Derealization is a thing. It's medical. It's not this place* . . . but something kept urging me to think differently. This land was on top of something, and it was powerful. There were miles of crystal beneath my feet, pulsing with energy, intertwined with something incredibly dark that wanted to take whatever it could get.

Whatever that dark thing was, it enjoyed feeding off human emotions.

Sound boomed around us, as if trapped in a vortex of vibrations. *"Anoche",* it said. The voice sounded like it was grating on metal and yet echoing within the walls of a cave. My knees gave out and I collapsed to the ground, holding onto my ears and closing my eyes. I curled into the fetal position. Right here, I felt safe. I felt connected. I felt whole and solid. Nothing else felt like that. *Anoche.* It reverberated within me, came to my eyes. The words. I wanted to scream that I knew its name.

Yet, when I opened my eyes, my face against the ground, it was like the earth grew beneath my touch. It glowed and opened. I threw myself back, hitting the back of my head against a stone. Everything rushed back at me. There was no growing, no glowing, no booming. Just little black dots in my vision, and I was very, very sweaty. I, too, wanted a shower.

"What the hell was that? What the hell!" Kennedy cried, pacing in front of me. I hadn't yet got my bearings and was woozy. "Did you see that? You had to have seen that! And heard that! It was like thunder but not from the sky, but from below our feet! It was awful! It was unnatural! This whole thing is unnatural!"

"I saw, I heard, Kenny," I said. "Help me get up."

She reached her hand out. Shakily, I got to my feet. I felt like I had a bad fever. My joints and muscles were weak.

"Well, we need to find Lukas or Harry and get you down flat. You're really, really pale, like a Malfoy pale," she said.

I laughed a bit. "We need to find Jenny."

"The rest of us can find Jenny, you need to rest before you have another fuzzy."

"Was all that a seizure or something?" I asked, looking at her, suddenly confused.

"No. If it was, I wouldn't have seen it too, but you hit your head again after," she said, leading me back to the campsite.

I was wobbling all over, not fully aware of my surroundings and likely to fall down if she wasn't leading me. *Anoche.* That had to be the thing's name, right? What else could it be? I could write that spell and place it before the house just to see what would happen. We could end it now.

Back at the campsite, we were all assembled, except for Jenny. No one located her. Tired and slumped over the picnic table I said, "It's too dangerous to keep you all here."

"What do you mean?" Gracia asked. "You said we could help!"

"And Jenny's gone missing!" I called.

"You rest," Lukas said.

"No, I have something," I said. "I got its name. I heard it. Kennedy probably did too."

"I think I did, I'm not sure. It sounded like gibberish to me. Ah-nah-key," Kennedy said.

"Yeah, that's what I heard, but I saw it too," I said.

Lisey jumped to her feet and ran over to get the empty inkwell, the pen, and parchment. "You can address it now. Ask it where Jenny is!" she exclaimed. She slammed the things down in front of me. I stared at the piece of paper, and then the inkwell, knowing I'd need to fill that thing with my blood.

"We should keep searching before we anger the house anymore, make sure she's safe," I said, standing up. The world spun quickly around me. Lukas put a hand on my back to steady me. It began to drizzle. "If you don't have the rain flaps on the tent, you need to do that now, and then let's get going." My tent was already weather proofed. August meant thunderstorms, if not tornados. "Come on everyone." No one moved with much speed. I put the parchment supplies back in a Rubbermaid.

"We need to find her before dark, but we should stay together," Harry said.

Lukas stepped aside to make a call. "Gary?" I asked, he nodded. If anyone was able to find someone who'd wandered off, it'd be him. I just imagined him in his ghillie suit with binoculars and night vision gear. Despite his wackiness, I'd feel safer if he was around.

Chapter Twenty Eight: August 14, 2016

Harry led us back toward the low ropes course. We fanned out a bit, calling her name in the ever darkening forest. A storm was pulling in, and the sky churned above, growling. "Keep an eye out for each other," Harry said. "I don't want to lose anyone else."

It may have been an hour of zigzagging through the forest before we were at the edge of one of the horse pastures. Now it was steadily raining, preventing most of us from seeing far ahead. It didn't take much to see Jenny though. She stood amongst the tall, golden grass, up to her waist, looking into the field. Her hair was long, but darkened by the rain, and clung to her shoulders and back. For a moment, the scene looked divinely beautiful. There appeared to be light on her despite the dark sky. She had a light that was all her own.

Yet, calling her, she didn't answer. She simply stood with an arm reaching out toward something unseen, perfectly at peace.

"What is that?" Lisey screamed, pointing past Jenny.

At first, I couldn't see anything, but as the grass far in front of Jenny started to move, I saw the antlers of a deer. Deer shouldn't have antlers at this time of year, so that stood out to me as strange. The head attached to the antlers had no skin, but it wasn't the skull of any ungulate I recognized. I knew that too well; it was very canine like, but it seemed to sneer with a wide, unnatural grin. The teeth didn't meet together, instead there were rows of short, sharp teeth going up toward where the ears would have been. It was moving toward Jenny, and she was beckoning it.

We all stood in a similar trance, looking at the thing. It was hard to move when seeing something so abominable, but at the same time, it was as if unreality was creeping in again.

Lukas put an arm around Jenny and hoisted her up and carried her away. She didn't scream. She didn't make a noise.

The creature bounded toward us. "Run!" I yelled at the rest of the kids. "Get back to the campsite!"

A snake-like tongue slid from the mouth of the creature, and it ran on human-like, clawed hands. Its back was bent and skeletonized. I hoped if I stood still, it would fixate on me and not follow the kids.

"It's not really there," a voice said, interrupting my thought. I jumped. Gary stood beside me, not in a ghillie suit, but regular khakis, darkened by rain, and a black coat. His hat was still on his head and there was a handgun at his side.

"Is this it? Is this what it looks like?" I asked.

"The house? God if I know," he said. "Get out of here you piece of shit!" It growled and turned its attention toward Gary. It had no eyes, yet it was easy to tell where it was looking. "Go on, go somewhere else you bastard. Done enough damage for one day." Gary sounded tired. It didn't back up or move. "Follow me, Miss Winters."

We walked backwards until it was out of sight. By then, all I wanted in the world was a hot shower and to go to bed and never see that damn thing again.

"That girl isn't going to remember seeing it. It was trying to get at her, but she was stubborn enough to fight it. I've seen that much before," Gary said.

"Was it trying to possess her?" I asked.

"Or just kill her. You're on its territory and it's not too happy about that," he said.

Back at the campsite, everyone was chilled to the bone from the wind and the rain. As a large group, we went to the shower house with a change of dry clothes. Lisey held onto Jenny, reassuring her, but Jenny didn't seem to understand what all the fuss was about. We decided that supper was going to be dry cereal, eaten inside the tents, and no one had any disagreements about that. Even Jenny. We had her favorite cereal, Reese's, and that meant all was well in her world.

I stood in the small shower cubicle at the very end of the row, shivering. My skin was wet and cold. The water slowly heated up, but in the meantime, I couldn't stop my own shaking. I was grateful that the building wasn't empty. As much as I loved being alone, I just couldn't be.

That *thing* in the field monopolized my mind. It ate away at me. Each time I closed my eyes, I saw it.

As soon as the warm water hit me, I breathed a sigh of relief. It wouldn't last long, so I quickly showered, scrubbing myself as clean as possible and took a razor to my legs. Another day and I'd be reminiscent of sasquatch. Just being clean, I felt a modicum better.

Right outside the shower house, Harry began, "We've all had a long day. How about we just take the rest of the evening to relax and keep dry. Feel free to raid the cereal and other snacks. We have a tote full of board games and card games. Try to stay warm." We hurried back, ducking as if we could avoid the rain.

Harry said to me, "I think you need to get some sleep. A lot of it if you can manage."

"Just what I was thinking," I said. "What do we do about the kids? I don't want someone wandering off again and getting lost."

"Before you get to your games, just make sure if you need the bathroom, please go in a group! Make sure to take lanterns as well. Everyone needs to watch out for each other," Harry called.

I crawled into my tent and happily collapsed onto my makeshift bed. With the rain being so heavy outside, the sound of rain hitting the tent was a nice steady noise that lulled me into a state of relaxation. Shortly after, Lukas came in. He stretched out and yawned. "I'm glad you're here," I said.

"Well, it'd really suck if you were angry I was here," he said, chuckling, looking over to me. It was that same, calm smile.

"I just feel . . . safer."

He reached out his left arm to me and I curled up beside him. He smelled of soap and rain. I rested my head on his chest with his arm around me. "I'll do everything I can to make sure all of you are safe. I should have finished it off a year ago."

I took a deep breath, relaxing, closing my eyes. "It's not only your responsibility. It's all of ours."

"Seeing it do that to kids . . . it makes me sick," he said. "And I don't want the damn thing to hurt you either."

He pulled his fingers gently through my hair and a shiver went involuntarily down my spine. I closed my eyes, and curled up against him, feeling the warmth from his body, the subtle smell of his skin behind the scent of rain and cheap soap. Just like that I fell asleep easier than I had in ages.

He was there through the night while the wind picked up outside and the sides of the tent shook. It was in one of these slight wakings, I felt the tell-tale tingling on the back of my head. The electricity I knew so well meant sleep paralysis was coming. Lukas was close. I could hear him breathe, but I knew he wouldn't be able to see what I was about to see. He couldn't save me from it.

Burning pressure slammed onto my chest, like something landed. I kept my eyes closed tight, struggling to get in good breath. A slurping noise caused me to open my eyes. It was the *thing* from the words. The skull glowed in the deep darkness of the inside of the tent. It had a light of its own. Unlike before, now it has eyes. Two small glowing orbs in the sockets, orbs that looked like those I'd seen across the camp. I feared that if I touched one, I would see things that would haunt me for the rest of my life.

Its long tongue was not a snake's tongue, it was reminiscent of a wet worm with no eyes or tongue of its own, sniffing the air, reaching for me. It reached my face and curled around me. The sound of squelching made me nauseous. Its body was curled up on my chest and stomach. I tried to scream, though I knew it was fruitless. Air screeched through my teeth, but not audibly. The *thing* laughed deep in its own body. I suddenly felt so small, like I shrunk onto the ground, overtaken by the earth. The creature stood above me, its back grew into an enormous hump with spikes. Its limbs stretched unnaturally. Surrounded by it, it growled and grew closer, as if crawling into the hole with me.

"Laurel?" The voice wasn't that of the beast. It was Lukas. The *thing* disintegrated into flakey ash before I was able to recognize reality for what it was. I was on top of my sleeping bag, not in it, but still lying flat. If I was smart, I'd realize that most of my sleep paralysis experiences happened when lying flat on my back.

Lukas was looking at me, his hand on mine. "What happened?"

"Sleep paralysis," I said.

"What did you see?"

"The thing in the field," I replied. My arms were cold with sweat. I hurriedly got into my sleeping bag and Lukas placed my blanket over me. "I think it was taunting me . . . but with its tongue."

"Uh, what?" Lukas looked both intrigued and disgusted.

"It's tongue was super long, like... a snake or an eel and it was all over my face," I said, and curled up tightly. I touched my face as if I was trying to sluff off the slime.

"You're safe, Laurel, you're safe."

"I don't feel safe," I said.

"It's hard to feel safe when there's a monster wandering around," he said, nonchalantly. There was a strange glimmer in his eyes. It wasn't one that made me fearful but put me on edge.

"What are you thinking?" I asked. He shook his head. I cocked my head to one side. "Lukas."

"Just a way to kill it." He sat cross legged, absent for a bit, deep in thought. His eyes always drifted away when he did that. I watched him for a moment. I could see each vertebra in his back, drifting down in a gentle curve. His hair was short, but wisps were caught in the weak moonlight. Eventually he said, "Do you want me to stay awake?"

"No, just near."

Chapter Twenty-Nine:

August 15, 2016

The rain hadn't let up even by morning. All of us were miserable, and cold. I was wrapped in a blanket and a hoodie when I slipped into the girl's tent.

"So what do we do up here when it's raining? I'm so bored! I want my phone…" Jenny whined. She'd taken up the largest spot in the tent, spread her things out quite liberally. It was exactly how I would describe a luggage explosion. The other girls, having been in my cabin for years, had their things nice and neat beside their sleeping bags.

"Well, first we need to eat," I said.

"Eat what? Cereal?" Jenny whined. The other girls glowered at me like they were at the end of their respective ropes.

"I thought you liked Reese's Puffs," I said. She held up an empty box and turned it over. I bowed my head. "Jenny . . ."

"What, am I not allowed to get hungry?" she asked. She also pushed an entire case of capri sun she'd drunk toward me as well. She had to have worked on that all night. Lovely. There were crumbs everywhere.

"Miss Laurel, we need to get to work on those spells. I don't know if they work if everything gets washed away by rain," Kennedy said. "The internet didn't say."

"That's because the internet isn't a witch and I think we need a real one," Lisey said.

"There are no real witches," Gracia pressed.

"Wiccans are witches," Lisey said. "They exist."

"Not with wands and Avada Kedavra," Kennedy said.

"Be careful with that!" Jenny yelled, laughing, lying back on her bed roll. The glowering continued.

"If the rain lightens up, we should try the spell," Lisey said. "You have a name to work with."

I sat down among them and took a deep breath. "I don't know how safe it is for you to be here when we do this."

"Why?" Gracia asked.

"This isn't a harmless experiment," I replied.

"I think we're all aware of that," Gracia said. "The boys too. Arty's a little freaked out, but he'll get over it. We all have a reason to be here."

"Seeking revenge can be dangerous," I said.

"Aware of that too," Gracia said. "But don't keep us out of it. Noah's not the only one who lost someone."

Lisey went through the tote and brought out the parchment, inkwell, and pen again. I dug through my backpack for my pocketknife. "Oh," Lisey said. "Yeah, I'm not looking."

The only one who looked was Gracia. It seemed stupid to cut my hand, and dangerous to cut my wrist, so I cut along my forearm, trying to coax the blood into the inkwell. Deep throbbing hit my arm, though shortly after adrenaline coated the pain a little. It became more bearable to milk out my own blood, hopefully just enough to write this letter.

"Ok, that's gross enough," Gracia said. "You're making a mess." She tore out a t-shirt and wrapped it around my still bleeding arm. Jenny crawled up to look. She was both fascinated and growing pale.

I dipped the pen in and scrawled out a rough equation of what Kennedy remembered from the internet. Many of her notes were waterlogged from the rain and the writing dripped from the page.

Anoche, may your darkness and hate return back to you and destroy you. You must go.

"That looks disturbing," I said at the dripping bits of my blood. "I need to get a first aid kit."

I slid out of the tent and removed the t-shirt, letting the rain hit the blood. The blood was membranous, holding to itself like a cobweb. The water washed it away and revealed the gash I'd made.

"What the fuck, Miss Laurel," Noah said. He'd been walking away from the bathroom and had seen me. He hurriedly slapped his hand on my back and pushed me toward the bathroom. Once inside, he opened his bag. "What did you do?" he asked.

"Blood for the letter," I said. There was more blood coming out of me than I thought was possible.

"People only cut longways if they intend on killing themselves," he said. "Oh."

"Did the house tell you to do this?"

"Uh . . . no," I said. Losing lots of blood would explain the lightheadedness.

He stuck my arm over the sink and rummaged through his bag. He came with his own full first aid kit. "You're not stupid enough not to know that. Did anyone see you do this?"

"The girls."

He shook his head angrily and turned the water on while he cut some gauze. "If you weren't a counselor, I'd slap you upside the head . . ." As soon as he yanked my arm away from the water, he wrapped my arm painfully tight. "Thankfully it was just one arm," he said, sitting down on a wooden stool. There was genuine concern and fear in his eyes. "You weren't trying to . . ."

"No, no, I just want to get rid of the house," I said, sitting down as well, exhausted. "You've done this before . . . haven't you? Taylor hasn't . . ."

"No, Taylor hasn't . . ." he said. "Riley, though. He has. Did. He was in so much pain after the fire that he did a lot of stupid stuff."

"What kind of stupid stuff?"

"Ten tons of pills. Cutting. Tiki torch fluid once... getting him to puke was not the highlight of my life. That's why Travis wanted me to watch him. Even when the pain got better, it became kind of a compulsion for him."

My eyes drifted to the innumerable cuts that scarred his arm. "You've stopped, right?" I asked, pointing to his arms.

"Yeah," he said.

"I'm glad, proud actually," I said. "Wow, I'm tired."

"No derp," he said, staring at my arm intently. "Never even think of doing that again. If we were smart, I'd take you to the ER."

"It's not that bad," I said.

"Once again, people only cut longways if they plan on killing themselves." His voice was dark.

"Well, I wrote the letter," I said.

"Going to need to keep adding to that bandage," Noah said. I didn't think he heard what I said. "You're not supposed to change it frequently, it'll make the blood clotting slow . . ."

The rain slowed to a drizzle later in the day. The 'ink' dried on the parchment. I had bundles of sage, a lighter, and was ready to do another stupid thing. My arm continued to throb.

"Let Gracia and I smudge the house," Lisey said, jogging to catch up to me. She had a big baggie filled with bundles of white sage and a wooden bowl. I looked at Lukas and he shrugged. Harry was biting his lip.

"What does smudge mean?" Jenny asked.

"Clearing the energy by burning sage," Lisey said.

"And that works?" Jenny didn't look very sure.

"Maybe?" Kennedy said.

"It's better than nothing," Gracia responded.

"'I'll go in there with them, in case anything weird happens," Harry said.

"Arty, Taylor, Noah and I are going to bury the black salt around the perimeter of the house," I said.

"With what?" Arty asked.

"There's tools in the House," Noah said.

"We need a few more buckets of salt," Kennedy added. "To surround the whole place."

"The earth around the House has been thoroughly salted," Lukas said.

"That's why we are trying something else," Gracia said.

We got to work, digging holes to bury the salt/dirt mixture, placing the mirrors upside down on them. The one bowl near the door was given the letter and that was placed between the bowl and the mirror. Then we buried them under heaps of mud, making cairns with stones in the surrounding area. The house rumbled angrily as we worked, especially as more smoke came from the windows.

"What in the sam-hell are you doing?" A voice echoed in my ears. I turned around to see Gary. He wasn't in a ghillie now either. I was almost getting used to seeing him in his civvies. He was wearing jeans and a long sleeved flannel but was still carrying a firearm.

"Do you have to have a gun around kids?" I asked.

"Do you have to have kids around the house?" he asked, cocking his head to one side.

"They know the risks, and they all have a reason," I responded. He rolled his eyes.

"All you're going to do is piss this thing off, Miss Winters, that's all."

"I know its name now."

"The Gatherer?" he asked.

"No, Anoche," I replied.

He shivered reflexively.

"How the fuck did you hear that name?" Taylor perked up in surprise and looked over.

"Mind your own business, boy!" he said.

"Hey, don't talk to him like that," I replied.

"Don't say that name out loud," he hissed. The house made a mad belching noise. Lisey shrieked but it was more out of surprise than terror.

"Are there children in there now?" he asked, eyebrows raising higher than I thought they could. "Get them out! Get them out!" He ran toward the house, full speed. I jogged after him as well.

Gary threw the door open. The trio just looked at him with wide eyes. They were fine. The house was shaking, though, but at this point, we were used to it doing weird things. "What part of *get out* didn't you hear! Git!" He sounded like he was talking to some horses.

They hurried out and into the clearing. "Ah shut it!" He banged on the wall with a fist. "Nothing to lose your gourd over!" It didn't stop.

"I'd advise you not to continue whatever you're doing. It stinks here."

"Sage," I said.

"Go back to your campsite," he said. "I'll keep an eye out in case they send something your way."

The kids looked defeated. "That didn't work," Gracia said.

"There was no change, at all," Lisey said.

"What are we expecting? For it to fall to pieces or dust?" Arty asked. "I really want to know what the end goal is here." There was a sound of a gunshot then. The only person who didn't react was Lukas.

"Was that . . .?" Kennedy asked.

"Yes," Lukas answered.

"The goal is to leave it harmless, or at least weaken it enough that it isn't going to keep hurting people," Gracia said. "Like it did to Riley."

"No offense, but Mr. Lukas did that," Arty said. Lukas nodded, looking down at his feet.

"No, Alina led him there even though she knew that he was pouring gasoline all over the place and was about to light it up," Gracia responded.

"Alina isn't real," Arty added. He adjusted the tarp below him so his khaki shorts would remain clean.

"She's part of the house," Gracia responded. "The lady people see on the hill, that's her. Everyone here has seen her at least once. For some reason, she followed him around, spoke to him."

"And did everything in her power to kill him," Noah added.

"He chose not to eat last summer. He chose not to eat before the summer even started," Arty said.

"He was in treatment for an actual condition. An eating disorder has nothing to do with *choice*," Noah replied.

"I'm pretty sure refusing to eat is a choice," Arty said.

"It's called anorexia," Noah hissed, holding up a hand. "This place aggravated—"

"What was already there," Arty said. "I know that; I'm not stupid. What I think we need to do is be more practical about all of this."

"Practical, hell," Noah grumbled.

Taylor said, "In Noah speak that means, it killed my girlfriend, I'm not going to be practical about anything."

Arty nodded and slapped his hands on his knees. "So what's next then?"

"Lunch," Jenny cried. "I'm hungry."

"I think I need to try to find Alina and talk to her," Taylor said. "I'll tell her that I'm here on Riley's behalf since we can't find him. Can I go to the clearing?"

"Alone?" I asked.

"Yeah,"

"Lunch!" Jenny yelled. "For God's sake, if we need something to eat."

"You're not going alone," I said.

"I second that," Harry said.

"I third it," Lukas added.

"Hello?" Jenny's voice upped a few octaves.

"If you want to go, I'll hide out in the woods, make sure you're safe," I said.

We made mac-and-cheese for lunch in a kettle over a damp fire that took an hour to get started. Jenny whined most of the time.

"I don't want macaroni. I want chicken . . ."

"Put a can of chicken in your bowl," Harry said.

"Canned chicken tastes like tuna," she said, grimacing.

"Then go without!" he yelled, exacerbated. She didn't even flinch in surprise. I'd never seen Harry upset. "Are you just not used to hearing the word 'no'?" She didn't respond, nor did her face change. After a few minutes she subtly rolled her eyes. "You'll have what everyone else is having, or you can go without, but there won't be any more late-night destruction of all of our supplies." She completely ignored him.

After eating, Taylor and I crossed to the clearing just east of us. "It hurt my brother and it hurt my friend. I have to find out why…" he muttered. I silently nodded and followed.

I hid behind a thick tree-cover in brambles and thorns. My jeans picked up burrs left and right, and so was my jacket, but I was happy it wasn't my skin. Kneeling down, I sank a bit into the mud, and watched. Taylor climbed up onto the roof of the house without difficulty and sat, facing away from me. I almost called out that sitting up there was dangerous, but the whole thing was dangerous. His voice was distant and hardly audible.

"Alina?" he called. "It's Riley's friend Taylor, I want to talk to you . . ."

Heavy breathing interrupted my listening and hair rose on my neck. The source of the breathing stomped its way through the brush and the trees. I imagined the bright red eyes and the serpentine tongue then shivered. Each step, it got closer, but it was ambling along at a comfortable pace. Then soft fur brushed up against me. It was Charlie. I wrapped an arm around him and buried the side of my face in his thick, dense fur. He sat down and just watched with me.

"Alina! We have to talk about what happened! Riley gave me the friendship bracelet he made for you! He hoped I'd see you this summer." He held up his wrist. "It didn't burn in the fire; can you believe that? You should have seen what happened to him, he was in a burn unit for weeks." He paused. "Alina! Did you hear any of that?" There was another pause. Charlie whined a bit and pawed at the ground nervously.

"Stay put," I whispered.

"Of course I came back," he said. "This place doesn't let anyone leave, does it?" Another beat. "Riley was angry you weren't there when he woke up. You said you would be." A shiver ran through me. Riley wasn't supposed to wake up in the hospital, he was supposed to wake up here. "Why did you even want to talk that night? Here? Could have been anywhere at camp." His voice wavered a bit, whether from bad memories or fear, I didn't know. "Were you trying to hurt him?"

My heart fell. Right now Riley is fourteen years old, as of a week ago. He was still a child who'd gone through way too much pain. All of these kids had. And now he went missing and only had us to speak for him.

"You didn't help him," he said. "He would have saved you if he could. Now he can't. But I don't really know who you are." He paused and took a deep breath. "Your name isn't Alina. It's Linnea. Noah told me."

The wind started to pick up and I held onto Charlie even harder. He didn't seem to mind. He just watched Taylor with all the focus he could muster.

"You lied to Riley. You wanted him to get killed." He grumbled from disappointment, sadness even. "He trusted you."

A long silence followed. "I know. Then help me."

Charlie's tail thumped the ground, and he moved like he was about to make a run for it. I held onto his collar.

"It is possible. It has to be." He was exasperated. "That's because you haven't tried!"

Charlie was about to howl or bark. I made him look at me and put my finger to my lips. He whimpered instead.

"Ok, ok, but we have to do it," Taylor said. He was looking to his right, as if someone was sitting beside him. Back behind me, at the campsite, the kids were working on building a log-cabin style fire as well as handmade hobo-stoves.

Taylor's voice fell and became inaudible. I strained to listen, but the buzz of the insects filled my ears. I sat down fully, simply waiting for something, anything. Charlie bolted forward as soon as I relaxed. I almost called out for him, but all he did was greet Taylor with a jump and a lick as Taylor came back toward me. "You saw her?" I asked.

He nodded. "I feel crazy that I could see her like he did, talk to her . . ." He took a deep breath and looked back and waved. "She knew you were watching and wasn't very thrilled about that. She said that she didn't know Mr. Lukas was going to do anything and she just wanted to see him. She claimed she tried to protect him."

"How?"

"I don't know," he said, throwing his hands up in the air. "But she doesn't seem to have an idea of how to get rid of the Gatherer, but she believes if it is destroyed, she can be free again."

Not knowing what to do, and expecting a ghost to tell a child how to do it was excruciating, and felt irrational, if not stupid. So, we played many rounds of mafia, Honey, I Love You (which was increasingly awkward with this group of kids) and BS. No one was interested in hiking. The campsite felt safe in comparison to the rest of the land. The kids exhausted themselves through games and went to sleep around ten. I stayed up for watch.

I tried to determine what could destroy the house. So many different things had been attempted before to destroy this house. Axes did nothing. Fire didn't touch it. Salting. Holy water. Magic spells. Yet, at the core of me, I knew something had to be able to destroy it.

I was shaken awake by the wind and the sudden permeation of light. I'd fallen asleep while on watch. Exhaustion clung to me. If it weren't for what I saw, I'd slip right back into sleep. The air was filled with luminous orbs, each of their own color. They were so near the ground, some within reach. A feeling of malignancy permeated the air, electric, and thick. There were hundreds of these orbs, some flashing like massive fireflies, hovering above our camp, leading back to the house. From my view, the house breathed. Its walls shifted in and out of place. A thick stench of death clung to the wind.

I stood on my feet, shakily at first and followed the smell and the orbs. I neared the object of my fear when my instincts told me to flee. I was so tired of the flight response; it was time to fight.

Coming upon the house, I saw where the stench came from. The clearing around it was littered with bodies of animals. They'd come silently and died silently. Rabbits, foxes, and coyotes.

I came to the front of the House. A rabbit's corpse lay draped across the cellar. I picked it up by one gelatinous ear and threw it aside. It'd been consumed by fast decay. Another gift this place had. I lifted the heavy lid of the cellar door and let it creak and crack before slamming into the dusty ground beside me. The smell of musty, airlessness wafted up from below.

I climbed into the cellar of the House, it's very belly, and sat in the dark, dank space. Above me, the cellar door was closed, and the only light I had was my lantern. I held the crystals in my hands, hoping they would offer some sense of protection. With my legs crossed and my eyes closed, I listened to the house breathe around me. It had its own heartbeat within the walls. It had its own musical quality. The energy inside the cellar sang and swirled around me. It was palpable. It clung to my skin.

"We are older than the trees and the hills. We created the hills by eating the earth. Our roots run deep, cradled at the center of the world. We have seen countless generations of men, watched them as they evolved into ruin and into dust. How short of a life you live. We were here at the beginning, and we will be here to shape the end," the voice was unrecognizable. It did not come from a single voice, but numerous as if chanted directly into my mind. "We are hungry, and your fear, your anxiety, your torment, is delicious. It sustains us. We have watched you long. We have seen your weakness. We see how you weep, and how your body betrays you. You cannot fight a power such as this. You cannot dare to become so powerful."

The lantern was extinguished, and an orb of light appeared before me. For a moment it floated, suspended, golden. It stretched into an image of Alina. The familiar figure we'd all seen on the hill, beckoning us. It changed into that of an Otoe man, sitting, calm and silent, before he became a hunched, biting menace. His arms and legs were elongated and broken, and he wore the fur of an animal on his shoulders. He sneered at me. Inches from my face, the image changed again, rapidly, to every child in the campground above, and then to an image of myself.

"You've become part of this land. You cannot leave. You are a part of us," the image of myself spoke to me. My energy drained significantly. It was getting its share of me.

"No," I said, the words fell out of my mouth.

"And you think that is enough?" The image of my own body looked at me and laughed. The mouth was wide, cutting across my cheeks, bleeding in places. My jaw cracked open, and the laugh became a surge of unholy mirth. The image grew larger and larger until it filled the space of the cellar. It was no longer me; it was no longer anything else recognizable. It simply *was*, broken smile and all. "What are you going to do now, little one?" The voice bellowed, shaking the earth, the house. It was like the image in the field but grown gelatinous with eyes about it. The teeth elongated and the hands became tentacular. I backed from it as fast as possible and hit the wall of the cellar.

I scrambled for the cellar door, not thinking of screaming or crying for help. The Gatherer's hand covered the exit, and it knelt down to stare at me with its empty eyes. It was there though, the spirit of the thing, but behind the eyes. Hiding its truth. "Let me out," I said. It was out of impulse rather than anything else.

Chapter Thirty:

August 15, 2016

Its whole body blocked the way out. Its hands and feet clung to the earth, digging into it. I could hear the soil, as if roots were growing through it, digging into the depths beneath us. Into all those pods of people. The face solidified once again, to the recognizable canine skull with deer antlers. The eyes produced enough light that I could see its features in the dark. It was lean, almost emaciated. The hide of it was flaking, the fur falling off. It seemed almost weak. A good blow and those ribs would crack, and it'd fall to the side.

It sneered, as though it could read my mind, and a crawling feeling covered my skin. Bugs. Spiders. Mosquitos. Anything and everything that could crawl, would crawl, was on me. They clung to my skin, digging into it, burrowing. The first thought that came across my mind was that I worked at a summer camp, and the weirdest one on earth, this wasn't the scariest thing I could imagine. It was uncomfortable, and slightly nauseating, but it was still a figment of my imagination. I closed my eyes. *It's not real, it's not real, it's not real, it's not real.* I repeated the mantra in my mind, yet the quick moving sound of insectile legs nearly got to me. Some weaseled into my ears, parted my lips, clung to my clothes.

A bit of doubt entered me. Maybe it was real. *Nope, nope, can't be real. Not that many bugs can live inside the cellar. Gary said it wasn't real.*

I reached out my hand, eyes still stiffly closed. I expected to feel bone or some kind of fur. The growling increased exponentially, but I wasn't about to stay in this cellar all night. So I shuffled forward, one arm outstretched, groping for the door to the cellar. The snapping sound of jaws collided next to my ear. My body lurched to the left, away from the noise, just out of instinct.

This was one of the few times I felt adrenaline actively course through me, burning, keeping every part of me alert and awake. I put my arm out again and went forward and one step to the right. *Ignore the biting noise. Ignore all the noises. Ignore.*

I focused all my energy singularly on finding the door, the familiar cold, metal loop that would lead me to freedom. Yet, in the snares of it now, I didn't know if there was freedom.

Something coiled around my leg. For a moment, I ignored that as well, but the smooth object tightened its grip and ripped me backwards. *It's real. It's really real.* Terror washed through me. Any confidence that lay with me before vanished. I could fight a figment, but I could not fight something in the physical world. Not alone, and I was alone.

I smacked the ground, on my chest and belly. The air shot out of me, and dirt clung to my teeth. I coughed, simply to get breath, then finally, opened my eyes. The creature was strangely twisted to fit into such a small space for its body, though I never considered the cellar small. One of its tentacular hands hit the floor in front of me, and it leaned down to lick me with its tongue. Shivers ran through me and the first audible scream I could manage ripped out. I was pulled again. I reached for something to grab, anything, but nothing was in my reach, not a single root, or object, just unyielding dirt.

There was only one other option, to flop onto my back and kick at whatever was dragging me- to face it. My mind became increasingly quiet with this singular focus. There was nothing running around in circles in there, just the need to free myself. To get back to the fresh air. Blood pumped in my ears loudly, mixing with the sound of my back scraping along the earth. The occasional little pebble or stone dug into my flesh. Hot dribbles of blood stuck to my clothing and mixed with my sweat. I reached for my right ankle, pulling at the tentacle. It was smooth, almost scaly in nature. It was muscle bound. As my hand slid over a stone, I took it and started to slam the stone into the tentacle. A faint, unholy screech came from the dark space before me. I continued to slam into the writhing mess, hoping desperately it would let go. Instead, the appendage, damaged from the trauma, fell apart and retreated.

Sitting in the dark, I didn't know where I was. There was no sense of direction. The lack of light was enveloping. With my hands around my ankle, I felt a slight dent in my skin. Exhausted, I lay down and stared ahead. I was lost.

I was too terrified to cry out for help. The emptiness of sound was vacuum-like, and I felt as though speaking would be dangerous. The air shifted around me, as if unseen things moved in the dark. At times, pinpricks of the smallest noises would permeate through. The back of my neck prickled and a sense that something was behind me was overwhelming. I stepped forward to turn around. Facing it made me feel less vulnerable than having my back exposed.

"Laurel!" A voice called. It was not a voice I recognized, and it didn't cut through the silence in any unholy way. It was as if it was part of the silence, moved with it.

Blinding white light entered my left eye. It was the girl on the hill. "Alina!" I whispered. She exuded moonlight with her white, lace dress, and milky skin. Her eyes were dark, but aware.

"Come with me," she said, motioning for me to hurry in her direction. Curiosity overtook me, though. She gave enough light for me to see what was lurking. The figure was so tall I could not see its head, only a very lean, emaciated figure. The skin clung close to the bone in a sickening way. If it moved suddenly, I'd imagine it'd creak. I jumped back. "Laurel!" she called. I ran in her direction.

She walked as though alive, without shoes, and with the dress scraping lightly against the ground. "Where are we going?" I asked.

"I've never been this deep beneath the house before . . ." she said, as amazed as I was about our surroundings.

"What was that thing?" I asked.

"An extension of the Gatherer," she replied.

We continued walking. My footsteps seemed to echo, louder and louder, as if the area around us was shrinking, tunneling. Then I stopped completely, but the footsteps faltered and continued. "There's something behind me, isn't there?" I asked. She nodded and hurried past me to stand between me and the monster.

"You can't have her," Alina said.

Perhaps this was its real shape. Standing tall, lanky, almost broken, with sickly colored skin that was almost translucent. In Alina's light, its eyes reflected back the same whiteness. Its jaw looked broken, hardly attached, hanging open, and bloody. Its purpose in life was to consume. Yet when I spoke to Anoche, it said 'we'. These were all pieces and parts of the whole. They couldn't be fought against because they weren't fully real, or even alive. It was the source that had to be destroyed.

"And why not?" The voice was a sneer of sound. It grated and cut through the air.

"You can't have her," Another voice echoed. Haley. I nearly jumped from my skin, turning to see her approach from behind, glowing as brightly as Alina. She stood at my side. It was bright enough now to see the outline of the tunnel. Rough crystal lined the tunnel, occasionally glittering in the light.

It stepped forward. "You have no power over me, girls," it said. "I brought you here myself. Why inhibit me from having a little treat to soothe my nerves?"

"No," It was yet another familiar voice.

"Riley?" I called, turning my head to see me. He raised his hand. Behind him came others I recognized, Charlotte Dahl, Edythe, Nicholas, Amalie, the whole family, crowding up this tight space.

The creature grew to exponential proportions out of anger, the earth moving with it. It was now made of the bones of its victims, skulls of every species held together with frayed and raw ligament and tendon. Riley took my hand. "You have to get out of here," he said. The light grew in the tunnel as more and more victims appeared.

"Go," Alina said. Haley smiled at me. My heart physically hurt. I could feel the tug on my arm. We were going *through* the mass of energy, further and further back. The space glittered more intensely with jagged edges of stone and quartz and chalcedony. Moments later I realized I was running as fast as I could. The tunnel shook with the power of the Gatherer behind us, being blocked only by light. Perhaps it lived in these tunnels, drew its power from these walls . . . but I didn't know.

"Where are we going?" I asked. He didn't answer me. "Riley! Where are we going?"

"Out," he hissed, pulling harder on my arm.

"Where is your body?" I asked. "We've been looking for you!"

He chuckled and shook his head. "I don't know," he answered.

I never saw the wall, so I didn't slow my pace. I slammed against a wall, face first. I felt around with my hands and found nothing around me but dirt, not the rough surface of the tunnel. My head, all shaken up, rang and pounded in my ears. I blinked rapidly in the darkness, as if that would help me see.

"Laurel?" Voices echoed around me, though I couldn't see where they were coming from.

"Miss Laurel? Was that thumping her? What is going on?"

"Arty, help me get this thing open!" It was Harry's voice.

"It's locked! I don't have pliers," Arty said.

"It's me!" I called up, seeing the faint outline of light above me. Riley took me to the entrance. I was inches away from freedom.

"We're all up here, Laurel!" Harry said.

"Get me out of here!" I could taste the blood in my mouth, mingling with cottony saliva.

"It's not budging!" Arty responded.

"Get some bolt cutters!" Lukas said. "There should be some around back."

I waited, fixated on the tiny crack of light. Behind me, there was a commotion that sounded like an unearthly thing screaming. I finally found the wood of the cellar door and pounded. "Get me out! Get me out!" I cried. The screaming grew closer.

"Step back, Laurel!" Lukas yelled.

"I'm not going back there!" I responded.

"You have to if you want out!" Harry said.

"I'm here, I'm here," Gary said, followed by what sounded like a yawn. "God, in the middle of the night too. You guys just can't do anything at the right time."

Growling echoed in the walls of the cellar and grew ever closer to my ears, causing everything to tingle and tighten. My stomach moved up to my throat. "You're all so feeble," the voice was right in my ear. "You'll never leave."

"For fuck's sake," A hatchet blade went through the door of the cellar. Moonlight sprayed in and the voice, and whatever produced the voice, retreated.

The hatchet continued to pound its way in until the door was obliterated. Lukas leaned down with a hand and pulled me up. The kids stood around, mouths open. I felt like shit. Gary said, "How did you end up down there?"

"I don't know . . ." I responded. My memory was cloudy.

"We need to get you cleaned up," Harry said. "Oh god, your face, your leg—what happened down there?"

"It's . . . it's alive. We gotta kill it. We gotta kill it now," I said. "Forget my face and my leg. We have to do something *now.*"

"And what do you suggest?" Gary asked.

The slimeball face of the Gatherer shoved its way through the hole in the cellar.

"Shit!" Jenny screeched. She ripped the ax from Gary's hands and threw it smack in the center of the creature. It whined and squealed before removing itself from sight.

"Nice!" Taylor high-fived her.

"There's tunnels beneath there . . . tunnels lined with crystal, going very deep beneath the house. That's where it really lives, but it's in so many parts," I said.

"Then we need to get it to focus on one spot," Kennedy said.

Chapter Thirty: August 15, 2016

"And how do we do that?" Jenny asked. "Especially if it's going to look like that."

Lukas wrapped his arms around me, and I buried my head in his chest and took a few moments to breathe. He rested his chin on the top of my head. For a moment I felt safe. Whole. "Like you said, we keep all of its attention here on the house, so every bit of it is in one piece." His voice crackled deep in his chest.

"I'll be right back," Gary said, shouldering his rifle and walking back towards his house. The night was clear, and the stars and moon were bright enough to illuminate our surroundings. The kids stood looking at Lukas, Harry, and I for instruction.

"I suppose we should get to work," Noah said, going toward the house.

I lifted my head up. "Where are you going?"

"To see if I can talk to Haley," he responded, carefully lowering himself into the cellar. I continued to remind myself, if it has no physical form, it cannot survive. This house was the physical form. To destroy it would, at the very least, grievously injure it.

Taylor said, "Noah told me there's a body down there. What if we properly bury it?"

"Could be a start, letting it have peace," Gracia said. "Though I don't know where the most sacred location to bury it is."

"Outside the clearing," Arty said. Gracia's eyebrows raised. Taylor, without another thought, went straight after his brother.

"Your gut telling you that too?" Lisey asked.

"Let's go get him," I muttered, turning away from Lukas. He held firm to my shoulder.

"You need to rest," he said.

"Rest? I don't think I could if I wanted to." I half laughed and went toward the cellar.

"You're just leaving us here?" Kennedy called, stifling her voice a bit.

"Yep," I replied.

"Uh!" Jenny exclaimed. "My dad would be so weirded out by this."

"Then don't tell him," I said, stepping back into the cellar.

Chapter Thirty-One:

August 15, 2016

The cellar smelled of musty dirt mixed with the body wash and odor of teenage boys. The light no longer seemed enough to illuminate our surroundings, and every hair stood on end, waiting for the Gatherer to reappear. This time, though, I felt calmer, safer.

"Taylor?" Arty called out. "Taylor?"

Lukas stepped past the fridge, which still lay on its side. He took a small bag from his pants pocket. "Like old times," he joked. We gathered the bones together. The skeleton was fully articulated, lying in a crumpled heap. The person's neck appeared broken. Age and filth discolored the bones to a dark, ugly hew.

Arty dug through the fine silt dirt to get the smaller bones so we wouldn't leave any bits behind. "Taylor!" he called again. "Where'd you go?"

"Here!" Taylor was somewhere deep in the cavernous system I'd just escaped from.

"Don't stay long!" Arty said. "And get your brother out of there too!"

"I'm right here," Noah said.

I jumped back, nearly falling, but someone's hand steadied me. His voice was low, defeated. When I laid eyes on him, his eyes were red, and he shook his head.

"What is it?" I asked.

"I can't leave her here alone," he breathed. "I can't, I just can't,"

"We are going to free her," I said.

"What if it doesn't work?" Noah asked, his voice rising higher.

"You can't talk like that," Lukas said. The bag of bones in his hand jingled a bit when he reached for Noah. They made direct eye contact. "You are not going to stay, not for her, not for anyone else. You're getting out of here with your brother."

"I can do it. I can be what the Gatherer focuses on," Noah said. "I know he can feel . . . everything."

"No," Taylor said. "You're not leaving me too." He grabbed his brother by the wrist and pulled him forcefully out of the cellar. "You've tried to leave me too many times. It's not going to happen. It's not fair!"

We followed. The fresh air hit me much clearer than just moments before. It was crisp, clean, and very welcome. I lay on the ground and stared at the stars. What I started I wasn't sure I could finish.

"Found a good spot to dig," Lisey said. "A nice grove of trees by the horse pasture."

We all nodded silently in acknowledgement. Even Jenny joined our trek. My watch said it was three in the morning. Lukas texted Gary quickly before returning the phone to his pocket. The blue glow the phone emitted seemed as unholy as the house. This was, after all, a funerary procession of a man we didn't know. He may have been the cause of this insanity. He may have simply been a victim, but his resting place needed to be outside of the vicinity of the house. Lisey lit sage while we walked, as a way of calming herself, and maybe the rest of us too.

The chalcedony was left in the jaw of the man, and in his ribcage. What was done there would not be undone by our hands.

It was strange to watch children digging graves, but Lisey and Arty insisted. Taylor held onto his brother tightly, feeling as though if he let go, he would lose him forever. Lukas's eyes kept flickering toward them. Still, he carried the skeleton. The vague outline of the skull could be viewed through the filmy bag. Strange to think something just like that lay under my own skin. I touched my face, pressing firmly on my cheek bones for the same curved features, and on my brow, where eventually there would be nothing but a cavity.

Lisey and Arty became tired and slowed. Harry and Lukas took up the spades to let them rest.

"I'll take it," Jenny said, holding the bag.

Gracia and Kennedy dug through papers, looking for some sort of prayer. I was entranced, watching the process unfold before me. So much pain and death and grief, all culminating, and out of what? Reckless hate? A deep need to consume? I wanted to put it to rest. Be done with it all.

Harry and Lukas climbed out of the hole, helping one another before Jenny carefully placed the bones, and not the bag, into the space. Kennedy said, "We return you to the earth, as the earth is your Mother so you may have peace and your soul may find freedom."

In the light of electric and battery powered lanterns, the grave was filled. The ground was patted down solidly, and we stood together for a moment, arms around one another. I closed my eyes out of respect. Someone patted my back. "Let's go back and finish what we started," Lukas said.

Gary's old truck puttered right outside the clearing to the house. It was packed solidly in the bed of the pickup. With the rifle strapped to his back, he approached. "I knew this would come in handy," he said, lightly touching the tarp covering his cargo.

"What is it?" Lukas asked.

"Explosives! Some military, some civilian," he picked up a motor-oil smelling piece of putty. "C4. Burns well, very controllable, in my opinion. Can learn a lot about them from online terrorist magazines actually. Then we have HMX, I prefer to mix it with good ole TNT. Don't touch it, it will give you some liver problems and do a hell of a lot of damage to your central nervous system." They were little round crystal looking balls, almost purplish in this light. "Some of the most powerful stuff I have here. No letting your little ones here handle it. I'm not going to be responsible for someone getting their hand blown off or losing their ability to walk because they got it where they shouldn't have. Got some Nitropenta, the stuff the shoe bomber attempted to use. Got it nice and wrapped up here and ready to go. Surprisingly easy to make if you know your chemistry. Then we have Semtex, the shit they use in IEDs. Easy to get too." He touched a strangely shaped hexagon of red." He sighed. "And gunpowder of course, gotta have something to make this thing go sky high. Even static electricity could make this whole thing go boom. Sounds good?"

"We're going to blow things up?" Jenny asked slowly.

"Not just things, that thing. Y'all have been doing stupid shit with this house. If I don't help you end it, it'll eat you up," he said. "It's mad enough anyways, I don't think it'll let this go."

"I tried burning it to the ground, why do you think this will make any difference?" Lukas asked.

"If people are brave enough to get into the tunnels, we should be able to take out the source with enough of a distraction. I can't promise anything, like this will be done forever, but it's better than nothing," Gary said. "Everyone get a lantern. You're going to go behind the fridge into the depths below the house. Anywhere that looks like a good place to put one of these, go right ahead. The adults will handle the HMX and lay the gunpowder when we are ready to go." Everyone grabbed their lanterns and gloves.

"Careful now," he said. "I've heard you tend to fall over things." His eyes landed on Jenny. She made a huffing noise but appeared to relish getting a task. We were handing explosives to minors. In any other context, I would question my motives and sanity.

"What if one of those creatures comes out?" I asked.

"Planning on it," Gary said, smiling. There was excitement about him, a high intensity energy. "We'll end it."

Inside the cellar, the kids often got lost, and we resorted to laying out tracks of friendship bracelet string to and from the piles of explosives. "I ran out of string!" Jenny called.

"What color are you?" I asked standing among four colors of string going in four different directions.

"Purple!" she said.

"Don't move," I called ahead, following the purple string. Light began to peek in from outside now. Morning was only a few hours away, but that didn't mean safety. Gary came in behind me, carrying a large tray of the little granules. I followed after Jenny. Where she stood, she shivered. The light shook in her hand.

"What is it?" I asked.

She shook her head. "Don't know. Don't care. Want out."

"Ok, let's go," I said, putting my yellow string back in my pocket. I led her out into the misty morning and got her to sit down on the picnic bench outside the clearing.

"It was like shit just kept going through me . . ." She put her fingers up to the center of her chest. "God, I'm tired, Miss Laurel."

"I know. Take a rest. If you need one of us, just holler," I said, beginning to stand back up.

She reached out for me. It was an oddly sweet gesture. "Don't let it get you, please."

"I won't."

With the explosives in place, we all returned to the light. It was six in the morning now. The sun was completely up, burning away the dew, though we were ankle deep in wet grass. Lukas interrupted the silence and said, "I want all of you to go back to the campsite."

"What? I thought we were doing this together?" Gracia asked.

"You guys did your part," he said. "Please."

He looked at Kennedy, Arty, Lisey, and Jenny, who all began to walk away. Noah and Taylor stayed put.

"Taylor," Lisey reached out for him. He looked between her and Noah repeatedly.

"Go with her," Noah said, nudging him.

"No, not if you're going to do something stupid," Taylor replied.

"Both of you, go," Lukas said. "And Harry, you need to watch them and make sure they stay in the campsite, no matter what they hear."

"I agree with the boy here," Gary said, slapping Lukas on the back. "The less of you there are here, the safer."

"I started this fight. I'm not going to leave," I added.

"Didn't say you had to," Lukas said. Harry sighed and put an arm around Noah.

"I have to make sure Haley is ok!" he cried.

"She's going to be ok. I promise," I said. He hugged me tightly, as if he was losing her all over again. Pain seeped out of him, out of every pore. He oozed hurt. I held him for some time, feeling hot tears hit my neck. "And so will you. Just keep Taylor safe. Keep each other safe."

Harry said, "I'll be happy not to see this thing ever again . . ." He sighed. "Come on you two. We can make some breakfast. I was thinking about pancakes. Seemed to be a hit the first time." Harry was depleted of energy, that I could see. He turned back to look at me with a tired smile.

A creature darted from a window in the house; it looked lean, skeletonized, with spikes along its spine. Its face was carnivorous, yet antlered like a stag and it had very human hands. It went straight at Harry, who instinctually covered the Halverson boys. The creature hit him with a solid thunk, and Harry landed on top of them. The thing screeched out loud enough it echoed off the hills and valleys, bouncing from one place to another. It reached out to touch Harry again and Gary shot it, right in the chest. It stopped for a moment, looking at its chest and then at us.

Lukas picked me up like a sack of potatoes and threw me into the truck, locking it from the outside with Gary's fob. Gary set up the site on his rifle once again and shot numerous rounds, only pushing the thing backward, not injuring it. Yet it grew in size and monstrosity as he angered it. It gathered more and more of itself into one body. The oozing substance I saw from the cellar grew into the body as if it was mercury, solid, yet liquified. The limbs grew longer and longer as well, until it towered over all of us.

While it was distracted and growing, Harry took the opportunity to hurry Noah and Taylor out of the vicinity and out of sight. The Gatherer looked at them—with its keen, predatory eyes—and bolted after them. The shots hitting its body did nothing to hinder it. Yet, when it reached the perimeter of the clearing, it stopped and squealed. It was as if it hit a wall. I almost expected to hear a noise, like air parting, but the only thing that could be heard was the frustration of this creature. The circle worked. I cheered internally, though I fought stupidly against the handle of the truck to open. I hated to have to sit aside while they were fighting this battle.

I had a right to end it.

Knowing it could no longer reach Harry and the boys, it turned back toward Gary. Gary struggled to reload, and Lukas stepped up with his arms in the air.

"What . . .?" I whispered.

"Take me and you can be free," Lukas said. "Then you can walk right out of this circle."

It looked at him for a long moment, and Gary stopped. Instead, he listened. The creature reached out with its tongue and touched Lukas's forehead. Lukas stood still, almost peaceful. He breathed evenly and slowly. *"Your pain is quite sweet. It can fill our hungry belly better than sorrow. You love as that boy loves, but your love isn't quite dead. Yet. I can collect her as well."*

The Gatherer stepped closer to Lukas. I screamed in the truck for him to get out, to flee. He was being stupid and impulsive. He was being himself.

"I always get what I want." It added.

Gary tiptoed around the two, toward the cellar of the house. I squinted, desperate to see what was in his hands. Matches. He had a box of matches. My heart twisted around my lungs and all systems wanted to come up and out of my throat.

I looked around the truck for anything to pry my way out with. There was a flimsy knife, piles of napkins from various locations, and a few pieces of plastic cutlery. My eyes flicked back to Lukas, who stood just as still as before. Gary now had a lighted match and briskly threw it into the cellar. Nothing happened. The Gatherer didn't notice, he was happily enjoying whatever emotion Lukas was letting out, breathing it in, digesting it. Turning to the backseat, I glimpsed something red and smooth. It was a fire extinguisher. I'd seen it in movies, maybe it'd work here too.

Gary made eye contact with me briefly, unshouldered his rifle and went into the cellar. I didn't understand what he was doing. My heart pounded faster and faster in my chest. There was no other word than sick. I struggled for the fire extinguisher under the pile of other odd items. Once I had it in hand, I struck it against the truck's window, and nothing happened. I readjusted myself and tried again. An explosion ripped out as the extinguisher went through the window.

The cellar. It'd blown.

With Gary in it.

I screamed instinctually, and the Gatherer looked at both me and at the cellar and screamed in response. It wrapped its tongue tighter and tighter around Lukas before liquifying completely. It climbed up his legs and was absorbed into his skin, joining with him. His arms and legs grew, cracking, breaking, making him a horrid, unnatural shape. He glowed slightly, even in the sunlight.

Chapter 32:

August 16, 2016

Gary was dead and Lukas was possessed by Anoche.

One shoulder rose up, snapped, and fell into its new position. The other shoulder did the same. His back arched painfully and ripped through the back of his shirt. Each vertebra of his was visible. With shaking hands, I took Gary's side arm he kept in the glove box, and with my elbow, busted out the rest of the glass so I could make my way out of the truck.

"Lukas! It's me!" I called. "You're in there, ok? You're in there!"

The house started to fall into the massive clearing below it that was slowly but surely getting larger. Explosions continued to go off steadily, growing wider, and deeper. The entire hill we were on was descending, all caverns were collapsing. They were collapsing on Gary. On the pods. The whole enclosed porch fell to the ground, screeching and crunching as it went.

Lukas approached me, his head cocked to the side. He was hardly recognizable. If I could get him to look in my eyes, I could bring him back. "Lukas, it's Laurel," I said calmly, though my voice shook. "I'm here. Come back to me. You can fight them. I know you can." He steadily walked toward me. His eyes became those of Anoche, emptied out lights that held only malice.

I lifted the gun, knowing nothing about them. I'd never held one in my life, but I knew there was a safety, which I turned off. I rested my finger on the trigger and tried to aim. As soon as he saw the gun, he moved with forceful speed out of my sight. Terrified, I lowered the gun and looked in the clearing around me. The second story of the house collapsed in on itself. At times it looked as though I was watching it flicker, going from a house to a cabin, to a wigwam. Large beams splintered and sang before falling in on themselves.

I bolted for the line of calla lilies and stood behind them for safety. The thing that was now Lukas easily passed through now that it had a body. My heart fell. I had to shoot. I squinted hard, trying to get my vision straight, and aimed for between his eyes. The bullet burst from the gun and lodged itself in Lukas's jaw, but it only stayed for a moment before a flattened bullet fell from him. I shot again, getting his cheek bone. Flesh tore from him for a moment before immediately returning to its initial place. For a moment, red, sinewy skin was visible and the slight white of bone. How many shots this thing had in it, I didn't know, but I was going to find out.

The whole house shook beside me as if it was seizing, then belching. A dark, gritty cloud spewed from it like an upside down sprinkler. This darkness remained within the clearing, even if Lukas could clearly leave. Another loud boom ripped through the house. It breathed, as though sighing from pain. Lukas was so close now, to me, to the kids, to all of us, as if the Gatherer wanted to take us all.

I raised the gun again, trying to stop the shaking and focused right between eyes I no longer recognized as that of my friend. I shot, but it landed in his nose. I howled out of frustration, crying. Just last night, he was the person I trusted, lying right beside me, breathing, smiling.

One of Lukas's arms turned into a spike, coming straight toward me. I tripped over, crawling away from it. Shivering, I hid beneath the truck. The spike drove itself through the bed of the truck, then ripped through the metal, and out again. The green truck's metal curled and twirled easily though the spike poured blood.

"Lukas, stop it!" I screamed. "It's Laurel! Lukas please!"

"You son of a bitch!" A voice yelled.

I stood up nervously. Gary, dusty and bloody, stood at the edge of the cellar. He was hunched over, grasping at his stomach. The house slowly crumbled behind him, deeper, and deeper into a cavernous space in the earth. It sounded like a war zone.

"Look me in the eyes!" Gary said, but not to me. "I've been fighting you my whole life, Anoche! You sad mother fucker." He shot once, right between Lukas's eyes. Lukas crumbled to the ground, pieces of him shrinking.

He shrieked in pain, every part of him was completely broken.

The venomous looking sludge exited his body and hurriedly tried to flee. Its home was in tatters, so it tried the surrounding woods. It couldn't leave the perimeter without Lukas's body. There was a mewling followed by an excruciatingly loud snapping noise. It came from the sludge repeatedly. I realized that Gary was filling the sludge with bullets until he completely emptied the magazine. Then he collapsed on the ground, his skull smashed against a slab of stone.

Lukas pointed at Gary, and I jogged toward him. I placed my fingers on his neck but felt no pulse. With my ear to his chest, I listened for anything- the sound of ragged breathing, a heartbeat. He was gone.

I curled up beside Lukas and picked up his head in my hands. "I'm here," I said. "I'm not going anywhere." He smiled and looked up. Blood was on his teeth, a small rivulet dripped down his jaw.

"I love you, Laurel," he said, gulping the air like a fish out of water.

I leaned down and placed my forehead on his. One of his arms reached up and touched my hair. He breathed in hitched, hard breaths that were painful just to hear. I rocked ever so slightly, my own tears flowing freely. I pulled out my phone and typed in 911.

"911, what's your emergency?"

"My name is Laurel Winters. I'm at Camp Kellova, on the hill, near the same place where there was a fire last summer. My friend's been hurt really badly. The cabin up here collapsed, there's one person dead . . ." I said quickly. "We need an ambulance, fast."

"Is he breathing?"

"My friend? Yes, but barely. His heart isn't steady. There's blood and broken bones."

"We have someone heading that way," she said. "Stay on the phone with me. Can you do CPR?"

"Signal's spotty," I said, and I hung up.

"You'll be ok," I said. "I promise."

I smiled and touched his cheek. He was clammy and his pupils were dilated. I caressed his cheek. He smiled slightly; his cheeks cracked with drying blood. "I really do," he said.

"You really do what, Lukas?"

"Love you," he responded.

"Sometimes you have a funny way of showing it," I said. He chuckled a bit, then grimaced in pain and held his stomach. "I can't feel my legs," he said softly. I took his hand and squeezed tightly.

"I still have you," I said. The ground moved beneath us as if the earth breathed and then let all the air out. The house was flattened. No structure remained. "We did it, Lukas. It's gone."

"Yeah…" he said. I squeezed his hand again.

"You feel that?"

"Feel what?" he asked. His eyes no longer met mine and he blinked. "Laurel?"

"Can you feel my hand?" I asked.

"No . . ." he said. "I—I can't see you."

"I'm here, I'm here. I'm not leaving you," I said, more tears coming to my eyes. He sighed as the earth settled and blinked one more time before he was at rest.

There was no house left. No pieces of building material. No nails, no planks, no windows, no glass. There was a scar left in the earth that showed large deposits of chalcedony and quartz, glittering in the sun, and it seemed to be growing. I dragged Gary away from the chasm in the ground and placed him by Lukas's broken body. Lukas's face was completely peaceful. I'd closed his eyes, and there seemed to be the smallest of smiles on his face. I wiped the blood from his mouth. I pulled my hand through his hair and kissed his forehead before hitching cries took over my bed. I wept and screamed.

"Miss Laurel?" Gracia's tentative voice interrupted my screams.

410

Harry enveloped me in his arms, and I crumbled into them, one hand remaining on Lukas's shoulder. "The house is gone…" Taylor said. "Gone, gone."

The distant sound of sirens wailed about us. They were coming.

August 19, 2016

Camp was closed; the Nomad room was raided by Officer Stevens, and Gary's home was also raided. No one has ever found Riley's body. The police placed the blame on Gary for Ezra's near-death experience. All odd things were explained away by Gary, the one with the illegal explosives. All of us, adults and children, knew that it was a lie, but Gary wouldn't have minded.

Camp Kellova wasn't going to survive this ordeal, and I didn't think Anoche survived either. Officer Stevens and my mother both destroyed me verbally. I was in shock from the events and massive trauma to my right arm. I knew I'd have a nice scar left there. A good place to get a tattoo.

I visited Ezra one last time at the hospital after a physical therapy session. With my cuts and bruises, and one arm wrapped up for stability, I looked like hell. This was the first time I'd seen him in real clothes since he got put in the joint.

"Hey," I said.

"You did it," he said. "You destroyed the house."

"I didn't," I said. "The ones who did it are dead."

"I'm sorry about Lukas, I know you two were close," he said, using a walker to slowly approach me. Tears welled up again in my eyes. These days it felt like anything and everything could cause me to cry. Just the drop of a pin, the smallest emotions.

"We did what we promised to," I said. "I'm leaving Greenville, by the way. I just wanted to tell you."

He looked confused. "Where are you going?"

"I don't know yet," I said, shrugging. "I'm staying with Harry right now in Des Moines. I have Charlie with me. I'll try to get a job and wherever that job is, that's where I'll go. You get better. Stick to the program, ok?"

"You're just walking away?"

"From what?" I asked.

"Everything."

"Do you mean you?" I added. He looked down, and in a way that signified to me that the answer was yes. "There's nothing there, Ezra. You have your life, and I have mine. I want to make you and Lukas proud. I want to make myself proud. To do that, I gotta get out of here."

"After this many years, and all those secrets and . . ." he sighed and rubbed his forehead. "All those late night talks."

"I suppose you'll always have a part of me in that way," I said, shrugging, my hand on his shoulder.

"You know more about me than even Jessica," he said, making eye contact with me. His eyes welled up slightly.

"I know," I replied.

He nodded slowly. "Ok."

"Make me proud too," I said, lightly punching him in the shoulder, smiling. I stepped up to hug him. I hugged him tighter than was comfortable for either of us in these states. "See you later, Ezra."

November 5, 2016

I sat down on the Saran wrapped chair at a tattoo studio on Fleur Drive in Des Moines. The artist looked like a hippy who lived on the side of the highway in a box, but his work was gorgeous. Harry was biting on his nails in a seat adjacent, watching. I was adding to my memorials. Lukas's tattoo would be reminiscent of his nomadic nature, an open sky above, an open road beneath, and a burning campfire. In the end, I also decided to add Gary and Riley to my arm. For Riley, I got a blackwork hunk of crystal due to the fact he may have delved deeper into the weaknesses of the House than any of us. For Gary, I got the image of a fox. He was sly, cunning, and a great liar, but also a great man.

Epilogue 2017

Noah Halverson drove three hours from Decorah to Greenville, slightly southwest. Gary Philips left the land in Greenville to Noah, and it was time to claim it. Free house. No mortgage, no rent, very few utilities to be paid for. It was hooked up with many solar panels after all. The place had been emptied by the police who seized all firearms and took custody of all the animals on the premises. A news story was spread about how the humane society in town was overrun with forty chickens that now needed homes where they wouldn't be eaten. The national news, on the other hand, was obsessed with Gary in general. A once trusted secret operative gone crazy conspiracy theorist.

Pulling into the hidden, gravel driveway, Noah parked beneath a shady, green tree. Taylor texted: *Let us know what it looks like.*

Noah smiled a bit, looking at the profile picture of his brother with an arm around Lisey, how young and carefree they looked, even if the carefree part was a lie. Noah closed his phone and jumped out of his 2015 Ford Impala. He was proud of the car. He was proud it was in his name.

Confident, he strode past his soon-to-be home with one thing on his mind: the clearing. He wanted to know what became of it. He felt pulled in that direction. He thought it was duty. This place was his burden now, something passed down by ancestors who didn't know what they were getting involved in, but he did. He knew precisely what he was getting into, because there was no surprise when he entered the circle of the clearing and saw the House standing right where it had last summer, as if nothing happened to it.

He took a picture with his phone and sent it to everyone who'd been there that previous summer.

It's Back.

About the Author

Nina Wilson was born in Des Moines, Iowa to Todd and Sharon Wilson in 1995.She graduated from Indianola High School in 2013 before attending and graduating from Coe College in 2017 with degrees in History and Creative Writing. In 2022 Nina earned an M.F.A. in Fiction from Albertus Magnus College. She's published a wide array of poetry, short fiction, and photography in literary journals and magazines. Nina currently works in Development at the Blank Park Zoo in Des Moines, Iowa and is an avid reader. Her hobbies include Historical European Martial Arts and hiking with her cat.

Thank You!

We are glad you took the time to read this book; if you will, kindly leave a review for the book as this gives the author kudos or feedback for improvement.

Both are very important to an author.

Warmly,
Lily Gianna Woodmansee
Executive Editor for Cactus Moon Publications, LLC

If you liked this book, you might like . . .

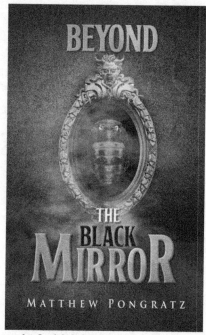

When 1980's party-boy, Billy Baxton, comes across a listing for the perfect fixer-upper in a neighborhood well outside his normal budget, he can't believe his luck may be changing for the better finally. Complete with an old swimming pool and a finished basement; housing an abandoned billiard table and an old Pac-Man machine-it has the potential to be the quintessential bachelor pad of which he's always dreamed. A chance to embark on the next chapter of his young life and escape his run-down apartment complex with smelly hallways, beer-saturated carpets, and paper-thin walls.

After moving in with his slacker roommate, Buddha, Billy slowly learns that the house harbors a morbid secret. One that immediately absorbs his insatiable curiosity. As he begins to dig deeper into the history of this house and previous owner, he is slowly drawn into a bizarre rabbit-hole of black magic, hidden rooms, portals, and beautiful, interdimensional creatures beyond worldly imagination.

Billy assumes he has discovered the key to a utopian realm, but eventually learns that there is a darkness that lurks beyond the fabric of this reality. A darkness that could potentially lead to the ultimate extinction-the extinction of mankind.

Made in the USA
Monee, IL
20 October 2023

44911077R00246